THE
BOOK
OF
KELL

Other Bella Books by Amy Briant

Romeo Fails
Shadow Point

A Heavenly Wilcox Mystery
Heavenly Moves

About the Author

Amy Briant is the author of four novels. A native Californian, she is startled to find herself living on the East Coast.

THE
BOOK
OF
KELL

AMY BRIANT

BELLA
BOOKS
2020

Bella Books, Inc.
P.O. Box 10543
Tallahassee, FL 32302

Printed in the United States of America on acid-free paper.

First Bella Books Edition 2020

Editor: Ann Roberts
Cover Designer: Judith Fellows

ISBN: 978-1-64247-104-5

CHAPTER ONE

The Field Trip

I hate field trips. That's exactly what I was thinking when the bus blew up.

I remember there was shouting. Then, a split second before the explosion, the crescendo of an intense high-pitched whine going from inaudible to ear-splitting in the blink of an eye. And then BOOM.

Hours before, they loaded the slouching, yawning, barely awake senior class—yours truly, eleven boys, eight girls—into a small bus for the ride up to the observatory. Field trips were everything that sucked about school, but worse. Crammed into a bus with my tormentors, I had nowhere to run.

It was fall. The beginning of my last year of school. I would've been long gone if I hadn't promised my Gran I would graduate. My mother had homeschooled me and Gabriel, but when she died during the Bad Times, Gran eventually decided we should go to school with the other surviving kids. I hated school. The only good thing about it was all the books the Settlement had in their library—fiction, nonfiction, poetry, reference, technical manuals. Almost a thousand books and I secretly vowed to read them all. But I hated being stuck inside a classroom, hated having to study things that no longer had any use or meaning in our world—if they ever did Before. But mostly I hated the other kids, who bullied and teased me like I was created for that very purpose.

That first day of school, my sister and I walked the five miles through the redwoods at dawn. I was thirteen and Gabriel was three years older. Side by side in the principal's office, Gabriel stood tall, doing all the talking as usual. I was silent, my eyes darting about the room, taking in the strangeness of it, a small, scruffy figure in my jeans and sweatshirt, baseball hat pulled low over my eyes.

"It's so nice to see you again, Gabriel," the principal told her. "Your parents were colleagues of mine in the psychology department Before. Fine people, both of them. And this must be, umm, your little brother, right? Kell, is it?" He squinted at the paper in his hand, then at me.

Gabriel looked down with the special smile she reserved just for me, her eyes questioning. She knew I was nervous about the whole school thing. I nodded once, just a quick up and down with my chin. She put her arm around my shoulders.

"Yes," she told the principal. "This is Kell."

The stupid field trip. The adults were usually stingy with fuel, although there was plenty left in town if you had the patience and the stomach to retrieve it. One of the grownups had been an astronomy professor at the university Before. He was just another Settler now. But he convinced the council that our young lives would be immeasurably enriched by viewing a passing comet through the one working telescope at the old observatory.

Like we gave a shit about comets. Or Before, which we barely remembered. The senior class was in kindergarten when the Bad Times began. Some people were even starting to just call them The Times, like bad stuff only happened in the past, or in a story. Like if enough years went by, only good things would remain. It had been seven years since the last attack, five since the last big quake. That's a long time for most people.

Friday morning, we'd assembled at the school with our backpacks and sleeping bags. Mr. Giovanni was checking names off a list with a pencil bearing his bite marks. He taught English and history to all the high schoolers, plus he was the Aptitude counselor for the seniors.

"...eighteen...nineteen...now who am I missing? Oh. Yes. Kell."

He shot me a quick, unsure half-smile as grownups so often did and made a final check in his little red notebook.

"Let's go, campers!" he yelled enthusiastically to the completely unenthusiastic group. He would be our driver that brisk October day.

The retrofitted bus lurched and shuddered its way up to the observatory on a highway long overgrown with weeds. It was a slow drive in a low gear. The road was marred with cracks from earthquakes, potholes, fallen trees and rocks, not to mention the occasional rusted-out skeleton of a Before car. Dense forest, mostly redwoods and pines, covered the rest of the hillside. I knew. I'd been up there before with Gabriel on one of our scouting expeditions.

Hunter Cohen and one of his equally dim-witted buddies sat in front of me. As usual, no one sat next to me. God forbid. I stared out the window and hoped they would leave me alone, knowing they wouldn't.

"What's in the bag, faggot?" was how it started. My backpack was on the empty seat next to me. I had automatically, defensively hooked my arm through the strap when I sat down. I couldn't afford to lose what little I had. I kept staring out the window, ignoring them, while surreptitiously tightening my hold on the pack. If it came down to a tugging match, I was going to lose. Hunter outweighed me by at least fifty pounds and his pal was even bigger.

Ignoring them wasn't working. They were bored. And I was prey.

"Probably just his bra and panties," sneered the pal. "Fuckin' little fairy."

Hunter reached over the seat and grabbed my pack. I held on with all my strength, but it was only a matter of time. His buddy giggled as he watched me struggle.

"Fuck off," I snarled at them both.

"Fuck off," Hunter repeated in a high-pitched, taunting voice. His buddy thought that was hysterical.

I wished them both dead with all my heart.

My ignominious and inevitable defeat was averted only by the arrival of Hunter's sometime girlfriend, who came swaying down the aisle, trailing her fingertips over the backs of everyone's seats for balance. Her name was Elinor Eastman, but the kids called her East. She was beautiful but unfortunately was well aware of that. Taller than I by at least three inches. Luminous, pale skin. Glossy, dark brown hair tumbling down past her shoulders, fine features, eyes an unusual shade of dark blue. Which didn't match the greenish shiner she had going on under her left eye. Maybe her stepfather had hit her. Maybe her oaf of a boyfriend.

Who, thankfully, let go of my backpack and the twisted fistful of my hoodie he had wadded up in his other hand. He shoved his buddy off the seat to make way for East. She glanced at me as she slid onto the padded bench, giving me just the glimmer of a nod. Or maybe I imagined that. Hunter didn't notice, being too busy running his sweaty hands all over her and leaning in for a big slurp of a kiss. Gross. I went back to staring out the window, wishing I was anywhere but there. Wishing the trip wouldn't last much longer.

Not knowing it was going to be the longest one of my life.

CHAPTER TWO

Lookout Dude

The observatory was ninety percent in ruins, but the council still used it as a lookout post. It was built on top of a large hill or small mountain, according to your perspective, at the crest of a highway formerly known as 17. Gabriel had shown me one of the old metal signs with the number on it, one of the few still standing by the side of the road. Presumably the sixteen other highways had suffered the same fate.

The man assigned to the lookout post had been an administrator at the university. Not too much call for that these days, but Everyone Must Contribute was a big rule, so they sent him up the hill to look out for—what? On a clear day, you could see the Pacific sparkling in the distance and plenty of forest on the surrounding hillsides, but not much else. I knew where our Settlement was to the south and west, but you couldn't see it from that vantage point. San Francisco was about sixty miles north. According to rumor, it was still faintly smoldering after all those years. A flattened, blackened, desolate no man's land. That was just a rumor, though. I'd never been further than the observatory summit myself, and I'd only made it that far because Gabriel had taken me on her explorations.

In history class, Mr. Giovanni told us that a lot of people had fled inland to Nevada, Arizona and other points east when the Bad Times began, anticipating the worst. Our town had been called San Tomas. Much of it was badly damaged in the first tsunami, but the university—University of California at San Tomas, or UCST for short—was perched high on a hill, so it was spared from that catastrophe, if not from the others. Whatever San Tomas had been Before—a college town, a beach town, a tourist town—it was none of those things now. Almost everyone in the Settlement had some tie to the university. Not as students—it was December break when Before had turned into Now. All the students had been home with their families. They were all gone now, one way or the other.

The lookout dude was kind of squirrelly looking, but he lived all alone up there so I figured he was entitled to his weirdness. What could he possibly have to do all day long? There hadn't been anyone or anything to look out for in years. I was glad that job was taken, though—I would have hated that Aptitude.

He was waiting for us at the checkpoint, a tight smile stretched over sunken cheeks. Probably hadn't had any visitors in months. Apart from the squirreliness, he was an unremarkable older white guy, average height and weight, brown hair going gray.

Mr. G. laboriously maneuvered past one last fallen tree and then into a cleared area a few hundred yards below the summit. As the bus rumbled to a stop, the seniors surged to their feet excitedly, eager to be released after the long, bumpy ride. No one was more eager than I.

"Settle down, settle down," Mr. Giovanni said loudly from the driver's seat, holding up a hand to get our attention and staring us down in the rearview mirror. He cut the engine and set the brake, then stood to face us.

"All right, you know the drill. We're just stopping here to pick up our guide, Mr. Larsen, from the observatory. We're going to take a ten-minute break, then finish the drive to the summit. I want you all back on this bus in exactly ten minutes, you got it?"

A mixed chorus of "Yes, Mr. G.," hoots and catcalls was his answer. I waited for the rest of them to exit, then got off with my pack on my back. The kids were spread out in the cleared area, running around and yelling at each other like a bunch of first graders. Mr. Giovanni had opened up the cargo space beneath the bus to pull out his backpack. From it, he was busy doling out little bags of trail mix which he made himself for school events. Nice man.

I eased past Lookout Dude who was poking around in the cargo space. I wondered about that for half a second, but I was more focused on getting my own gear out of there. I was supposed to hang with the group and then get back on the bus like I was told, but I was never very good at following rules. And no way I was getting back on that bus—I had decided I would walk up to the summit and meet them there. I needed the fresh air.

Lookout Dude flicked me a glance as I hauled out my sleeping bag and tent. There was sweat on his brow although the temperature was in the low fifties. Blue skies, a light breeze—a perfect fall day. He stared at the nametag on my gear.

"Dupont," he said. "That a French name?"

He didn't sound too happy about it. Some people blamed Europe for the Bad Times, others the Middle East. No doubt some of the folks over there (if there were any left) were busy pointing their fingers at us. As far as I could see, there was plenty of blame to go around. The triple whammy of radical climate change, domestic political dissent and international unrest had altered a lot of things.

My Gran, as usual, had her own take on the situation. "People ruin everything," she told me more than once. "They just can't help themselves."

Lookout Dude was staring at me, all beady-eyed and twitchy. What was his problem anyway?

"You don't look French," he said argumentatively.

"I'm American," I said and walked away. I'm a mongrel, as Gran used to so proudly proclaim. In addition to French, our family tree had Chinese, Pawnee, Welsh, Cuban and who knew what else in its branches. Out of this mixture came me: short, skinny, brown eyes, brown skin, cropped black hair that refused to obey either a comb or gravity. My sister got all the looks in the family. The charm too, Gran would have cackled. So fine, I wasn't the pretty one—but I didn't think I was ugly either. I was quick, but not muscular. Smart enough, but not talkative, which for some reason really bothered people. When they looked at me, they saw someone who didn't fit in, someone who didn't fall into one of their precious preordained categories. They saw someone they couldn't figure out and that made them nervous. Nervous as in mean. Curious. Confused. Aggressive.

I just wanted to be left alone.

I told Mr. Giovanni I'd see them at the summit.

"Kell…" he said, disappointed but understanding. He was always trying to get me to play well with others. Which would have been great if the others didn't insist on beating the crap out of me.

"All right," he sighed and handed me a little cloth bag of trail mix. "Be careful out there."

The school bus was far more dangerous to me than the forest, but there was no point in debating it. I thanked him and set off up the hill. My fellow scholars were sitting on the fallen trees and boulders that formed the perimeter of the cleared area, eating their snacks. The path leading to the observatory wound through a stand of three enormous redwoods fifty yards up the hillside and I headed that way. The ground was soft underfoot with a cushiony, slippery layer of pine needles. The cool clean air was spicy with their scent. The gentle breeze had the treetops and the brush in constant, delicate motion.

There was a great view from up there. Through a gap in the trees, you could see miles of rolling hills, all the way to a glimpse of the ocean. The Settlement was on the far side of one of those hills. I wondered who else was out there—other groups like ours? Someone like me? Yeah, right.

Beyond the three giant redwoods was a natural bowl-like depression, perhaps fifty feet in diameter, before the hillside resumed its ascent to the peak. I paused there for two quick adjustments. First, I wanted to strap my sleeping bag and tent to my pack so it was all on my back, leaving my arms free. Second, after a long bus ride, I really needed to pee. There was no one else around and the broad base of the nearest redwood was more than sufficient cover. I was thankful I didn't have to deal with the usual hassle of peeing at school. If I went in the boys' bathroom, I was likely to get roughed up. If I went in the girls' bathroom, they would shriek and freak out. I normally tried to hold it until lunchtime when I could duck behind the handy ruins of some former campus building and piss in peace. I never understood why it had to be so complicated. Why they thought I couldn't be allowed in either place. I mean, everybody's got to pee sooner or later, right?

Having watered the first redwood, I crouched down at the foot of the second one, organizing my gear. I froze as I heard a rustle in the bushes and then a girl's voice.

"Come on, Hunter, let's go—we have to get back on the bus in like a minute."

The girl—East—and Hunter Cohen appeared around the trunk of the third giant redwood. He backed her up against the tree and kissed her neck, intent on getting what he wanted. She saw me, though. Down on one knee, with my gear spread out on the ground before me. Our eyes met. I tried to tell her with a look that I'd be gone in a moment if she would just give me that chance. If she would just let me disappear.

I heard Mr. Giovanni call from below. "Let's go, campers! All aboard!"

"Hunter…Hunter!" East said, finally pushing him off her to get his attention.

"What?" he said, aggrieved, half slipping on the pine needles. Then he saw me.

"Are you spying on us, you little queer?" he angrily demanded. He took a step toward me.

I donned my pack with my gear finally secured and started walking away, downward into the bowl-like depression. There was no point in talking to him. The only reaction he was capable of was hatred. He didn't even know what or why he hated. He certainly didn't know me.

"Did you hear me, faggot?" he yelled. I kept an eye on them with my peripheral vision, but kept moving. East grabbed one of his arms. He dragged her with him as he followed me. There was shouting from down the hill now too. Shouting and screaming. One voice rose above the others.

"Long live the Ship of State! Death to all traitors and cowards!"

In a split second—a bone-jarring, ground-shaking split second—a high-pitched whine like a mosquito seemed to start deep inside my brain, but then was suddenly all around us, unbearably, impossibly, painfully loud.

BOOM.

CHAPTER THREE

Graduation Day

The bowl-like depression in which we were standing was fifty yards up the hill from the bus, behind and below the stand of three giant redwoods. Those trees saved our lives. They blocked the force of the blast and much of the shower of debris that ensued. Although we were a few steps down in the bowl, we were all knocked off our feet by the violence of the explosion. I was the first to scramble back up and ran—stupidly, in retrospect—to the tree line. I was abruptly stopped there by what I saw. I was already deaf from the explosion, but then I wished I were blind as well.

The scene was horrendous. I could hardly process what I was seeing. The bus was blown in two. Black smoke was billowing from the wreckage and flames twisted throughout. Bodies—mostly parts of bodies—as well as pieces of the bus and camping gear were everywhere, littering the formerly cleared space with flesh, blood, metal and Gore-Tex. With all the smoke, it was hard to see, let alone make sense of what I was seeing, but as far as I could tell, there were no survivors. It looked like everyone had been on or near the bus. Everyone—except me, East and Hunter. They stumbled to my side, white-faced and shocked. East looked desperately into my eyes. Her lips were moving, but I couldn't hear anything. The total silence added another layer of eeriness to the grim display. Time stood still while we stared at things no one should see.

When my stunned brain could once again form a coherent thought, it was: this kind of stuff isn't supposed to happen anymore. The Bad Times are over, the adults had told us. Over…

I walked slowly down the hill, careful where I was stepping. My legs felt simultaneously heavy and numb, like they belonged to someone else. I could hear something now, but it was only the sound of my own blood, pounding in my ears. In an unhurried manner, matching my measured pace, background noises began to reemerge. The wind in the trees. The awful crackling of the fire. Birds chirping. Birds—I wondered how long it would be before the crows and condors showed up, but thrust that thought away from me with a shiver. The smoke was noxious, choking me. Some of the bodies were whole, or nearly so. I checked each one. All dead. I had met Death before, seen it creep up slowly on my Gran and finally devour her. This Death-in-the-blink-of-an-eye was much different and yet the same. And no improvement.

Thirty feet from the bus was a cluster of young pine trees and scrub brush. Thrown in their midst like a rag doll was the observatory lookout guy. His eyes were open. Blood trickled from his ears and nose. There was a lot of blood on his clothes as well, presumably his. I knelt down beside him.

"A…bom…" he said.

"A bomb," I agreed. I figured he was dying. There was nothing I could do for him, except wait with him for his imminent departure.

"Noooo…" he labored to say, then lapsed into a weak and agonized coughing fit.

No?

I glanced back over my shoulder up the hill toward East and Hunter. They hadn't moved.

Lookout Dude seemed to get some strength back for a moment. I tried to offer him a sip of water from my canteen, but he pushed my hand away, almost angrily, I thought.

"A...bom..." he said again. It seemed important to him to get it out, so I leaned in to hear him better. There was a rattle in his throat now.

"Abomination," he whispered hoarsely. "You...and your kind...nothing but an abomination..."

I recoiled from him, both amazed and horror-stricken that those were the words he would choose for his last. There had to be more, I thought. But it appeared that was it. His eyes slowly closed, the rattle faded.

God, I hate field trips, I thought with all my might.

Lookout Dude had a gun in a holster on his hip. I hadn't noticed that before. Guns were not uncommon around the Settlement, but ammunition was strictly rationed. Gran had taught Gabriel and me to shoot. After she'd died, I traded most of her weapons and livestock for items I needed more. I thought with a pang of the shotgun hung over the fireplace in our little cabin. I hadn't thought I would need it for a school camping trip. But there were snakes and bears in these woods—mountain lions too. Maybe some two-legged predators as well. I put the gun in my pack after making sure the safety was on. Lookout Dude did not protest.

I hiked back up to where East and Hunter awaited me. She spoke, her voice low and quavering. "Is there anyone—? Are they—?"

"They're all dead," I said flatly. She flinched, then looked searchingly into my face as if she might find more of an explanation there.

I turned away. I needed to get out of that place. And I had already decided I wouldn't be going back to the Settlement. There was nothing there for me. Nothing and no one. I took a step, but East stopped me.

"Where are you going?" she demanded.

"I'm out of here," I told her and Hunter.

"You can't just leave," she said, outraged. "We have to..."

"Have to what?" I said.

She was silent, staring at me intensely with her dark blue eyes huge in her pale face, her hand clamped tightly on my arm. I looked down at it and then back up at her tear-streaked face. She withdrew the hand. It was trembling.

"There's nothing we can do for them now," I told her, as gently as I could. "And we need to get out of here, to somewhere safe."

"But shouldn't we…bury them or something?" More tears were welling. Even in her distress, she was beautiful. I silently berated myself for thinking that with death and chaos all around, but I couldn't help it. I shook my head, trying to shake that thought out of my skull. It was nothing but a waste of time. It always had been.

Hunter was still standing there, staring down at the devastation in utter shock. He hadn't said a word since the bus blew up. Which was a welcome relief.

I said bluntly to East, "There's too many. It would take too long. We need to go—now."

I nodded up the hill, which was more or less north. She looked confused.

"But we have to go back," she insisted, pointing southwest toward San Tomas. "We have to go back to the Settlement, back to school…"

"I don't know about you, but I just graduated." My voice came out harsh and cold. I didn't mean for it to, it just did. "Look, I'm out. I'm not going back. You do what you want."

Hunter had slowly sunk to his knees while we argued. He was making small, wordless sounds. The smell of what was burning below was sickening.

East said fiercely, the outrage again uppermost in her voice, "You can't leave. We have to go back. Or wait here, at least—someone will come for us. They'll come get us when they realize what's happened." She grabbed me again, as if she would forcibly make me stay.

To the southwest, there was a "whoomp" kind of noise. And then another. A small, but distinctly shaped, cloud formed in the distance.

A mushroom cloud.

CHAPTER FOUR

Mile One

"Get a pack!" I screamed at East and Hunter. The latter was still on his knees, his face now in his hands, shoulders shaking.

East screamed back frantically, "It's on the bus!"

Not your pack, ANY pack, I thought, but I didn't want to waste time explaining it to her. We needed to get the hell out of there. The prevailing winds were offshore and San Tomas was on the coast. So with any luck, that mushroom cloud wouldn't be blowing our way. Still, we were far too close for comfort. We needed to put some distance between us and them (whoever "they" were) and pronto.

Most of the bus and what had been on it was blown to gruesome smithereens. But a surprising amount had simply been blown clear by the force of the explosion. I darted down the hill to snag the nearest backpack. We each needed a pack with some kind of provisions to have any chance at surviving the days ahead. Mine was on my back, along with my sleeping bag and tent. I reached down for a large blue pack with an aluminum frame and froze. It was Mr. Giovanni's pack. I could tell that because of the nametag and also because Mr. Giovanni's hairy arm was still entangled in the straps. The rest of him was nowhere to be seen. I shut my eyes and my mind to the horror of it, focusing instead on the need to get the backpack and then get out of there. Another dirty bomb or missile or whatever might be headed our way any second for all we knew. I grabbed the backpack, which had a bright smear of fresh red blood down one side, managed to shake the arm loose without looking directly at it and ran back up the hill.

East had hauled Hunter to his feet, although he still looked dazed and traumatized and was clinging to the big redwood tree for support. Even better, she had found a couple of sleeping bags that had bounced into the bowl.

"Here," I growled at Hunter, slamming the backpack into his chest as hard as I could. In part to snap him out of his funk. But mostly because I didn't like him. "Put it on and let's go."

He fumbled with the straps, shuddering at the blood, but managed to get it on. I strode hurriedly past East, who followed me, clutching the sleeping bags. She stopped to pick up something off the ground. I started to yell at her to keep walking, then saw that what she had retrieved was a water bottle. Which was smart. Maybe there was more to her than I'd given her credit for.

I was moving fast. I wanted to get up and over the hill, putting that physical barrier and as much distance as possible between us and that mushroom cloud. The other two stumbled along behind me. There was no time to think of what had happened to the bus or the Settlement. Of who or why or how. I kept my mind blank.

As soon as I could, I got us back on the remnants of Highway 17. Speed was more important than stealth at that point, and it was easier going than through the woods. Plus, it was headed in the direction I wanted to go. North.

Before she left, my sister Gabriel told me a few things. I was fifteen then, too old to be blubbering like a baby, but I couldn't help it. I hated that she had to leave. She wasn't just my big sister, she was my best friend. My only friend, actually.

"But, Kell," she told me gently. "It's my Aptitude. I have to go. You'll understand when it's your turn. And that's only three more years. Just think, you'll probably be a Pioneer like me and you can come join us in Segundo then."

I knew she was excited to be part of the group that was leaving the Settlement to establish a new community—Segundo, they named it. They'd had a contest to come up with the name. The math teacher, Miss Sanchez, who doubled as the Spanish teacher, submitted the winning entry. The master plan was to build a network of small, self-sustaining communities, each one hundred miles from the last. The hope was that we could reconnect with other survivors of the Bad Times, maybe even reconnect with whatever remained of the old United States of America.

Well, it was all fine and dandy for Gabriel to be excited about being a Pioneer, but that left me stuck with Gran, not to mention trapped in that hellhole of a high school for three more excruciatingly long years. At fifteen, I thought Gran would live forever. It never occurred to me that she would leave me as well. My sister must have recognized that possibility, though. Gran too. Before they left me in their different ways, they made sure I knew a lot that the other kids didn't.

Like the location of Segundo. Or, at least, where they planned it to be. One hundred miles from the Settlement. Gabriel drew me maps in the dirt with a stick until she was sure I had it in my head.

"Highway 17 will take you over the hill," she said, drawing a big "Y" with her stick. "The hill" was what everyone called the small mountain on which the observatory perched. In the past, it had separated San Tomas from San Jose, Silicon Valley and the rest of the greater San Francisco Bay Area.

"So first get yourself over the hill," she continued. "When you reach the fork in the highway, that's the bottom of San Francisco Bay. Don't go up the left fork—that's the peninsula that leads to San Francisco."

We both shivered at the thought of that graveyard city.

"You want the bay to be on your left," she told me. "Just keep going up this right fork. They say 17 eventually turns into what used to be the old Interstate 80. It runs northeast for a while, then turns straight east."

"Why not just go straight east toward Nevada from here? Why head north at all?" I asked her.

"There's no easy way over the mountains if you head due east, they say. Or at least there didn't used to be. Maybe the quakes have changed that…But in the old days, they'd go north up 17 to 80 and follow it east. There's a pass through the Sierra Nevadas there. Or at least there used to be."

We both knew why they didn't head south. South was where the trouble had come from in the Bad Times.

"Anyhow, Kell," my sister concluded, tapping the stick on her dirt map for emphasis, "when you've traveled a hundred miles, more or less, you should find us here." She drew an "X" in the dirt. "That'll be Segundo."

As maps go, it wasn't the greatest.

* * *

After two hours of high-speed hiking, East and Hunter were ready to drop. They lived inside the Settlement with their families, so they didn't walk five miles to school every day like I did. Settlement kids were soft. Shit, Gabriel and I had been all over the campus, had ranged for miles through the woods and on the beaches. Even made some forays into what was left of San Tomas. Stupid Settlement kids probably never even left the campus. I knew I could travel much more quickly without them, but my conscience wouldn't quite allow me to ditch them. Not yet, at least.

Only two hours and already they weren't looking too good. Hunter's face was dirty, with sweat (tear?) streaks carving a path through the grime. Not looking so tough today, big boy, I thought. Like the arrogant idiot he was, he had dressed for the field trip in a T-shirt, shorts and sneakers. Fine for a fashion statement on the bus, not so fine for a serious trek. East was more appropriately garbed in jeans, a jean jacket and hiking boots. As usual, I wore a hoodie, cargo pants, work boots and my baseball cap.

We went single file at first, but then East caught up with me. Hunter clomped along a ways behind us. He was carrying a lot more weight than either East or I—Mr. Giovanni's pack was unexpectedly heavy. I hoped it was full of food, but we hadn't had an opportunity yet to take stock of our limited resources. At least Hunter was good for carrying stuff. Although a mule would have been more pleasant company. Probably smell better too.

When East caught up with me, I glanced over at her. She gave me a cautious nod. Her face was still pale and drawn—I daresay mine was too, although I could feel my jaw muscles were clenched with grim determination. I nodded back at her, but kept moving. With her long legs, she matched my pace with no problem. Out of the corner of my eye, she seemed to be searching for the right words.

"I guess we've never really talked before," she said eventually. "I'm Elinor Eastman—people call me East."

She was attempting to put me at my ease, I realized with some astonishment. The princess and the commoner. How very regal of her.

"Kell Dupont," I replied shortly. It wasn't the time or place for social niceties. Besides, we'd been in the same class for more than two years now—did she really think I didn't know her name? She started to say something else, but I cut her off before she could get started. "We need to keep moving."

"Five-minute break?" she said tentatively, doing a little head jerk back toward Hunter. He had fallen even further behind as we talked. He scowled as he saw us looking back at him, then stopped. He shrugged out of the heavy pack and bent over, hands on his thighs. He waved an arm, imperiously summoning us. I hated to waste the time, but realized it was probably quicker to take the break than to argue with them.

"Five minutes," I said to East.

I stepped off the road and found a place to sit in the shade under the trees. East hesitated, then followed me. I didn't know if anyone was looking for us, but it seemed prudent not to hang out in the middle of the road waiting for them. Would anyone even know we were missing from the bus? Probably not—a census of all the miscellaneous body parts at the blast site would take quite some time and still come up inconclusive. On the other hand, a tracker could easily find our trail. I mean "tracker" as in footprints and broken twigs, not GPS and satellites. They said the satellites all went down, literally or functionally, during the Bad Times. No one knew if that was just a rumor or really true. Still, only a fool would lounge in plain sight on the highway.

Hunter finally realized we weren't walking back to him and noisily tromped to our location. He threw his pack to the ground, narrowly missing my feet, then took a seat next to East.

"What happened back there?" he asked.

It was the first thing he had said in a while. He drank from the water bottle she offered him, then drew a shaking, filthy hand across his mouth. He was staring at his sneakers, which was good because I was looking at him like he was crazy. East glanced at me expectantly, which I found strange. I figured the two of them were having a conversation, not me.

"The bus blew up. Everyone's dead," I finally said, stating what I thought was the obvious.

"I know that, asshole," Hunter said testily. "I mean, was it an accident?" He finally raised his head and looked me in the eye.

"I heard that observatory guy yell something right before the explosion," East said. "Something about the Shiprights. At least, I thought it was him."

According to history class, the Ship of State was a far right-wing militia group, one of many spawned during the heatedly divisive times Before. Their philosophy of "righting" the ship of state was rife with senseless violence and fearmongering. The group's many followers—zealots, bigots and flat-out lunatics—became known as Shiprights. That's what they taught us in school, at least. Gran had her own version.

"Most people need someone to hate, Kell. It's in their DNA," she told me not too long before she died. "It's what we're put on Earth to rise above, I believe, but hardly ever do. And the easiest one to hate is the one who's different—different skin color, different language, different way of looking at things. Different is dead, Kell. And you're different. You're smart and you're a hard worker and you got a good heart, kiddo, but all most people will see is how different you are. Don't get me wrong—I'm proud of all your differences and mine too. They make us special, but they make us stand out. You're just like me in that regard. You look different, you act different, you talk different."

"What's wrong with the way I talk?" I said, incensed that yet another aspect of my personality that I thought was just fine had been identified as a defect.

"Not a thing, except for swallowing that dictionary. Now, come on, don't make that face!"

I must have frowned. Besides, if I talked funny, it was her fault. Who else encouraged me to read all those books? Who else did I have to talk to except a batty old woman? No wonder I sounded weird—I sounded just like her! But she wasn't done.

"Just understand, kid, most people don't like to be challenged. They think boys wear pants and play sports, and girls wear dresses and play with dolls. If you don't fit in one of their little boxes, they can make your life mighty uncomfortable. Different is dead, Kell—don't ever forget that."

In school, there were a few books about grandmothers who baked cookies and told bedtime stories. Apparently Gran never read those.

"So what am I supposed to do?" I asked. "Pretend to be someone I'm not?"

"Oh, hell no," she said. "You'll never pull that off. Nope, Duponts just have to be Duponts, I guess. But you'll never win any popularity contests, I guarantee you that. Lord knows I never did!" She cackled her way into one of her coughing fits. In the end, the cackles were few and far between, the coughing relentless.

"Maybe something was wrong with the bus," Hunter was arguing. "Maybe the gas tank caught fire and that's why it blew up."

"I think it was a missile," East retorted. "Or a bomb. Did you hear that noise right before it blew?" Neither of us answered her. She turned to me. "What do you think, Kell?"

I was startled again that she included me. Like she'd said, we had never really spoken before. Oh, maybe a word or two, here or there, in class when the situation demanded it, but an actual conversation? No way. In school, nobody ever talked to me. To be fair, I never talked to them either. Silence was one of my best weapons.

"I'm not sure," I said slowly. Missile or bomb? Did it matter, when the result was the same? "I did see that Lookout Dude poking around the luggage compartment when I got my gear out."

"Why would he blow up the bus?" Hunter argued, looking at me the way he always did—as someone to take his aggression and insecurity out on. "He was from the Settlement, for chrissake. He was one of us."

"But he was the one yelling that Ship of State stuff," East pointed out. She looked at me like I was supposed to jump in and referee. Fat chance.

What was the point of wrangling over the details? The mushroom cloud over San Tomas made it clear the Bad Times were back. I noticed neither one of them had mentioned that yet. I gazed up at the sky—still clear, still blue. The movement of the treetops told me the wind was still blowing east to west. Good.

"So where are we going anyhow?" Hunter asked, his petulance a poor mask for his fear. East said nothing, but looked at me.

"I'm going to Segundo," I said.

"Segundo!" Hunter crowed derisively, like I'd said I was going to the moon. Picking on me seemed to be perking him right up. "You're crazy. We don't know where that is. Nobody's even heard anything from that group."

"I know where it is," I said staunchly. "Gabriel drew me a map before she left."

"That's your sister, right?" East asked me. "Gabrielle? One of the Pioneers?"

"It's Gabriel and yeah, she's my sister."

"Isn't Gabriel a boy's name?" Hunter said with his usual ugly smirk.

What in the world did she see in him? But I merely responded, "My parents named her Gabriel, like the angel, and they named me Kell. Just like your parents named you Hunter and her parents named her Elinor. Got it?"

"Yeah, Hunter, be cool," East urged him. "Let's not fight, okay?"

There was a brief silence. In spite of the awfulness behind us, and the shock and the horror that we all three were feeling, it was still a beautiful fall day. Sun shining, birds singing. People destroy, but nature abides, Gran used to say.

"Look," I tried again. "All we basically have to do is follow the highway for a hundred miles. At twenty miles a day, we'll be there in less than a week. That was their plan, you know—to establish the next Settlement one hundred miles away, to the north and then east."

I said it like it was a piece of cake, but in reality, I knew it wouldn't be easy locating Segundo. We could walk for weeks and never find a trace of them. It made sense that they would follow the highway and establish the new village nearby, but there were a hundred different reasons why they might do something else. It didn't matter to me. Ever since my grandmother had died, my plan was to first honor my promise to her to graduate, then set out on my own to find Gabriel and Segundo. Maybe I was crazy to think I could do it, but I was pretty confident in my skills. I'd done all right on my own after Gran passed. And it wasn't like I had any better options in life. I wasn't going to live alone in Gran's cabin forever. I sure as heck wasn't going to stay in the Settlement. I was an outsider to those people. I'd never felt welcome there. No one would miss me if I left.

Although, there was the question of the Aptitudes. Gabriel was certain that I'd be a Pioneer, just like her. That would have been cool, but I had my doubts. Gabriel and I weren't that much alike. Our physical differences were easy to see, but I knew that we felt and acted differently too. She was extroverted, easygoing, a conformist, to tell the truth. And I thought I understood the reasons for that. Why fight the status quo when it's working so well for you? It was people like me and Gran—"subverters of expectations" was Gran's fancy phrase—who stuck out like sore thumbs, who were stubborn about getting our own way.

I was sure the testing and evaluations that led to one's Aptitude had uncovered that I wasn't anything like my big sister. Maybe I was meant to be a Scavenger, part of a small team devoted to retrieving resources from what was left of San Tomas. I knew I would hate to be a Settler. In theory, it was possible to reject your Aptitude—but they said no kid had ever done that.

Screw it. All bets were off now.

"Let's go," I said, standing up and tightening the straps of my pack. "A few more hours, then we'll find a place to camp for the night."

CHAPTER FIVE

The First Night

The long-gone manufacturer of my tent optimistically described it as a four-person model per the still-existing label over the door. For one small person such as myself, it was spacious. I loved sleeping out under the stars, but I could see fog creeping over the tops of the coastal mountains to the west. There would be no stars to see that night. The temperature would likely drop into the forties, if not lower. I was extremely thankful I had left the bus with all my gear on me.

We stopped in the late afternoon to make camp. Gabriel had taught me that one of the first rules of camping is to make sure you've got plenty of daylight to set up. There had been no sign of anyone following us. Which didn't mean they weren't back there, but I was trying to focus on the positive. East and I gathered wood to build a fire. Hunter found a flint in Mr. Giovanni's pack, along with clothes, food and cooking equipment. All of which I had in my own pack, but it was good to have spares. Particularly the food.

I knew the fire would give away our location to anyone searching for us, but we needed it, for the psychological comfort as much as the light and heat. I didn't really think we were being followed. After obsessing about it all day, I concluded that the Lookout Dude was nuts and had blown up the bus. Maybe he was in cahoots with whoever bombed the Settlement. Maybe, since he couldn't be part of that, he had unilaterally decided his contribution would be to take out the senior class. The bottom line was he and everyone else in the vicinity was dead—the three of us were on our own. By the time anyone realized we had survived—if anyone even cared—we would be days ahead of them on the trail. I hoped.

"It's kind of small, but we can all sleep in my tent if we stash our packs in the trees," I offered. Quite graciously, I thought. East was about to speak when Hunter interrupted her.

"I'm not sleeping anywhere near you, girly boy," he said with a curled lip. "And neither is she."

"Hunter!" East said loudly, her tone a warning.

"Maybe you should give that shit a rest," I said to him. "Things are a little different now. Hun-ter." I gave his name some extra emphasis.

"You little—" he started to say, arising from where he'd been crouched by the fire. But East stood in his way.

"Knock it off, Hunter," she said. "Kell is right. Things are different now. We need to pull together, not fight with each other."

He looked from her to me, his eyes narrowed to slits, then abruptly turned on his heel and stomped off into the bushes, grumbling under his breath.

"Sorry," East said to me. "He's just upset, you know? He's not always like this."

"I know exactly what he's like," I told her. She looked taken aback. Every time I opened my mouth, in fact, she looked surprised that I had the power of speech. Not to mention an opinion.

"I guess I better go find him," she said after a moment.

I shrugged. "You're still welcome to sleep in here if you like. It's going to get pretty cold tonight."

"Thanks," East said. "I appreciate it. I'll see if I can change his mind."

I meant she was still welcome, not him, but whatever. It looked like there was finally going to be a silver lining to his hatred—I'd be cozy in my tent, he'd be freezing his big bullying ass outside. Sounded good to me.

The three of us didn't talk much at dinner that first night. I think we were all still stunned by what we'd seen. What we'd so narrowly missed being a part of. At least we had plenty to eat for a day or two thanks to the food in Mr. Giovanni's pack. I had decided not to share with them—at least not yet—the list of what I had in my backpack. Living alone in the woods, I never left the cabin without some basic survival tools and supplies, like my flint, compass and hunting knife. Things that could mean the difference between life and death in the wilderness. And I certainly didn't tell them about the gun.

But I silently thanked the universe for the extra food. The only problem was Hunter ate more than East and I did, combined. I tried to tell him we needed to ration the food. He threw an empty can at my head. And missed. I gathered up the trash and buried it. No point in leaving more of a trail than we had to. Even if the Mad Bomber wasn't after us, there might be others out there without our best interests in mind. Most survivors in the area had made their way to the Settlement in the past several years, but there were stories about people still living on their own out in the woods or the ghost towns. If the stories were true, I hoped to avoid those people.

Later, snug in my sleeping bag in my tent and glad of at least some semi-privacy, I closed my eyes. My body wanted to sleep, but my mind kept cycling through the moments just before and after the explosion, over and over again. I couldn't stop it, no matter how hard I tried. Then I heard East's voice. Eavesdropping was a welcome distraction.

"Don't cry, Hunter," she said softly, "we're going to be okay."

I heard a strangled sob. I couldn't catch everything he was saying.

"My mom and dad…everybody…and Ronnie…He was my best friend since we were little kids…Ronnie's *dead*, East…"

Ronnie was the guy sitting next to him on the bus, the one who had laughed while Hunter tried to twist my arm out of its socket and steal my backpack. Ronnie, over six feet tall, had once spat into my hair as I passed him in the hallway at school. Usually, though, his role was merely to snicker and applaud as Hunter verbally or physically assaulted anyone who was weaker or smaller or different. I just didn't have it in me to grieve for Ronnie.

But Mr. Giovanni was a good guy. And there were people at the Settlement who had worked with my parents at the university for years. Gran had a few friends who had been pretty decent to me. So many people gone in a moment…I kept feeling the unfairness of it like an electric shock in my stomach. Not to mention the pictures in my head of the blood and the bodies…

I doubt any of us got much sleep that night.

CHAPTER SIX

Animals

In the morning, my first thought was to get us moving, but my second thought was to keep an eye and an ear out for water. I had my canteen and East had the water bottle she'd found. Mr. Giovanni's pack had a full water bottle in a side pocket, but all three of us were running low. None of the containers held more than a quart.

We broke camp early, but not too early. I didn't say anything to the other two, but I didn't want to be out at dawn with a couple of greenhorns bumbling through the forest and making a racket. Dawn and dusk were when mountain lions hunted. Bears, formerly rarely sighted in the urban sprawl of the Bay Area, had made a comeback after the Bad Times. Wild animals, in general, had flourished. It was humankind, the depredator, who had been systematically wiped out, mostly by each other during those Times. With the top of the food chain suddenly vacant, Mother Nature was back in charge. Still, as a rule it was rare that any wild animal would attack an adult human unless provoked. Everyone knew to give mother bears with cubs a wide berth. Cougar attacks were unusual, but not unheard of. Wild boar were known for their nasty and unpredictable tempers. And, of course, snakes didn't give a damn about any rules—we needed to be careful about snakes.

There had been stories—tall tales—of exotic beasts escaping from the zoo in San Francisco, but surely that wasn't true. The zoo was a flat, black, scorched place now, like the rest of that doomed city. It was also said—and much more likely true—that some farm animals, like horses, cattle, sheep and goats, continued to thrive, grazing on the grass now covering many areas that had once been urban.

We'd had experience at the Settlement of another formerly domesticated animal. Many dogs were abandoned by their owners during the Bad Times. Coyotes picked off the little ones and disease thinned out the purebreds. But in the way of dogs, the remaining previously cuddly pooches had gotten together and formed packs. Several years and doggie generations later, they had reverted to wild dogs. Whatever breeds they had started out as, they were all pretty much just basic Dogs now. Short-haired, more or less brown, thirty to forty pounds, with tails that curled up over their hindquarters. If you came across one of them in the woods, you could usually scare it off with a few well-thrown rocks and a show of belligerence. The problem was, there was never just one of them. Fido and Fluffy were now soldiers in a highly efficient killing machine—the pack.

The good news, however, about all this burgeoning wildlife was that some of it was available for us to eat, instead of it eating us. There was fruit and nuts and plenty of other growing things to eat. I knew we were fortunate to be in this bountiful region, with lots of fresh water, plants and animals. We probably wouldn't starve to death. Probably. My concern was the time it took to find and prepare food. Time I would rather be spending on getting to Segundo as quickly as possible. The one-week timeline I'd given East and Hunter was a joke. There was no way those two could do twenty miles a day, even if we knew exactly where we were going. And we wouldn't be going far without food. I resolved to keep my eyes open for anything edible as we hiked along. As far as meat, all we had to do was catch it somehow. I couldn't waste ammo on it, though. I'd checked Lookout Dude's gun in the privacy of my tent—six bullets and that was it. I was thinking along the lines of something small that I could trap, like rabbit or squirrel. Maybe quail. Fish would be good.

For fish, we'd need to find some water. San Tomas had been a beach town Before, but nowadays, most people avoided the water. The tides and currents were just too strong, and unpredictable to boot. The sea floor was constantly shifting due to underwater earthquakes, they told us in science class. The Bad Times had taught a lot of people to fear nature. I guess there was a lot to be afraid of, if you thought of it that way: storms, earthquakes, floods, animals. But Gran pointed out that an earthquake could just as easily strike the Settlement as it could our cabin in the woods. It was important to respect nature, she taught me and Gabriel, and to try and understand it as best we could—but fear was just not an asset in our lives. We're all going to die anyhow, she would cackle. Might as well enjoy the fresh air while we can.

So while other kids stayed with their families within the confines of the Settlement on what had previously been the university campus, we went back to living in the woods after the worst of the attacks stopped, in the cabin Gran had built for her retirement Before. Strangers passing through San Tomas found the Settlement easily enough. None of them ever stumbled across our off-the-beaten-path cabin deep in the forest. Maybe we were lucky. I knew they were—Gran was armed to the teeth. She built some wicked booby traps too.

As a little kid, I slowly came to understand the adults weren't entirely clear on who the enemy was. The drone planes that terrorized us were unmarked. Were they from a foreign invader? From those homegrown terrorists, the Shiprights? Could they have been a mistake, a misguided assault by our own government? We never saw the face of our attacker—just the bloody aftermath of his bombs.

My memories of those childhood years were murky and piecemeal, which was probably for the best. I remembered all of us from the Settlement huddled together in the darkness of the bomb shelter, which was the basement of the campus bookstore. I remembered the acidic smell of the grownups' sweat, a smell I still associated with fear. I remembered the group getting smaller as the months went by. I felt jealous of the ones who had left us because they got to be with my parents. I remember Gabriel holding me as we sat together on the gritty concrete floor while Gran conferred with the other adults, making decisions that would enable the group to survive.

I brought my mind back to the present. I couldn't waste my time on memories—most of which weren't even that great—when the here and now demanded one hundred percent of my focus. Water was uppermost on my mind as we continued hiking down the hill from the summit. By my best guess, we'd gone about ten miles the day before. Only ninety more to go, I told my smartass self. Less, in fact, since the bus ride to the observatory gave us a head start. The slope was flattening out as we neared the bottom of the hill. What lay ahead of us, according to Gabriel's hazy knowledge of the terrain from her Pioneer training, was several miles of flatland along the side of San Francisco Bay, then a gentle ascent to the northeast to the spot where they planned to build Segundo. If everything had gone as planned. If they hadn't been eaten by mountain lions. If they hadn't gotten lost and ended up far from the planned spot. If they hadn't decided the hell with it and moved to Nevada.

I shrugged those thoughts off. "No point in worrying about what you can't control" was another one of Gran's favorites. I missed her. I missed Gabriel. But I was used to being lonely.

We stopped for a break mid-morning. A massive sequoia had fallen alongside the freeway, providing us with a place to sit while we drank the last few drops of our water. East took a sip, then held out her silver water bottle, turning it upside down to demonstrate its complete emptiness. Her expression would have been comical under different circumstances.

"We'll find a creek or a pond sooner or later," I told her. "Especially now that we're off the hill."

"What does that mean?" Hunter said crossly. He never spoke to me except to argue or attack. Very tiresome. I considered him for a moment before I answered. I saw East flick me a glance out of the corner of my eye.

"It means water runs downhill," I said neutrally, although I knew he would find a way to be antagonized no matter what tone I employed. "You'll find water in a valley."

Having no answer for that, he made a scornful face.

"Just listen for the sound of running water, okay?" I told them both. "We need to find some today."

"But we're still going to follow the highway, right?" East asked. She seemed to find some comfort in clinging to 17, the artifact of our former life. Actually of our former former life.

"As best as we can," I answered. "It's supposed to form a 'V' pretty soon." I showed them with my hands how the highway supposedly forked—the left side running up the west side of the Bay and the right side the east.

"And we want east?" East said, then smiled for just a second at her east/East statement. It was the first time I'd seen her smile since the explosion. Which was less than twenty-four hours prior, but in a weird way seemed already far distant. Probably because I didn't want to think about it, even though in the back of my mind, the images and sounds from the day before continued replaying. The screaming. The explosion. The bodies...

I gave myself a little shake, physically willing those thoughts away.

"Yes, East, we want east," I told her, which sounded funnier than it was. She and I shared a small smile. Hunter noticed. I could tell he didn't like it. He narrowed his eyes and looked at her and then me. I wiped all expression from my face and got to my feet. "Let's go find some water," I said.

I figured he had to agree with that. Plus, I wanted to distract him before he could come up with another reason to pound on me. They reluctantly stood and followed me back to the road.

The temperature rose as the sun climbed higher in the sky. It had been in the fifties the day before, but it was starting to feel more like seventy. Gran had told me the weather used to be much more predictable, with cool falls, cooler winters, a mix of sun and rain in the spring and sunny, moderate summers in our region. That, like so much else, had changed in the last few decades. Although the adults hated the uncertainty of the weather, I knew it might help us on our trek. Hot spells were confusing to the plants and animals too, sometimes tricking them into thinking it was an early spring. Even though the calendar said October, with a little luck, we might find some fruit or birds' eggs to eat. You never knew.

CHAPTER SEVEN

The Apple Tree

It was birds that led us to the water, late that afternoon. I had maybe an ounce left in my canteen. I could tell East was hurting for a drink and considered offering her a sip, but the practical part of me was thinking she had to learn to manage her water better. She'd given Hunter some of hers the day before—liquid she could have sorely used now. It had been a long, hot, dry hike that day. We needed to stop and make camp soon. I wasn't looking forward to hearing their complaining if we had no water overnight, not to mention first thing in the morning.

East was walking slower and slower. I lessened my pace to accommodate her. Hunter trudged along in front. We still hadn't come to the V in the highway. I wasn't sure whether or not to be worried about that yet. This section of the highway had been carved out between two plump hills. The one to the west was smaller with a steep grassy slope. A single tree punctuated the ridgeline. A hundred feet ahead of us, Hunter stopped, staring up at the tree and shading his eyes with one hand.

"What?" I called to him.

He pointed up at the tree. As we got closer, we could hear the raucous chatter of birds coming from it. It was an apple tree. The birds were feasting on the fruit, zipping in and out of the branches with abandon. The sun was low in the sky, shining through the leaves and limbs, illuminating the tree with a golden glow.

Hunter started up the hill without waiting for us. The ground was soft and a bit muddy due to recent rains. Slipping occasionally and falling once, he persisted until he reached the top, one hand resting on the trunk of the tree while he caught his breath. It wasn't a very big tree. It looked young and alone, standing all by itself, a few feet below the summit. East and I had followed Hunter up the slope, but I didn't like it—it felt much too exposed. If anyone was watching.

But the apples sure looked good. My stomach grumbled in agreement. The birds ignored us, continuing to squawk away, enraptured with the bounty. A few rotten, much pecked fruits littered the ground. Hunter gave the trunk an experimental shake to see if any of the apples would fall to the ground. Nope. He dropped his pack, then went down on one knee.

"Come on, East," he wheedled. "I'll give you a boost."

He held out his interlaced fingers.

"No way," she said.

"Well, then, you give me a boost."

While they bickered about it, I checked out the ridgeline. If we were going to be up there, I might as well have a look at the view. The hillside was so steep, I couldn't see anything until I was right at the top. Once there, I found that the ground fell away sharply, almost vertically—clearly, a landslide had happened not long ago. The raw earth was rain-soaked and dark. Down at the bottom—a long way down—a creek rushed and foamed. Boulders and smaller rocks dotted the hillside, dislodged by the slide. The sound of the creek, which cut northeast through the landscape, was drowned out by the birds' frenzy. I felt elated, but cautious. The ground beneath my feet was soft and yielding. Too soft. I could feel it wanting to give way and slide down to the bottom. I carefully edged back from the lip, then turned to tell my companions the good news.

Hunter was up in the branches. He tossed some apples down for East to gather. There weren't that many whole ones left—the birds had beaten us to it. The slender bole of the tree quivered under his weight. The branch he had a foot on made a creaking noise.

"Take it easy," East said anxiously. He laughed, tossing her another apple. Then aimed one not so gently at my head—which I managed to catch.

In the soft earth, the young tree was definitely listing to one side under the burden of his bulk. He set his sights on the one remaining full apple still hanging. The birds were cawing and shrieking, scolding him for interrupting their dinner. With one hand holding on to the trunk, he reached for the dangling red fruit. He was about two feet short.

"Hunter…" East said warningly.

He grunted, shifting his weight while stretching six more inches toward the apple. The tree creaked again, more loudly.

"Just come down, all right?" East pleaded. "We already have some apples."

"Yeah and I see one more," he said, precariously leaning forward. Which forced him to loosen his grip on the trunk.

The tree was tilting even farther off its axis in the soft loamy ground.

"Look," East said, trying to be reasonable, "if you fall and break something, it's not going to be good."

"No worries, babe," he told her with a nauseating smirk, "I got it under control." He sidled another few inches forward on the branch, which bowed under his weight.

"This is stupid," I said. "There's a creek down below. Let's just go get some water, okay?"

"Shut up, faggot," was his not unexpected reply. "I'm getting this apple."

The fingertips of his right hand were now just barely brushing the trunk. His left hand was outstretched as he slid his foot one more inch down the branch. The birds, which had grown quieter and quieter as we squabbled, suddenly all took flight as if there'd been a silent signal. I think we all jumped. Hunter yelped and flailed, then there was an almighty CRACK as the branch he was standing on broke clean off the tree. It was only about eight feet off the ground, so the fall itself wasn't too bad, but it pitched him forward, up the slope, right up to and onto the lip of the cliff overlooking the creek.

"Hunter!" East screamed.

He was motionless for a long moment, then slowly rolled over onto his back.

"I'm okay," he told us, still smirking as he started to sit up. He put his hands down on the ground to push himself up.

That was when the entire section of lip he had landed on collapsed and sent him headfirst over the precipice.

East screamed again, a scream that became a wail. She started to rush up to the edge, but I stopped her.

"The ground's too soft. We can't go running up there or we're going over too."

She struggled to free herself from my grasp, even as another big chunk of hillside broke off and went crashing down the hill. That got her attention.

"Look, I'm the smallest, so let me take a look. You stay here, okay?"

She nodded, eyes huge in her white face, tears somehow intensifying their hue. I let her go, then removed my pack. Picking a point several feet from where Hunter had fallen, I slowly belly-crawled up to the lip, sensitive to every tremor in the soil. I already knew it was a long, steep way down. I had no hope he had survived. He'd probably gone into the creek and been swept downstream. But when I finally, carefully popped my head over the edge, I was surprised to see him—crumpled up at an awkward angle by one of the big boulders about two-thirds of the way down the hill. I stared, looking for any signs of life, but he wasn't moving. At all.

"Hunter!" I yelled. Nothing.

Well, shit. I belly-crawled back to safer ground, then got to my feet. My pants and hoodie were now grass-stained and caked with mud, but it's not like it was ruining my look.

"Did you see him?" East asked in a quavering voice. She stood rigidly by the tree, her fists clenched. For a second, I wondered—was she hoping for a yes or a no?

"He's about seventy feet down the slope, by a big rock. He's not moving, though."

"We've got to go down there then," she said urgently.

I nodded. We had to go down there to get water anyhow. I seriously doubted he was alive. If he wasn't dead, but badly injured, we would have a difficult decision to make. I blanked my mind to that, concentrating instead on how to get us down there without further disaster. The trick would be to descend safely without setting off another landslide. And/or killing the rest of us.

"Come on!" East commanded. She had donned Mr. Giovanni's pack. I could see from the bulging pockets of her jean jacket where she'd stashed the apples. I mentally applauded her for having the sense to do that. Not to be cold-blooded, but whether Hunter was dead or alive, we still needed to eat.

I put on my own pack and picked up the two sleeping bags she'd been carrying before. I glanced back once as we walked away from that lone apple tree on the hill. The big broken-off branch lay at its base. The spot where it had so violently been severed looked like a wound in the red rays of the setting sun. Far above, hanging at the end of a slender branch was a single apple, bobbing gently in the breeze.

The safest way down was on our butts, inching warily along, abruptly halting at the first trickle of loose dirt. It was slow and painful and not pretty, but it got the job done.

Hunter was unequivocally dead. He must have smacked headfirst into the big boulder we'd found him by. Bashed-in skull, broken neck, no pulse. Boulder 1, Cohen 0. East made a choking sound in her throat as she knelt beside him.

She didn't cry, though. That surprised me. Maybe she was feeling as numb as I was by the sudden advent of way too much death and destruction. She seemed to need to stare at him for a while, so I let her be. I kept an eye on our surroundings. Eternal vigilance and all that. As I turned to gaze back up the slope, a sudden movement at the top registered in the corner of my eye. I didn't really see anything, just sensed some motion. A bird? A rabbit? I scanned the cliff's edge for a while, but saw nothing moving.

"Kell."

I glanced at East. She looked shaken, but like she was trying to hold it together.

"Will you help me bury him?" she said in a small voice.

Why did she have to be so damn beautiful? Making me want to help her do things I absolutely did not want to do? I didn't give a rat's ass about Hunter Cohen. Truth be told, I hated the son of a bitch. Was I glad he was dead? Hell, yeah.

"Please," she said faintly. Those remarkable navy blue eyes. What a sucker I am.

I said to her, "Let's get some water first. And we'll find some sticks or something to dig with."

I held out a hand, which she took, and pulled her to her feet. Her hand felt soft and warm in mine. Not like gooey soft, or pillow soft. Firm and strong, but somehow delicate too... like a really good soft. I let her hand drop. Crushing on Elinor Eastman was not going to help me get to Segundo and that was all that mattered.

The creek was pretty, busily rushing along and sparkling in the waning light of the day. The water was clear and cool. Hunter lay dead on the hill. So strange how the world kept turning.

We had to walk upstream a ways before we found a good place to fill our containers. I warned East not to drink any until we had a chance to boil it. Down in the gorge, twilight was nearly upon us as the hill to the west blocked the setting sun. We had another hour, at best, before complete darkness fell. Having found the water, I was reluctant to leave its side. If we followed it northeast, we would reconnect with the highway in the morning. I turned to East to tell her we would camp in the gorge that night.

There was no warning. Simply an ominous rumble that seemed to pass under our feet like a wave, then a violent shaking as the San Andreas fault readjusted itself as it had so many times before. The whole thing took less than ten seconds. The quake was mild compared to some I'd been through, but it still knocked us both to the ground. Where we watched, open-mouthed, as the hillside above Hunter gave way yet again, burying him in a few tons of dirt and rock.

CHAPTER EIGHT

The Aptitudes

The quake was over before we could even regain our feet. As I jumped to mine, my no doubt inappropriate reaction was heartfelt gratitude that we wouldn't be doing any digging that evening. My next thought was that the gorge no longer seemed like such a swell place to camp. The hills which rose on either side of the creek seemed menacing now, like they were closing in on us. But I was torn—I still wanted to stick with the water.

East had gone down awkwardly and was stuck like a turtle on her back, Mr. Giovanni's heavy pack weighing her down. I helped her up. Back on her feet, she clung to me tightly. She was crying and gasping for breath. I thought she was winded from her fall, but then I saw the panic on her face. Her teeth were chattering, her body rigid.

"Hey," I said to her. Then, "Hey!" more sharply. She looked at me then, but her eyes were unfocused and wild.

I managed to pry myself loose from her grip and took a step back. I stooped to pick up my fallen canteen, then realized this was the perfect moment to throw my water in her face. I always wanted to do that to somebody.

She was sputtering then, pissed off and still crying, but at least I had her attention.

"We're going to make it," I said with as much conviction as I could muster. "You and I are going to Segundo and we're going to be fine." Frankly, I needed the pep talk almost as much as she did.

"B-b-but what if they're all d-dead too?" she said, tears glistening on her cheeks. That was my worst fear as well, but I didn't see any point in talking about it. She started to shake.

Oh, crap, I thought, but stepped in for the hug. Which was made clumsy not only by the heavy packs on our backs, but the apples in her pockets. Not to mention my keen awareness of her breasts. *Classy, Kell. Her boyfriend's a corpse and you're thinking about boobs.* When the worst of her distress seemed to have passed, I let her go.

"Come on," I told her. "Time to find a place to camp."

"Not here," she said with a shudder and a glance toward the mound of dirt that marked Hunter's final resting spot.

"Not here," I agreed.

We headed upstream in the dwindling light. Two good things happened along the way. One, there were no aftershocks. Two, as the creek meandered northeast, the hill on our right petered out. We found ourselves on the verge of a great grassy flatland, just as Gabriel had described it. With the last few dying rays of sunshine, we made camp by the creek.

There was plenty of driftwood along the banks, deposited there by the rushing waters when they were much higher in the spring. By the light of a crackling fire, we ate our apple dinner, supplemented by the last of the trail mix. Having water again was major—I felt immensely relieved, both physically and mentally.

East was quiet. She was obviously distressed and I couldn't blame her. I was just glad she wasn't going off in total hysterics like some girls would. Or asking me questions I couldn't answer—like what had happened to the Settlement. Or how exactly I planned to find Segundo in a vast unknown wilderness.

"How come you never talk?" she finally said after we'd finished eating. We sat side by side on the largest of the driftwood logs, the creek murmuring to itself in the background.

"I talk," I said. It sounded defensive, even to my ears. "When I have something to say."

"You never talked in school. We've never even had a conversation before."

"And that's my fault?"

That gave her pause.

"Okay," she said slowly. "I guess not. I guess that's on both of us."

There was another long stretch of silence broken only by the gurgling of the creek and the hiss of the fire. The stars in the limitless black sky above us were amazing as always. Gran had told me you couldn't see the stars at night in San Tomas Before. She must have been pulling my leg on that one. There was no way to make a million blazing stars disappear.

"So how come you never talked in school?" East persisted, poking at the fire with a stick.

I considered my answer for a moment.

"I don't like to lie," I finally told her. "I'd rather be silent if I can't speak the truth."

"But—" she started in again.

I stood up abruptly, wanting to change the subject. She seemed to take the hint. I grabbed Mr. Giovanni's pack and started going through its contents. A whistle, a flashlight powered by squeezing and a bar of soap were all keepers. I put all the good stuff in the pockets of my cargo pants. My plan was to remove all unnecessary weight from the pack, but to hang on to anything useful.

I pulled out the clothes for East to sort through. I had some of my own clothes in my pack, but she had only what was on her back. None of Mr. G's garments was her size or taste, but she set aside a few items. She held up a pair of way too big wool socks for my inspection.

"Keep 'em," I advised her. "At least they can keep your feet warm at night. Or you can use them for mittens when it gets colder."

"When it gets colder?" she echoed with some dismay. "Just how long do you think we're going to be out here, Kell? Shouldn't we be in Segundo by the time it starts getting really cold?"

"I hope so."

She frowned, then balled up the socks and threw them at me. I stuck them in my pockets—far be it from me to waste a good pair of wool socks. I dug deeper into the backpack. There wasn't much left in there. We'd already eaten almost all his food.

"Here, see if I missed anything."

I traded East the pack for her fire stick. As I leaned forward to tend the flames, she upended the empty backpack and gave it a shake.

Something small tumbled out.

"What's that?" I asked. The teacher's secret stash?

East felt for it in the dark, then picked it up. A little red leather notebook. I remembered seeing Mr. Giovanni jotting notes in it at school. Diary? No, too small for that.

She leafed through it, which seemed wrong. Whatever was in there, he had never meant for us to read it. But he was gone... Everyone was gone.

"What does it say?" I asked her, returning to my seat on the log. I was not so much curious as hopeful for a distraction from the dead.

She held the tiny book up to the flickering firelight, which, in case you don't know, is hell of hard to read by. I inched down the log to see. My leg brushed hers. She didn't seem to notice. I inched back.

"It's some kind of list..." she said, peering intently at the cramped handwriting. "I think it's a list of us."

"His attendance list from yesterday?" Yesterday. A few centuries ago.

"No. It's the names of everyone in our class on one side of the page and on the other..."

Her nose was all but touching the paper.

"So what, did I flunk the last history test?"

"It's not grades, Kell," East turned and pinned me with those big eyes. "It's the Aptitudes."

The sky chose that inopportune moment to start raining on us. And I mean a cold, hard, drenching rain. Sometimes the rain would be a gentle mist and sometimes it came down in buckets like somebody up there was mad at us. This was one of the latter. It began with a few fat drops, then the deluge commenced in earnest. The fire went out in seconds. Fortunately, my first task when making camp was always to set up the tent. East clutched the little notebook to her chest and ran for it. I was right behind her with the pack and the armful of Mr. Giovanni's clothes she'd set aside for herself. The rest of our gear was already inside the tent, so at least not much got wet.

I'd been planning to sleep outside by the fire under all those stars, giving her the privacy of the tent, but the rain cancelled those plans.

After a few breathless moments of figuring out how two people, two packs, three sleeping bags and a few miscellaneous other objects could fit into a very small, very dark, confined space, we each found a place to sit. The whirring noise of the squeeze-operated flashlight was overwhelmed by the intense drumming of the rain on the tent.

East sat cross-legged on her sleeping bag, drying her long, dripping hair with one of Mr. Giovanni's shirts. My hair was so short, I just ran my hands through it a few times to shed the excess water. She had draped her wet denim jacket over the larger pack, while I did the same with my sodden dark green UCST hoodie. Not surprisingly, Mr. Giovanni had also had a dark green UCST hoodie in his backpack. The Scavengers had found several hundred of them in the wreckage of the university bookstore's storage room, each one clean and soft and new, individually sealed in airtight plastic, sizes XS to XXL. All dark green. So we'd had a generous supply of those for the foreseeable future.

As if the future could be foreseen.

It was funny, not to mention random, the things we'd had so much of back at the Settlement, compared to the things we desperately craved. Gran always grumpily said we had everything we needed and more. But then she had already mastered off-the-grid living long before the Bad Times hit.

East, shivering a bit, pulled on the way-too-big hoodie. I had to smile as her head popped through the opening. She just looked so damn cute. I was less so, but probably warmer, in Gran's old brown wool sweater. It was going to be a cold night, particularly with no fire. Thank goodness we had the sleeping bags. I was keenly aware just how thin the line was between our survival and us not making it. I would need everything I'd been taught to keep us alive long enough to find Segundo.

"Kell, can you hold the light for me?"

East had the tiny red notebook open again, flipping through the pages. I held up the flashlight so she could read, although part of me felt like I could care less what the Aptitudes had been. That was all past now.

But I guess I was a little curious after all. Curious enough to want to see what they thought my Aptitude was. After all the testing and analysis the school had put us through…Maybe Gabriel was right and they'd made me a Pioneer just like her.

Suddenly, it all felt wrong.

"East, wait," I said, moving the light away.

She looked at me quizzically.

"Maybe we shouldn't look. I mean, do you really want to know the Aptitudes for all those kids?"

All those dead kids was what I didn't say, but she knew what I meant. I thought the knowledge might upset her. Heck, I thought it might upset me. She stared at me intently for a moment, then looked down at Mr. Giovanni's notebook in her hands. She closed it abruptly, then handed it to me.

"I don't know," she said, biting her lip.

"Does it even matter?" I asked. "It's not like we're going to *do* our Aptitudes when we turn eighteen." *If we turn eighteen*, I didn't add.

"But it's our Aptitudes," she said, looking surprised. Like it was a done deal that of course we would do exactly what our elders had decreed.

"East, think about it. Like, if I'm a Pioneer and you're a Settler or whatever, what exactly are you going to settle?"

"Oh, you just assume I'm a Settler?" she flared up at me unexpectedly. I thought girls like her all wanted to be Settlers.

"And you're so sure you get to be a Pioneer like your sister?" she went on in the same fiery manner. "It's not automatic that we get the same Aptitude as our brother or sister, you know."

East had an older brother—Baird. Two years older than us. Baird Eastman was quite the Golden Boy. Tall, handsome, good at sports, good student, popular with his peers, respectful with the adults. I guess no one was surprised when he received one of the rarer and more prestigious Aptitudes: Messenger.

I should probably explain a little more about the Aptitudes. Not every role was assigned every year. It wasn't about filling a quota. The testing and assessments every student at the Settlement school underwent were what determined one's Aptitude. And they weren't just academic tests—I'm talking full-blown physical, psychological, intelligence and everything else evaluations. From strength and agility tests to an analysis of your ability to understand spatial relations to an appraisal of your communication skills. Gran was often impatient with all the former academics in the Settlement ("Got no more sense than a billy goat" was one of her favorite observations), but they formed the majority of the population so they made the rules.

Anyhow, if one senior class produced only Settlers, so be it. Settler was the most common Aptitude and the one that needed the most warm bodies, so that worked out. The next class might be a mixed bag of Scavengers, Pioneers, Engineers, Educators— you name it. Some Aptitudes apparently called for such a rare mix of skills and attributes that years would pass before someone got that assignment. That's how it was with Baird Eastman. I had never even heard of the Messenger job before him. Even Gran couldn't remember the last time it had happened. The Messenger's mission was simple on paper: to carry a message from the Settlement to Washington, DC. The message was simple too, something along the lines of, "Yo, we're still here!" Of course, the tricky part was who knew if Washington even existed anymore? Not to mention the three thousand mile-plus trek to get there. Baird the Golden Boy had squared his broad shoulders and set off the previous fall after completing his months of specialized training. No one had expected to hear anything from him yet. Frankly, most people never expected to hear from him again, period. That was the brutal truth behind his particular Aptitude. And yet those same people clung to one small sliver of hope that he might be successful—that he might actually make it back there and find whatever remained of the federal government. And that something good would come of it all.

It must have been hard on East, even if she missed her brother only half as much as I missed Gabriel. I'd heard the other kids say she and Baird were close. Their mother had died during the Bad Times, a few years after her first husband disappeared. A lot of people went missing in those days. Unfortunately, before their mom died, she had remarried and rather poorly too, to a drunken lout who was lazy when he was sober and belligerent when he was not.

This was the stepfather the two kids were left with when their mother died in the Monterey flu epidemic. The three of them had shown up at the Settlement, starving and bedraggled, toward the end of my ninth-grade year. East had been cooking and cleaning and dodging fists, if not worse, since she was a little kid was how I heard it. I hoped she was enjoying her vacation from domestic strife.

But she was still glaring at me, having taken offense at my "settler" remark.

"Sorry," I said, hoping to placate her. I hadn't meant to insult her in the first place. This was yet another reason I hadn't talked much in school—all the teenage drama was a pain in the ass.

"I'm just not sure if it's going to be a good thing for us to know," I said.

"Isn't it better to know than not to know?" she asked. "Isn't that what they taught us?"

I was confident she and I had been taught entirely different things in school. She learned that a pretty girl often gets her way. I learned not to get caught alone in the corridor between classes.

We both looked at the book in my hand.

"Dude, your hands are really small," East said by way of a non sequitur. I don't know why that rattled me, but it did.

"Fine," I said, shoving the notebook back at her. "Read the stupid thing."

"I'm going to save ours for last," she said with a gleam in her eye. Apparently, this was something like fun for her. Which it really wasn't. I carefully shone the light on the page as she slowly began to read, struggling to make out Mr. G's chicken scratch.

"Anderson, Kristy—Settler. Bautista, Enrique—Engineer. Cohen, Hunter—"

Her voice cracked on that one. I thought she was wiping a tear from her eye, but then realized she was lightly tracing the fading bruise on her cheekbone.

"Cohen, Hunter—Settler."

She made a big deal of skipping over Dupont and Eastman while averting her eyes and turning the page. By the time she got to the Witkowski twins, Adam and Astrid, I could feel the tension in the pit of my stomach. Which was ridiculous. Even if we'd still been in school, I probably wouldn't have done their dumb Aptitude. It was my life.

"Eastman, Elinor," she read her own name. Her eyes were shining. Her lips curved as she read her Aptitude. "Pioneer."

She looked over at me. "Ha!" she said victoriously. I rolled my eyes at her, but couldn't help but smile back.

"Dupont, Kell." Her eyes widened as she read the word that followed. She paused, for effect, I could only assume, then took a deep breath. No smile this time. "Are you ready?" she asked me solemnly. I nodded.

"Kell Dupont—Messenger," she said.

"Yeah, right." I grabbed the little book from her, certain she was joking.

Wow. No joke. It really said "Messenger" right next to my name. For a second—a paranoid second, I admit—I wondered if it was just their way of getting rid of me once and for all. Shipping off the misfit, the outsider, the unwanted freak...But Baird Eastman was a Messenger—no flies on him, the Golden Boy.

Was it a mistake?

Did they really think I could do it?

I glanced over at East. Two tears had trickled down her cheeks. She met my gaze defiantly. I could not figure that girl out.

"My brother Baird is a Messenger," she said.

"I know."

"He's not dead," she added almost angrily.

"Okay," I said neutrally. And paused a moment, unsure what to say to her in her fragile mood. I handed the book back to her. "Are you all right?"

"Aren't you scared?" she suddenly yelled at me. With the wind whistling outside and the rain now lashing the side of the tent. She threw Mr. Giovanni's notebook at me, but it sailed harmlessly past my ear. "Why the fuck aren't you scared?"

As quickly as it had come upon her, the fit of anger seemed to pass. She sagged from her sitting position into a curled-up S-shape on top of her sleeping bag. She wasn't even crying, or at least not much. I think she was more exhausted, physically and emotionally, than anything else.

I reached over and put a hand on her shoulder. She did not respond.

"We'll be all right, East. All we have to do is stay sharp and keep walking. We'll find Segundo. I'm not going to stop until we do."

We stayed like that for a few moments, she lying there in the fetal position, me with my hand on her shoulder. Finally, she gave a sigh and climbed into her sleeping bag. I did the same.

The third sleeping bag stood mute in the corner. I'd have to decide whether to keep it in the morning.

"Goodnight, Kell," she said quietly, sounding tired.

"Goodnight, East."

My last thought before sleep took me was: Me? A Messenger? Holy shit!

CHAPTER NINE

The Naked Truth

When I awoke, the sun was on the rise and had warmed the tent considerably. I could hear water dripping from the trees, but the rain had stopped. I got up and out of the tent without waking East. It was a glorious morning, temperature in the sixties, little to no wind. The sun sparkled and danced on the creek. Except for a hawk doing circles high above, I saw no other living creature.

I ate an apple for breakfast, then busied myself with spreading out our wet garments on a flat rocky ledge by the creek to dry. At least the rain the night before had washed some of the mud from my hoodie. I buried the no-longer-needed third sleeping bag and the items we had discarded from Mr. Giovanni's pack. No point in lugging that stuff—it would only slow us down. There had been no sign of man or beast following us so far, but I thought it prudent not to leave obvious markers of where we'd been.

After that, East still wasn't up, so I decided to take advantage of the sunshine by indulging in a much-needed bath. A few yards downstream, by the rocks on which our clothes were drying, the bank of the creek curved. A sandbar had formed, creating a shallow pool no more than three feet deep, protected from the current by the sandbar's embrace. With a little luck, I'd be washed, dried and dressed before East arose. I would have preferred the pool to be a little further from our campsite for privacy's sake. On the other hand, if East woke up and I was nowhere to be found, she would freak for sure. I stripped down to my T-shirt and boxers and stuck a cautious toe in the pool. It was cool, but not too cold. Nothing like a brisk dip al fresco to get your blood going in the morning. I took one last look around and listened hard as well. Nothing from the tent. No critters or people within range, except for the circling hawk and a smart-alecky-looking blue jay who was eyeballing me from across the creek.

I pulled the bar of soap from the pocket of my cargo pants where I'd left it, dropped the rest of my clothes on the bank, gritted my teeth and plunged in. The water temperature encouraged me to move fast and I did, scrubbing and lathering furiously, all the while trying to keep an eye out for anyone watching. Especially East. I'm no prude, but having her see me naked was way down on my list of things to do. I sat down with just my head above the surface for the final rinse. The cool, clear water felt absolutely marvelous on my body. I don't think I'd even realized how dirty I'd been. I dunked my head to wash the soap out of my hair. It was Settlement soap, so it didn't smell that great, but it did what soap is supposed to do.

When I came up for air, I saw East standing in front of our tent, staring right at me.

"Don't look!" I yelped, instinctively ducking back down. I didn't think she could have seen much, what with the angle and the distance. A part of me wondered why I even cared. Everybody was dead, everything was gone—did it even matter anymore?

But old habits died hard, so I yelped "Don't look!" When she didn't budge, I hollered an indignant "Go back in the tent!"

She shrugged once, then turned and went back in the tent, zipping the flap up behind her.

I was still sitting hunched over in the pool. Crap. Why had I told her to go back in the tent? Now she had a perfect view if she wanted to spy on me with her eye pressed up against the zipper. I sat there for a moment longer, but there was no way out of it. Either she was going to look or she wasn't, and there wasn't a darn thing I could do about it. I took a deep breath, stood and strode out of the creek with as much dignity as I could muster onto the bank where I bent down for my clothes. The blue jay cawed loudly from his perch in a rude avian fashion. I toweled off with my shirt and got dressed. Speedily.

I heard the tent's zipper being opened in a hurry. East practically ran down to where I stood. I avoided eye contact while I took my time tucking my damp T-shirt into my cargo pants.

"I knew it! I knew it!" she crowed triumphantly.

Crap. I didn't say anything, just got my hoodie off the rocky ledge, then crouched down to launder it at the water's edge, my back to her.

East was excited. I was…relieved?

She continued to babble. "I mean, I kind of suspected—a bunch of us did, we all talked about it, but I didn't know for sure, but I thought I knew and I'm right! I *knew* it!"

I paused in my scrubbing just long enough to turn my head and say to her wearily, "Knew what, East?"

As if I didn't know.

"That you're a girl, Kell Dupont—you're a girl!"

CHAPTER TEN

Right Field

So fine, fuck, whatever—I'm a girl. On the outside.

I absolutely hated the idea that they'd been talking about me. Even though I knew all along they probably were. Still, that didn't prepare me for the pain of hearing her say it. Why? Why should it hurt? Why did I even care what they thought?

I'd always been a tomboy, as Gabriel had put it, even when I was so little I couldn't remember it. Always ran around, got dirty, climbed trees. Always wanted boys' clothes, had demanded to wear them as soon as I was old enough to demand. I'd always known I was a boy on the inside, although the world said I was a girl. It's a damned odd feeling to not have your outsides match your insides. But early on, I understood that I was just me. A boy born in a girl's body. Felt like a boy, looked like a boy, acted like a boy. Was, in fact, a boy. It wasn't my fault the factory shipped me with the wrong parts. I was a boy. I had no desire to dress like a girl or be girly. It wasn't happening. It simply wasn't in me.

My family loved and accepted me. I was just Kell at home. No big deal. There was Mom and Dad, there was Gran, then

Gabriel and me. When I was little, life was just about perfect, I thought.

Then the Bad Times came and with them a storm of violent change and misery for everyone, not just me. But I still had Gran and Gabriel and their unconditional love. But I was only five when those Times started—a lot of it was a blur to me. A period of some stability then followed. Gran continued with our homeschooling for several years and we lived more or less happily in her little cabin in the woods. We made occasional trips to the Settlement, but Gran decided our family was fine on its own. My days were filled with lessons from Gran, chores, more chores and—whenever I could—adventures with Gabriel. Expeditions, she called them.

And it never occurred to me that I was doing anything wrong or even particularly different. I was just being me, being a kid. Being Kell—a boy who hadn't yet realized what a burden his female body would be.

Gran's decision that we should attend Settlement school changed all that. I hated that decision at the time, but it eventually dawned on me—as Gran's health declined from middling to bad to worse—that this was her way of preparing me for the world. It was a painful pushing from the nest, but I came to understand it had to be done. The truth is, the world is a wonderful place. It's people that make it shitty. It was the people I needed preparation for.

So off I went to Settlement school at age thirteen, in my jeans and sweatshirt and '49ers baseball cap. I'd always worn my hair short—that was the way I liked it. I'd always kept my nails short—that was just common sense. Maybe my brows were a little messier and heavier than the Settlement girls. Probably because I never bothered to pluck them. I thought they did a fine job of separating my eyes from my forehead, so why change 'em? Maybe my voice, when I bothered to use it, was a little lower than their voices. Frankly, the teenaged girls were astonishing to me. Astonishingly silly and loud and annoying. I felt much more at home among the boys. My silence didn't seem to bother them as much. And I was just as agile and athletic as any of them, more so than many. What I lacked in size and strength, I made up for in speed and guts.

Everyone—grownups and kids—seemed to take it for granted that I was a boy. Fine by me. All our classes were coed, many with mixed grade levels to make the best use of the limited teaching resources. We had recess, but no formal physical education classes. There wasn't enough staff for that. Didn't matter—I was getting more than enough exercise between my chores at home and my ten-mile round trip walk to school each day. During recess, those first few days of eighth grade, I'd either find a quiet place from which to observe or take part in one of the boys' games if it appealed to me. I loved baseball—two teams of nine was way better than the two-person version Gabriel had taught me. On rare occasions, we could cajole Gran into pitching for us. That's how I learned about trash-talking.

Gabriel let me choose my own course at school. She, of course, was making friends left and right. Like I've said, she and I were never much alike. I loved my sister, but I never aspired to be like her—certainly not in appearance. At sixteen, she was curvy, feminine, long-haired, outgoing and charming. Everything I wasn't and never would be. She seemed to easily fit in at school, with the girls liking her and the boys all agog.

At first, I thought I too might make some friends. There was one kid, scrawny and short like me, but a few years older, who was more interested in bugs than baseball. Everyone always called him by his last name—Burroughs. While the other teenaged boys played a quick game of baseball during recess, Burroughs would haunt the edge of the field, looking for caterpillars or butterflies or beetles. On the third day of school, I spotted him from my place in right field, engrossed with something by the foul line. I was secretly burning to make a spectacular play and show them all I deserved to man third base, or at least center field, but no one had hit anything near me all game. And Burroughs made me curious. He seemed like a nice guy. I thought maybe he could be my first new school friend.

"Whatcha got?" I asked, wandering over. I squatted down next to him to see his latest catch-and-release specimen, a gorgeous Monarch butterfly gently resting within his cupped hands. The pitcher struck out the hitter while we admired it.

"Check out the faggots!" came the yell from the next hitter at bat. Hunter Cohen, thirteen years old.

I straightened up, shocked and surprised. Was he yelling at me? At Burroughs?

The rest of the boys laughed, pointing and jeering at us. Burroughs let the butterfly go and quickly walked away from me and the game, disappearing into the trees at the edge of the playing field. The Monarch flew once around my head, then also had the good sense to depart. I was still standing there, looking around like an idiot, not sure what was happening. I wasn't even sure what a "faggot" was at that point.

Hunter was now making obnoxious kissy noises from home plate.

"Oh, poor little faggot! Your boyfriend left you all alone."

This led to increased hilarity from the rest of the ball players. I'd seen the feral dogs in the woods circle and then suddenly come together as a snarling pack, so I finally recognized what was going on. Although I still had no idea why.

"Are you talking to me?" I called to him, trying the direct approach. It's important to not let the dogs know you're afraid.

"Yeah, I'm talking to you, pretty boy," he yelled back. "What's your name again? Smell?"

That knee-slapper brought on a fresh round of sniggering from the pack. So much for making friends in school. The irony was, they all absolutely believed I was a boy. The ridiculous part was, they pegged me for a gay boy. A boy who liked boys.

When the truth was a lot more complicated than that.

CHAPTER ELEVEN

Three Questions

East stood there looking at me with a big cake-eating grin on her face. Her words—"you're a girl"—still rang in my ears. Well, no point in denying it. My body was a girl's body. I actually felt kind of glad she knew. The older I'd gotten, the more of a hassle it had become to hide my identity from the Settlement. Or what they would call my identity. In my mind, it was crystal clear. I was Kell—boy soul, girl body. Some might have thought I was confused, but I wasn't. I'm just Kell, I thought. Why can't other people get that?

Back at the Settlement, they had all kinds of names for me—the kids and some adults too. Faggot. Homo. Freak. Mistake. How can a person be a mistake? That didn't even make sense. Oddly, the people who called me a "mistake" were the same ones who liked to say their God didn't make mistakes. Those people were always a little short on logic, but full to the brim with hate.

Gran had told me it used to be different. The San Tomas of the past was famous for its free-wheeling radicalism, its open acceptance of one and all. "Hippie-dippie" was her technical term. But in the years that led up to the Bad Times, something went wrong with the world. Or the wrong that had been there all along grew stronger. Little by little, old ways began to trickle back—ways of fear, distrust and animosity toward those who were simply different. Even the university, formerly a bastion of liberality, found itself transformed by a rising tide of right-wing ideology and so-called conservative thinking.

"But how?" I asked Gran once. "Why did it have to go so wrong?"

She eyed me as if sizing me up, checking to see if I was old enough to hear whatever she was going to say. Finally, she sighed and with no trace of her usual humor said, "You have to understand something, Kell. For most people, it's all too easy to become the worst versions of themselves."

I put together more of the story with bits and pieces overheard from the adults through the years, and from what Mr. Giovanni told us—and didn't tell us—in history class. In those twisted, toxic years preceding the Bad Times, it became fashionable for the Before people to share loathsome messages on their communication networks. An increasingly repressive government fanned those ugly flames with poisoned rhetoric and the abolishment of protections. Cruelty and lies somehow became things to admire and emulate. The punishment for dissent was swift and brutal. It was around then when people started to go missing. And those who were left became afraid to speak the truth.

So after a while, the truth changed.

When I was a little kid, I had a book of stories about magic and princesses kissing frogs and happy endings. I spent countless hours yearning to awaken from my spell one day to find that I was a boy on the outside as well as on the inside. If that had ever happened, I would have welcomed it as a quick and painless fix, and happily lived my life without a single glance backward.

But instead, I grew older and my previously unremarkable child's body began to change. There was no doubt I was a girl on the outside then. The boys' clothes I wore easily concealed that from everyone else, but I knew. I didn't hate my body. It was me—the outside me—just like what I felt on the inside was me. It would have been easier, no doubt, if I'd been born in a boy's body, but who has an easy life? Anyone? Overall, I felt pretty lucky. I was alive, for starters—not one of the millions who had died during the Bad Times. I had a home with Gran and Gabriel. I had books to read. I knew in my heart it wasn't weird to be me. Not at all. What was weird was other people's expectations—if you look one way, you must act one way. No coloring outside the lines. Even though people come in all different shapes and sizes and variations, even the "normal" ones. So why demand that everyone fall into such strict and limited categories?

Why? I wanted to shout. Who cares? Where did all these rules come from anyway? And why does everyone else automatically know them and I don't?

One night, after an exceptionally trying day at school, I was upset. In the midst of railing against the world in general, I asked Gran those questions. Being Gran, she had her own special way of explaining it to me. She was enjoying some of her homemade blackberry brandy with dinner that night.

"People are assholes, Kell," she informed me, gesturing emphatically with the hooch sloshing perilously close to the rim of her blue speckled mug. "They're hard-wired that way. It's in their goddamn genes, I'm telling you. High time you found that out. What have they been teaching you at that school anyway? And is there any pie left? You kids better not have eaten all the pie…"

So back in eighth grade, my brief baseball career came to an abrupt and inglorious end. I don't think Burroughs ever said another word to me. After that, I mostly read at recess. I got a lot of reading done at that damn school.

Tenth grade was even worse than eighth and ninth, which I would not have thought possible if someone had warned me ahead of time. The girls developed, the boys started shaving. Couples formed, split and re-formed with different partners, a process that was as mysterious as it was fascinating to me. Even though I was remote from my classmates and thought most of them were pretty worthless, it nonetheless hurt that no one— no one—showed any interest in me. I knew I was no beauty, but I didn't think I was so awful-looking. Maybe I wasn't attractive in their conventional ways, but I wasn't a total beast either. I was reasonably smart, thanks in no small part to all that reading at recess. I was lean and nimble. But the things I had to offer were nothing anyone there was looking for.

In the end, it was just easier to let them see what they thought they saw. Easier than trying to explain, that was for sure.

An explanation was clearly what East was expecting now. I could see it written all over her face. It was kind of ticking me off that she was so thrilled to have figured it out. I wasn't there for her freaking entertainment.

"Well?" she said.

"Well, what? Fine, I have a vagina. You solved the mystery, genius."

She was brought up short by my curtness. "Well, I mean…" she started and then faded out. "I mean, do you want to talk about it?"

"Nope."

I finished washing my sweatshirt and laid it out on the flat rocky ledge next to her jean jacket. I brushed some dried mud from the cargo pants I was wearing, which only revealed the grass stains underneath. East took a seat on the rock next to my damp hoodie and carefully spread it out further on the rock ledge for maximum drying potential. The creek babbled happily along, accentuating the stark silence between us.

"You can take a bath if you like," I said, not looking at her. "I'll go in the tent. I won't look."

"Okay." There was another pause. I was hoping she was done.

No such luck.

"Can I ask you a question?" she said.

I sighed, but it was only to be expected. I took a seat on the ledge, the wet garments separating us.

"I'll give you three questions," I told her. "Just like in the fairy tales. Then we gotta get moving, all right?"

Her face was serious, but her eyes were dancing. I'd only spent two days with her and I was already a little alarmed by her emotional swings. Depressed and traumatized one moment, angry the next, and now tickled pink by her Momentous Discovery. This is what I hate about girls—they always have to make such a big fucking deal out of everything. Plus they never shut up.

But maybe that was her way of coping. There's only so much death and devastation our brains can handle before we have to take a break, even if it's just for a moment. I'd learned that the hard way myself, when my Gran lay dying in her bed, coughing away the last days of her life.

"Three questions," East repeated mischievously, her eyes sparkling, a curve to her lips that she was trying to fight.

If I'd thought putting a limit on her inquiries would make it less painful for me, I was apparently wrong. I so did not want to answer her questions.

Which didn't mean I wasn't thinking about how it would feel to touch her at that very moment. Those lips…that body…

"Okay," she said. "First question—why?"

"Why did I let everyone think I was a boy?"

She nodded. She was leaning back on the rock on her elbows. Her dark brown hair tumbled down past her shoulders, gently stirring in the morning breeze. She was wearing a white T-shirt and jeans. Leaning back on her elbows somehow made her breasts a focal point. I felt like she'd done that on purpose. Some women are like that, I'd noticed—only happy if they're controlling the situation with their sexuality. She caught me looking and I glanced away, blushing probably. I'd caught a glimpse of her bra strap on her shoulder. I had no need for a bra—I was still as flat as I'd been at eleven and it didn't look like that was going to change. Thankfully.

"Well?" she verbally nudged me.

Did I even owe her an answer? What difference did it make, considering the circumstances? My instinct was to tell her the truth—no, that's not right. My first instinct was to keep quiet like I'd successfully done for so many years. But that was all out the window now...

"I always knew I was a boy on the inside," I found myself telling her. "It never felt right to dress like a girl."

"Or act like one."

I looked at her sharply to see if she was laughing at me, but she merely looked interested.

"But you are a girl—physically, I mean. Right?"

"Right," I said shortly. "And that was question number two."

"Hey!" she said, dismayed.

"Rules are rules and they exist for a reason," I quoted with a smartass smile—one of the many Settlement tenets we'd had bored into our brains.

"Fine. Question number three," she said, drawing out the words as she thought about what to say. She was thinking way too hard. That wiped the smile off my face. A feeling of dread began to grow in its place. Surely, she wouldn't dare. Despite the schoolyard heckling, there were certain subjects that simply weren't discussed in the Settlement. Or maybe that taboo was the root cause of the heckling...I'd never really thought of it like that before. I looked back at East. She had one eyebrow cocked and that gleam was back in her eye. I could tell that question three was going to be a doozy, as Gran used to say. Whatever the hell that meant.

"Question number three," East repeated, rolling the words off her tongue like they were delicious. There was something about the shape of her lower lip that very nearly undid me, when I allowed myself to look. "Do you like boys or girls, Kell?"

I'd halfway expected it, but still I was shocked. People just didn't talk about that kind of stuff. Even Gabriel and I had never had that conversation, although we might have if she hadn't had to leave. At least I liked to think that. Of course, Gran knew my truth—she knew everything.

She'd given me the basic "how babies are made" talk years before. Since we'd had goats and chickens at the cabin, the mechanics of it were pretty obvious to me and any other child who'd grown up around farm animals. Gran's version of it was long on the mechanics—she'd been an engineer Before. Her speech was short on sentimentality (no surprise there), but she did throw me a few nuggets.

"Here's the deal, Kell," she'd told my younger self. "Some folks will tell you there's only one way to be in life, but that's pure horse puckey."

"What do you mean, only one way?"

"I mean folks'll tell you boys like girls and girls like boys and that's all she wrote."

"Who? Wrote what?" I asked, confused.

"No one. It's just an expression. Never mind. Are you paying attention to me?"

"Yes, ma'am. But I'm not ever marrying a boy," I told her stubbornly. "No way."

I think I was eight or nine at the time. We were sitting on the cabin's porch steps, watching our rooster scrabble in the dirt, his ridiculous puffed-out chest and fancy white feathers belying his low-down, mean temper. The chickens wisely kept their distance.

"You'll find your own way, kiddo," she said with a grin. "That's what Duponts do. And don't ever let anybody else tell you you're wrong for what you feel in your heart." She poked me in the chest with a bony index finger. "You remember that, Kell—love is the most important thing you can find in this life. And nobody gets to choose who they love. It's fate."

"What's fate, Gran?"

"Fate is that beautiful girl you're gonna meet someday who will make you very, very happy."

"And then can we get married?"

"Shack up for a while first," she said, sounding like the chickens as she cackled away. I had no idea what she was talking about. "Always best to kick the tires and take 'em for a test drive 'fore you make any big decisions." She whooped with laughter, which ended in my pounding her on the back as she coughed and coughed.

Back in the present, I was shocked and not a little embarrassed that East had so brazenly asked me about my preference. I didn't know what to say, so I did what I did best—I said nothing.

"Come on," she said, teasing. Like that was an effective strategy. "We had a deal—three questions and three answers."

More silence.

"Oh, come on!" she said, exasperated. "Just because the stupid grownups are too uptight to talk about sex doesn't mean we can't. Kids talk about it all the time."

Really. That was news to me. Of course, the other kids didn't talk to me, period. I gave her the look of death, hoping she'd take the hint and shut up.

"Okay, look," she tried again, this time with her best persuasive voice and facial expression. "You tell me and I'll tell you. Hey, you can ask me whatever you like. Give me three questions, Kell. C'mon, I want to play too."

I could tell she was not going to let it go. I could either tell her or listen to her garbage all the way to Segundo. And hadn't I planned to start my Brave New Life after graduation anyway? I'd only kept my mouth shut in school as a matter of daily survival. Once I turned eighteen and graduated, though, I'd envisioned a whole different existence. An honest life—even if that meant I had to be alone.

I snuck a glance at East. She was now fully reclined on the flat rock ledge, lying on her side, with her head propped on her fist. I'd noticed before—in school—how at ease she seemed with her body. I envied her that. Must be nice to be a girl on the inside *and* a girl on the outside, I thought wistfully. My life would have been so much easier if I had been the gay boy they all thought I was.

But I wasn't. I stole one more look at East, who met my gaze. I took a breath. I said to her three of the words that I'd never actually said to anyone. Never even said out loud to myself.

"I like girls," I said. Then looked away from her, across the creek, away from that dark blue eye contact that made me feel like I was an electric circuit in danger of shorting out. The lights we'd used on special occasions at the Settlement were always arcing out with small but spectacular displays of red and gold sparks.

I felt, rather than saw, East ease herself off the ledge and walk over to stand beside me, her face on the same level as mine. Her bare hand brushed my arm. I couldn't look. I struggled desperately to keep my focus on the opposite bank.

She said, "I like boys and girls."

We both listened to the stream rushing by for a moment. A long moment. I didn't say anything—there was nothing to be said. She had to be shitting me, I figured. So she was a mean girl after all.

What else did I expect?

I threw a pebble into the water, then stood, stretching past her to gather up my still-damp sweatshirt.

"Well, you'll have your pick of both at Segundo, so let's get a move on," I said with no expression.

Nonchalance was also one of my best things.

CHAPTER TWELVE

Welcome To Deadwood

We didn't talk as we followed the creek on its winding northeasterly path. My compass confirmed we were headed in more or less the right direction. My plan—well, my hope—was that it would intersect 17 at some point. I hated to leave the water source behind, but at the same time, I was eager to find the highway again. Freestyling it off the road was an excellent way to get lost. The last thing I wanted was for us to end up on the west side of the bay, on the peninsula which ended in San Francisco. We needed to find the V that my sister had told me about and make sure we went up the right fork, not the left.

The silence was peaceful as we trudged along. It wasn't total silence, of course. There was the creek and the birds and the wind in the trees. I loved the sounds of nature, the sights and smells. I much preferred the woods and the water to the company of my fellow human beings. If it weren't for the nightmarish quality of the circumstances, I would have been having a reasonably good time.

We walked for hours. We hadn't come across 17 yet, but I wasn't too worried. Yet. I knew we were headed in the correct direction, although the creek was taking us more north than east. The sun was directly overhead, beating down on us warmly, but not unbearably hot. I was looking for a spot to stop for lunch when the creek took us around another bend. Up ahead the land rose sharply, forming a ridge that ran at an angle to our path, like the spine of some giant sleeping animal. 17!

I stopped and turned to East happily.

"What?" she said.

"We found the highway again," I said, pointing and grinning like a fool. I hadn't realized how anxious I had been. The relief was exhilarating.

"Didn't know it was lost," she said shortly. I'd already learned she got grumpy when she was hungry. My own stomach was growling.

"Let's break for lunch," I told her, still delighted with having found the highway.

She brightened at the mention of food, but there wasn't much to be had. We were down to two apples and some jerky.

"That's it?" East said, sounding outraged.

"At least we've got plenty of water," I said, trying to make the best of it.

I got a little fire going, just big enough to boil some more water for the road. Food was definitely a concern. Once we found the V and headed up the right side of the bay, though, I had hopes of finding some sustenance along the shoreline—crabs, shellfish, something. I wished I had fishing gear with me, but no such luck. There were fish in the stream beside us, but they were far too quick and wily for me to catch with my bare hands. Although I might have had a shot with a sharpened stick...I decided to keep an eye out for a good stick as we continued our hike. With any luck, we'd be camping on the eastern shore of the bay that evening and enjoying a seafood dinner.

At least that was the rosy picture I painted for East after lunch. We were back on the highway and I kept thinking we'd find that elusive V any minute. But minutes and then at least an hour had passed and there was still no sign of it. The landscape looked the same all around us—the high coastal hills to our west with the ever-present fog starting to peek over the top. The flat plain extending to the north and east, where more hills awaited. No sign of the V, no sign of the bay.

But whereas we'd started our journey in the forest and then continued alongside a creek, we were now in an area that had formerly been inhabited. We could see the remains of what had been a town on either side of the highway. The Bay Area had, of course, been heavily populated Before. The stretch of 17 which ran through the forest was the exception, not the rule. I knew we would encounter the ruins of previously bustling cities and towns as we progressed along the highway, but I didn't like it. I much preferred the woods to these ghost towns. I remembered some of their names from a lesson at school: Sunnyvale, Mountain View, Pacifica. Somehow only the pretty-sounding ones stuck in my head.

Not so pretty now. We might find some food in a town, though. Not in the burnt-out or toppled wrecks of buildings. I was sure those had all been thoroughly scavenged by whatever people still found themselves alive there during the Bad Times. I hoped those people were all long gone. In the residential areas, however, we might find the descendants of the fruit trees and vegetable gardens some of the Before people had in their yards. That kind of foraging required leaving the highway, though, and was not without danger. You never knew who or what might be lurking around those old buildings. Something as simple and stupid as stepping on a rusty nail in the urban rubble could spell disaster for us. Plus, the roving packs of wild dogs seemed to like the cities for some reason. Memories of better days? I decided we would keep going and find the V. That was more important than foraging for that afternoon, at least.

Although as soon as I made that decision, I wondered if it was the wrong one. I could hear Gabriel's voice in my head with another of her survival lessons: "The time to look for food, Kell, is when you're full, not when you're starving. Remember, it takes time and energy to find food. Never leave it to the last minute."

"Think there's anything to eat in there?" East asked.

She was pointing at a building off to our left, at the bottom of a freeway off-ramp. It was an old gas station. This I knew from my ventures into San Tomas with my sister. Gabriel had pointed out similar structures to me there and explained their purpose. There were still some buildings standing in what had been downtown San Tomas and likewise in this nameless town, despite the passage of time and who knew how many earthquakes. This building appeared to be in fairly good shape. Of course, the windows were all broken out and the door was boarded up. A large sign teetered from a pole by a single screw, creaking as the wind rocked it. The elements had greatly faded it over the years, and some of the letters and numbers were missing, but it still proclaimed the price of super unleaded to be $57.99 a gallon. Cash only. What a deal.

It hadn't been that long since lunch and already my stomach was grumbling again. Fine, I told Gabriel's voice in my head—food it is.

I looked at East, eyeing her somewhat skeptically. She'd done all right with the hiking so far, but was she up for searching for supplies in the post-apocalyptic city?

"What?" she demanded. "What's the problem?"

"No problem. Maybe you should wait here, rest for a little while and I'll go see if I can find us some food."

"Oh, hell no, Dupont," she said, color surging to her face. "You are not leaving me here by myself. Wherever you're going, I'm going and that's that."

She grabbed the straps of her backpack and shifted its weight to ease the burden, staring daggers at me, daring me to argue.

"Okay, okay," I shrugged. "But if we're going into town, we need to be really careful, all right? Watch where you step. Keep an eye out for animals. And we have to be very quiet. If there's anybody else in there, we don't want to draw attention to ourselves, okay?"

She looked a little scared, but nodded.

"Gimme a minute," I told her, reaching around to undo one of the external pockets of my pack. To her amazement, I pulled out the gun I'd taken off Lookout Dude.

"Where did you get that?" she said, her eyes bugging out.

"Never mind." I made sure the safety was off. "Stay close. And be quiet, will you?"

We walked down the crumbling off-ramp toward the beckoning sign. As we drew closer, I saw that somebody had placed another old sign at its base. It too was faded but still legible—Redwood. Population 67,000. Someone had scratched a new name, though, with a knife or some other sharp implement: Deadwood. The scratches gleamed in the afternoon sun. They weren't neatly done. They looked more like slashes, like someone had hacked at the metal sign in a fury. It gave me a bad feeling in the pit of my stomach to look at that sign.

But the next one made me feel even worse.

"Shit!" I cursed loudly. I couldn't help myself. East clutched my arm in alarm.

"What?" she said in an undertone. "I thought you said we had to be quiet."

"We do," I said, getting control of myself. "But it's just—" I gestured wordlessly at the third sign, on the far side of what had been the street, directing long-gone drivers toward the highway. Highway 101 North, with a big white arrow.

"What does that mean?" East said impatiently, tugging on my arm. I turned to face her.

"We missed the V," I told her. "We're on the 101, headed for San Francisco. We're on the wrong side of the bay."

San Francisco. Even just hearing me say the words made her flinch. She let go of my arm and took a step back. San Francisco—city of the dead.

"How close?" she whispered. "Are we…there?"

"No," I said in a low, but more normal tone of voice, trying to sound reassuring. "We're still a good thirty miles south, I'd say. And we're not going any nearer, so don't worry."

"But the radiation…" she said, still in that hoarse whisper.

Now it was me clutching her arm.

"Listen to me, East. We're not that close. We'll just find some food here and then head back south. We'll find the V today or tomorrow, I'm sure."

Actually, I was thinking how in the world had we missed it, but it wasn't the time to share that with her. San Francisco had become a horror story, a tale to scare bad children with. I could tell East had heard it too many times. Personally, I was a lot less worried about ten-year-old radiation from Frisco than I was about three-day-old radiation—albeit on a much smaller scale—coming over the hill from San Tomas. Although, who was to say it had been a dirty bomb? I suspected any kind of explosion big enough to blow up the Settlement would create a mushroom-looking cloud. I mentally shrugged—whatever had happened had happened. The only thing that mattered now was finding the V.

East was still staring at the 101 sign, her eyes wide, her breathing shallow.

"Come on," I told her.

I hated the idea of backtracking and all the wasted time and energy that entailed, but there was no choice. San Francisco was literally a dead end and it wasn't like we had a boat to sail across to the other side. Hoofing it was our only option and that meant curving back south and east around the bottom of the Bay. I kicked myself for being such a dimwit. How could I have missed the junction?

"So where's the food?" East asked. She took a step toward the gas station building and I pulled her back. I shook my head at her. I'd been with my sister many times in downtown San Tomas—we did not want to go in the buildings.

"Not there. This way."

I led her up the street, which was choked with weeds and scrub brush. The trampled plants beneath our boots gave off a pungent but not unpleasant scent. We were headed west now, up a slight incline with the coastal ridge maybe five miles in front of us. The afternoon fog had spilled over the top and was tumbling down toward us ever so slowly, stretching out long fingers of grayish white mist through the densely forested hillside. Although we were tromping through weeds, the cracked concrete pad of the gas station had been remarkably free of vegetation. I thought about that as we slowly walked up the hill.

The street was quiet. Just the wind in the trees—lots of pines, eucalyptus, palms and others I couldn't name. I could hear the buzzing of insects and an occasional cry from a bird. Once in a while, there'd be a rustle in the undergrowth or the snap of a twig behind us, but that could have been any number of small, harmless creatures. And if it wasn't, I had the gun. It was heavy in my hand, but a comforting heaviness. I kept my head on a swivel, alert with every sense for both the food we sought and any sign of a predator.

Our target was a residential neighborhood, but this area had clearly been a commercial district. A few buildings were still more or less intact, but the majority had collapsed or burned. Sometimes there was a faded sign or some other indication as to the nature of the business. I figured that, like the layout in San Tomas, the shops and offices would have lined the freeway with the houses further up the hill. But not too much farther, I hoped.

To our left was the remains of an enormous parking lot, with several multi-story buildings either still shakily standing around it, or imploded into immense piles of rubble. HOSPITAL, read a sign dangling from a rusted chain. Or H SPI AL, rather, but I'd always been good at word games. Instructions in dull red paint on the side of one building, bleached by the sun from its former vividness, pointed us toward the emergency room. Well, we were in a bit of an emergency, no doubt, but there'd been no one to help us in Deadwood for quite some time. The wreckage of a crashed helicopter punctuated the weed-filled driveway of the ER.

A few more blocks up the hill, the neighborhood turned residential. Small houses, or the charred remains of small houses, or sometimes just the concrete pad the small house had sat on, appeared at regular intervals. I slowed our pace even more, my head turning from side to side as I looked for what we needed.

"What are we looking for?" East whispered in my ear, her breath tickling my neck.

"Roses," I breathed back.

"Roses?"

"Yeah. They're not native, so if we see roses growing wild, we'll know we've found somebody's old garden."

"Like those?" A tangle of pink and white roses was growing in the yard to our right. I looked at her. She grinned. "Beginner's luck."

Part of the house was still standing, though the roof had fallen in long ago and all the doors and windows were boarded up. The houses on either side were burnt-out hulks. There goes the neighborhood. Broad concrete steps led up to a wraparound porch. We were standing in what had been the front yard. I tried to imagine what the house had looked like Before. Like a picture from one of the books back at the Settlement. Maybe it had been a cute little white wooden house, with pink and white roses in the green grassy yard. Maybe a swing on the porch. Maybe a bomb shelter in the basement.

We cut around to the back and were rewarded with the sight of an orange tree and walnut tree, both bearing fruit, so to speak. Thank you, global warming. While East gathered nuts and oranges, I scoped out the ground level. If we were really lucky, we'd score some vegetables too. A potato would be nice. I stuck the gun in the back of my pants and bent down. I found a few strawberries and put them in my pocket. I was down on my hands and knees looking for more when I heard the growl. I looked up to meet the gaze of a surly-looking dog about twenty feet away. It was bigger than average, a yellowish brown with a ruff of fur standing up all along his back. Three more dogs slunk out of the bushes behind him as I slowly rose to my feet.

"East," I said in a low, but urgent, voice. I pointed my gun at the dogs, who seemed to recognize it as a weapon. Who had taught them that? They watched me with intelligence and caution, ears pricked, tails up, as I carefully backed toward the house.

East was picking oranges off the tree by the back steps of the house.

"Oh, crap," she said when she saw the dogs.

"Yeah," I replied. "Move slowly, but get up on the porch."

When dogs hunt in packs, one or more of them will circle around behind the prey so you're trapped between them. We needed something against our backs, in this case the house. There was no way we could outrun them. Four dogs, six bullets. Probably not enough.

The floorboards of the porch were old and rotten, creaking ominously beneath our feet. There was already one big hole in the wooden steps, where it looked like someone's boot had gone through in times long past.

"Gimme an orange," I said out of the side of my mouth to East. Our eyes were pinned on the four dogs, who had now been joined by a fifth mangy cur. I yelled as loud as I could, startling East, and hurled the orange at the lead dog, the first one I had seen. I missed him but nailed one of his cohorts on the nose, causing him to yelp and turn tail. East screamed something and threw an orange that went high and wide. The remaining dogs had spread out in a semicircle and were starting to slink toward us. What we needed here was less citrus and more bullets. I brought the gun up at arm's length, holding it with both hands and carefully sighted down the barrel. Just the way Gran taught me.

Several things happened so close to one another I hardly knew which came first. Out of the corner of my eye, I saw a man come around the side of the house. He lifted something like a long, skinny tube to his lips. There was a small, quick sound somewhere between a "pffftt" and "snick." A dog yelped. I refocused on the pack and saw that the yellowish brown leader was now drunkenly staggering sideways across the yard. Something was sticking out of his neck—a tiny dart. Small feathers with a brilliant hint of green where the sun struck them adorned the shaft. The dog stumbled, then one of his forelegs suddenly collapsed beneath him. His chest on the ground, back legs still upright, he pitifully fought to regain all four feet. His eyes were bulging, the whites showing crazily. His chest heaving, his jaws opened and closed, snapping shut on nothing but air. As the other dogs barked and milled about in confusion, one of them slunk in and bit the leader, as if to snap him out of his bizarre behavior. As the lead dog went down in a twitching heap, a second "pffftt snick" shot out of the skinny tube, unerringly finding the neck of the other dog. When it too collapsed, the rest of the dogs seemed to lose heart and ran away, snapping and snarling at each other irritably.

All of this happened in mere seconds. East had screamed when the man appeared, bumping into me hard and knocking the gun out of my hands. It skittered across the floor of the porch and fell into the hole in the steps. Instinctively, I dived for it, but it was out of my reach. I looked up from my hands and knees (again) as the man came around the corner with a hunched and shambling gait to face us.

And a strange-looking man he was. He was old, maybe fifty, with a thatch of matted dark hair and beard gone gray and growing every which way. He was stringy and stooped, but still considerably taller than I. In his hand was the tube, which I now saw was a thin metal pipe. His clothes were dirty and tattered and he stank, but he had undeniably saved our bacon.

I was awkwardly sprawled on the steps. Before I could get up, before I could even open my mouth to thank him, he reached down and grabbed me by the collar of my shirt, yanking me to my feet. In a flash, he had me pinned up against him, his scrawny arm around my neck, half-strangling me.

"Don't fight me, boy," he rasped as I struggled. "I can make this easy or hard on you."

"Hey!" East shouted. She wisely stayed out of reach up on the porch. I was doing my damnedest to send her a psychic message with my eyes to get the gun out of the hole in the steps, but she didn't seem to be picking up on it.

"No worries, Pretty," he said to her nastily. "I got plans for you too. This boy here won't make more than a morsel, though…"

East seemed to be thinking about beaning him with an orange but then decided on diplomacy.

"Look," she said, still loudly, but in an attempt at calm. She held out her hands, palms down, in a non-threatening gesture. She took a deep breath. I could see her struggling to not freak. "We can work this out, right? Let's start over, okay? My name's Elinor. What's yours?"

I didn't think making friends with the crazy bastard was going to be a successful technique, but at least she was buying us some time. I couldn't see his face, but something about the way he was breathing told me he was considering her words.

"You can call me...Matteo," he said, with a burbling, phlegmy laugh that was truly a horror. I didn't get the joke. I was continuing to struggle, doing my best to wriggle away from him. His rank body odor being just one of my motivations.

"Boy, you better quit," he said to me, shaking me hard enough to make my teeth rattle. I couldn't get away, but in that shake, I caught a glimpse of his face—filthy, with only a few blackened stumps of teeth and one milky, wandering eye. I also caught the metallic gleam of the gun in its hiding place under the porch. And Matteo's dirty feet in some kind of homemade sandals with rope straps.

If I could just get away from him, I thought desperately. Early on, Gabriel had taught me how to defend myself. Sad to say, I'd had plenty of practice over the years against schoolyard bullies, most of them bigger than I was. Gabriel had equipped me with a whole toolbox of dirty tricks that I was itching to try out on this guy. I was embarrassed he had caught me unawares. The whole thing had just happened so fast.

East was still trying to talk to him as if he were a sane person. I shot her a look and mouthed the word "gun" at her, but she merely stared back at me in puzzlement.

And then something really awful happened.

He *sneezed* on me.

His involuntary paroxysm resulted in his grip on me loosening, just for a second. And that was all the time I needed. In that moment of slackness, I wrenched myself out from under his arm and stomped on his exposed foot as hard as I could with my work boot. He screamed, then doubled over as I'd hoped and expected. Which meant his descending jaw met my ascending fist at high velocity. He went down like a ton of bricks. I then kicked him in the crotch for good measure.

"That's for sneezing on me, asshole," I told his prone and unconscious form.

I snatched the gun from under the porch and held a hand out to East, who still stood there gaping.

"RUN!" I yelled at her.

We ran.

CHAPTER THIRTEEN

The Three-Legged Race

We ran back down the weed-choked street toward the highway. The uncertain footing and our backpacks slowed us more than I liked. East was huffing and puffing beside me.

"Why," she huffed, "didn't…you…shoot…him?"

I was a little shocked to hear that coming from her. Bloodthirsty much? It hadn't even occurred to me to shoot him once I had disabled him. Temporarily disabled him. I cast a quick uneasy glance over my shoulder. Nothing and nobody back there that I could see. Good.

I probably should have at least grabbed his metal pipe thingy. Or…something.

I shrugged, both mentally and physically. It's always easy to second guess after the fact. If I started doubting myself out there, I would never stop. All I could do was keep trusting my instincts—instincts that had kept us alive so far.

Probably should've shot him, though. Well, maybe I could shoot the next crazy bastard we ran into. We were abreast of the gas station, our pace already slowed to a jog, our packs uncomfortably lurching up and down with each step, when East put a foot in a gopher hole and went down hard.

"Aw, fuck," she said between gasps for air. She lay still for a moment, face down, trying to catch her breath. I ran back to give her a hand.

"Are you okay?"

She pushed herself up to balance on her hands and one knee, the other one obviously hurting. Her face twisted in pain as she tried moving her right leg.

"I think I sprained it," she said.

"Disaster" was the word that immediately formed in my mind. Well, at least it wasn't broken.

"Can you stand?" I asked, scanning around us and up the hill for any signs of danger. All clear for the moment. I was ready for us to be out of Redwood/Deadwood ASAP. Our sojourn there just kept getting worse. I bent down and put my hands under her arms to haul her back to her feet. She winced as she put her right foot on the ground, holding on to me for balance. The knee was not allowing her to put any weight on it.

"We need to keep moving, East," I told her in as stress-free of a voice as I could muster. I had a bad feeling about the gas station. My gut told me it might be the home of our new friend Matteo. And by home I meant den. Lair. Hole.

"Just give me a minute," she said peevishly, the pain stoking her ire, which I well understood.

We paused there for about thirty seconds while she took deep breaths, trying to marshal her resources while I thought of all the perils we were exposed to by standing still in the open. The Crazy Bastard being Number One. If we stood there long enough, we were bound to attract other predators: dogs, snakes, cougars, bears. We really needed to get a move on. I took a deep breath of my own and draped her arm over my shoulders.

"We can do this." I put my arm around her waist. "Let's at least find a place to hide."

She nodded, the tense set of her jaw an indicator of the pain level. Cursing softly under her breath with every step, we limped slowly up the off-ramp and back onto the freeway. The wrong freeway. 101. We still had miles to go to get back down south to find the V. I fervently hoped East's knee was only mildly sprained and she'd be better soon. Like any minute.

There was little cover on the freeway. Despite my firm intention to head south and not north—not one foot nearer to San Francisco—a clump of cars about a hundred feet to the north caught my eye. My innate preference was for the woods, but being on the pavement did have two distinct advantages: we could travel more quickly on it than we could through the brush and we could easily see anyone or anything approaching us for quite some distance. Of course, they could see us too. For a quick, temporary hiding place, however, the cars would have to do. I spoke words of encouragement in her ear as we gimped toward them, telling her that was our destination.

We had seen other cars on the highway, of course, earlier in our trip. Rusted-out skeleton cars. It was best not to look inside as you passed. Not long after the Bad Times began in earnest, there weren't too many functioning cars left or drivers to drive them. Most people who could leave had already left the state by that point. And of the remaining vehicles not physically destroyed, something in the attacks seemed to have fried their electronics.

There had been plenty of warning signs of the impending catastrophes for those paying attention, both from Mother Nature and the federal government. The state government, however, had been desperately trying to hold things together. State employees—including the faculty at UCST—were told to stay at their posts, especially if they wanted to keep their jobs and benefits and retirement pensions. Some did, out of loyalty or fear or misplaced optimism. Thus our Settlement was born—a bunch of loyal, fearful, foolish optimists. And a few others, oddballs like Gran. Latecomers like East's family.

The vehicle East and I finally stumbled our way to was a really old van. Even Before, it would have been considered old. I'd seen a photograph of a much younger and bell-bottomed Gran standing in front of a van like this. It was a funny looking thing, a rectangular box on wheels with a rounded top. Snazzy two-toned paint with baby blue on the sides and white on the top that extended into a triangle on the front, where a chrome symbol something like the peace sign Gran was making in the picture was displayed. Except that van was shiny and new, kind of like Gran was too at that time.

This van was rusty and a complete wreck. It was tipped over on its side, for starters. It was hard to tell who had T-boned whom, but a demolished sedan was propping up the van. All the windows in both cars were busted out. The van's windshield was cracked and starred but still in place. We went around the far side so no one approaching from the south could see us. I got her settled on the ground, leaning against the van's undercarriage. She gratefully accepted my canteen and took a big drink.

"How you doing?" I said to her. She had her head back, her eyes closed. She nodded without saying anything. I knelt down beside her and touched her jean-clad thigh lightly. She opened her eyes and looked at me questioningly.

"Okay if I take a look?" I asked.

She shrugged, but I could feel her eyes on me as I gently manipulated her knee, checking to see if the joint was still moving all the ways it was supposed to, trying to feel with my hands if there was any grinding or any sign of a broken bone. Not that I was any kind of a medic, but I knew all about falling out of trees, leaping without looking, and the resultant bruises, bangs and bumps. East bore it all without complaint, although there was a sharp intake of breath at one particular movement. She squeezed my shoulder tightly.

"Ow. That hurt."

"Sorry." I used one of Mr. Giovanni's extra-long socks to bind up the knee. I gave it my best shot, which was clumsy and probably all wrong, but East gave me a wan smile when I was done and said it felt a little better. I pulled her to her feet and let her test it, taking a few tentative steps to and fro behind the cover of the van. She kept a grip on my arm for balance.

All this time I had kept my ears cocked for any sound of pursuit. It was hard for more reasons than one. The wind had picked up. The fog, which had started as delicate white tendrils creeping over the top of the hills, had now grown and revealed itself to be a huge bank of epic proportions. The clouds had proliferated and darkened as the afternoon progressed. The very air felt ripe with the need to rain, but so far not much had come down. Just an occasional sprinkle here and there. And I'd be lying if I told you East's grip on my arm wasn't a bit of a distraction. The way she'd pinned those big dark eyes on me when I touched her thigh. Something electric jumped in my stomach when that happened. It was not really that enjoyable of a sensation. Maybe because my stomach knew it was way out of its league.

And it was dumb to think about that anyhow. This wasn't a date. This wasn't even school. Or if it was, I hoped we lived through the final. Survival 101.

"Kell, I think it's feeling better now. Maybe if I keep it moving, it won't stiffen up so much."

"Great," I said with relief. We simply could not afford injury or sickness. Not then. Not there. The walk we had ahead of us was not going to be easy, but I hoped we could at least make it back to the point where the creek had intersected the highway. We could camp there and resume the hunt for the damn V in the morning. Presuming East's bum knee was indeed just a minor strain. I took a deep breath. No point in worrying about everything under the sun. Just put one foot ahead of the other.

I was about to tell her the plan when a wild shriek rent the air. Ducking down, I glanced around the side of the van. Something else Gabriel had taught me—if you have to stick your head around a corner, don't do it at eye level where someone watching expects you to appear. No need to make it easy on a sniper or other enemy. Take a different angle and you might just gain that split second that is so often the difference between life and death.

Matteo had climbed onto the freeway a hundred feet south and was babbling and keening to himself.

And he'd brought his little metal pipe with him too.

CHAPTER FOURTEEN

The Bridge

"Pretty! Boy!" he roared as East and I huddled behind the van. "I know you ain't far! And I'm comin'…"

He looked like a madman, which no doubt he was. Who wouldn't be, after living all alone in a ghost town for ten years or more? Surviving on who knows what…I snuck another quick peek. He was looking up and down the highway, apparently trying to decide which way to go. He looked uneasy, uncomfortable perhaps at being out in the open on the freeway. Like a wild animal out of its accustomed territory.

"Okay," I turned to East, who was huddled by my side. "We need to get going now."

"What if he comes after us?" Her eyes were as big as saucers. "We can't let him get too close with those darts."

I showed her the gun. She nodded without saying anything. I suppose I could have tried to shoot him from behind the van, but I was not that confident of my ability to hit him at such a distance, with an unfamiliar weapon and with the wind picking up. I had no bullets to spare for target practice. The gun would have to be a last resort.

And honestly, I didn't want to kill him or anybody else. I just wanted him (and everybody else) to leave us alone. But I didn't think a courteous and well-reasoned request was going to do the trick.

"I see you now! Where's your little friend?" Matteo yelled.

How could he have seen us? I snuck another peek. He was facing south, gesturing wildly. I squinted. There might have been something moving in the distance—a deer, maybe? It didn't matter. This was our chance.

South was not an option at that moment. My hope was that we could sneak over to the side and disappear in the bushes without him noticing us. I grabbed East around the waist and we frog-marched as fast as we could to the non-Deadwood side of the freeway. Unfortunately, Matteo must have caught our movement in his peripheral vision before we'd gone thirty feet.

"Hey there!" he screeched as he whirled around. "Get back here! You don't want to be late for dinner!"

That last bit was accompanied by a nasty laugh. He started after us, but I noted with a grim sense of satisfaction that he was walking mighty funny. His pace wasn't any quicker than ours.

"Keep moving," I muttered to East, although I might have been talking to myself. We turned to head north, the exact opposite of where we needed to go, but we had no choice. As soon as Matteo had seen us, I gave up on the idea of disappearing into the brush. He probably knew every inch of the countryside around there. I could see the next off-ramp coming up, this one headed east toward the as-yet-unseen bay. If we could keep our distance from him until the next burnt-out car or other cover, maybe we could lure him close enough so I could put him out of his misery once and for all. Or maybe he'd get tired and give up. Yeah, right. Hungry cannibals do that all the time.

Just keep going, I told myself. And breathe.

"Hey, Pretty! Come back here!" Matteo was gaining on us. I disengaged from East and told her to keep moving. I wasn't going to waste a bullet on a warning shot, but I picked up a rock from the road and heaved it back at him. It missed, bouncing in front of him, which seemed to startle him. But he kept on coming.

"Stay back!" I yelled at him. "Don't make me shoot you!"

"Don't run," he answered. "I like dark meat." This amused him greatly. What a funny guy.

I threw another rock as East hightailed it, nightmarishly slow, for the next off-ramp. If he got within poison dart range (whatever that was), I would have to shoot him, I thought with despair. He dodged my rock, but in doing so lost his balance, stumbled and fell to his hands and knees. He watched us pull further away and gave an angry howl.

"The bridge is out," he yelled. "You're trapped, you little—"

He stopped as I continued backing away, staring at something high in the sky. I didn't look up. Gabriel had taught me the old fake-like-you're-looking-at-something-horrible-behind-your-enemy trick when I was eight years old. I wasn't about to fall for it now. I wondered what bridge he was talking about. But I didn't care as long as we were getting away from him. I turned and hurried to catch up with East.

As I put my arm around her waist, a quick glance over my shoulder showed him painfully scuttling back toward Deadwood as fast as his skinny legs would carry him. I looked up then to see what had caused this powerful reaction. What I saw stopped me cold in my tracks.

"What?" East gasped in between heaving breaths, bent over and clutching her knee.

I mutely pointed skyward to a sight I'd only seen twice before in my short life—the vapor trail of a fighter jet which streaked high above San Francisco, an emphatically straight white line in the dark gray sky. We both just stood there, gaping in astonishment like a couple of boneheads, for far too long. I think our brains were simply stupefied with way too much information.

Finally, I was snapped back to my senses by an ice-cold raindrop hitting me smack dab in the middle of the forehead. The good news was two-fold. Matteo had turned tail and run back to his hole, never to be seen again, hopefully. And we had reached the off-ramp we'd been aiming for. A large orange sign saying "Bridge Closed" was riddled with bullet holes. I hurried us down the ramp as the rain intensified. We were getting pretty good at the two-stepping in sync. If nothing else, I was finding her increasingly easy to work with.

"We need to get under the ramp," I told her. "In case they're looking for things that give off heat. You know, like people-type things."

"Like a drone? Infra-red?" We'd been taught this in school, along with fire drills, earthquake drills, nuclear attack drills and how abstinence was the best birth control method ever.

"Exactly." We found a spot underneath the freeway, in a convenient pile of rubble that sheltered us with concrete on all sides but one. There was a triangular wedge of open space amongst the rubble with enough room for us to squeeze in. As a bonus, it appeared to be snake-free. The concrete slab above our heads was a good six inches thick. I hoped it would keep us safe from any scanning, although I was starting to redefine the word "safe" on an almost hourly basis.

East and I sat on our packs, welcoming the chance to rest. Our view was back the way we'd come, so we could see if Matteo or anyone else was headed toward us. Thankfully, we saw nothing but asphalt, weeds and rain. And an occasional seagull swooping past. The bay must be near, I thought. East and I sat very close together by necessity in the small space. I could feel the warmth coming off her body.

"Is it them?" she whispered, meaning the jet. She looked scared, but not panicked. I was probably poker-faced as usual. I had learned early—and perhaps too well—that showing no reaction was helpful when dealing with bullies, snoops and other assorted assholes.

Who exactly is them, I thought. I had no idea what the jet was looking for or who had sent it. It was far too distant for us to make out any markings on it. Us? Them? Figuring that out seemed not only impossible, but moot. The only "us" at the moment was me and East. Until we found Gabriel, that was how it would remain. I shrugged, which was the best answer I had to her question.

"How's your knee?"

She massaged it gently with both hands, as if my question had reminded her it hurt. "It'll be all right, I guess."

We were both silent for a while, staring out into the rain. A random thought struck me. What if there were only about twenty-seven people left in the whole world, and Number Twenty-Seven happened to be a jet fighter pilot? Just out for a spin. It was ridiculous, but it made me smile for a second. A tiny snort escaped my nostrils as well.

"What?"

I shook my head and shrugged again. "Nothing."

"You do that a lot, you know. It's fucking obnoxious," she said. Pissed off again.

I was genuinely taken aback. "I'm sorry." I tried to explain. "I just thought of something stupid and it made me laugh inside my head. You know what I mean?"

"I'm right here," she said, sounding more and more angry. "You could share some of your precious thoughts with me once in a while."

I didn't understand what she was so mad about. Hello to another arbitrary mood swing.

"Sorry," I told her again. "I guess I'm just not used to having someone to talk to. And most of my thoughts are not really that brilliant."

I described my image of the twenty-seventh person left on Earth, the fighter pilot out for a spin. She shook her head.

"That is truly asinine." But she was smiling.

"I warned you." I smiled back at her. I had a sudden compelling urge to pick up her hand from where it lay on her thigh. To hold her hand in mine. My fingers even started to move on their own, but my brain made them stop. I clenched my fists. What the hell was I thinking?

"You used to do that a lot in class too," East said. "That secretly-smiling-to-yourself thing."

"You were watching me in class?" I asked skeptically. I certainly had never noticed that. On the other hand, at school I was usually trying to keep my head down and just get through the day without conflict. Sometimes I would even learn shit. She nodded.

"Why would you do that?" I said, still skeptical.

She went back to rubbing her knee. "I don't know...I guess I thought you were..."

Bizarre? Repellent? Contemptible?

A freak?

She finally looked up and caught my eye. "...interesting."

What a cop-out. I kind of hoped she would go on. And I kind of hoped she would shut up.

"And cute," she added. There was a new look in that dark blue eye now. Was she making fun of me?

Probably. And yet, there was something in the way she said it...

I was having a little trouble with my breathing. Most of the air seemed to have fled from our little concrete haven. How did that happen? If she was yanking my chain, I could always throw her off the bridge Matteo had mentioned.

"You thought I was a cute boy? Or a cute girl?"

"Just...cute," she said with a grin and a shrug. "That whole androgyny thing is kind of hot, you know."

Androgyny. I'd come across that word for the first time the year before. In a book, of course. I looked it up. How strange to find my whole life summed up in the dictionary, in words so dry they practically choked me when I said them out loud. I never knew there was a word for people like me. Never knew there *were* people like me.

I think Gran tried to talk to me about it once, toward the end. "Transgender" was the word she used as she went off into one of her stories about Before. I didn't understand at first that she was trying to talk to me about me. When I did, it got awkward. And embarrassing. When she started talking about surgery, I was horrified. In the Settlement, surgery was an absolute last resort and not something most people survived. If the operation didn't kill you, the infections would. And then a coughing fit shut Gran down. Between her coughing and my embarrassment, somehow we never quite made our way back to that conversation. I tried to look up transgender in the big dictionary at school, but that entry had been censored like so many others.

I searched East's face for a clue as to whether there was even one percent of truth in what she was telling me. Her grin widened.

"I'm trying to give you a compliment, dumbass. This is where you say thank you. Or maybe you tell me I'm cute too."

She knew she was cute. She knew she was beautiful. She didn't need me to remind her. I'm sure she'd heard it ten thousand times already in her first seventeen years. I didn't trust her.

"You like little brown mutts, huh?" I said with no humor in my voice. There was a warning in my tone if she was bright enough to hear it.

"Well, you may be little, but you're strong." She picked up my left hand and showed it to me. "See? Strong."

My skin looked dark next to her whiteness. It was kind of a nice contrast, though, I caught myself thinking. Her hand was warm and dry. I was highly conscious of my heart beating in my chest. Could she could hear it too?

"People used to say you and your sister were exotic looking," she went on. "But I always thought you just had a nice face."

I could not think of a single thing to say. Silence. Rain falling on pavement outside. More of a light drizzle now. *Say something*, my brain commanded.

When I said nothing, she gave me a small woeful smile. She let go of my hand.

"Sorry," she said. I didn't know what she was apologizing for. Maybe she didn't either. "I guess I just wanted to say...I'm glad you're here with me."

Of course she was. She would probably have been dead five times over by then without me.

Oh, well. At least I was useful.

And...cute?

We waited for a half hour or so, during which the rain stopped, started and stopped again. The sky could not make up its mind. I set one of the cooking pots out to gather the rainwater, but it only yielded about half a cup for each of us. If the point of our being indoors wasn't to hide, I would have been more aggressive about collecting some drinking water.

When I finally poked my head out of our cramped little shelter, there was no sign of the fighter jet. It might have been lurking behind the gray clouds massing above the bay, or the fog bank which had crept further down the hills as we hid. But we couldn't stay where we were forever, the plane was nowhere to be seen and I couldn't seriously believe they—whoever they were—would send a jet to look for two stray teenagers. If that scanning stuff was even true—a lot of what they told us in school seemed pretty outlandish to me.

So it was time to move on. But where, exactly? If it weren't for Crazy Bastard Matteo, the logical thing would have been to go back down 101 South and find 17. I had confidence (well, some) that once I got my bearings again on 17, I could lead us to the V that would put us on the right side of the bay. But neither East nor I wanted any further encounters with Matteo and his darts. From the way he'd run off when the jet appeared, I didn't think he'd come after us if we stayed out of his territory. But if we walked right back into his clutches again, East's hurt knee would hamper our efforts to avoid him.

So South did not seem to be an option. North would dead end in San Francisco—definitely not an option. West was the opposite of where we wanted to go. East? We were on a road headed east, to a bridge that once spanned the bay. If it still formed an unbroken connection to the eastern shore, it was the perfect and most direct choice. The adults told stories of Before, when there were no less than five bridges across the bay, with the Golden Gate, of course, being the most famous. It had been the first to go, blown up by homegrown terrorists in the early days of the Bad Times. War, weather and earthquakes had all taken their toll on the other bridges. No pun intended. None of them had been passable to vehicular traffic for years. I wondered what kind of shape our bridge was in. Despite the standard piles of debris and weeds poking up through the asphalt, the road was still walkable. I knew no car or truck could get over the bridge, but how about an agile and athletic person such as myself? If we could get across the bay via the bridge, we'd be saving days of travel time.

I decided to give it a try. Worst case scenario, we would camp overnight in some well-hidden spot, then backtrack in the morning. It was worth a shot. I explained my thought process to East as we shouldered our packs and started walking toward the bridge.

Eyebrows raised, she said, "Uh, not to be rude, but are you sure we're going the right direction?"

I had to admit it was a fair question, all things considered. We'd been running all over the place, first this way, then that. We both knew the old maps we'd seen in school could not be trusted. Too much had changed during the Bad Times. Geography itself had changed, what with all the earthquakes and violent storms. The afternoon sky was too dim at that moment to reliably find the sun starting its descent in the west. I searched for another landmark, something to convince both of us that we really were headed east. The road began to rise as we approached the beginning of the bridge. I was cheered by its sturdy appearance. Well, sturdy by post-apocalyptic standards. The side railings were missing in some spots. There were the usual abandoned vehicles here and there, and plenty of potholes. But so far, at least, we hadn't come across anything insurmountable.

As the road climbed, we gained a commendable view of our surroundings. Below were marshy sloughs, stretching for miles in both directions. North and south, if I was right. Straight ahead, we could finally see the turbulent steel gray waters of the bay with whitecaps dancing. In the distance was the eastern shore. The East Bay, they used to call it per history class. Cities like Oakland and Berkeley had been there. Behind the cities, further to the east, loomed an impressive peak called Mount Diablo. I pointed it out to East to confirm we were going the right way. Once we reached that far shore, we'd make a left and head north again.

"If Diablo's on your right and the bay's on your left," Gabriel had told me, "you're on track."

Now all we had to do was skip across several miles of open water. San Francisco Bay is not some cozy little pond. It's pretty much like the ocean. It's big and cold, with waves and currents and sharks.

I really wished I hadn't thought of the sharks.

CHAPTER FIFTEEN

The Toll

The first five miles or so of the bridge were easy. East's knee didn't seem to be bothering her too badly. There were places where the middle lanes had collapsed, but we could still ease our way along one of the sides. There were a few spots where we had to jump over small gaps, the water visible below. One ten-foot gap was too far to jump, but a downed light pole allowed us to safely scoot across on our butts. All in all, so far, so good, although I was acutely aware that every mile we walked was a mile we'd have to walk back if we found something that blocked our progress. I pushed that thought to the back of my mind and hoped for the best. Maybe Matteo was wrong about the bridge being out. The guy was mental, after all.

As usual, I was highly alert and checking behind us, in front of us, on both sides and keeping an eye on the sky as well. But I saw nothing. Heard nothing but the wind and the waves and the birds. Big metal power towers on concrete pedestals ran parallel to the bridge, their bases white with guano. Cormorants were clustered on several of these. The birds ignored us, but they got me thinking about nests and eggs. And dinner, always one of my favorite topics.

The view was astounding. The bay was vast and we could see miles of it on either side of the bridge. A delicate mist hung over the East Bay, but we could discern the ghostly, bombed-out skyline of Oakland. Or maybe it was Berkeley. No skyline in San Francisco, of course, but the remains of the Bay Bridge could be seen to the north. From a distance, these sights were striking, beautiful even—as long as you didn't know the ugly history. I was never much for history, though. Lots of the grownups were stuck in the past, obsessing over things they couldn't change. I was all about the present. If we could survive that, we'd make it to the next bit of future.

But walking on the vast, deserted bridge, with the vistas of bay, sky and land to feast our eyes on, was something I knew even then that I would never forget. It was gorgeous, even on a cloudy day with intermittent sprinkles to refresh our faces. East had unearthed Mr. Giovanni's yellow slicker from her pack, but I always liked the feel of a little rain on my skin. The tantalizing eastern shore grew closer with each step. The air, so fresh and clear right off the water, was cold, yet invigorating. Like it was infused with extra oxygen or something.

Ahead was yet another tangle of abandoned vehicles, this one larger than usual. Some big trucks, including an eighteen-wheeler, were at the center of the wreckage. About a dozen rusted-out vehicles were scattered across the bridge, forming a wall of metal that would have blocked anything substantial from getting through.

But we were small. We approached the line of cars with caution, but they were empty hulks. We threaded our way through, then found out why everybody had slammed on the brakes and crashed together in a pile.

The bridge ended. A fifty-foot section was simply gone, no doubt at the bottom of the bay, covered with barnacles. And/or minivans. Fifty feet of no bridge, then the structure picked up again, looking robust and saucy on the other side. So near and yet so far. The bay surged below, mere feet beneath us. I'd seen pictures in books where the water was considerably lower under the bridges on the bay, but global warming had melted a lot of ice over the years. San Francisco Bay, along with the world's oceans, had noticeably risen as a result.

Fifty feet of air to the other side. It felt so close, like we could almost reach out and touch it. Too far to jump, though. There were some crumbling concrete kiosks on the other side. I remembered hearing about people working on the bridges, collecting money from each car as it passed. Maybe that's what the kiosks were for. Or maybe they housed the electrical stuff for the light poles which monotonously dotted both sides of the bridge every hundred feet or so. My grandmother would have known what they were, with her mechanical engineering background. An all too familiar feeling of desolation arose in my chest, but was blocked by the lump in my throat. I missed Gran so much. And Gabriel. The only people who loved me. And I might never see Gabriel again…

Shut up, I told myself. Shut up shut up shut up. Focus. You've got business to take care of. I took another look at the far side. Beyond the kiosks, the bridge sloped downward. Just another mile or so and we'd have been on the eastern shore. Dang, so close! The thought of having to walk all those miles back made me feel sick.

A rumble of thunder summed up my mood nicely. There were more clouds in the sky and they were a dark, ominous gray. The wind was picking up too. We were going to be drenched soon, no doubt about it. I glanced behind us—nothing back there but a long soggy walk awaiting us. I turned to look again at the fifty-foot gap between us and the rest of the bridge. I had to get us over there. Had to. But how?

East came up next to me and wrapped both her arms around my right arm. A week before, I would have found that unimaginable. The day before, I would have found it intrusive. Now, I think we both needed the consolation of a little contact.

"What do you think?" she said, looking down at the dark heaving waters of the bay.

Something stirred inside me. Frustration, impatience, stubbornness, strength, will—call it what you want. A feeling that I would not—could not—be denied.

"Can you swim?" I asked her. She gasped and let go of my arm. I took that as a no.

"Are you nuts? We can't swim across that!"

She gestured incredulously at the waves below. They weren't that big, I thought. Only a foot high or so. And it was only fifty feet. I knew I could swim that far—no problem. Gabriel had taught me to swim when I was little. Although this wouldn't be like swimming in a pond or one of the little sheltered inlets by the beach in San Tomas. There were the waves to contend with, currents as well, and hopefully all the sharks were taking the day off. Fifty feet…it wasn't that far. I just had to convince East.

She was still staring at me like I had a screw loose. Hands on her hips. I realized with a jolt of recognition that she was just as stubborn as I was.

"What about our packs? Did you think about that?"

Crap. I had not thought about that. But there was no way in hell I was walking five miles back to 101 and then all the way down south to where we'd started out that morning. Several freaking lifetimes ago.

"Kell, come on," she said anxiously, pleading her case. "You know these packs won't float. They'll sink like rocks. And drag us down with them!"

"Well…" I said, trying to come up with a solution. She was right—we couldn't ditch our packs. I had some lightweight, but ultra-strong utility cord in mine as part of my usual camping gear, but I couldn't swim and tow the pack behind me. It would sink like she said. I'd once read a book where a boy lassoed hundreds of sea gulls so he and his friends could fly away from a sticky situation. The gulls on this bridge were not of such a cooperative bent, however. Think, I told myself severely.

What kind of tools and assets did we have on the bridge with us? I turned around to survey the available resources. Old wrecks of cars wouldn't help. Ditto hunks of concrete. We needed a boat or a raft. Or at least something that would float…

"There!" I exclaimed, pointing.

"There what?" East said, exasperated. "Look, whatever you're thinking, just stop, all right? I can't fucking swim!"

"Maybe you won't have to," I said to her over my shoulder as I jogged back to what I'd seen. One of the vehicles in the pile-up was a pickup truck. Its front end was smashed, but the cargo in the back had survived undisturbed—orange plastic barrels. I had no idea what they'd been used for—probably something terrible for the environment—but that didn't matter. What was important was that not only does plastic last just about forever, it floats. The barrels were filthy and some had lost their tops, but they were otherwise just as good as new.

"Kell," East said nervously, joining me as I examined the barrels, trying to decide which one was best for our needs. "What are you doing? Are you listening to me? Seriously, I can't swim!"

I jumped down from the truck. If we were going to cross the water together, I needed her to not freak out. "I'm listening. Look, it's okay if you're not a good swimmer. I can tow you over there—it's really not that far. It'll take like two minutes."

Dubious was the word to describe her expression. A wet lock of her hair hung down the side of her face, framing her cheek. I wanted to reach out and gently push it behind her ear. Stop it, I told myself. She's not your friend. She's one of them.

"Have you ever swum in the ocean?" she asked pointedly.

"Yes," I said confidently. It was even true. "That's where Gabriel taught me to swim back in San Tomas. I'm an excellent swimmer, East. You gotta trust me."

She trembled a bit as I said the town's name. Perhaps from the cold and the wet. Perhaps from the memories. Since our conversation about the Aptitudes, both of us had shied away from talking about the past, especially the traumatic events of the extremely recent past. It was just too hard to think about.

"What about sharks?" she said with a scowl, arms rigidly folded across her chest. "Let's just walk back, all right?"

"The bay is huge, East. The chances of a shark being in the same fifty-foot stretch of water we need to cross are super low.

And anyhow, those sharks are looking for fish to eat, not people who are bigger than they are."

I hoped she didn't remember from class that one of the Before towns that lined the bay was called Tiburon. Which is Spanish for shark.

She turned her back on me to stare across the gap. Maybe I was winning her over after all.

"East?"

Whoa. So not winning her over. She whipped around and grabbed both my arms fiercely, but she wasn't just angry. She was scared.

"I can't swim!" she yelled at me. "And you want me to jump in the freezing cold shark water like it's no big deal! Well, it is a big deal—to me!"

She slumped suddenly, her hands slipping down my arms as if she'd lost all her strength. Sitting at my feet on the wet concrete, she pulled her knees to her chest, then put her head down. She was rocking slowly, from side to side.

"Why can't we just walk?" she said, sobbing. "I just want to go home."

Oh, hell. Crying girl alert. Crying *tall* girl alert. If I sat down next to her, I wouldn't be able to put my arm around her shoulders. I got down on my knees and awkwardly hugged her from the side.

"Don't cry, Easty," I murmured. "It's gonna be okay."

I continued with the meaningless, reassuring drivel for a while. I don't know if she believed that stuff any more than I did, but that was apparently what people did in these situations. Eventually, she stopped sniffling and wiped her nose with her sleeve. I pulled out of the hug and rocked back on my heels.

"Did you seriously just call me Easty?" she finally said, with tears still on her cheeks, but the beginnings of a smile in her eyes and on those lips that I wanted to kiss so, so badly. Back in our school days, I'd sometimes fantasized about what it would have been like if I'd been born in the right body. When East came to our school for the first time as the new girl at the end of ninth grade, I could have been all charming and nice, showing her around. Maybe she would have liked me. Maybe she would have been my girlfriend...I couldn't even imagine that level of happiness. To be part of a couple.

Yeah, right.

We were definitely going to die out here if I couldn't stay focused on the task at hand for more than a minute at a time. Why did she have to be such a distraction? Heck, if I were alone, I would have probably already made it to Segundo.

I stood up abruptly and went back to what I'd been doing before, selecting a good barrel. They were pretty much all the same, so that was easy.

"We can't walk," I said over my shoulder to East as I wrestled the barrel out of the truck. My tone was objective, just laying out the facts for her with no emotion. "It's not just the time and the distance and the backtracking. We have to be realistic. Every minute, every hour we're out here, we're in danger. Swimming fifty feet and saving days of backtracking is a much better option—and a much lower risk—than having to go past Deadwood again and being out here for extra days and nights. We need to get to Segundo as quickly as we can. And I know you're scared about the swimming part, but I can do it, East. For real."

She stared back at me bleakly, not speaking. After a moment, she got up and walked over, looking deep into my eyes as if she could see the truth in my soul if she looked hard enough. Finally, she slowly nodded and held up her hand, palm facing me. "Okay. I'm in. And if you drown me, I'll kill you."

I high-fived her to seal the deal. We worked together to load up the Chosen Barrel, which seemed reliably watertight with its lid screwed on. The molded plastic lid had handles built in—perfect for attaching a length of utility cord.

It was going to take three trips—one with East, a second with the barrel full of my gear and a third for her gear. We couldn't fit all the gear in the barrel no matter how we configured it. On one hand, that was okay—it might have been too heavy for me to tow. On the other hand, I wasn't sure how well I'd be doing making multiple trips in cold and increasingly rough water. Was

I being pigheaded and stupid to think this would work? Was laziness the real reason I didn't want to walk all the way back and then around the bottom of the bay? These weren't idle questions. If I made the wrong decision, I was gambling with not only my life, but East's as well.

I knew what my Gran would have said. *When all your choices are bad, you've still got to make a decision. So pull the trigger, kid!*

I sighed. Time to pull the trigger.

We walked through the plan a few times to make sure I'd thought of everything. Then East climbed down first, stopping a couple of feet above the water line. Slowly and tentatively, but she made it. The steel framework holding up the bridge had plenty of hand-and footholds built into it, so at least that was no problem. The spots where waves splattered were slippery, but we both knew we needed to be careful. I lowered her backpack and other gear down to her. She found places to hang all that from the structure, using bungee cords as needed to secure them.

The next step was the barrel itself. I'd tied two lengths of utility cord to its handles—one shorter, one longer. It must have weighed about twenty pounds when it was empty and was much heavier with nearly all my possessions packed inside. The clothes we'd both just stripped off were in there too along with East's water bottle. The chilly air off the bay was an additional incentive to work fast. East had helped me manhandle the full barrel to the side of the bridge by a gap in the railing before she descended. Now I tossed her the shorter of the two lengths of cord. She made sure it too was firmly secured to the framework.

The plan was for me to gracefully lower the barrel via the longer cord into the water. But the hell with that—it was heavy, I was cold and time was of the essence. Either it would float or it wouldn't. I pushed with all my might. It teetered on the edge for a moment, then hit the water with a tremendous splash. My heart was in my mouth for those few moments before it resurfaced, bobbing like a cork on the waves.

I'd kept back two of my precious items, hanging them on a final bit of cord around my neck: my knife, which I usually carried in a sheath on my belt, and the flint. I was glad I'd thought to do that. Which made me worry about what I'd forgotten. I climbed down to join East.

"You ready?"

She didn't say anything, but nodded. Her eyes were big in her pale face. We were both shivering already, wearing just the essentials. I'd been trying to visualize a quick and successful swim from point A to point B, but my mind kept helpfully inserting brief images of all the cars, boats and planes that must have been down there in the murky depths. And God knew what else. Shut up, I told myself firmly. Just concentrate—it's only fifty feet.

East had agreed she wouldn't panic, wouldn't strangle me, wouldn't do anything except follow my directions and basically just float. All she needed to do was keep calm. Simple, except I could tell she was petrified.

Now that we were right on top of the water, the waves looked bigger than they had from above. Or maybe they had grown in the time it took us to get ready. The sky had further darkened, without a doubt, and the wind was picking up. Perfect day for a swim. Not.

I took a breath and jumped. The water was cold enough to take that breath away, but I knew I would warm up once I started swimming. The bright orange barrel bobbed nearby. A coil of roughly seventy-five feet of my utility cord was attached to it. I tied the free end to my wrist. The idea was to tow East and the long cord over to the other side on the first trip. That way, she could pull and I could push the barrel on the second trip. Maybe I'd inherited Gran's mechanical engineering genes. Maybe.

"Jump, East," I called to her as I treaded water. "The sooner we start, the sooner we're done. Let's get this over with."

She clung to the bridge. She looked scared. Her hair was blowing every which way.

"You can do it," I yelled, trying to be encouraging. A wave rose up and slapped me in the face, giving me a nice drink of salt water. I choked and spit, which is challenging when you're trying to look cool and in charge.

"East!"

I swear I saw her dig down deep and find the resolve within herself to do it. Her jaw tightened, her shoulders straightened, she shut her eyes and leaped off the girder into the water, landing almost on top of me. That splash of water went up my nose.

I grabbed her immediately, securing her within my arms. She had landed facing me so we were nose to nose. I was treading water for both of us, but instinctively, she was kicking her legs a little too. I tried not to dwell on the fact that her body was pressed up against mine in several noteworthy places. I got her turned so we were both facing west, got a good grip and started one-arm backstroking us across the gap. Fifty feet and closing.

"Okay," I said tranquilly into East's ear. "Nice and easy. You're doing great. Just stay relaxed."

She hadn't struck me before as someone who'd be good at following instructions, but so far our team effort was going well. Once we got a rhythm established, it wasn't as bad as I had feared. There was a current which was making us drift to the south, but I kicked and I stroked and I fought to keep us on track. Forty feet to go. Thirty.

"Halfway there," I said between gasps for air. She didn't answer. She had her eyes closed, her face clenched like a fist. I could feel the power of her will. It was remarkable. To hold her in my arms, feel her against me and feel her energy, her spirit—and all without saying a word. It was uncanny, like nothing I'd ever experienced.

Was she thinking about me? Probably wishing I'd shut up and swim faster.

Just ten more feet and I was still going strong. See, I told myself jubilantly—I knew I could do it.

"We're here," I breathed into East's ear as we glided to a stop at the foot of the next bit of framework holding up the bridge. God, even her ear was adorable. I wondered—not for the first time—what it would be like to live your life in such a beautiful body. She opened her eyes and smiled at me. I smiled back and let her go, helping her as best I could to clamber up onto the framework after transferring the cord tied to my wrist to hers. From my vantage point below her in the water, she looked nothing short of magnificent as she stood tall above me, one arm wrapped around a metal post, the other raised to pull her long, wet hair from her face. Water streamed from her pale limbs and torso. Dressed in nothing but soaked-through bra and panties, she was quite the vision. If she were a siren and I a passing sailor, I'd have been a goner for sure.

"Get going!" she hollered at me impatiently, with a peremptory gesture to the far side where our gear awaited. Even visions want a sweater now and then. Her teeth were chattering, her body wracked with shivers now that she was out of the water and in the cruel teeth of the wind.

The trip back was quick as I sliced through the waves solo, only raising my head for a brief gulp of air a couple of times. Climbing up to free the line securing the barrel was but the work of a moment. One slash of my knife and I was back in the water after giving East the signal to start pulling. Even with her help, pushing it in front of me was slow going, but it worked. After a decade or two, I made it back to the other side where the first flaw in my plan was exposed. The barrel was too heavy and awkward for us to lift up to the bridge no matter how we tried. With me in the water helping to raise it, East didn't have the strength to haul it up. With both of us on the girder, we were fighting each other for space and non-slippery spots. Meanwhile, the wind was picking up and the sky darkening with each passing minute.

After several failed attempts, East lost it. "What the fuck!" she bellowed at me, shivering and shaking. I was shivering too, but at least my hair wasn't whipping in my face.

"Okay, okay—we'll have to open it in the water."

"Do it!"

I jumped back in. The barrel had progressed from gently bobbing on the waves to bouncing up and down in the rougher water, but I tied it to the bridge as tightly as I could with both lines. The hardest part was removing the lid with benumbed fingers, but finally I unscrewed it—only to have it promptly sail off toward San Jose as a powerful gust of wind caught it. Oh, shit. Well, I could get another lid on the other side.

We pulled everything out as quickly as possible. East got dressed in a hurry while I joined her on the girder to secure my gear. I was feeling pretty proud of how well my little plan was working.

Pride goeth before a fall, Gran said in my head. The waves were now cresting at two and three feet, with whitecaps everywhere. The sky above was close to black. I would have thought it was eight o'clock at night if I hadn't known for a fact it wasn't yet suppertime. But we were used to dramatic changes in the weather. The "normal" weather they'd had Before wasn't even a memory for me and East. Too long ago.

Big churning clouds loomed above us in the darkened heavens. The rain was back, stinging and pelting us with cold, angry drops. I was glad East had the slicker. I needed to get back in the water for the final two laps to recover some of its faux warmth. My muscles were tensed, my lungs filled with air and I was half a second away from jumping when East grabbed my arm.

"Kell—DON'T!" she shrieked in my face.

"What the hell?" I yelled right back at her.

It was her backpack and sleeping bag which still needed to be transported, so I didn't understand her change of heart. Until I looked north where she was pointing.

A fierce black waterspout had formed about a mile up the bay. Even from that distance, we could see the turmoil it was causing in the water as it carved a path straight toward us. As we watched its deadly, chaotic dance with awe, a second skinny funnel dropped out of the sky and took furious root in the bay. Waterspouts—like tornadoes on the water.

And headed right for us.

CHAPTER SIXTEEN

Two Little Pigs

I quickly gauged the distance between us and the oncoming twisters.

"I can make it!" I shouted to East, struggling to free myself from her grip. "Let me go—we need your pack!"

"Are you insane? Screw the pack, Kell—I need you more than it!"

We both glanced as one at her pack and sleeping bag, hanging on the bridge framework, a scant fifty feet away, then back at the waterspouts. They were definitely closer, even in that small amount of time. I generously decided to change my mind. I really didn't want to be caught in the water when those things bore down upon us.

"Yeah, okay," I said hurriedly. Now it was my turn to get dressed in record time. I used my knife to cut the cord to the barrel, stuffing several feet of it in my pocket. East donned my pack while I grabbed my sleeping bag and the tent. I slung their cords over my head and one shoulder to keep my arms free. We would have to run for it. Again.

Even in that minute or two, conditions had noticeably deteriorated.

"Listen," I yelled above the now roaring wind and waves. "We're going to climb back up to the bridge, then we're going to head for those little huts or kiosks or whatever you call 'em. We can take cover in there. Just be careful, okay? Now is not the time to fall."

She nodded and gestured with her jaw that I should go first. With equal parts speed and caution, I climbed up the slick framework. East was right behind me.

I had never heard the sound of a freight train or any other kind of train, but that was the simile the grownups always used to describe the incredible din of a dangerous windstorm. The waterspouts were closing in, almost like they could see us. Like we were their chosen targets. I don't know if East took my hand or I took hers, but we ran like hell, hand in hand, for the nearest kiosk, a small cube of concrete. It wasn't far, only about a hundred yards, but we were dodging the usual potholes, debris (much of it now flying past our heads) and trashed cars. The wind was almost overpowering, threatening to blow us right over the side of the bridge. The howling of it was terrifying—I never dreamed it could be that loud. It drowned out everything, drowned out my own thoughts, replacing them with an elemental, primitive fear that all but overwhelmed me and tasted like metal at the back of my throat. Massive waves had kicked up and were slamming into the bridge from both sides. The whole structure was shaking from the violence of the tempest. So was I.

The first kiosk had its entrance on the far side, which at least gave us a little bit of respite from the wind. The door was sealed tightly shut, however, and we couldn't kick it in. There were no windows. We ran to the second kiosk, thirty feet away, stumbling and weaving in the ferocious gusts of wind. We were almost out of time. My ears felt like they were going to explode from the terrible pressure. The door on this hut was on the eastern side—the bay side. It had long ago been wrenched nearly off its hinges, but all I cared about was the fact that it was open. There were all kinds of crap blocking the entrance, however—so much so that we couldn't get in without getting some of it out.

"Kell!" I thought I heard East scream, but the storm snatched the sound away immediately. The pack on her back made her even more vulnerable to the wind. Frantically, we reached into the kiosk and started heaving things out. An old chair, a milk crate, boxes of who knew what, decayed and ancient computer equipment—as I cast them aside, the wind caught them and sent them soaring aloft. And some of that shit was heavy. I pushed East inside, then dove in behind her. An old desk was on the back wall. We moved it sideways across the open doorway to form at least a partial barrier. Not to keep the storm out—to keep us in that tiny room, maybe eight square feet. Loose papers and trash were swirling madly about, being sucked out the doorway. I hoped we were too heavy for that to happen to us. The storm screamed outside. It was almost completely dark, but I could still just make out the dim forms of the cluster of abandoned cars on the other side of the bridge. Where we had been less than an hour ago. East and I huddled together on the filthy floor, as far from the doorway as we could get (which wasn't far), holding on to each other for dear life. There was an old heating unit bolted to the wall beside me, so I linked one of my arms through it, hoping we could stay connected to the building as the waterspouts passed by. And that the building would stay connected to the bridge. And the bridge...

"HOLD ON!" I screamed to East. I doubt she heard me. She had her eyes closed and her face buried in my shoulder, her arms around my waist like steel bands. I held her as tight as I could with my free hand, winding my arm through the backpack strap and clutching her to me. Our legs were intertwined. I could feel a heart pumping madly, but wasn't sure if it was hers or mine.

The next three minutes were the most intense I have ever experienced. The noise level was simply staggering. I wished I had fingers free to plug my ears, but the best I could do was hunch my shoulders and press one side of my head into East's hair. The air above our heads was a hellish whirl of flying objects. The old wooden desk we'd pushed up against the doorway was jumping and shaking like it was alive. I watched in horror as it bowed, then suddenly snapped into tinder, bits and pieces flying out the door like bats pouring out of a cave at dusk.

And then the darkness became total. In the pitch black and violence of the storm, it was impossible to say how close the waterspouts were. If it had been a direct hit, though, I doubt we would have survived. The floor of the kiosk, the very bridge itself, was shuddering beneath us. I could feel, more than hear, the impact of stuff hitting the outside walls of our kiosk. I was glad there were no windows. Glad our shelter was made of concrete. An image of the Big Bad Wolf blowing down the Three Little Pigs' houses popped into my head and I laughed out loud, one short, sharp bark of laughter edged with hysteria. I had never been more frightened.

East was closer to the door than I was. When the desk blew out, I could feel her start to be pulled away. She clung to me with a desperation I matched. Slowly, inexorably, we were both being drawn toward the open doorway. This was a tug-of-war we were going to lose unless the waterspout kept moving. If it sat on the bridge, we were dead meat.

My muscles were being stretched to their limits. The pressure was unbearable. Millimeter by millimeter, East was being torn from my grasp. The awful slowness of it was agonizing. Everything I had—fingernails, biceps, willpower—was concentrated on hanging on to her. Hanging...on...

And just like that, the pressure was gone. The screaming winds, the objects smashing against the kiosk, the blackout conditions—in a heartbeat, they disappeared. It was still gloomy outside, still raining, still a storm, but the waterspouts were gone. We had lived to tell the tale.

"East! We made it! Are you okay?"

She was still in my arms, but I relaxed my hold on her from "death grip" to "very close friends." Then relaxed it quite a bit further when I realized just how tightly we were wound around each other. It seemed dumb to still be so nervous around her considering all we'd been through, but I couldn't help it. I jumped to my feet, then helped her stand on wobbly legs. She was pretty shook up.

"It was pulling me out the door," she kept mumbling. She was shaking, white-faced. I helped her out of the backpack, then had her sit down on it. I took advantage of the downpour outside to refill our water containers, giving East the first sip. I helped guide her shaking hand to her lips. I felt almost giddy. I was so surprised and happy that we were both still alive, I wanted to laugh and dance and yell at the top of my lungs. Since East was having the exact opposite reaction, I kept all that inside. She'd gone quiet on me again.

"Hey, we're okay," I told her, giving her a quick hug. "We made it. Everything's fine, all right?"

I could feel something in her jacket when I hugged her. I stuck my hand in her pocket and retrieved, incredibly, an orange. Rather squished and sad looking, but an orange. I was amazed it had survived all our adventures. I quickly peeled it and shared it with her, knowing it would give us both a little boost. Just a simple moment, but by the time we'd finished, the worst of her shakes was gone and the sun had even started to peek out from behind the clouds. As long of a day as it had already been, it was not over yet. We still needed to get off the bridge and find some shelter for the night.

"Come on, Easty," I told her with a grin as I hauled her to her feet yet again. I reclaimed my backpack and tossed her the sleeping bag and tent. "Let's go find a place to camp."

"How much farther?"

"A few more miles. Just one more hike, then we'll find somewhere good—maybe even on the beach."

She liked that, I could tell. We emerged from the kiosk into full daylight. The sun had returned, the fog and clouds blown away with the storm. To the west, the formerly fifty-foot gap between us and the rest of the bridge had more than doubled. The waterspouts had taken out another chunk of the span, including the cluster of cars that had lined the edge. That reminder of the storm's fearsome power was all the more striking with the sun now gently shining down upon us, the bay returned to a friendly blue with only the occasional whitecap. You would never have known what destruction had just swept through there with killing force. One more not-so-gentle reminder from Mother Nature about who was in charge around here.

CHAPTER SEVENTEEN

The East Bay

I was grateful for the sunshine helping to dry us out, grateful for the daylight that would allow us to find a place to camp before night fell and grateful for our full water bottles. The loss of Mr. Giovanni's pack was a blow, but even that had a silver lining—less weight to carry meant we could travel a little more quickly.

So it was with a relatively light heart and a bit of a spring in my step that I headed east once again. As we left the kiosks behind, I stole one final glance over my shoulder. For a split second, I thought I saw a figure standing on the far side of the gap in the bridge. I blinked and it was gone. I shaded my eyes and stared intently, scanning for any activity, but saw nothing untoward. Matteo? A figment of my imagination? Maybe I'd seen a bird's movement and my hypervigilant brain had filled in the rest.

"Come on, Dupont," said East who obviously hadn't seen anything. She'd done another of her mercurial changes in mood. "Who's lagging now?" she said in a teasing, semi-flirty tone I remembered her using on the guys in the Settlement—both our age and the adults.

I was uneasy about the distant figure, real or imagined, but shrugged it off. If it was anyone at all, it was probably Matteo and he was history. There was no point in scaring East with futile speculation, so I kept it to myself.

I was also uneasy at being on the receiving end of her not inconsiderable flirting skills. I wondered what had brought out that side of her. I flicked her a glance but decided to ignore the tone.

Another half a mile and we were finally off the bridge and on a highway bisecting the eastern shore of the mighty bay. The shoreline wasn't a nice sandy beach. The bay first dwindled into a swampy marsh, then stretches of salt flats, then some nasty chemical flats in strange and vivid colors near the ruins of large industrial buildings.

This had been a well-populated area Before. The many buildings, large and small, demolished or still semi-standing, were evidence of that. Nature had reclaimed the region for the most part. The warm afternoon air was heavily scented with the fragrances of plants as well as the bay itself.

We were headed inland, which made me a bit jumpy. I was completely unfamiliar with this part of the world. I knew from Gabriel's dirt map that yet another highway ran north and south, paralleling the bay. We needed to find that highway—the old Interstate 80—and follow it north.

But not that night. A safe place to camp was our current top priority, with food a close second and sleep in third. I could feel my body starting to crash after all the exertion and excitement of the day. I couldn't believe we had awakened beside the creek that morning.

The chemical flats on both sides of us were starting to peter out into just plain dirt and bushes. I felt reluctant to leave the Bay behind since it was potentially a good source of food. If we headed directly north, we'd still be going in the right direction and we could keep close to the Bay for a little bit longer. We could cut further inland the next day and hook up with the interstate then.

A narrow dirt path, an animal trail, beckoned off to the left. It looked like a good jumping-off point for us. I wanted to sleep where I could hear the water, for one more night at least. I was trying and mostly succeeding at not worrying too much about someone following us. If I had seen Matteo, I couldn't imagine that he would follow us all the way into the East Bay. He didn't seem built for long-range pursuit, either mentally or physically. Not to mention, I was pretty sure I'd broken at least one bone in his foot when I stomped him. In any event, taking a random path off the side of the highway seemed like a good way to thwart anyone trying to track us down.

"Think what they'd expect you to do," Gabriel had told me when I complained to her about bullies chasing me after school whenever she wasn't accompanying me. "Then, do something totally different. And kick their asses, if you can manage it."

I'd followed her advice as always. The next time those dipshits chased me in the forest—Hunter Cohen leading the way—I circled back behind them, found a good hiding place and pegged two of them in the head with well-thrown pinecones. Gave one of them a bloody nose. They lost interest in the let's-chase-Kell-into-the-woods game after that.

East hadn't mentioned Hunter's name in a while. Me neither.

I was tired. My feet were dragging. My stomach was growling. Our dirt path was taking us alongside yet another marsh. Sea birds were having a hoedown there, which seemed to be a prime feeding area for them. Scores of white and gray birds of varying sizes and species wheeled and shrieked in the sky, dove into the water or bobbed placidly on top of it, according to their preferences. I guessed they were feeding on insects. East and I weren't that desperate yet. Give it another day or two, I thought.

We plodded onward. At the edge of the marsh, dozens of snowy white birds whose name I did not know had built nests. They stared beadily at us, opening and closing their bills with a clack, spreading their wings to look bigger, but not making any other sounds. They were clearly not happy with our intrusion into their nesting grounds. To me, though, nests meant only one thing—eggs.

I stopped and took off the backpack, donned my sweatshirt, then pulled up the hood over my baseball cap and drew the strings tightly around my face. I pulled a worn pair of old suede work gloves from my pack.

"Put that on," I told East, nodding toward my backpack. I pulled a mesh stuff sack from the pack's side pocket. The camper's best friend. "Wait here. And get ready to run."

"What…?"

As soon as I stepped off the path into the marsh—with a big squish—I wished I had hip waders. Well, sometimes you have to get dirty to get dinner.

The birds freaked as soon as I set foot into their swamp. Their nests were built on little hillocks of grass amongst the muck and shallow standing water. My best bet was to get in and out as quickly as possible and then run for it. The shrieking and squawking and general clamor was earsplitting. Much flapping of wings and hissing too. They were mean little suckers, those sea birds. Of course I was stealing their unborn children. *Sorry, birdies*, I said to them in my head, and meant it. Gabriel and I had been brought up to respect and honor nature—we'd been taught to apologize to an animal before we killed it and to thank its spirit before eating it. Maybe it was silly, but it seemed important to keep that Dupont family tradition alive.

I felt bad for the birds, but a lot worse for me and East. I splashed my way from nest to nest, collecting eggs somewhat smaller than what our chickens had produced and stowed them carefully in the mesh bag. The flock was incensed, with some of the bolder members dive-bombing me and pecking at my hoodie, which was alarming but did no real damage. They crapped on me too, whether by design or out of sheer frustration I did not know. That strategy eventually proved effective in driving me away from their nesting ground, but not before I gathered close to a dozen eggs. I couldn't really run, at first because I was in a swamp and then because I didn't want to break the eggs, but I've never walked faster in my life.

East was waiting for me down the path.

"You're covered in bird shit," she laughed.

"You might want to be nicer to the person who's got your dinner," I told her, running a hand through my hair. My head felt nibbled on, but no blood had been drawn.

We found a place to camp for the night a few minutes later. The path took us through tall pine trees, all of which leaned eastward, blown that way by the wind off the bay. The water was out of sight, but I sensed it was not far away. All was quiet and serene as we hiked through the forest-like setting, years of pine needles soft and slippery beneath our feet. We topped a small rise where the path led between two gnarled and ancient trees to find a beach spread out below us. A real beach with white sand and the mild surf of the bay rolling up on its shore. Remnants of a pier or breakwater could be seen jutting up through the waves. Trees and shrubs formed a border to the east. The beach wasn't very wide, but it was long. It ran northward as far as my eyes could see.

"Oh, let's stay here!" East said, a look of delight upon her face.

"Sounds good to me."

We pitched the tent in the trees where it wasn't so obvious and then camouflaged it with some leafy branches. We weren't exactly hiding. We weren't exactly not hiding. Didn't hurt to be cautious when we had that luxury.

After setting up camp—which was easier now that we had fewer possessions—we built a fire in a sheltered spot behind a sand dune. This provided some protection from the wind, but it also kept the fire from being a blazing beacon on the open shoreline. As the sun set, East took charge of cooking the eggs while I rinsed my befouled hoodie in the surf. I thought about looking for more food, like crabs or clams, but was too dog-tired to do anything more than think about it. Tomorrow, I thought. Maybe we could fish as well. Scrambled eggs that only tasted a little weird and a handful of walnuts from East's pockets was our menu for that evening.

The temperature dropped rapidly when the sun set. As we ate dinner by the fire, exhaustion settled upon me like a thick dark cloud. By the time we finished, I could hardly stand up or walk straight. East grabbed my elbow and guided me to the tent. It wasn't that late, but we were both pretty wiped. I'm sure I meant to have some kind of meaningful conversation with her about how we were going to handle two campers and one sleeping bag, but in the end, I simply collapsed on top of the bag and was out like a light before my head hit the pillow.

I awoke to the pale pink light of dawn. I had slept so deeply, it took me a minute to figure out where I was and what was what. Cold crisp air streamed in through the fine mesh window panel in the door of the tent. The door itself was zipped shut.

Tickling my nose was East's hair. My cheek was pressed into the crook of her shoulder. I could feel her deep, rhythmic breathing as she slumbered.

I felt sore, but good—relaxed and peaceful. The meal and the sleep had greatly refreshed me. I stretched, but only a little. I didn't want to wake up East. My astonishment at waking up in her arms was total. She was so beautiful and I was so...me. I didn't want to think. I just wanted to hold on to the moment for a long, long time. I closed my eyes and breathed her in. I touched my lips to her neck, very gently so as not to rouse her. Not even a kiss, just the lightest brush of lips on skin.

She made a small sound in her throat, somewhere between a sigh and an *mmmmm*. I froze. She moved her body against mine, finding a more comfortable position in the sleeping bag. She slept on. After a while, I fell asleep again too.

CHAPTER EIGHTEEN

A Day At The Beach

My intention was to rest for just a few more minutes, but the next time I opened my eyes, I was alone in the tent and there was full sunlight outside.

Damn it, I thought. That meant we had lost hours of daylight—hours that could have put us closer to Segundo and my sister. I jumped to my feet—well, I tried. No one in a sleeping bag has ever successfully jumped to his or her feet, but after fighting my way out of the bag, I quickly pulled on my pants and boots.

Then I stopped. When exactly had I taken off my pants? East must have pulled them off before she put me to bed. Which would have been quite an accomplishment in and of itself—cramming an inert form, even one that barely cracked a hundred pounds, into a sleeping bag. She'd probably put the bag around me, instead of me in the bag. I shook off the thoughts of East undoing my belt, then gently pulling my pants off since I had no idea what to do with that information.

I hopped out the door of the tent, still struggling with a recalcitrant boot. It was another absolutely picture-perfect day in the Bay Area. Brilliant blue skies, no clouds, beautiful bay breaking onto the beach in front of me, the incredible panorama of the peninsula across the water, with the bridge we'd come across the day before to the south. Looked like about eleven o'clock in the morning based on the sun's position. East was sitting by the fire pit we'd built the night before. She'd been working—a large stack of driftwood was piled up next to her. Which we couldn't carry if we got going like we needed to.

"Hey, Kell!" She waved me over.

I bent down to tie my boot and noticed my fly was open. Smooth. I turned away in a fit of modesty and zipped up, hoping my blush would subside by the time I tromped through the sand to her. The opposite seemed to be happening, though. My face felt aflame as I sat down next to her. Maybe she wouldn't notice.

"Wow, you really got sunburned yesterday," she said.

Having no answer to that, I shrugged. I felt tongue-tied and self-conscious. Nothing even happened, you bonehead, I told myself. Therefore, there was nothing to be embarrassed about.

"I think I got a little sun too," she said, turning around and pulling down the neck of her T-shirt a few inches to show me. With her other hand, she held her hair off her neck. Her lovely, lovely neck. "Can you see? It feels kind of hot."

I nodded wordlessly.

"I kept the fire going," East went on, proud of her diligence. "And look—we'll have plenty of firewood for tonight too."

I said something intelligent like "hmmph" and poked at the fire with a stick. She squinted at me, confused by my lack of response. But my tongue would not unstick. I needed to tell her we weren't staying there that night. I needed to tell her it was time to get moving. I needed to tell her...

"Why'd you take my pants off?" I suddenly blurted out. My face was on fire.

She stared at me, cocking her head to one side. "Are you blushing?"

"No," I said belligerently, sounding completely unbelievable.

"Well, the pockets of your cargo pants were so full of stuff you were clanking. I didn't want your jackknife or whatever poking me in the back while we were sleeping. And honestly, I thought you'd be more comfortable too. Did you sleep all right?"

She sounded sincere. She sounded kind. She could have teased me, but she simply answered my question. I felt something slip a little inside me when she did that. Like the tiniest crack in my heretofore impenetrable defenses.

Oh, no, I thought. No, no, no. I cannot be having these feelings for Elinor Eastman, of all people. I'm like a...bug or something to her. A pet, at best. But insignificant. Inferior. For chrissake, she barely knows my name.

"Kell?" she said, awaiting my answer.

"Yeah, I slept okay," I grudgingly admitted. Then, as an afterthought: "Did you?"

"Oh, yeah," she said with a smile, stretching her arms above her head luxuriously. "I slept just fine."

"You didn't think it was..." I lost my nerve as the end of the sentence arrived.

"What?" she prompted.

"Weird?"

"No. It was too cold to sleep outside the sleeping bag, and I didn't want either one of us to freeze. So...common sense, right?"

She shrugged. I could not fault her logic. Still...

"It doesn't freak you out?" I asked her. I was embarrassed, but I needed to know.

"No. I told you—I like girls, remember?"

I remembered all right.

"Especially to sleep with. Girls are nice to cuddle with. Soft—not all awkward and bony like boys. Right?"

"Right," I said weakly. Like I knew.

"So," she said, rising to her feet and dusting her hands off on her thighs. "What's for lunch?"

We were done? That was it? Apparently so. And come to think of it, I was starving. As usual. Which was not good, since we had zero food and only a little water. I kicked myself for failing to follow Gabriel's teachings. One of these days, that might just kill me.

East said, "I was thinking, maybe we could spend the day here, find some food and rest, you know? Just for a day." She hurried to add that last bit when she saw my face.

I opened my mouth to argue, but she beat me to it.

"Please, Kell. After all that...yesterday...I just need a day. Please?"

Fine. I caved. Probably not for the last time. Damn her hot girl superpowers.

But if you're going to wake up starving, the beach is not a bad place to be. I went back and raided the birds' nests again, royally pissing them off.

"Now what?" East looked at me expectantly, holding the mesh stuff sack with just six eggs in the bottom. Not a major haul, but my head was still sore from the previous day's pecking. She had appointed herself Official Food Carrier, which was fine with me. I didn't want to leave the eggs unattended and have some other predator steal them away after all the shit— literally—I'd gone through to get them.

"That way," I said, pointing north. "We'll check out the shoreline on our way up and the bushes on the way back. And bring your water bottle."

I grabbed my own canteen, my suede work gloves, the drawstring sack for the sleeping bag and the cooking pot with its lid. Not exactly ideal hunting and gathering equipment, but I'd been trained to make do with what I had. And then improvise.

Just up the beach, there was a jumble of large boulders right at the water line, extending into the surf. We walked toward it at a leisurely pace, taking it easy on her still gimpy knee. I was looking for food and water, but as always, I kept an eye out for anything dangerous like people or animals. It seemed we were alone on the beach, though. Our footprints were the only ones to be seen other than those made by birds. There were plenty of shells and sand dollars, along with intermittent piles of kelp, but nothing edible. East exclaimed over a brilliant blue piece of beach glass which might have been the neck of a wine bottle long ago. When she bent to pull it from the sand however, it was just the lip and about an inch and a half of neck. Where the rest of the bottle might be—and perhaps the message it had carried?—there was no telling. She held it up for my inspection.

"Pretty, eh?"

"Matches your eyes," I said without thinking. Which was true, but came out sounding like I was sucking up. Which I wasn't. East smiled humorlessly to herself without comment, fingering the smooth glass, careful to avoid the jagged edge. After a moment, she turned and threw the chunk of glass as far as she could into the water.

"No need for pretty out here," she said.

The tide was receding from the boulders but was not yet at its lowest point. It was frustrating to have so much undrinkable water in view. Water was constantly on my mind, constantly guiding us or limiting us. There were ways to get drinkable water from seawater or even out of kelp, but I was foggy on the details. It rained often enough in the Bay Area that I'd never needed to try those methods.

"Kell, look!" East cried excitedly, pointing at the boulders where the tide surged, then retreated. Crabs! Several decent-sized crabs could be seen in the cracks and crevasses between the boulders. I was able to snare a few after I found a long stick and added a loop of utility cord. East was loath to carry the live crabs in the pot, shrieking when I went near her with the first one, its fierce-looking pincers slowly flexing.

"Get that thing away from me! Can't you kill it?"

"No, you have to cook them live or they can make you sick. Come on, you're the Food Carrier. Besides, how am I supposed to catch any more unless you take it?"

We worked it out. When the pot was full, I stood on the topmost boulder taking a quick visual survey of our surroundings. There was still no man or beast in sight, save the sea birds. No boats on the bay. Something shiny glinted out of the corner of my eye. The sun on the water? No, it had been closer than that, down below me on the sand. There was kelp and driftwood together in a heap at the foot of the rocks. Then the breeze picked up and I saw the gleam again—clear plastic fishing line tangled up with the kelp! With a whoop, I jumped down from boulder to boulder until I reached the sand.

"What is it?" East asked.

"Fishing line," I told her gleefully. It was beyond tangled, all clumped and knotted into a ball nearly the size of my fist, but with patience and care I thought I could extract a useable length of it. Hooks would have been nice, but I could carve those out of wood or maybe find some bits of metal that would do. Even a hard shell could be used as hook material.

East was digging in the sand where I'd found the fishing line. She uncovered a chunk of driftwood. Underneath that was something plastic. A horseshoe-shaped handle, semi-transparent, maybe four inches long. I think we both thought it would be like her blue glass wine bottle neck, but as she tugged and dug, she found herself pulling out a true buried treasure—a one-gallon water jug with the cap still firmly attached. The jug was empty but in great shape. Say what you will about those Before people—they knew their nonbiodegradable plastics.

"Good job, East!" I was thrilled at the find. She looked startled at my enthusiasm, but pleased as well. The water jug was a major boost to our scant belongings. Now all we needed was some water to put in it.

We scouted the bushes and trees on our way back, hoping for a creek. No such luck, but we did find a huckleberry bush heavy with fruit. As I filled up one of the big pockets on my cargo pants, I offered up a silent "thank you" to the universe—I knew how fortunate we were to find all this food. We would eat well, sleep well and be fortified for the trek on the morrow.

We walked deeper into the woods, but found nothing more. I headed due west thinking it would lead us straight to the tent. So much for shortcuts—a large rock formation blocked our path. It wasn't a jumble of boulders like the beach, just one enormous chunk of rock, almost as big as Gran's cabin. The trees overhead, thinning as we neared the shore, provided some protection from the sun. That gave me an idea.

"Hang on," I told East. "I want to check something with this rock."

"What, the local snake population? Let's just be safe and go around, all right?"

I had my head thrown back, still studying the rock.

"Kell," she added plaintively, "I'm starting to smell like crab."

I laughed at that. "It'll just take a sec."

"Shit," she muttered.

I climbed up the rock, keeping an eye out for snakes like I always did, but I was in search of something much more desirable. Water. I was thinking of all the different ways you could get water. Obviously, you find fresh water in streams and lakes and springs. There is pure cold water flowing underground in inaccessible black rivers. There is water in small but drinkable amounts in certain kinds of plants. There's water in the early morning dew. And sometimes water falls right from the sky.

That's what I was after—rainwater. After a storm, you might find a pint or two in depressions in rocks or even the boles of trees. Wait too long and it will be nastily stagnant and growing skeeters or have evaporated altogether, but we were still within a reasonable timeframe, I thought. And if we could find some water, we had the fire to boil and sanitize it.

On top of the big rock, I was elated to find two hollows full of yesterday's rainwater. The first was nearly a foot deep, but only about five inches in diameter and tapering toward the bottom.

"Toss me up your water bottle," I called to East, who looked bored and grumpy. She brightened, however, when she realized I'd found some water. I filled her bottle as best I could and then tossed it back down to her. I warned her not to drink it yet, which bought me a glare and more vile words muttered not so under her breath.

My canteen wouldn't fit in the hole, but there wasn't much left in it anyhow. I turned my attention to the other spot. This was not so much a hole as a shallow depression, about three feet long, three inches wide and maybe two inches deep. There was a good amount of water there, but it was so shallow and narrow and awkwardly angled, I couldn't scoop it up with any of our containers.

"Are you coming down?" East sang out from below.

"There's more water here—I just need to figure out how to get it."

"I'm coming up," she announced.

I went to the side and peered over the edge.

"No, East, you can't leave the food—it would only take a second for a dog or something to sneak up and steal it."

She looked around nervously. "A dog?"

"Look, I'll be down in a minute, as soon as I figure out—oh."

It had finally dawned on me how I could transfer the water out of the depression and into the canteen. If I soaked up the water into a piece of fabric, I could then squeeze the water out of the fabric and into the container. I looked down at my T-shirt. It was filthy. Plus, I wasn't wearing anything underneath.

"Hurry up, Kell!" East said with some urgency. Her shirt looked a whole lot cleaner than mine. She looked up at me, shading her eyes with one hand. "Why are you looking at me like that?"

"Take off your shirt."

"Excuse me?" she replied, cocking an eyebrow at me. Looking like she didn't think I had it in me to form those words into a sentence.

"I need your shirt," I said impatiently, although conscious of how my request must have sounded to her. "To soak up the water so I can squeeze it into the canteen."

Still she hesitated, peering around like someone might materialize, point a finger at her and shout, "Aha—nudity!"

"We need the water, East," I said neutrally.

"Yeah, yeah," she replied, sounding dubious, but peeling off her top and throwing it up to me. I caught it and got to work on the water. Which is not to say my brain hadn't registered the sight of her, standing there in her beige bra, her skin pale, her form slender and yet with the definition of muscles showing in the arms and torso as she tossed the shirt up to me. I added it to my stock of mental images of Elinor Eastman, a girl I hardly knew until a few days before. And did I know her now? Was she being nice to me only because she needed my help to survive? Was she manipulating me, the way I'd seen her manipulate guys at the Settlement? For all our differences, I wondered if she kept her true self locked up inside her just as tightly as I did.

The shirt idea worked like a charm. I could almost feel Gabriel's hand on my shoulder, her voice in my head congratulating me. It wasn't gallons of water, but it was way better than the nothing we'd had before.

I climbed back down to ground level and gave East her clammy T-shirt, doing my best not to gawk. Hiking boots, jeans riding low on her hips, hint of abs, beige bra, tousled head of long, dark brown hair and those uncanny navy blue eyes. I could have stared at her for hours and still not have drunk my fill. Be cool, I told myself as I bent to pick up the crab pot—I knew she hated carrying it—and the eggs.

"Back to the beach?" she asked.

I nodded, tongue-tied again, and gestured that I would follow her. I thought she would put her shirt back on, but she merely slung it over her shoulder and started down the path. Dappled sunbeams streamed through the tree limbs, the path winding sometimes through light, sometimes through shadow. I loved looking at the curves and musculature of her bare back, particularly since I could stare unreservedly. She probably knew.

Everything looked as we had left it back at camp. Even the fire was still faintly burning. After lunch, our bellies full, we rested, alternately dozing on the sand and splashing in the shallows, relaxing in the warm October sun. I took advantage of the time off to do some dry fire training with East. I had no intention of sharing the gun with her, but if something happened to me, she needed to know how to shoot. I drilled "breathe, relax, aim, slack, squeeze" into her head until she seemed to have it down pat. It wasn't the same as actual target practice, but it would have to do.

I also drew Gabriel's map with a stick, showing East how far we'd come (as best as I could guess) and where we were headed.

Although a nagging voice in the back of my head begrudged the lost day, I had to admit it was nice just chilling on the beach. It was probably best for East's sore knee as well, which seemed to be on the mend.

As night fell, the question of who would sleep where became the elephant at the fire pit, at least in my mind. A part of me wanted to sleep with her so badly, entwined as one in the dark in the little tent that had become our home. Our haven.

On the other hand, contrary as usual, another part of me absolutely recoiled at the thought. It was one thing to have more or less passed out the night before and then awakened in her arms. It was quite another to cold-bloodedly (so to speak) worm one's way into an already occupied sleeping bag. I wasn't used to being touched much, not even in passing. I'd seen the other kids at school routinely hug and grab and pat. Seen the older ones, who were dating—as much as one could "date" within the confines of the Settlement—hold hands and sneak kisses when the adults weren't looking.

People went out of their way not to touch me, of course. God forbid they might catch what I was carrying. With first Gabriel and then Gran gone from my daily life, if someone touched me, it was by accident and usually a shock to both of us. I didn't like casual touching. I wasn't the touchy-feely type. Other people seemed to think nothing of it when they put their hands on each other, but to me, there was a kind of unspoken information exchanged with touching. Too *much* information.

But it was different with East. I found more and more of my time was consumed with thoughts of touching her. Of her touching me. In ways I'd never been touched before. Ways I'd only read about. Or dreamed about.

My mind, always creative when imagining the worst-case scenario—and then the worster—went blank when I tried to conjure the picture of what might happen once we were both in the sleeping bag together. In the dark. Would there be conversation? Or would only a dumbass expect small talk in such a situation?

Would we be face-to-face? Who got to turn first? Where did all the hands go?

Jesus H.

And it wasn't like I'd had any indication from East that she wanted to do anything more than sleep in the sleeping bag. She'd acted like it was no big deal for us to share the bag. She'd said it just made sense, so we wouldn't freeze. And, of course, she was right. But still…

Sex. Did you just do what you felt? Or were there rules unknown to me? Probably. Rules about who led and who followed? Eyes open or shut? Maybe there were things that should *not* be done that I didn't even know about. Or were these things renegotiated each time? I had a feeling I was thinking about this all wrong.

Jesus, what in the hell *was* I thinking? Elinor Eastman could not possibly be interested in me. Elinor Eastman could have her pick of anybody she wanted. Guy or girl.

Except…there wasn't anybody else to pick. Just me.

I was in such a lather, such a welter of confusion by the time bedtime rolled around, I didn't think I'd be able to sleep a wink.

We were in the tent for the night at that point. The squeeze-as-you-go flashlight was our only source of illumination, propped on top of one of East's hiking boots in the corner. Clouds obscured the moon and the stars, so it was truly a very dark night. Wind rushed and swelled among the trees and bushes, sounding almost like the sea. Despite the breeze in the treetops, the bay itself was oddly still. Like it was thinking.

I was still dithering like an idiot about the sleeping bag situation, still fully clothed and my mind nowhere near made up. East didn't seem to notice my distress. Or maybe she did, but didn't think mentioning it would improve the situation. She sat cross-legged on the unzipped and open sleeping bag, wearing only an oversized T-shirt of Mr. Giovanni's that had somehow ended up in my pack, her panties and the wool socks of his that she had reclaimed. With one of those lithe, elegant moves so natural to beautiful women, she reached inside her T-shirt, did a shrug and a twist and somehow magically came out with her bra in her hand. She tossed it to the side, where it landed on top of her jeans.

I did not know where to look. And it was such a small tent. I shut my eyes tightly and took a deep breath, hoping for…I didn't know what I was hoping for.

East cleared her throat. I opened my eyes. She was staring right at me.

"Are you all right, Kell? You don't look so good."

She eased herself into the bag and down onto one elbow as I watched. Her long brown hair fell about her shoulders. I was trying desperately not to stare, but my gaze had a mind of its own. It lingered—just for a moment—on the jut of her breasts under the thin cotton of the T-shirt. Her nipples were hard with the chill of the night.

"It's getting cold," she said with a yawn and a shiver. "You better get in. I won't look if it bothers you."

Great. With all my angst about sleeping together, I hadn't even thought about the part where I'd be taking off my clothes in front of her.

No problem. The flashlight chose that moment to flicker and fade to black. I quickly stripped down to my T-shirt, underwear and socks, just like her. It seemed like the decision was making itself. It was too cold to even think about sleeping outside. I felt my way over to the sleeping bag, finding its zippered edge with my outstretched hand in the pitch dark.

"Climb in and pull the zipper," East murmured. She sounded half asleep already.

Pulling the zipper meant pressing my body against hers. She was facing me. I squirmed around so that my back was to her front. I could feel her warm breath on my neck. Her thighs pressed against me. Her breasts. She sighed, then withdrew her arm from the bag and put it across me, gently pulling me closer to her. Into her.

Even if it was all a lie, even if it was all wrong, it felt good in that moment. I breathed in and then out, and felt myself drift away.

CHAPTER NINETEEN

Rain Rain Go Away

The rain came sometime in the night. At daylight, it was pouring. No leaks in the tent was the good news, plus the chance to fill all our water containers. The bad news was the further delay. If it had just been me, I would have packed up camp and slogged through the rain for several hours. Sitting around on my butt was never one of my best things. But I knew I'd never get East to walk through the torrential downpour. Short of physically dragging her, I had no choice but to wait it out. I could only hope it would quickly pass.

East seemed glad enough to turn over and go back to sleep. I was restless. Once I was up, I was up. Unfortunately, there was nowhere to go. I busied myself with sweeping the floor of the tent with a sock and otherwise tidied up the homestead. Which took all of two minutes. I didn't have to worry about waking East—the noise of the rain covered up any small sounds I was making, plus she was out like a light.

I borrowed the giant-sized slicker which was almost more trouble than it was worth. Outside, I filled everything that could hold water, even the cooking pot and pan, and drank deeply of cold, clear rainwater. I made a trip to the huckleberry bush we'd found the day before and picked the remaining fruit. With no fire, it looked like that was it for breakfast. Lunch and dinner too, maybe. There were no signs of life in the woods except for a few bright yellow banana slugs oozing along the forest floor. All the red-blooded critters were smart enough to stay out of the rain. Except me.

The sky above was uniformly gray and overcast. No patches of blue to indicate any clearing. It looked like it might rain forever. The bay was angry, dark white-tipped waves frothing higher on the shoreline of our little beach than I'd seen them before. But our tent was in no danger just inside the tree line, which protected it from the worst of the wind as well. If I'd known we would be staying on the beach for an extended period, I would have moved the fire closer to our tent and constructed some kind of shelter for it. As it was, it was a cold, damp morning with no hope of a cheery blaze to warm us.

Back inside the tent, I sat on my pack and ate some berries. I wished we had some jerky or crackers or—I forced myself to stop that train of thought as it led nowhere good. Be grateful for fruit and fresh water, I told myself. I glanced at East—still asleep. I wished I had a book to read. We didn't even have Mr. Giovanni's little red notebook anymore as that was in the pack we'd lost on the bridge. Although re-reading the list of Aptitudes would probably not have improved my mood.

The Aptitudes…It surprised me that I felt a tiny tug of obligation to fulfill mine. That was dumb. I didn't owe those people anything. Gran must have instilled some extra honor and duty in me when I wasn't looking. I still couldn't believe they'd made me a Messenger. If I couldn't find Segundo, I might as well just keep on walking, head to DC and give those assholes a piece of my mind.

I decided to be productive and work on untangling the ball of fishing line I'd found on the beach. I wound it around a stick I'd collected during my morning ramble. About an hour and ten feet later, East finally deigned to join the world.

"Good morning," I said from my perch on the pack. I felt kind of funny. Hot but cold. Amped up but tired. Probably just nerves from being cooped up.

East nodded, squinting at me in the grayish light. She sat up and ran both hands through her hair. The rain was drumming on the roof of the tent, loud in the absence of all other sounds.

"Coming down hard," she said, yawning.

I nodded.

"What's for breakfast?"

I pointed toward her water bottle. Next to it, I'd piled some berries on a large green leaf.

"Oh, that's so sweet! Thanks, Kell."

She seemed genuinely pleased. Which made me feel a little funny in the pit of my stomach. Or funnier. I shrugged it off and returned to my fishing line. By the time East had finished her meal, I had the fishing line all neatly untangled and wrapped around the stick. My next task was carving hooks out of wood. This was very boring. Would the rain never stop?

East put the slicker on for a trip outside, but came back with her hair all wet, hanging in dripping strands around her face.

"What'd you do that for? You're getting everything wet," I chided her as she dried herself with Mr. G's all-purpose shirt.

"Sorry," she said. "But I couldn't resist the chance to wash the salt out of my hair."

That was such a good idea I had to follow suit. Except I just unzipped the door and stuck my head out for five seconds. One more upside to having short hair. If it had been warmer, I would have thought about stepping out into the rain for a quick shower in the buff, but it was too cold for that.

We idled another day away. Hours that would have been much better spent walking were instead spent talking. I couldn't remember the last time I had talked so much. It had to have been before Gabriel left. By unspoken agreement, East and I avoided the most difficult subjects. There were quite a few of those.

We talked about our childhoods, our families, things we liked and things we didn't. We shared our few murky memories of Before. As I'd grown older, I noticed many of the adults talked about Before like it was perfect. Clearly, it wasn't or it wouldn't have led to our present predicament. And by "our," I mean all of us—the human race or what was left of it. Although the adults spoke so glowingly of their precious past, it didn't sound that great to me. It sounded like a time when people were selfish. And greedy and stupid. It sounded to me like they didn't value what they'd had, and they'd had just about everything. Talk about spoiled brats. Brats with nothing better to do than play with their toys and pick fights with each other over nothing. Over who was better. Foolishly, maliciously, arbitrarily deciding this group was good, this group was bad. Weren't we all just people? Doesn't everybody want the same things? Food, friendship, love, sex, a roof over your head, a good book to read…

Of course, the topic of sex came up. She wanted to know if I'd ever been kissed. I thought about lying. I thought about telling her to mind her own business. I thought about asking her who the hell did she think would ever have wanted to kiss me?

I thought about telling her I wanted to kiss her.

In the end, I just told the truth.

"No," I said quietly, staring at my boots, listening to the rain pummel the tent. I was sitting on the pack, and she was cross-legged on the sleeping bag. Our chosen spots.

There were a few moments of silence. I wasn't exactly embarrassed. Not exactly. I mean, I was only seventeen, I had lived in a very small community with only a few other kids my age and frankly, I'd rather be un-kissed than be kissed by someone I didn't care about. East had had a lot more kissing opportunities than I'd had, that was for sure. I stole a glance at her. She looked deep in thought, like she was cooking up another question for me, one I probably wouldn't like any better than the last one. I decided I'd better come up with a question of my own. I caught her eye.

"So did you like kissing Hunter?"

She seemed to flinch a bit when I said his name, but held my gaze.

"He was okay, I guess."

Since I would have willingly kissed a dead possum with rabies before ever locking lips with Hunter Cohen, I thought "okay" was likely an exaggeration.

"Boys are always in such a rush, you know?"

I did not know, but I'd heard. And I'd read some books. I braved another question.

"So are you saying you like kissing girls more than you like kissing boys?"

She hesitated, which made me wonder again if she was lying. Made me wonder if she even liked me at all, or if she liked me simply because I was there. I'd seen her play the chameleon at school, being whatever the people around her needed her to be. Going along with whatever the other popular girls ordained. Flirtatious for the boys. Compliant for the adults.

I was increasingly suspicious that she wanted me to think she liked me because she needed my survival skills. Because that was *her* survival skill. A lot of doubt flickered in my brain during that second East hesitated.

At the same time, I couldn't deny my growing attraction to her.

"Well, what's better?" she finally asked me. "Sunrise or sunset?"

I rolled my eyes at her.

"No, listen," she said, exasperated. "I'm trying, but it's hard to explain. It's like…"

She screwed up her face and stared at the ceiling, searching for a comparison I would get. She snapped her fingers and pointed at me.

"Okay, you tell me what's better. Your first choice is roast beef."

The Settlement had cattle. There had been a small herd at the university Before for its agriculture and veterinary programs. Cows were even more important After. Milk, cheese, meat, leather…I loved cows. And I loved roast beef, but I was not at all sure what "beef" was in East's metaphor. I also thought it was highly unfair of her to bring up food when I was so hungry I could almost eat a banana slug.

"What's the other choice?" I asked cautiously.

"Hmm," she pondered some more. She was really getting into this. "How about a chunk of warm cornbread with butter melting on it and honey drizzled over the top?"

"Those are two totally different things," I argued. "How am I supposed to choose just one when they're both…oh."

I finally got her point. She smirked from her corner of the tent. I felt like she'd tricked me.

"No way," I told her, still arguing. "I am not a piece of cornbread."

"Maybe you're the roast beef," she said, still grinning.

I shook my head adamantly. "Look, East, not to be rude, but I still don't see how you can like guys and girls. They're so different. They're *too* different."

A frown clouded her face.

"Of all people, I thought you'd understand, Kell," she said. Now she was the one looking at the floor. I felt like a jerk. Felt like everything I was trying to say was coming out all wrong. I groped for the right words, but finally just blurted out what was in my heart.

"How could you like Hunter? That guy was such an asshole."

For a moment, I thought she wasn't going to answer. Then she shrugged and spoke softly without looking at me.

"I guess I didn't want to be alone."

We were quiet then for a while. In my opinion, being alone was far superior to being with an asshole, but there was no point in saying it. I was quite aware just how far apart my opinions set me from my peers. And how well they generally reacted to that.

I remembered a conversation I'd had with Gran when I was younger. She'd caught me silently crying into my pillow after a hard day at school.

"Why?" I asked her forlornly, tears streaking my face. "Why do they have to be so mean?"

Gran sat on the edge of my bed, gently patting my back. She was always a comfort in her own way.

"You *will* meet good people in this world, Kell," she said reassuringly. But then followed that up with a solid whack of truth, in typical Gran fashion. "But even they will have some bad in them. It's just the way we're built."

"Everybody?" I sniffled, wiping my nose on my sleeve as I sat up.

"Everybody," she said flatly. But then smiled, albeit a little woefully. "Even you and me, kiddo."

"You're good, Gran," I insisted, thinking what a weird argument this was. Me trying to convince my beloved grandmother that she was a good person. She was only the best person I'd ever met in my whole life. Not to mention the smartest. And hands down the funniest.

"I'm good," she agreed. But then couldn't help adding with her wicked grin, "But only ninety-seven percent."

"Grannnnnnn," I said, rolling my eyeballs while she cackled away.

"Well, anyhow *I'm* good," I staunchly tried. I was very young, after all. "I'm not mean like the rest of those kids."

"You never wished they were dead? Or punched one of them in the gut? Called 'em names under your breath?"

I looked sideways at her, still wanting to argue, but finding nothing to say. Gran put her bony arm around my shoulders and pulled me in for one of her quick, fierce hugs.

"Don't worry, Kell," she told me. "I love every bit of you. And you're about as good as they come. Sometimes it just takes folks a while to figure that out."

"And if I punch 'em in the gut?" I inquired, knowing I would inevitably need to revisit that issue. Probably sooner rather than later.

"Go for the face," my grandmother sagely advised me. "It's more discouraging."

CHAPTER TWENTY

Cannibal Germs

We headed inland the next day into the rising sun, looking for Interstate 80, the highway that ran north and south alongside the bay before eventually curving due east. Since we'd cut straight across on the bridge, we were intersecting the right fork from Gabriel's dirt map several miles up from that pesky V. I was pleased when we found the interstate after less than an hour of walking. Once back on the pavement, we turned north. Toward Segundo, I hoped.

East's knee was back to one hundred percent. On the other hand, I wasn't feeling so great. In point of fact, I felt distinctly peculiar, but at least it was a sunny day. Sunny, but cold. Even well away from the water, the strong wind had a bite to it that we hadn't experienced before on our journey. I stumbled along, letting East take the lead, feeling alternately hot and chilly, sweaty and parched, hungry and nauseated. Oh no, not sick, my foggy brain said distantly, but mostly I was too miserable to form an opinion. Oh no no no no…

"Are you all right?" East asked me when we paused mid-morning for a water break. She looked at me intently.

"I'm fine," I said shortly, avoiding eye contact. Somehow, it seemed incredibly important to me that I keep up the front of being tough, of not letting her see any vulnerability. That was another Dupont family tradition. Gabriel and I had learned that stoicism from Gran, who'd continued it to the very end, gruffly telling me she was fine, just fine, while she wiped the red blood from her lips.

East and I sat on the side of the highway for our break, dangling our feet off the edge which dropped down sharply. Beneath us was a steep dirt slope to what had once been a busy street running parallel to the interstate. We might have been in Oakland or Berkeley. I wouldn't have been sure even with a clear head. Whatever city it had been, it had sustained devastating damage during the Bad Times. From where we sat, facing inland, our shoulders and knees touching, East and I were looking out over a vast landscape of rubble and scorched earth. Nothing moved. Hardly anything was higher than ten feet. Most of it was unrecognizable after years of exposure to the elements. Just an immense jumbled wreckage of concrete, steel, asphalt and bones, bleached by the sun, pitted by the wind.

I'd had nothing to eat that day, my insides rebelling at even the thought of solid food. My belly rumbled as I took another swig from my canteen, then lurched as I suddenly puked. Fortunately, I was looking away from East when that happened.

"Oh, no, you are sick," she said with dismay. I drew a shaking hand across my mouth and ineffectually tried to fend her off, but she clapped a hand to my forehead. "Damn, Kell, you're burning up!"

"I'm fine," I told her again, hoping to persuade at least one of us. I hardly ever got sick, so this was as unexpected as it was unwelcome. Maybe it was all that swimming in the bay. Or being out in the rain. The disgusting memory of Matteo sneezing on me suddenly sparked in my brain. Gross—cannibal germs! God only knew what foul disease he'd afflicted me with.

"I'm fine," I mumbled one last time, the taste of bile in my mouth. I closed my eyes for just a second. I was shivering and East put her arm around me to warm me up. I thought that was awfully nice of her, considering my somewhat puke-ified condition. So far, we'd survived a terrorist bombing, an earthquake, wild dogs, a homicidal lunatic, immersion in the chill, shark-infested waters of the bay, two waterspouts and a whole lot of general deprivation/starvation/wandering in the goddamn wilderness. Brought down by a sneeze, I thought blearily. What a way to go…particularly for such a badass like myself.

"Do you want to go back to the beach?" East asked with a tremble in her voice. She looked worried and upset.

"No!" I said, astonished that she'd suggest it even in my feeble state. "We've got to keep moving north."

I gathered what little energy I had and found the will to stand. And walk. I took a step. And then another.

"We're walking," I told her although I felt like shit, more so with each passing minute. "Let's go."

In retrospect, it might not have been the wisest of decisions. All around us, as far as the eye could see, was the urban wasteland. And the thing about wastelands was there's nothing to eat. We needed to find food that day and I had no idea how long the wasteland would continue. But the fever was upon me—impairing my judgment, weakening my limbs. All I could think, all I could do, was keep walking north.

That day was agonizing. East stopped trying to get me to talk after a while, but I could see how concerned she was. She kept giving me looks—the furrowed brow, the frowny face. I might have thought it was sensitive and caring of her if I wasn't mindful of the fact that without me, she'd be dead meat.

Only my will kept me going as the morning turned to afternoon, and the afternoon turned to evening. I didn't think it was a hallucination that I was hearing Gran's voice in my head: "You can do it, Kell. One foot in front of the other. One more… one more…"

The sun was near to the horizon when East took my arm, the sky a dull pewter gray. The temperature had dropped drastically. It felt like it was in the forties, maybe lower, especially with the wind chill. I was shuffling by then, shivers wracking my frame, my breath rasping in my chest. I had almost forgotten she was with me. It felt like a week since we had left the beach that morning.

"Drink this," she said, tipping the last of the water in my canteen down my gullet. My hands were shaking too badly to hold it myself. We had come out of the wasteland a few miles back. Nature had first modestly, then boldly reclaimed the land on both sides of the freeway. Just ahead, a prominent hill arose from the otherwise flat landscape, its flanks lushly covered with pine trees. A few hundred feet up the road, the freeway split to form another V—one route heading west around the shoreline of the bay, the other continuing north.

Every bone in my body ached. I felt like I wanted to die and was aware that was a viable option if we didn't find some cover for the night.

"Why are we stopping?" I said hoarsely to East, my throat, my head, my lungs on fire.

"I think I see something," she said, gesturing toward the hill.

I squinted, but my vision was blurry along with everything else.

East put her arm around my shoulders.

"Come on," a voice said. It was either hers or Gran's. "We're almost there."

That final leg was an absolute nightmare. I was almost on the point of collapse, but East's strong arm kept me upright and moving.

"Almost there, Kell."

Her breath was cool on my feverish brow. She led me up the hill, into the trees as the day began to fade. There was a light winking ahead of us—flickering amongst the pines, leading us on. I was too sick and faint to wonder what it was, too exhausted to warn her that a light probably meant other people, and other people could only mean trouble.

I slipped out of her grasp and fell heavily to my knees as we reached a clearing in the woods. First one, then another snowflake grazed my cheek like cold, wet, ghostly fingertips, melting as soon as they hit the ground.

"Kell!" I heard East cry as I slowly toppled onto my side, but it was like I was hearing her from underwater. The world began to recede. I knew I was hallucinating then as I breathed deeply of the pine needles on the forest floor and beheld a tiny log cabin in the gloom of the clearing. A bright white light winked on and off from its front window. I lost consciousness as East began to drag me toward the door, the snow falling ever faster.

CHAPTER TWENTY-ONE

Cabin Fever

I was neither asleep nor awake, but in that wonderful place in between. I didn't want to wake up, but I couldn't remember why. Slowly, gradually, I became aware of three things. I was warm. I was lying on a bed. The fever was gone.

I opened my eyes. Gentle pale yellow light crept through curtains framing the window at the front of the cabin. It was early morning, but of what day? My internal clock told me a significant chunk of time had passed.

Soft rhythmic breathing was the only sound. I turned my head to see East asleep at my side. Her hand was loosely in mine. Flannel sheets, a heavy blanket and a quilt covered us in the full-sized bed. The air had a lingering warmth to it as well—I turned my head the other way to see the remains of a fire still glowing in a fireplace.

I sat up slowly, careful not to disturb East. I felt weak but good. I could feel my strength, that essential "me-ness" at my core returning. I stood, noting along the way with surprise that the clothes I was wearing—socks, long johns, T-shirt over my long johns' top—were *clean*. My body felt clean too—I decided not to speculate about that for the time being. The rest of my clothes and gear were neatly stacked by the door. I finished dressing and packed my bag since it was all laid out for me right there. There was a mini solar-powered camping lantern on the windowsill. That must have been the flickering white light that had drawn us to the cabin. I threw that in the pack as well. An Army green knapsack made of tough canvas was also by the door. Looked like East had found herself a new bag. I took a peek inside. Beside her few clothes, it was full of protein bars and other food. Maybe she was trainable after all.

The cabin had a tiny bathroom and kitchen, both with running water. There must have been a well on the property or a rainwater catchment system. Either way, the cabin's owner seemed to be well prepared for life off the grid.

A large sturdy box made of bright orange plastic was open on the kitchen floor, its hinged lid propped open. A veritable prepper's treasure trove of nonperishable food, tools and other useful objects lay within. It looked like East had already delved into the box, as there were various items on the counter next to our plastic jug from the beach, now full of water. My canteen and our other water containers were there as well, all full. Ripped-open plastic and foil packaging alongside was marked "water purification tablets." Since East was still breathing—I checked the bed once more—it seemed safe to assume it was okay to drink it. I drank long and deeply, quenching the thirst the fever had induced.

As hungry as I was, the Dupont in me made sure I stashed our water containers with our bags before I ate. You never knew when you might need to leave in a hurry.

All the food packages had U.S. government markings on them. Expiration dates still had a year or two to go. I tore into an MRE (meal ready to eat), scarfing it down cold. Gnawing on a protein bar, I took another look at the lid of the orange box. More official markings: UNITED STATES GOVERNMENT ISSUE SURVIVAL BOX, FAMILY OF FOUR and a bunch of letters and numbers that meant nothing to me.

I knew what it was, though. I recognized it from Gran's stories. It was a Tucker box, so-named for some assistant deputy underling of the Department of Homeland Security called Alonzo Tucker. Mr. Giovanni had mentioned him in history class too. When things started to go downhill right before the Bad Times began, Mr. Tucker was instrumental in developing and distributing the bright orange survival boxes to just about every family in America. Besides food, each box contained other emergency supplies like a first aid kit, a few basic tools, a space blanket, water purification tablets, etc. It was said that each box could keep a family of four alive for a week, as long as that family had water and no life-threatening injuries or diseases. Of course, since the Bad Times lasted a lot longer than a week, some thought they were a colossal waste of the taxpayers' money, but there was no doubt that Tucker boxes were highly valued. The occasional find of one by the Settlement's Scavenger team was always cause for celebration. Gran had one at the foot of her bed that she used as a linen chest.

Having satisfied my most immediate needs, my curiosity and powers of observation were both returning. I noticed there was a thick layer of dust on the floor and other surfaces. Crumpled wrappers and used plates and cups in the kitchen bore testament to several meals East must have eaten. I didn't see any indication that anyone else had been there. The dust pointed to an absent owner as well. Where was the cabin's inhabitant? Or inhabitants? I thought uneasily of another book in the Settlement's library— the one with the bears coming home to find the girl asleep in their bed.

On the other hand, we'd been there for days with no problem so far. I looked in a few drawers and cabinets, but I didn't find any clues as to the identity of the cabin's owner, other than it was probably a single, large, adult male based on the clothes I saw. Maybe it was Alonzo Tucker's cabin, I joked to myself. Ha.

Munching on my second protein bar, I took the first aid kit, an entrenching tool, a space blanket, some water purification tablets and an armful of MREs from the open box on the floor and added them to my backpack. We wouldn't be able to tote an entire box with us, but at least I could fill my pack with as much as I could carry.

I poked around the rest of the cabin for a bit, still being quiet although I don't know if wild horses would have awakened East, who was now gently snoring, one bare foot sticking out of the covers. As I pulled the quilt over her foot, I caught a glimpse of orange under the bed—three more Tucker boxes down there.

The sunlight was growing stronger outside. I peeked out the window to see patchy snow on the ground, brilliant among the pines, with blue skies overhead. There were coats hanging on hooks by the front door. I grabbed a dark green parka which was only about nine sizes too big for me, and eased outside to explore some more.

It was amazing how much better I felt. I guess you never really appreciate your health and your body until something goes haywire. I felt full of pep, ready to resume our trip to Segundo. The snow and cold weather was a bummer, though. In days gone by, we probably never would have seen snow that early in the year and certainly not that close to the bay. These days, the weather did what it wanted when it wanted and the humans just had to deal with it. I was glad to have the parka as I investigated the outside of the cabin. Besides the nip in the air, the winds were really starting to pick up.

A cord of wood was chopped and stacked on the porch, so someone had obviously planned ahead for the cold. The cabin was a one-story rectangle with the porch across the front. The front door was the only entrance. Beyond the clearing in front of the cabin was forest on three sides. We weren't on the top of the hill—the peak rose above and behind us.

On the side of the cabin with the best sun, a small garden was enclosed inside a chicken wire fence. Weeds looked to be the main crop. I didn't see anything edible other than a few shriveled tomatoes drooping from their stems.

Behind the cabin, a rocky cliff rose some forty to fifty feet. A large lean-to had been built against it, which I guessed was the barn. I approached it cautiously. All I heard was the twittering of birds and the gusts of wind in the pines. The lean-to was enclosed at both ends. The door was closed but not locked. With some difficulty, I finally succeeded in wrenching it open with a horrible screech that seemed to echo off the hillside.

I paused at the entrance, allowing my eyes to adjust to the dimness within. It was pretty much a cave, with the roof sloping down at a forty-five degree angle. A pen had been constructed—for a goat? A pig? It looked too small for a horse or cow. The gate to the pen was open. It was empty of everything but dried-up dirt and straw. Tools and even more Tucker boxes were stored along the walls. A hatchet hung from a peg. I took it down, wishing I'd brought the gun with me. The thick layer of dust on everything was just like the cabin. Plus cobwebs galore—kind of spooky.

On the far wall of the pen, three wooden barrels were lined up, blocking my view of what lay beyond. I wished I had brought the flashlight. There was enough light to see by with the door wide open, but it was darker in there than I liked. I could no longer hear the birds tweeting outside. There was a dank and musty smell to the place.

I edged past the empty pen and reached the barrels. As I turned to peer in the shadowy recess of the end of the lean-to, I stopped.

I had found the owner of the cabin.

He'd been there at least a year, I thought. The skeleton was mostly intact, although the bones had settled with the passing of time. The skull had tipped jauntily onto the left shoulder, the eye sockets staring up at me blankly. There was no flesh, no smell, just clean white bones. The closed door had kept out the bigger varmints, but time and insects had done their jobs. A perfectly round hole in the side of the skull showed me how he'd exited this vale of tears. Poor bastard.

In his lap, another smaller skeleton reposed, this one four-legged. But also with the perfectly round hole in the skull. The man had come out to the lean-to, closed the door behind him, sat down with his faithful hound and blown both their brains out.

I could understand why.

I stood there for a long time, thinking of those I had lost. And those whose fates were still uncertain.

Finally, I shrugged, trying my best to shake off such dark thoughts. I sank the blade of the hatchet into the nearest barrel, gave the skeleton a sketchy salute and said a silent thank you that he hadn't done it in the cabin. I left his rusty gun undisturbed amid the bones.

It was with relief that I returned to the fresh air and bright sky. I breathed deeply of the pine trees and felt grateful that I was still alive. That we were still alive. I smelled wood smoke in the air. Puffs of smoke from the cabin's chimney told me East must be up.

She stepped out onto the porch, wearing the other jacket I'd seen hung by the door—a light brown corduroy jacket with sheepskin-lining. It was also way too big on her, which somehow made her look cute, while my giant parka no doubt made me look like an idiot. She was shading her eyes with one hand, looking for me. I smiled and started to wave, but froze as the unmistakable and unnatural whine of a drone came to my ears. It was far off, but getting closer.

I sprinted for the cabin, nearly knocking East down as I thundered past. She gaped, looking at me like I was crazy.

"DRONE!" I screamed. "DRONE! GRAB YOUR STUFF, WE GOTTA RUN!"

That last bit probably came out more like *grabstuff*RUN, but she picked up on the panic, if not the actual words. Her new knapsack was right next to mine. I threw it at her, hauling my own pack on at high speed, then seized the sleeping bag and tent.

"COME ON!" I roared at East, who was looking desperately about the cabin as if wondering if she could fit it in her pack as well.

"But—" she started. I simply pushed her out the door, caught her hand and ran for the trees as the high-pitched whine of the drone passed right over our heads.

CHAPTER TWENTY-TWO

You Will Not Be Harmed

Down the hill was the freeway, which was our best chance of finding Segundo. So where did I run?

Up the hill.

Sigh.

Stupid, maybe, but instinct told me to run up the hill, so that's what we did. We were under the trees in the thick of the forest in just a few seconds. There was no clear pathway, but I made a path, crashing through the undergrowth in full-blown flight mode, dragging East along behind me. After about five minutes of that, my brain kicked back in, coincident with my lungs giving out. I wasn't completely back from the fever yet.

Huffing and puffing, the two of us huddled behind a tree. I was trying to listen for the drone, but couldn't hear anything over my own heart pounding and gasps for breath for a minute or two. I strained to hear the whine or any other giveaway noise, but the forest was eerily silent, except for the blustering of the wind.

"Do you hear it?" East whispered, her face taut.

I shook my head.

"What's the plan?"

I looked at her, trying to think. We'd been taught that the drones were spies. I didn't know if this one had been on a routine patrol or if the smoke from the chimney had drawn it. Either way, we were moving on. The drones had cameras and computers onboard. The one that had just flown over the cabin had no doubt already reported back to its masters. We wouldn't want to be there if and when they came. It wouldn't take much to blow up such a little place. One well-placed grenade ought to do the trick.

The drone might now be looking for us, but I still didn't hear anything. It might have been recalled by whoever sent it, or continued on its rounds. There was no way for us to know. Maybe it hadn't seen us at all, but there was no way it had missed the cabin with the telltale smoke coming from the chimney. If we were really lucky, they would deem the cabin unimportant and not send anyone at all. If we were a little lucky, it would take them a day or a week or a month to send somebody. And if we were unlucky...

The staccato beat of a helicopter's rotors was coming in our direction.

"Oh, fuck," I said.

East looked terrified. She clutched the front of my ginormous parka with both hands, but didn't say anything, her eyes huge. I looked around us, but saw nothing but trees and more trees. There was nowhere to run. No time to run. I could hear the chopper hovering. I assumed it was over the cabin and was glad the clearing was too small for them to land.

"Get under my jacket," I told East, shrugging out of my pack and holding the extra-extra-large dark green parka open. I thought her beige coat would be too easy to spot from the air. We huddled together under the parka. I threw handfuls of pine needles, dirt and grimy snow over the rest of our gear to make it blend in with the forest floor. It was the best I could do under the circumstances and I knew it wasn't nearly enough. I dug through my backpack frantically and pulled out the gun. If this was it, I wanted to make sure I had at least two bullets left. One for her and one for me. I'd heard stories of other people being captured by the enemy and they weren't pretty.

The helicopter began to slowly move over the forest, methodically searching for us. East was shaking as she clung to me under the parka. I was fighting back the fear rising within me, knowing I needed to focus, but distracted by the nasty metallic taste at the back of my throat.

I could hear the change in the engine tone as the helicopter hovered over another section of the woods, maybe half a mile away. Maybe farther—without a visual, it was hard to pinpoint either distance or direction. It sounded like some sort of announcement was being broadcast from the chopper, but with the wind whipping, it was impossible to make out any of the words. After a minute or two that felt much longer, the chopper began its search again, quartering the forest for its prey. It was getting closer and closer.

A pinecone fell with a thump to the ground about a foot away and I damn near shot it. I looked up—the boughs of our tree and its neighbors were rocking to and fro from both the natural and helicopter-produced wind gusts. The chopper was visible through the branches, hovering over us like a giant malevolent hornet. Monstrous and scary, it was black with large, official-looking white letters painted on its side and underbelly. I could only see it in snatches through the treetops, but the letters appeared to read FBSA, which meant nothing to me. The strong winds were buffeting the helicopter. The pilot must have been fighting for control. Down on the ground, we were struggling to hold on to the parka. Pine needles and dirt were flying everywhere in the powerful downward draft from the chopper. I sent up a silent, urgent request for them to immediately crash and burn, but that went unanswered. As usual.

Could they see us? They were hovering practically overhead. If they had infra-red technology to see our body heat, then hiding under the parka was just foolish. On the other hand, they hadn't shot us yet, so I was sticking with the hiding plan for the moment.

The racket alone from the helicopter was overwhelming. But suddenly an even louder noise boomed from it—the apparently pre-recorded announcement.

"THIS IS THE FEDERAL BUREAU OF SURVIVOR ASSISTANCE. WE ARE HERE TO HELP YOU. YOU WILL NOT BE HARMED. PUT DOWN YOUR WEAPONS AND COME OUT WITH YOUR HANDS UP."

East and I goggled at each other underneath the parka, but they weren't done yet.

"WE HAVE FOOD, WATER, SHELTER AND MEDICAL ASSISTANCE TO OFFER YOU. WE CAN HELP YOU LOCATE FAMILY MEMBERS. THIS IS THE FBSA. YOU WILL NOT BE HARMED."

The deafening announcement then repeated in Spanish and (I guessed) Chinese. While this was going on, East and I tried to talk.

"I've never heard of the FBSA. Have you?" I yelled at her.

She shook her head.

"Maybe we should accept," she yelled in my ear, then pulled back a little as if fearing my reaction.

"Are you fucking kidding me?" I hollered in disbelief.

She grabbed me and put her mouth right up to my ear, still having to yell to be heard over the chopper.

"Listen to me, Kell. If they are the government and they know where Segundo is, they can take us there in about ten minutes in the helicopter. Think of that. You could be with your sister in ten minutes."

Her breath was hot and moist on my ear. I shrugged out of her grasp and stared at her. Ten minutes...so easy...Then I came to my senses.

"It's too risky," I told her fiercely. "We can't take the chance, East. We've gotta be smart."

She drooped and wouldn't meet my gaze.

The helicopter had finished blasting its trilingual announcement. Either a bigger gust of wind caught it or it drifted a little too close to one of the pines. There was a nasty sound of the blades shearing off some branches, then the pilot recovered and sharply corrected the chopper's position. A moment later, it rose, turned and then soared back toward the west, the direction from whence it had come.

The silence was as startling as their abrupt departure. I surmised the winds had become too powerful for safe hovering. Or at least I hoped. The nearest place they could land was probably the freeway—which wasn't all that far away. A vision of armed men trooping up the hill to find us was extremely alarming. I waited another minute to make sure it wasn't a fake-out, but the chopper did not return. I jumped up, tucked the gun in my waistband and pulled East to her feet.

"Come on, we gotta go!"

"Okay," she said, starting back toward the cabin.

"Whoa, where are you going?"

"Can't we at least get some more supplies from the cabin?"

"No, East—they might be landing on the highway and coming up the hill for us right now. We gotta book, all right?"

That got her moving. She followed me silently as we fled up the hill. My plan, half-assed as it was, was to climb up and over the peak, go down the other side, then circle back to the highway when it looked safe.

After a rapid and panicky hike of only ten minutes, we stumbled across the other area where the helicopter had hovered. I knew this because it looked like a blast zone. Pine needles and snow had been blown about, exposing the topsoil beneath. Why had the chopper hovered here? What had they seen? My inner alarm bells were going off. I stopped short, trying again to simultaneously catch my breath and listen. East bumped into me and shot me an irritated look. I pulled out the gun, holding it down by my side.

"Now what? Why are we stopping already?"

I looked around us carefully. Nothing but trees. No one in sight. No sounds but forest sounds and wind.

"What?" East said again, this time with an edge.

"The helicopter hovered here as well," I told her quietly. "Why?"

"They saw us," she said with a strong element of "duh" implied.

"Right," I agreed. "And they hovered right over us when they found us. I think they saw our heat. So what were they hovering over here?"

"Maybe it was a deer."

Oh. That made sense. I didn't know if their technology could tell the difference between people heat and deer heat. If it hadn't been a deer, though…

I scanned the area again, trying to use my vision like Gabriel had taught me back home. To look for what was out of place. Or what was missing. But it was all so windblown and torn up, nothing was standing out to me. The urge to continue our flight up the hill was strong—but was there another enemy in the forest? Waiting for us? Or worse, watching us now?

Fear was welling up inside me, threatening to blot out rational thought. It was fear of the unknown, I recognized, trying to push it back down. There was no imminent danger at the moment, although that could change in a heartbeat. I took a deep breath and pulled myself together, trying to think it through. There might or might not be someone else in the forest. If there was, and he or she had any sense, that person would be hightailing it out of there to get away from the black helicopter and any soldiers who might or might not be coming up the hill behind us.

The bottom line was standing still was not an option. We simply had to keep going, balancing speed and caution. Keeping our eyes and ears open for potential enemies behind us and ahead of us. A tricky proposition, but not impossible. Not all that different from every other day in the recent past, come to think of it.

Another half an hour and we were over the top, scrambling down the back side of the slope. It was only a hill, after all, not a mountain. A steep, rocky, treacherous hill that descended into a region marked by deep ravines and stony hummocks.

We camped that night in a well-hidden spot in a canyon. Despite my fears, we had not encountered any other people during our flight. East had hardly spoken to me all day, nor was she making much eye contact. She seemed dispirited and sad. I wasn't feeling all that awesome either, but at least we were still alive, I told myself. Again. And we still had our gear, with the addition of some much-needed Tucker box food and supplies.

At our lower elevation, we'd left the snow behind, but the evening was still bitterly cold with the wind continuing to howl. We could have used the warmth and comfort of a fire, but I didn't want to give away our position to anyone who might be looking. We huddled together in the tent wearing most of our clothes, eating cold MREs with the baby lantern providing the only light while I attempted to strike up a conversation.

"I can't believe they didn't blow up the cabin," I said. Not the cheeriest of subjects, perhaps, but it was on my mind.

East gave me a dark look. I didn't think she was going to say anything, but she did. "You know winter is coming, Kell."

I did know that since we were freezing our asses off, but I merely nodded encouragingly.

"We could have survived all winter in that cabin," she said resentfully.

"And had the storm troopers in for tea?" I responded with a little too much sarcasm. But it's hard not to be sarcastic when that's one of your strongest talents.

"You don't know that they came back!" she fired back angrily. "For all we know, we could have lived there forever. You don't know anything. You don't even know where Segundo is! You're going to get us killed out here, Kell!"

I knew she was upset. That was the easy part. Figuring out how to calm her down was not so easy, especially when there was a lot of truth in what she was saying. But getting angry myself was not an option—there was no point in tearing each other apart. We were all we had. So I swallowed my temper and spoke softly to her.

"You know what? You're right, East. I don't know. We may never find Segundo. We might miss it, or they might have moved on…or they might all be dead…"

My voice broke on that last word, but I continued.

"But what I do know is we have to try. We have to, East."

There was more I wanted to say, but my throat closed up on me. Dumb throat. Hot tears prickled my eyes. I looked over at East and saw there were tears on her face too.

"Look," she said with a catch in her voice, "I'm a Pioneer, right? That's my Aptitude. So all I want to do is find a safe place and settle down. But you're a Messenger. You're never going to settle down. You're just going to keep going and going until you go off and leave me like my brother did."

"I'm not going to leave you," I protested. "And you're not a Pioneer and I'm not a Messenger. We can do whatever we want with our lives, East. We don't have to do what they told us."

She looked at me without saying anything, then busied herself with laying out the sleeping bag.

"Come on," I said. "Like I'm really going to accept their stupid Aptitude?"

"Maybe I don't think it's stupid," she said sharply. She pulled off her hiking boots more forcefully than was necessary. I'd count myself lucky if she didn't chuck one at my head, the way the conversation was going.

"You really think we should follow our Aptitudes?" I asked her, but without the sarcasm.

I couldn't see her face since she had crawled into the sleeping bag and turned away from me. It wasn't that late, but there wasn't much to stay up for on a pitch black, icy cold night with the wind howling and nothing to do but argue.

Then I heard her crying.

"Oh, East," I said, my heart breaking for about ten different reasons. I turned off the lantern and joined her in the sleeping bag.

"I just want to go home," she said with a sob. "I just want this to be over."

"I know," I said softly, stroking her hair and holding her close in the dark as she began to cry in earnest. "I know."

CHAPTER TWENTY-THREE

Never Name Your Food

The next day was a challenging hike over hill and dale. Just when it seemed like the land might be leveling out, we would come across yet another hill to climb or another canyon that might lead somewhere or might be a dead end. I did my best to keep us moving in a more or less northwestern direction, figuring that would get us back to the freeway eventually.

Thankfully, there was no sign of the helicopter or any other human threat. The countryside we passed through seemed uninhabited and might have been farmland or pasture for grazing in the past. At least it was getting a little warmer as we slowly made our way down toward a distant valley we had glimpsed from the rolling hills behind us. The weather was still cold but not freezing.

East and I resumed our habit of only discussing "safe" subjects. I thought of one I had overlooked as I reached for her hand to help her across a small but energetic creek, quick with snow melt.

"Thanks for taking care of me back there," I said as we paused to fill our water containers. "At the cabin. When I was sick, I mean."

"I know what you mean, Kell," East said, with a wry smile she sometimes used on me. It always made me feel about eight years old.

"Sorry. I should have said that before."

"It's all right. You would have done the same for me. I mean, heck, you take care of me all the time, right?"

"I guess we take care of each other now."

We glanced at each other, crouched together at the side of the boisterous, rushing little creek and shared a smile.

And then I heard it. A piercing cry that cut through the white noise of the stream. We both jumped to our feet.

"What the hell was that?" East said, the whites of her eyes showing as she nervously glanced about.

Before I could answer, the banshee wail came again. It sounded like it came from farther down the hill from where we were. The creek curved around a corner and disappeared from view downstream.

"Is it a person?" she whispered.

"Sounds like it's in pain, whatever it is," I said.

Part of me thought we should just ignore it, be on our way and not go looking for trouble. But what if it was a person? A person who was hurt and needed our help? Or would that be the oldest trick in the book, to lure in two dumbass teenagers?

What if it was the person I suspected might be following us? If it was, I wanted to get a look at him. Or her.

The agonized wordless cry came once again. East raised her eyebrows at me.

"Oh, shit," I said. "Let's go check it out. But we have to be careful."

The bawling continued as we crept through the brush. The closer we got, the more I was convinced it wasn't a person. It definitely sounded like an animal. An animal that was hurt or trapped or otherwise in distress. The desperate cries were heartrending. And also not smart, since they might draw the attention of creatures more dangerous than East and myself. I was still wary, knowing that one of the most important components of any trap is the bait.

At the bottom of the hill, the creek fed into a large pond in a meadow dotted with tiny yellow wildflowers. The edges of the pond were well-trampled. It was clearly the watering hole for the local wildlife. On the far side, the dirt became a morass of sticky mud. And there we saw not a banshee, but a cow, stuck in the mud nearly up to its neck. It looked pitiful and exhausted. I guessed that it had been thrashing to try and get out of the mud, but was now reduced to just mournful moos.

"Ohhhh," East exclaimed, her voice filled with sympathy.

"Shh," I told her, a finger to my lips. I was still on the alert for a trap. Could that crazy Matteo really have followed us all this way and organized a devious cow-in-a-mudhole plot? Probably not. Still, I made East follow me as I carefully circled the pond at a distance, making sure there was no one lurking in the trees.

Nope. It was just us and the cow. East and I sat on the bank and studied the poor creature. It stared back with its great brown eyes, too worn out to be afraid of us.

"Poor little cow," East crooned to it, then turned to me. "How are we going to save it?"

I must confess, I was thinking more about pot roast than rescue at that juncture. The cow was firmly mired in the mud. It would have been cruel to simply leave it there. On the other hand, I was loath to waste a precious bullet on a mercy killing. I also didn't want to announce our presence to the neighborhood by firing a gunshot. Slitting its throat would be messy, but effective. My brain juggled the two puzzles: how to kill the cow in the most humane way possible and how to break the news to East that we had to kill the cow.

The cow bawled again, but halfheartedly. It seemed to be weakening. East poked me in the ribs. I jumped.

"Ow. What?"

"Come on—how are we going to get it out?"

Getting it out looked like a lot of filthy hard work. Which meant a whole lot of time and energy expended, and for what?

A half-dead cow? I wasn't entirely sure we could do it even if we tried. I made a face and looked back at East without saying anything.

"Kell! We have to help it."

She stood up suddenly, putting her hands on her hips while staring down at me belligerently. The breeze ruffled her long hair slightly. Her eyes grew darker, yet blazed at the same time.

"Kell," she said again, commandingly, and held out a strong, slender hand to pull to me to my feet.

"All right, all right," I said, giving in. Again. I took her hand. I knew I was caving, but I couldn't help it. Maybe I felt like I owed her for taking care of me when I was sick. Maybe I just couldn't say no to her when she had that look on her face.

"What do we do first?" she asked.

I looked at the sky, which was a pale, washed-out blue. It was mid-afternoon already.

"First, we set up camp," I told her decisively. "Over there looks like a good spot."

"But the cow—"

"The cow will be fine for a little while longer. Cows are tough, East. We need to make sure we're set up for the night, then we can rescue the cow."

I had never seen her work so hard and fast at setting up camp. As I pulled the entrenching tool I'd got from the Tucker box out of my pack, I gave East her next assignment.

"Find some branches that can form a path for it to walk on once I've got it out of the mud, okay? The bigger, the better. Something to give it a little purchase."

"And what are you going to do?"

I unfolded the entrenching tool. It was essentially a small shovel, a very useful tool in many different ways. Like the obvious.

"I'm going to dig."

There were plenty of fallen tree boughs on the ground nearby. East stayed close to the pond, each of us in sight of the other, while she gathered enough for the planned pathway. The mud was cold, sticky as molasses and it didn't smell that great either. Being several hundred pounds lighter than Bossy, I didn't sink into the mud more than a few inches. The cow eyed me with trepidation as I approached, but seemed resigned to its fate. At least it had stopped mooing. It wasn't long before I was covered with just as much mud as the bovine. I managed to free up one of its front legs and it started heaving and moving, trying to get out.

"East, get the cord from my pack!" I called to her. "Let's put a rope around its neck, okay?"

I didn't want the damn thing running off into the forest the moment my hard work had sprung it from the mud. Maybe I wasn't going to have steak for dinner that night, but it seemed silly to just let it get away.

East was not eager to wade into the mud with me and a hyperactive cow, but she at least found the cord and tossed it to me. I tied a quick slipknot and draped the loop over its head, during which it managed to bump into me and knock me on my butt in the slimy cold mud. Shaking my head at my own foolhardiness, I gathered up the rest of the line and tossed it back to East who secured it around a stump near the water's edge.

Another half of hour of digging with the entrenching tool and the cow was nearly free. East had finished laying down the tree limbs to form the path. The cow was not impressed with our impromptu sidewalk and continued to flounder around with no success. Finally, after dumb luck resulted in its two front hooves striking a solid surface, it seemed to warm to the plan. It bucked and lunged and with a mighty push from me on the hindquarters suddenly freed itself from the mud with a loud sucking noise and staggered up the pathway onto dry land, where it stood, head hanging low, wobbly with exhaustion.

East strode over, patted its broad back, beamed at me and said, "I think we should call her Nancy."

"Oh, no, no, no!" I retorted, scrambling up the bank to join them. "You never name your food, East. My grandmother taught me that."

"Food!" she said indignantly. "We can't eat her. Not after all that. And I mean, literally there's no way you and I could eat a whole cow. Ninety-five percent of it would go to waste. What would your grandmother say about that?"

I was pretty sure Gran, if she had been there with us, would have said, "Where's the barbecue sauce?" but I let that pass. East did have a point. We would eat extremely well for one night, maybe two and then have to walk away from about a thousand pounds of rotting meat. It was also a lot of work to butcher a cow and I was pretty wiped out from Operation Banshee Rescue. I wiped a muddy hand across my muddy forehead and sat down to think.

"Besides," East went on, "I think she's a girl cow. Maybe we can milk her!"

She started to sluice the mud off the beast with pond water she'd collected in our plastic jug. She rinsed off the rear end first, which took several jugs worth, then moved on to the middle. While she was busy with that, I rinsed off as best I could at the water's edge, then changed into clean (well, cleaner), dry clothes.

Out of the bog, "Nancy" was undoubtedly female. With East's help, she was transforming from a dark brown to a pleasing black and white combo. The cow shook her mud-spattered head vigorously, then lowered it to the ground to take a mouthful of scrubby grass. Munching contentedly, she flicked her tail and gave me a look out of her big brown eyes, which were framed by ridiculously long lashes. If I didn't know better, I might have thought she was trying to tell me something. Maybe all our time together in the mud had meant something to her. The cow blew heavily down her nostrils, snorting and twitching her ears.

Jesus. I had bonded with a cow. Now I couldn't eat her.

"She's beautiful, isn't she?" East said, admiring her work. "Aren't you, Miss Nancy?" She poured another jug of water over its back, then pulled up a fistful of grass and offered it to the critter.

"Why, East?" I asked in mock despair.

"Why what?"

"Why Nancy?"

"Oh. Well, I had a doll when I was a little girl and she had beautiful brown eyes and long lashes. And that's what I called her—Nancy. The name sort of popped into my head just now. It's funny. I haven't thought about that doll in years. My mother gave her to me…"

Her voice trailed off. She was still for a moment, then seemed to shiver. She said nothing, but returned to sluicing off the mud, which was thickly clumped around the cow's neck.

"Hey, what is that?" I said, peering more closely. Rinsed free of mud, I'd expected to see my loop of cord resting on black and white hide. Instead, there was something else around Nancy's neck.

A bell.

CHAPTER TWENTY-FOUR

The Vineyard

At first, East could not understand my alarm upon the discovery of the bell around the cow's neck. I finally got through to her, sputtering out the equation of cow plus bell equals a human being somewhere in the mix. All the while cutting my eyes around to see if the rest of the herd or the herdsman would appear.

But we were alone in the meadow by the pond. East still didn't seem that concerned.

"Maybe it's one of the cows from Before that went wild," she said.

I could tell she was way too attached to the stupid cow. Nancy, my ass. And I was no farmer, but even I could see that cow was nowhere near ten years old. It had obviously been born long after the Bad Times. The braided leather strap from which the bell hung was neither tight nor loose. It was comfortably snug—a perfect fit. I wanted to take it off, but Nancy would have none of it, shaking her head and snorting when I tried. She didn't seem to mind my laying hands on her, it was just the futzing with the collar that was upsetting. After she nearly trod on my foot, I gave up. I stuffed one of Mr. Giovanni's wool socks up in the bell so it wouldn't ring. I knew those socks would come in handy.

It was starting to get dark and I eventually convinced myself that the cow was a stray that had wandered off from its herd. Hopefully one far, far away. We'd certainly come across no evidence of a herd of cattle in our trek thus far. We'd already made camp and nightfall was imminent, so it made sense for us to spend the night there as planned. I calmed myself down enough to realize it was smart to be aware of the dangers we faced, but even smarter not to panic. Panic led to bad decisions and bad decisions all too often led to death. I was determined to be a survivor.

"So Kell..."

I looked up from the fire, which I had built while I brooded. East must have been watching my face, waiting for my expression to clear before she made her next request.

"Are you going to milk her?" she asked hopefully.

We both looked at Nancy, who was placidly chewing her cud a few yards away where East had tied her rope to a tree. Fresh milk did sound awfully good. Gran kept goats at our cabin, but we never had a cow. I figured it couldn't be all that different from milking a goat—right?

Wrong. For starters, we had no bucket or stool, and it was getting darker by the minute. Still, I decided to give it a shot. I got East to hold her collar and feed her grass while speaking soothingly to the beast.

"About what?" She wanted to know.

"It doesn't matter! It's a cow!"

"All right, all right, chill out."

I knelt by Nancy's side and hoped she wouldn't kick me. I was holding the flashlight with my mouth and could already feel the drool starting to run down my chin. Her equipment was way bigger than our frisky little goats, but the principles had to be the same. Amazingly, after cleaning the teats with a warm wet cloth, and a few false starts, I was able to fill our cooking pot with milk. More milk ended up outside the pot than in it, but I got the job done. I think Nancy was as happy as we were.

East congratulated both the milker and the milkee with pats on our respective backs, then carefully carried the pot back to the fireside. It was fully dark by then. I removed my cord from the cow's neck and tried to shoo her away when East wasn't looking. Nancy serenely ignored me and continued to graze nearby while we ate our own meal by the fire.

In the morning, she was still there to East's delight and my dismay, reposing comfortably under a tree. She arose when we did. I tried milking her again—just a few pints was the result, but that was more than sufficient for our breakfast. Having only had water to drink for quite some time, the warm milk was particularly delicious.

We broke camp and continued our trek toward the distant valley, following the winding stream again as it exited the pond and headed downhill. We would catch glimpses of the valley when we climbed yet another of the gently rolling hills. There was no particular reason to head for it, except we (well, I) needed a goal and I felt fairly confident that we would cross the freeway if we aimed for that valley. Despite the undulating topography, our overall direction was downward and more or less northwest.

A strange couple of days ensued, wherein I was never quite sure if we were following the cow or the cow was following us. Either way, two days later, the three of us were still keeping company. In the late afternoon, we had finally come down from the rolling hills into the narrow and beautiful valley. It bothered me greatly that we had not re-crossed the freeway, but I kept my growing concerns to myself. No point in alarming East or confirming her fears that I had no idea what the heck I was doing. After all, highways didn't always run perfectly north or west. Maybe the highway was just over the next hill.

The western wall of the valley was a steep, almost mountainous hillside that was densely forested. Was it the coastal ridge? But how could it be, if we were on the eastern side of the bay? I was confused and tired and footsore. And sick of milking that damn cow every morning. The novelty had long since worn off. The milk was starting to seem more gross than delicious—I was never a big milk fan even when I was a little kid. I did miss the goat cheese Gran used to make. I even missed the last of our goats, a spunky little yellow creature which my grandmother, for reasons unknown to me, had named Velveeta.

That recollection made me miss Gran so bad, it was like a punch in the gut. So I shoved those thoughts back in a far corner of my brain and tried to think of something else. At least East wasn't bugging me as much anymore. She was pitching in more and more with camp duties, asking fewer dumb questions. It was almost kind of nice to have another human being around, to have someone to care about on a daily basis.

Whoa. I caught myself. You better knock that shit off, I told myself sternly. If you think Elinor Eastman is your friend, you're delusional. Stop being a jerk and focus on the mission.

The area through which we were walking must have been rich and fertile farmland Before. I could still see traces of the farmers' efforts. Although overgrown and untended now, we were in what must have been a vineyard. There were a few wild grapes on the vine which East and I sampled, savoring their juicy sweetness. Nancy plodded ahead of us, tail swishing back and forth. She had no interest in grapes or history, but acted like she knew where she was going. I admired that.

As we stepped out of the last row of untended vines, we found ourselves on a broad dirt road. The field of grapes before us was not in disarray. In fact, it looked extremely healthy and well looked after, with row after row of vines laid out in a geometrically precise fashion. As the implications of this sunk into my brain, the cow chose that moment to moo. Loudly. I jumped. She made a hard right and trotted off down the road purposefully.

"Hey, where's she going?" East said in protest.

"Forget the cow," I said, grabbing her arm with belated urgency, "we need to get off this road—"

But it was too late. Around the bend came two riders on horseback. As they saw us, they urged their horses into a gallop. Puffs of dust flew up from the hooves with each stride. They passed Nancy without a second glance, heading straight for us. The cow scampered out of sight around the corner. There's gratitude for you. There was no time to run. In the few seconds it took them to reach us, I observed two points of interest. Both riders were women. And both were well-armed, with rifles tucked into scabbards on their saddles and handguns on their belts.

The taller one reined in her horse in front of us. She was an African-American woman of about forty with close-cropped hair and a weary expression. Her companion, a short, squat Hispanic with long black hair in a single braid down her back, circled behind us on her chestnut mare. She rattled off something in Spanish at the other rider that I didn't catch. I spoke a little *Español* thanks to my grandmother's Cuban heritage and a year of lessons in tenth grade from Miss Sanchez. Gran's knowledge of several colorful Cuban epithets had not helped me in my academic pursuits, but they continued to come in handy at trying times in my life. Like the present.

"So what have we here, Marta? A couple of cattle rustlers?" the weary-eyed woman asked her companion with a trace of a smile. I was glad she spoke English.

Marta didn't answer, but I could hear the leather creak as she shifted in her saddle behind me. I didn't like her being back there—my neck tingled with her unseen presence. I glanced at her. She steadily returned my gaze with no expression whatsoever.

"We didn't steal your cow—we brought her back!" In her outrage, East bent the truth only a little.

The tall woman looked her up and down without a word, then her gaze passed to me. Our eyes locked for a moment, then I deliberately looked away. Her look was piercing and intelligent, like she knew exactly what I was thinking. I hoped not, since what I was thinking about was my gun. It was on my right hip in a makeshift holster I'd fashioned out of Mr. Giovanni's other wool sock, a bandana and some cord. It was too heavy to carry in my hand as we'd walked along each day. And I'd grown tired of it banging against my leg or slipping down inside the waistband of my pants. With everything that had happened, it seemed ill-advised to carry the gun in the depths of my backpack. So it was securely tucked away in the sock holster, strapped to my upper thigh, barely concealed by my untucked flannel shirt. It wouldn't take more than ten minutes or so to whip it out. And then what? A pitched gun battle with two women who were armed to the teeth and had the drop on us? Who might—or might not—be foes? Unless our lives were threatened, I wasn't willing to use the gun. I decided to bide my time and see what they had to say.

"What's your name?" the woman said to East.

"Elinor," she said after flicking me a glance. "And that's Kell."

I was happy to let East do all the talking as long as she didn't tell them anything about Segundo. All of my concentration was focused on the two women. My neck was getting a crick in it already from constantly turning to look at one, then the other. Marta's poker face was unnerving. The African-American dismounted and walked over to us.

"What are you kids doing out here? This is private property. And we don't take kindly to trespassers."

"We weren't doing anything wrong!" East flared up again. I knew the anger was just a front for her fear. I thought the adults knew it too. They seemed amused by us, not threatened. "We found Nancy stuck in the mud and we rescued her, then we came down here—"

East faltered at their reactions. Marta—or maybe it was her horse—snorted behind us. The African-American woman had an odd look on her face.

"What?" East said. "What's wrong?"

"You called the cow Nancy?" the woman said, fighting a smile that shone in her eyes. Her eyes didn't look so tired when she smiled. They were warm and brown. Very expressive, in contrast to her no-nonsense appearance. She looked over our heads at her buddy. "What do you think of that, Marta?"

I turned in time to see Marta shake her head and roll her eyes in disgust. This time, I caught more of what she said. "*Ay, nunca nombra su comida.*"

Her irritation evident, East said, "Why are you laughing?"

"Because *my* name is Nancy," the woman said, letting the smile loose. It was worth waiting for—she had one of those terrific smiles that made *you* want to smile. She was no beauty, but in that moment, I found myself drawn to her somehow.

East shot me an "oops" kind of look. Nancy—the woman— seemed to have reached a decision about us.

"You are welcome to come with us, *chiquita*," she said, still addressing her remarks solely to East, "but the boy cannot. It is women only here at Tres Hermanas."

"What boy?" East said, confused.

I was not, and yet I found I was unprepared for it. Again. Would it ever end? There were times—too many of them, I admit—when I wondered if I would ever find a place where I could just fit in. Not be the freak. What had I ever done to be eternally cast as an outsider, an undesirable…a monster. I swallowed and closed my eyes for a moment against the harsh slanting rays of the afternoon sun. I would have to explain. I hated that. I opened my mouth to speak, but nothing came out.

Nancy-the-woman said, "You'll have to make up your mind, Elinor. You can come with us, or you can move on with him. But the two of you cannot stay here on our land."

East stopped looking bewildered as she finally got it. She even laughed a little with relief, then abruptly stopped when she saw my face. She waited a moment for me to speak, but when I didn't, she said, "Kell's not a boy. She's a girl. Go on, tell her, Kell."

This time, I didn't look away. Chin up, shoulders straight, I looked into Nancy's eyes, daring her, asking her to see me— Kell, a person—through all the barriers, cloth and otherwise, that separated us.

She shaded her eyes with a hand that looked large and hard. She looked me up and down one more time. And again. Perhaps she noticed the absence of an Adam's apple. The absence of facial hair. She must have seen the flat chest and unplucked eyebrows. She must have noticed the bulge of the gun. She probably saw dirt and sweat. Hope and fear. Fight or flight.

"Ah, I see," she finally said as if to herself. I had no idea what she meant. I heard Marta shift in her saddle, then cluck softly to her horse to move up beside me.

"My apologies, Kell," Nancy said. "Of course, you shall both come with us."

She said it like we had a choice, but it was clear to me we did not.

"But first I must ask you for your weapons."

She held out that large hand peremptorily. There was no doubt or hesitation in her manner, like it was automatic I would just hand my gun over. East froze, staring at me.

"How do you know there aren't ten more of us?" I asked Nancy, finally finding my voice. "Maybe we've got *you* surrounded. Maybe you need to hand me your guns."

"Nice try, kid, but you've been on our land for quite some time now. Our sentries have been following your progress closely. It's not a coincidence that Marta and I found you here."

She said all that with just the hint of a smile, not like she was laughing at me exactly, but letting me know who was in charge.

"How about East, I mean Elinor, and I just turn around and go back the way we came? Like you said, we'll get off your property. We don't want any trouble."

She considered me for a moment. Then, she said, "How old are you two?"

I said "eighteen" at the same time East said "seventeen." She heard my lie and cut her eyes at me as I glared right back at her. I hoped she was reading my mind and getting the SHUT UP I was so fervently trying to send her.

"And how much food do you have?" was Nancy's next question.

Again East and I spoke simultaneously. East, her pride evident, said, "We've got plenty. We found MREs and—" while I yelled "East, will you shut the fuck up!"

She shot me a wounded look, but stopped talking.

Nancy was giving me that considering look again. I didn't like it. I much preferred to be under the radar. I decided that since we apparently couldn't fool her and we surely couldn't outrun them, I would just lay my cards on the table.

"Look," I said. "I'm not giving you my gun. So everybody just be cool and nobody gets hurt. We'll be leaving now."

I gestured to East and started to turn to walk back up the road. Before I could do that, I heard a click as Marta cocked her weapon.

"Sorry, Kell," Nancy said with a serious face. "I can't let you do that. I can't let two underage girls go off into the wilderness by themselves."

In a world where life expectancy was a big fat question mark, the adults still found magic in the number eighteen. I didn't see what the big deal was myself. Just another stupid grownup rule.

"We don't need your help!" East flared up again. "We've been doing fine on our own for like a month!"

I caught her eye. She looked at me uncertainly.

"Shut up?" she asked. I nodded tiredly. "Sorry."

I realized it was a foregone conclusion that I would hand over my gun. It had been since the two riders came around the bend in the road.

"Easy," Nancy said as I reached for the gun. I slowly pulled it out, making sure I was giving them no cause for alarm as I walked the few paces over to her and handed her the gun. So long, gun. It wasn't even mine. For a second, for the life of me, I couldn't recall where I'd gotten it. Oh, yeah. Dead Lookout Dude at the observatory. And the bus…the bodies…

"And now the knife," she said.

I slowly pulled my hunting knife from its sheath on my belt and gave it to her, hilt first.

"*Gracias*," Nancy said as she stashed both my weapons in her saddlebag. "Anything else on either one of you that could hurt you or us?"

We shook our heads no, but were nevertheless subjected to quick, efficient pat-downs and bag searches. My respect for this strange authoritative woman was growing—unlike a lot of other adults I'd met, she knew what she was doing.

She mounted her horse, then deftly maneuvered it over to East. She had East put a foot in the stirrup, then, with one swift, strong motion, she held out a hand and pulled her up behind her. Marta did the same for me.

"Just an hour's ride," Nancy told us as we set off down the same road which Nancy-the-cow had taken. She said something in Spanish to Marta and this time I did understand it.

"We'll take them to Simone and let her decide."

I missed my gun already. I rubbed my thigh where it had so recently rested.

Who the hell was Simone?

CHAPTER TWENTY-FIVE

Tres Hermanas

An hour later, my butt was numb, but my brain was abuzz. We had left the vineyards behind, first riding through an area of paddocks, barns and other outbuildings, then a ramshackle collection of living spaces. There were tents, yurts, tepees, lean-tos and tiny shacks constructed of odds and ends of building materials like boards, sheets of tin, scraps of tar paper and whatever else their scavenging occupants could find. As best as I could tell from the curved dirt roads we bisected at regular intervals, the place was designed more or less in a circle. The fields were the outermost ring, the paddocks and barns the next layer and the residences were one away from the inner circle. After an hour's leisurely ride—and by leisurely I mean hellishly uncomfortable, bumping along on the back of the bony, stumble-prone steed, forced into close proximity to Marta, who herself smelled of horse, hard work and cinnamon—we had made it to the center.

The most striking feature was a round amphitheater, built in a natural hollow surrounded by towering eucalyptus trees. A broad unpaved street of yellowish dirt circled the amphitheater, providing access to it at four equally spaced entrances—north, south, east and west. On the other side of the street were buildings, better built and larger than the hovels in the residential area. Signs on some of the buildings identified them: clinic, library, supply, security. Other structures were unmarked.

The biggest building was the kitchen—half enclosed, half an outdoor cooking area with a canvas roof held up by poles, with canvas sides that could be rolled up or down depending on the weather. Next to the kitchen was an open grassy space with wooden tables and benches, shaded by trees. Smoke emanated from a chimney. Whatever they were preparing for dinner smelled really, really good. The late afternoon sun shone down on a few dozen women who were already in line for the evening meal, which had not yet begun.

Obviously, this place was large and well-organized. As big or bigger than the Settlement. My rough estimate of the seating capacity of the amphitheater was well over three hundred. This place didn't look like it had sprung up overnight. Perhaps it had been in existence Before and had, by some small miracle, survived the collapse more or less physically intact. It was, as Nancy had made clear, a community of women—I saw no men, although we did come across some women tending to a group of small children, both girls and boys. We had passed a few people on the ride in without comment, but now that we were "in town," so to speak, we were attracting a lot of inquisitive glances. I felt tension and hostility in more than a few of the looks directed at me. I felt extremely self-conscious, but yelling, "I'm a girl, damn it!" didn't seem like the answer. Especially when I wasn't—not at my core. Nancy merely smiled and waved at the inquiries from the bolder ones. Marta remained stolidly silent. East was looking around her with cautious interest much as I was.

Marta said "*Está allí*" and pointed. Nancy nodded. She told East and me to dismount, which was music to my rear. She also got off her horse. Marta took the reins from her and presumably headed off to the stables.

At the far end of the dining area, three women sat at a table in the shade of a magnificent redwood tree. Nancy led us to them. One white, one Hispanic, one Asian. Behind them was an old trailer. There were a few of those at the Settlement, leftovers from Before. Like those, this one had probably once been fancy and state of the art, all gleaming chrome and shiny paint. Now it was a dull leaden color, with patches of rust in places. A wooden sign above the door had "office" burned into it in Western-style script.

"What's this?" the white woman said to Nancy. A mug and a notebook lay before her. She did not arise as we approached, though her two companions did, taking up protective flanking positions. Which seemed odd, since it was just me and East. The seated woman was old, in her fifties if not sixties, with wild-looking flyaway white hair. Short on the sides and back, longer on top. It didn't look unclean, it just looked like she had made no attempt to comb it. Ever.

"We have some visitors, Simone," Nancy replied. Her tone was courteous, but somehow I could tell there was no love lost between the two of them.

"Kids, this is Simone, our leader and the founder of Tres Hermanas," Nancy told us. "That's Violet and Rain Cloud behind her. And this is Elinor and Kell," she finished, presenting us to the trio. There was a moment of silence as they collectively scowled at me. I waited for it.

"The man-child is not welcome here, Nancy. You know our laws."

"They're just kids, Simone," Nancy said mildly. "And they're both girls."

Another long pause as they took a second look. What was I supposed to do, drop my pants and show 'em my lady parts? Fuck that. I crossed my arms and stared back at them, pretending I was tough. And not at all humiliated. Not me.

"You are vouching for this…person, Nancy?"

Simone's voice was as cold as her gaze. There was something going on between them that had nothing to do with me.

Nancy met her gaze calmly and unflinchingly, but firmly said, "I vouch for both of them. I'd like to bring them to the meeting tonight if that's all right with you."

"Fine," Simone said briskly, as if dismissing this petty matter from her busy schedule. It looked to me like she'd been drinking coffee and shooting the shit with her buddies when we walked up, but maybe she had plans for world domination in her notebook. "We'll take care of it tonight. Secure their belongings, get some dinner and then bring them to the meeting."

She stood up and turned to go into the office trailer. One of her minions—I hadn't caught who was whom—jumped to open the door for her. The other jumped to get the coffee cup and notebook.

"Thank you, Simone," Nancy said politely, but the leader of Tres Hermanas did not reply. The trailer door banged shut. Marta had silently rejoined us at some point in the conversation and put a hand on East's bag. East flinched and took a step back, looking at me with alarm.

"Hey, wait a minute—" I said.

Nancy made a "let's all calm down" gesture with her big hands.

"We need to store your bags. You heard her—'secure your belongings' is what she calls it."

"And what do you call it?" I said, tightening my grip on the straps of my own backpack and also taking a step back. I did not like the way this was going at all. I absolutely hated losing control of the situation. Not to mention that backpack was everything I had in the world.

"It's standard for new arrivals. We're not thieves, Kell. You'll get your gear back."

"When?"

Nancy and Marta exchanged a brief look, loaded with meaning I could not divine.

"First things first," was her reply. "Marta will take care of your packs and then we'll eat. After dinner is our weekly meeting. Simone will introduce you to the sisterhood then."

That damn cow had a lot to answer for.

CHAPTER TWENTY-SIX

Captured By Amazons

The dinner bell rang as Nancy led us to the back of the chow line. I was, of course, seriously concerned about our situation and the loss of our liberty. On the other hand, the thought that we would eat that night, that we would have water to drink, and not have to worry about where to set up camp…It was an incredible relief, at least for a moment, to not have to work so freaking hard at just staying alive.

There were lights strung amongst the trees that formed the perimeter of the dining area. A few of them started to flicker on as the daylight waned. I hadn't heard any generator sounds. I assumed they had solar power. The delectable aroma from the cooking tent was making me light-headed. East's arm bumped lightly against mine as the line moved forward. She took my hand and I squeezed hers back as she anxiously smiled down at me. I wanted to warn her, to tell her what not to say, but there was no opportunity for a private chat. It hadn't occurred to me previously to have the What-If-We're-Captured-By-Amazons? conversation.

I was afraid they would separate us soon. That's what I would have done. Nancy was right behind us in the line, but at the moment was talking with the women behind her. Marta had not yet returned from wherever she had gone with our gear. I stood on my tiptoes to whisper in East's ear one urgent sentence.

"Don't tell them anything about Segundo."

She looked surprised but nodded.

After loading up our trays with food, we sat down with Nancy at a long communal table crowded with other women. I caught sight of Marta at another table, seated next to a young woman who resembled her. The meal was simple, but mind-blowing to me and East. A delicious beef and vegetable stew. Warm rolls with butter and honey which caused East to cry "Bread! They have bread, Kell!" much to the amusement of the others. I kept my eyes and ears open and tried to learn as much as I could from the chatter around us while stuffing my face. There was cheese and fresh fruit and even cobbler for dessert. I tried not to overeat, knowing it would only make me sick later, but it was hard to resist. My hands were shaking as I lifted a mug of cold spring water to my lips, more from emotion than any physical reaction. After weeks of scant rations and constant worrying about food, to sit down to such a dinner was almost overwhelming. I tried not to let anyone see.

Nancy was sitting across from me and I met her gaze more than once during the meal. She ate slowly and sparingly and seemed to be studying both me and East with great curiosity. There was compassion in her gaze as well, or at least I thought so. I hoped I wasn't misreading her.

Each table seated about twenty. There were more than a dozen tables, all of which were full or nearly so. I could see several more women working in the kitchen, bringing out fresh dishes and clearing the tables as diners finished. Nancy had mentioned sentries, so there had to be more security personnel out there working. There were two hundred plus women eating dinner, plus the kitchen staff, plus security…plus who knew how many more. I was impressed with the size of the community. I was even more impressed with their infrastructure. We had washed our hands and faces before dinner at a spigot set in a gravel-paved area just across from the kitchen. These women had plumbing! And solar power. And roads and vineyards and cattle. I was curious about their organizational structure. Was Simone the supreme and only leader? Had she been elected? Perhaps the town meeting would provide some insight into that.

East was seated to my left. She was attracting a lot of attention. As usual.

"Where are you two from?" The question came from a beefy woman with a bowl cut who had plunked down next to Nancy. It sounded as if she were asking both of us, but she was completely focused on East. Both of us had gotten a lot of stares throughout the meal. East's were of the admiring variety. Even as grubby and disheveled as we were, her beauty stood out in that crowd. I noticed almost all the women were at least in their thirties. The majority were in their forties or fifties. A few were even older.

"Oh, uh, you know, south," East replied with her easygoing smile. She shot me a glance then to check on my reaction. To make sure I approved. I knew she had felt my leg stiffen under the table next to hers when the woman asked the question. If I hadn't been there, I felt certain East would have spilled all our beans. She was way too trusting, in my opinion. It was probably only a matter of time before the truth came out, but I thought it best to be wary at this point. These women were strangers to us. Dangerous, unknown strangers with their own agenda. Just because they were female didn't mean they were our friends.

Across the table, Beefy McGee was still making conversation with East. *Hitting* on her, I realized with a jolt. I had never been around another queer person before—or if I had, I'd been entirely unaware of it. My very limited knowledge of such matters came from a few books, things I'd overheard other people say and the thoughts in my head. I still wasn't sure if I believed East's declaration of going both ways. I looked around again at the tables full of women eating, drinking, laughing and talking. A few had their arms around their companions' shoulders. As I scanned the crowd, I saw one couple kissing. Good heavens, were they all gay? My eyes must have been as big as the dinner plates. Across the table from me, Nancy watched me watching the crowd with a wry twist to her lips. Was she gay?

"So are you a couple?" the beefy woman asked East.

East laughed nervously, flicked me another glance and said, "Uh, yeah…I mean, no. Not really."

She looked again to see if I approved of her answer. Was her off-hand "not really" her honest answer, or was she bluffing them? We hadn't kissed or really done anything…There'd been a lot of up-close-and-personal in the sleeping bag, but that was out of necessity, not romance. But still…I was surprised how much it hurt me to hear her say we weren't a couple. As if Elinor Eastman and Kell Dupont could ever be a couple. I stared at the empty plate on the table in front of me and tried to block out everything for a moment, to make that sharp pang in my heart go away.

What would that even be like? To be part of a couple? Maybe I'd have my arm around her waist. Her hand would rest lightly on the back on my neck as she leaned in to brush my lips with hers.

The dinner bell loudly rang again to announce the end of the meal, jarring me out of my foolish distraction. Three distinct clangs then sounded, which I correctly guessed meant the meeting was about to start. People around us were getting up and ambling over to the amphitheater, but Nancy held us back for a moment.

"Don't be scared of the meeting, kids. It's just a good way to introduce you to everyone."

"What's going to happen?" East asked. Despite Nancy's words, she looked frightened, which was exactly how I felt. East put her hand on mine under the table. Wait—was that something a non-couple would do? I was totally confused. I slid my hand out from under hers and stuck both of mine in my pockets.

"Well, it's our regular weekly meeting," Nancy explained. "It's a chance for the group to get together, talk about how we're doing and discuss any problems. Simone will lead it. She'll introduce you, I'll vouch for you and then you'll probably be assigned jobs. We all work here and you'll be expected to pitch in."

East and I looked at each other but said nothing.

"Don't worry," Nancy said with a smile. "You'll be fine, I promise."

Great, a promise from a strange woman I'd met at gunpoint just a few hours earlier who had taken away everything we owned. I felt better already.

She led us down to the bottom of the amphitheater and showed us where to sit. Front row and center. She then climbed onstage and took a seat with several other women on two low benches behind Simone, who had her own large and ornately carved chair. Marta appeared out of nowhere—I had a sense she was good at that—and slid into the seat next to me.

Wild-haired Simone strode to the front of the stage, slowly raised her outstretched hands and loudly said, "Sisters."

The place was instantly quiet. The natural acoustics of the bowl-shaped amphitheater easily carried Simone's words to the audience. She sounded kind of phony to me, like she was putting on an act, but the women were all listening respectfully, just like she wasn't a jackass.

There was still a little light in the sky to the west—a faint gleam of pink, all that was left of the sunset. The first stars were shyly glimmering overhead. Several large and intense lights hung over the stage from a metal framework, powerfully illuminating Simone and the women seated behind her. In the audience, a few subdued lights shone just brightly enough so you could find your seat, or climb one of the four sets of stairs running from top to bottom of the bowl.

"Good evening," Simone said to the attentive crowd. "Our agenda tonight will be old business, status reports from the crew leaders and new business. Violet, is there any old business still pending from the last meeting?"

"No, Simone," answered the Asian minion from stage right, referring to a paper in her hand. She seemed to be taking notes although nothing much had happened so far.

"All right, we'll move on to status updates."

It turned out the women sitting on the benches were all in charge of some vital function. Each stood and addressed the crowd when called upon by Simone to report the latest news or problems with their work areas, which included Admin, Farm, Health, Kitchen, Laundry, Security and more. Some had nothing to share. Most of it was surprisingly tedious to me— heck, it was worse than school. Here I was, trying to learn all their deep dark secrets, and they were yapping about showing up on time for your shift, being quiet around the tents of the women who worked at night and slept during the day, and other earthshaking matters. The Farm crew leader, who covered both crops and animals, had a lot to say about irrigation schedules, which was as exciting as it sounds. I wanted to turn in my seat and study the crowd behind me but felt constrained by Marta's dour presence at my elbow.

Simone called out "Security" in her booming fake voice and a lean blond woman with a crewcut took the stage. She looked like she spent a lot of time outdoors. Green eyes blazed in her tanned face. I thought she was about thirty, maybe five foot seven, one hundred twenty very fit pounds. The stage lights added drama to elegant cheekbones and her sculpted frame. She wore tan carpenter's pants, a form-fitting navy T-shirt and suede boots with some serious lug soles. I was trying not to stare, but the woman was mesmerizing. I wasn't the only one who thought so—I heard a murmur of appreciation from the row behind me. She launched into her update with no preamble.

"One of our patrols riding the vineyard perimeter encountered an intruder this afternoon—a man."

Angry muttering from the crowd was the immediate response. Crap, was she talking about me? I hoped not. The back of my neck grew hot. I eased myself a little lower in my front row seat.

"No shots were fired, but he is believed to be armed. The patrol attempted to detain him for questioning, but unfortunately, he eluded capture."

The angry muttering swelled and broke into a buzz of irate voices—some frightened, some questioning, some demanding more information from the security chief, whose name was Pinto according to the people yelling at her. Well, at least she wasn't talking about me. I sat back up.

Pinto held up her hands and asked them to quiet down, which they grudgingly did.

"I've put extra patrols into the field. At first light, we'll resume our search. He may have already fled the area. We believe this man was simply a wanderer who strayed onto our land by accident. We've all learned the hard way how important it is to be vigilant. Please keep your eyes and ears open, sisters. Be watchful and let Security or Sarge know if you see anything."

"What's he look like, Pinto?" somebody called out from an upper row.

"White male, age forty to fifty, medium length dark hair and beard going gray, approximately five foot ten, hundred and fifty pounds, dirty clothes, walks with a limp."

Oh, fuck. That sounded kind of familiar. I wondered if the man they were looking for had pursued me and East into their community. Had we unwittingly brought him here to their doorstep? But I still couldn't believe that cuckoo Matteo could have followed us all this way. It didn't seem like he was physically capable of it, let alone mentally. But if it wasn't Matteo, who could it be?

"We've dealt with these kinds of situations before," Pinto was saying reassuringly. "My crew knows what to do if and when they find him to ensure Tres Hermanas remains safe."

"Shoot his ass!" someone yelled which got a big laugh and lots of heads nodding in agreement.

"Any questions?" asked Pinto, who was unsmiling and all business. I could see the flash of her green eyes from my front row seat. The bright stage lights caught the delicate down on her cheeks and the back of her neck as she turned her head. I had never seen such a gloriously hot androgynous female before—except in my dreams. In my peripheral vision, I could see that East was looking at me. I closed my mouth, took in some air and pretended I was cool.

There were no questions, just a few more shouts of "Go get him, Pinto!" as she returned to her seat on the bench. Nancy was the last one sitting there who had not yet spoken.

"Utility?" Simone said.

I didn't know what "utility" was, but Nancy merely rose to her feet, said "Nothing to report, Simone" and sat back down again, so that was sort of an anticlimax after the big news from Security.

Simone once again took the floor, her wild fluff of white hair looking theatrical in the lights. I uncharitably speculated that that was the point. I didn't trust her one bit. Sometimes, you just have a gut reaction to a person and my gut did not like Simone at all.

"Thank you, crew leaders," she said. "And now we move on to new business. There are two items this week. First, I want to remind you that our annual harvest festival begins in just three short weeks."

Cheers and applause filled the air at this happy news. I had a feeling these gals liked to party.

"We have a lot of work to do before then, but I know we will all pull together to get the harvest in on time so we can celebrate. And now for the other item—"

The crowd quieted again, although there was a feeling of excited anticipation in the air, as though they'd all be waiting for this. I suddenly realized "this" was us. Me and East. We were the New Business. Nancy was gesturing to us to come up on stage.

Simone said, "Sisters, I am happy to announce we have two new recruits joining us today."

Recruits?

East stood and tried to pull me up. My legs would not cooperate. I absolutely did not want to go up on that stage. Marta helpfully gave me a shove and between the two of them, I suddenly lurched to my feet. East grabbed me and dragged me with her up on the stage. The lights were blinding. My mouth was dry, my stomach full of large and pissed-off butterflies.

"What are their names again?" Simone said out of the side of her mouth to Nancy, who quietly answered.

"Sisters, please welcome Elinor and Kell!"

There was a smattering of uncertain applause, a few hoots and catcalls, and one angry shout which cut clearly through the cool night air.

"Looks like a guy to me, Simone!"

More irate mutters. The general consensus did not appear to be in my favor.

Simone said unconvincingly, "I am told both are girls."

It was almost like she was trying to embarrass Nancy or at least put her on the spot. I watched both of their faces. Nancy was calmly awaiting her turn to speak. She caught my eye and gave me a nod.

"Do you vouch for them, Sarge?" somebody yelled.

I wasn't sure who Sarge was, but to my surprise, Nancy stepped to the edge of the stage and answered in a strong voice that left no doubt as to her meaning.

"I vouch for both these girls," she called out to the crowd, emphasizing the "both" and the "girls."

There was more murmuring in the crowd, but I heard someone near the front say "Well, if Sarge says so, that's good enough for me."

Simone seemed irritated that the attention had shifted away from her.

"Who will have them?" she cried.

East shot me a scared look and clutched my hand. I had no idea either what was going on.

The crew leader in charge of the kitchen (the aforementioned Beefy McGee, to my dismay) yelled, "I'll take the hottie!" which got a lot of raucous laughter from the crowd and the women on stage. Nancy frowned. East couldn't help but smile a little bit. I felt like shit.

Simone declared, "Elinor is assigned to the kitchen crew then per Buffalo's request. Who will take the other?"

Silence. No one yelled out they would take me. No one called me a hottie.

Damn. Just like high school.

"I'll take her," Nancy said to Simone. Their gazes locked for a long moment.

Simone turned to the crowd. "Kell goes to Utility."

She then turned sideways to face me and East, while still addressing the crowd.

"The new recruits will stay with us for thirty days and work for their meals. After thirty days, their possessions will be returned to them and the board will convene to decide on their permanent membership."

There was so much wrong with that declaration, I hardly knew where to begin. I opened my mouth to protest, but Nancy caught my eye. She shook her head just slightly, just one quick left-right movement. "Now is not the time" was what her glance was saying. I decided to let caution be the better part of valor, but I was far from happy. Recruit, my ass.

"Is there any other new business?" Simone called out.

There was, but it was just a mix of complaints, requests and other boring junk that was quickly dispensed with. In a matter of minutes, the meeting was over. The kitchen crew leader and her staff descended upon East and spirited her away. I don't think she had realized until that moment that they would be splitting us up. There was nothing we could do. She shot me a fearful look as they walked her away from where I stood with Marta and Nancy, my fists balled, my jaw rigid. I thought I saw her lips form my name, but then she was lost in the crowd.

"She'll be okay, kid," Nancy said to me. "They're just taking her to the kitchen crew's quarters. She'll be working with them now."

She gestured in the opposite direction. "Let's go," she said to me and the ever-silent Marta, who nodded.

I had no choice but to follow them. I thought we were going to their tent, but we had a stop to make first—the showers.

Many things, in fact most things, were both communal and outdoors at Tres Hermanas. Including the showers. We found some in a small tree-ringed glade between the residential ring and the main inner road. An area had been dug up, leveled and then a floor of gravel put in place. There were two parallel lines of pipe held up by posts, each pipe with four shower heads. No separate stalls. No privacy. Just an open space where you and seven friends could get naked and bathe under the open sky. With pedestrians strolling past, perhaps pausing to offer commentary or words of encouragement. How delightful.

To Nancy and Marta, it was the norm and not worth commenting on. There were two other women already in there. The area was lit, although not brightly. A stooped, gray-haired old woman was the worker assigned to the showers, doling out towels, soap and shampoo as needed. Open-ended wooden cubby hole boxes were available to stash your clothes in while you bathed. Nancy and Marta did so and strode naked toward the shower heads, exchanging greetings with the other two already in there.

Gran had taught me that life would offer many experiences. Some good, some bad. Many could be perceived as either good or bad simply depending on one's point of view. "Adjust your attitude, adjust your outcome" was another one of her sayings.

As I hesitated by the cubbies, I thought: On one hand, a public shower with four other strange women could be considered a total nightmare unless you were an exhibitionist.

On the other hand, it was all women, so who cared, right? It was just skin…

And I was so freaking filthy…

"Hurry up, kid!" Nancy yelled at me. She reached over and turned on the shower between her and Marta, then gestured at me to join them. "You only get five minutes of hot water once you turn it on."

Modesty, cleanliness and other considerations aside, I recognized that taking a shower would put to rest any doubts about my anatomy and help gain their trust. I wasn't sure how long we'd be staying—not long, if I had my way—but getting these women to accept me was good strategy. I had no doubt they would accept East. They already had based on the comments at the town meeting. Whether we were guests or captives, it made sense to get along with them. At least for now.

I gritted my teeth, took a big breath and stripped, then walked to the shower head between Nancy and Marta, trying extremely hard not to look at them or the other two. But they were so naked! And so right there! Not that it was the good kind of naked. Far from it, in fact. I tried not to look but couldn't help but get a few glimpses. Of the four, Nancy had the best body, but although fit and well-muscled, it was a forty-year-old body. Several noticeable scars, surgical and otherwise, crisscrossed her torso and limbs. One unfortunate and accidental glance at Marta's squat form was more than enough. The other bathers were pale and a bit tubby.

I closed my eyes—tightly—and concentrated on the amazing sensation of hot water and soap suds sluicing down my frame. Looking up was another safe visual option. As I stared at the stars above and pondered just how much had changed for me and East in the past twenty-four hours, I had to take a moment to just *be*—to enjoy my clean, well-fed body under the cascade of water. And to try not to think about any of them looking at me. Yikes.

The water chose that moment to run cold. I involuntarily yipped and scrambled to turn it off. The old lady was there with a smile, handing me a clean towel for which I thanked her. I wasn't looking forward to redonning my dirty clothes, but yet another surprise awaited me back at the cubby holes where Nancy and Marta were getting dressed.

"Here," Nancy said, "these are for you." She pointed to a neatly folded stack of navy blue sweats and a pair of thick clean socks. "So you can sleep in clean clothes tonight. We'll get your other clothes washed by the laundry crew, okay?"

Even as she spoke, the old lady was collecting my pile of clothes and taking them away. I hurriedly dressed in the sweats which were too big, but way better than naked. There was a big yellow "Cal" in the center of the chest on the sweatshirt. I didn't know who Cal was, but silently thanked him or her for the loaner.

It was about a ten-minute hike to their tent's location in the residential ring. On the way, Nancy explained that many women bunked with their work crews, although it wasn't mandatory. Couples, women with children and those who preferred solitude had the option to find or build other housing to suit their needs.

"Are you all, uh…" My question lost steam at the end.

"Queer?" Nancy finished for me with a flash of her white teeth. It was fully dark now and I was stumbling along at her side with Marta behind me, all of us following the beam of Nancy's solar-powered flashlight on a well-trodden dirt path. Every ten yards or so, we would pass another dwelling, most with lights showing and women inside. We collected a lot of "Good night, Sarge!" and "*¡Buenas noches, Marta!*" along the way.

Was "queer" the word I was looking for? Hell, I didn't know. But I nodded cautiously at Nancy. Or Sarge. Whatever her name was.

"All women are welcome at Tres Hermanas, Kell," she told me quietly as we walked along. "Many of us are lesbians. Some prefer the word queer. Some identify as bisexual, transgender, genderqueer, gender non-conforming, asexual. Some prefer not to be burdened with a label. A few are straight who feel more secure and comfortable in a community of women in these challenging times. We've taken in lots of stragglers in the last several years. Did I answer your question?"

I nodded, in truth feeling a bit overwhelmed by all that information. But, since she seemed open to my inquiries, I tried another.

"Are you and Marta a couple?"

She smiled at that and said something in Spanish over my head to Marta, who snorted behind me. We were nearly at the end of a row of similar tents which looked semi-permanent— large, sturdy, off-white canvas structures with wooden floors that were built on blocks a few feet off the ground.

"No," Nancy said. "I met Marta and her sister on the road many years ago, when I was traveling from Oakland to here. We are friends and coworkers, but we're not a couple. For one thing, I'm gay and Marta's straight. She lost her husband during the Bad Times. That's when she and her sister decided to come to Tres Hermanas. It was known as a gathering place and safe haven for women even Before."

We had reached the last tent. A single light gave off a soft golden glow within. Past the tent, darkness swallowed up the path and the trees. I could hear the wind moving gently through their unseen branches. A gaunt Hispanic woman sat on the steps. She stood as we approached, conferred briefly with Marta, then set off down the path back toward the central area. Marta folded back the tent flap and disappeared inside.

Nancy took a drink from her water bottle and offered it to me. I shook my head.

"How come they call you Sarge?" I asked her. "Were you in the army?"

"Marine Corps," she said with a hint of pride. And sadness. "And then I was a police officer in Oakland for ten years. You may call me Nancy or Sarge—I answer to both."

"Okay," I said.

"Any other questions, *chiquita*?"

"Where's my friend?"

"The tents where the kitchen workers sleep are on the other side of the residential ring," she said, pointing off into the darkness. "I'll show it to you tomorrow if you like. And don't worry—you'll see your friend at meals and during free times. In the morning, though, you start work with us on the Utility crew."

"What does—"

She cut me off with a tired smile.

"That's enough for one day, don't you think? It's time for sleep now, Kell. There'll be plenty of time tomorrow for more questions and answers. For both of us."

She pulled back the tent flap and gestured me inside. Two sets of metal bunk beds were on opposite walls. The canvas ceiling was ten feet high—no need to stoop in that tent. Marta and her sister (I presumed) were already ensconced in the top and bottom bunks of one bed. I took the upper on the other since Nancy's pajamas were laid out on the lower bunk. I was pleased to find mine was already made up with sheets, warm blankets and even a pillow, while Nancy turned out the light and changed into her jammies.

"Good night, Kell," she said softly. I heard the springs creak as she climbed into the lower bunk.

I lay there with my eyes open, feeling the fatigue hit hard even as a part of me savored the comfortable bed, snug and warm in my blankets. My mind fought to stay awake and make sense of the events of that very long day. I tried to sort out what I was feeling at that moment. Was I afraid? Not exactly…Was I safe? I had no idea. Was I numb? That was more like it. My eyes closed just for a moment and I was gone.

CHAPTER TWENTY-SEVEN

Living In Lesbo Town

When I awoke, it was morning, but just. A pale gray light illuminated the interior of the tent. I could see my breath when I exhaled. I sat up and took my first good look around the space in the daylight. Besides the two bunk beds, the walls were lined with a battered chest of drawers, milk crates and wooden boxes for additional storage, three mismatched chairs and a card table. An ancient Turkish rug, fringed and threadbare in tones of blue and red, covered the floor between the bunks. A variety of other personal articles perched on top of the boxes, or hung from the bedposts. Nothing fancy, but it was a cozy, homey place. Close quarters, though, for three—now four—people. It felt odd to have slept indoors again and in a bed no less. I wondered how East was faring.

Marta was just climbing down from her top bunk. Her sister was already up, sitting on the edge of her bed with her hands clasped. She was clearly the younger sister, probably not much older than I was. She was a shorter, rounder version of Marta, just as brown, just as squat, with the same long pigtail down her back. She kept sneaking shy peeks at me, but wouldn't meet my gaze.

I climbed down too, to find that Nancy's bed was empty. The tent flap stirred and she came inside, carrying something under her arm.

"Oh, good," she said when she saw everyone was up. "Kell, I'd like you to meet Marta's sister, Alma. Alma works with the laundry crew. She doesn't speak much English."

"*Hola, Alma*," I said, hoping to score style points with Marta who, as usual, paid me no mind. "*Me llamo Kell.*" My name is Kell.

Of course, then I realized I probably should have kept my rudimentary knowledge of Spanish under wraps. You never knew what might be an advantage. Crap.

Alma giggled and did not reply. Marta, who had swiftly dressed during this exhilarating exchange, said something in Spanish to her sister and the two of them walked out together. Alma looked over her shoulder at me as she went out and waved. Surprised, I belatedly held up a hand, but they were out the door.

Nancy said, "Alma has Down syndrome. Do you know what that is?"

I wasn't sure what to say, exactly. I hadn't been expecting a pop quiz first thing in the morning.

"I think so," I said haltingly. "There was a little boy at our... There was a little boy where I lived who Alma reminds me of. His body grew up, but his mind stayed a child."

Nancy nodded. "Alma is a good friend to have here, as you will see. And these are for you."

She handed me the bundle she'd brought in. It was all the clothes that I'd worn yesterday, plus the few additional garments from my backpack. And both of Mr. Giovanni's wool socks. All were clean and dry. They smelled marvelous.

There was one change to my meager wardrobe. The gigantic dark green parka I'd grabbed at the cabin was gone. I can't say I missed its oversized, ill-fitting, reeking-of-campfire presence. In its place was a well-worn, but still in good condition, black leather jacket. The soft leather was cracked and faded, the satiny interior patched and aged—but it fit! A warm jacket that was actually my size. I looked up at Nancy, speechless. And wrestled with my conscience. Could I accept this? Should I? On the other hand, if they'd confiscated Old Greenie, did I have a choice? I needed a coat to survive.

Nancy gave me a ghost of a smile as if sensing my turmoil, but merely said, "Why don't you get dressed and join us outside? We'll walk to breakfast and then start work."

Thus began a routine that filled all my waking hours for many days. The four of us would get up, eat breakfast with the rest of the sisterhood, then work for eight or ten or twelve hours. Sometimes even longer. I didn't mind. I liked hard work, especially if it was outside. What I didn't like was being held captive against my will, even if it was in the politest way possible. I could have left—they weren't physically restraining me. But without my gear, I wouldn't last long on the road. It was as simple as that. They knew it, I knew it. So I played along, and kept my eyes and ears open.

Simone had said we could have our stuff back at the end of thirty days. Maybe she was lying, but that was okay. I had no intention of sticking around for thirty days. As soon as I figured out where my gear was and nobody was looking, I was gone. In the meantime, I listened more than I spoke and found out a lot about Tres Hermanas and its inhabitants.

Also in the meantime: there was cake! And hot water! And an occasional softball game, where Marta, unexpectedly, unleashed a wicked fastball.

As the days went by, I heard more than a few stories from the women of how they had come to Tres Hermanas. They had a doctor there, a French woman who gave both me and East a clean bill of health on our second day. In her exquisite accent, she told us she'd been on vacation in the wine country when the Bad Times hit. Stranded in Northern California with no money, no way to get home or even communicate with anyone in Europe after the Internet and all telephone services failed, she had made her way to Tres Hermanas with some dykes on bikes she'd met at a bar along the Russian River.

As an aside here, I have to mention that the women at Tres Hermanas were a mixed bag, looks-wise, just like any diverse group of women, but that doctor was smokin' hot. And that accent! Ooh la la. I heard someone say she was Pinto's girlfriend, but I decided to ignore that, preferring to cling to the belief that Pinto was secretly holding out for me.

Pinto herself, Nancy told me, had been a sheriff's deputy in the area around Bodega Bay. Quite a few of the Tres Hermanans were former law enforcement or military, which explained their apparently good security. Women skilled in agriculture, construction, healthcare and education were also well represented. There seemed to be a place and a job and a purpose for everyone, no matter what her background was.

I understood that East and I were being recruited. Yes, they were detaining us against our (well, my, at least) will, but they were doing so in an awfully hospitable fashion. They needed us—the majority of their population was forty and up. Tres Hermanas was a city of old women, getting older every day. There were no other new "recruits" as far as I could tell. The community desperately needed to add some younger members to keep things going for the future. That was clear to me.

Was it clear to East? I wasn't sure. She appeared to be having a good time being held captive by the Amazons, which totally pissed me off. As always, her looks ensured her popularity. I would see her laughing and joking with the other kitchen workers, yukking it up while I trudged by with a shovel or a sledgehammer over my shoulder. She and I didn't see much of each other at first. I presumed they were keeping us separated on purpose to facilitate the brainwashing. Of course, I was glad East wasn't suffering or in distress—but did she have to be the freaking life of the party? It was disconcerting to be so jealous—jealous of the attention lavished upon her by her adoring public...jealous of the women who got to spend time with her, look at her, hear her laugh...jealous of the possibility that maybe East would find someone else to share her sleeping bag…I tried to shut down such dark thoughts when they came upon me and concentrate on my mission: get my gear back, get the hell out and find my sister. Find Gabriel. Find Segundo—with or without Elinor Eastman.

The work of the Utility crew took us all over the compound, which was a great way to learn about the place. The crew was just me, Nancy and Marta. "Utility" turned out to mean doing all the jobs the other crews did not. Or filling in if another team was short-handed. We dug ditches, picked grapes, fixed fences, cleared brush, chopped firewood—you name it, we did it. Except security—I would have enjoyed doing a shift or two with the Security crew, particularly if my imaginary girlfriend Pinto were involved, but that assignment never came. I wouldn't have put the new arrival on security detail either. It was a good reminder for me that these women weren't stupid. I needed to keep my wits about me. And that wasn't always easy for me in Tres Hermanas.

It was a dizzying (I was going to say "heady," but this is serious) experience for me to be in a town of all women. Almost all of whom were queer. In my wildest dreams, I could not have pictured it. Well, maybe I could have, but I had never let myself picture it. I had grown up thinking—knowing—I was going to be alone my whole life. That love would never be an option for me. That I might never even know another queer woman, let alone have a girlfriend. A lover.

And here they all were.

Yet they were my enemies. Anyone who stood between me and finding Gabriel was my enemy.

It was all very confusing.

And it's not like living in Lesbo Town was perfect. I was disconcerted to find that, having finally met a bunch of lesbians, I didn't like a lot of them. On some level, it felt wrong, disloyal even, to think a queer woman was a jerk. Like I should treasure each and every one of them simply because they were so rare, mathematically speaking. But rare or not, a jerk is a jerk.

Some of them were loud. Some were rude. Far too many of them were coarse. Nancy tried to explain it to me once, about the lack of civility, the crudeness passing as humor. We were eating breakfast in the common area at my favorite table under a large shady maple. She saw me wince at the noisy and nasty banter from the next table. Nancy started by telling me I was too young to remember or understand what it had been like for gay people Before. I silently swore to myself that if and when I became an adult, I would never tell a kid he or she was too young to understand something.

"The thing is, Kell," Nancy said earnestly, "there was so much we couldn't do Before. For a lot of us, despite the horror of those bad years, this is finally a time of freedom and equality. We had to hide so much before—you couldn't hold your girl's hand in public, much less kiss her. If you dressed differently, or walked differently, or acted differently, you were in trouble. You couldn't even say you were queer without paying a terrible price. You'd lose your family, your friends, your job...maybe even your life. So for those of us who lived through that, to now have the opportunity to do and say as we please...well, some of them go a little overboard, I know. But they're just reveling in the liberty they never thought they'd live to see."

"That's great, Nance," I replied, a bit caustically, "but I'm just trying to eat my breakfast in peace without hearing a bunch of rude shit that makes me want to hurl."

"Yeah, I know," she said, her brow creased. Probably worried the recruiting effort would fail if they grossed me out too much. Plus, I think she secretly agreed with me. Nancy had the right stuff.

"Some of them don't know any other way to behave," she admitted with one of her wry smiles. "But we've got some good people here, Kell. Don't be too quick to judge us."

"Nancy, how come you're not in charge of security?" I asked, wanting to change the subject. I was curious as well. With her military and police background, it seemed like she was the obvious choice. Despite my ridiculous crush on Pinto, even I could see that. Heck, I thought she should be running the whole damn place. I wasn't attracted to Nancy physically, but I admired her—her strength, her honesty, her compassion. The way she absolutely refused to take any guff from anybody.

She met my eyes for a second, then glanced away. She looked sad, which made me regret bringing it up.

"Pinto wanted the job. And I did not," she eventually answered.

The silence hung between us like she was daring me to ask why not. She flicked me another look, like she was gauging my character. Again.

"I'm sick, Kell," she finally said.

I was shocked. I stared at her.

"No, Nancy…"

"Yeah, kid, I am. I have lots of good days, but I never know when a bad one will strike. It's why I came to Tres Hermanas. You reach a point in your life where you need other people. You need their help sometimes. Even if they're rude and obnoxious and make too much noise—they're still family."

I ignored the little dig at my judginess and stared at the ruins of my breakfast.

Fuck them. They weren't my family. My family was Gabriel. And sort of East. Maybe. That was my family. Not all these new people I didn't have time to care about.

For the thousandth time, I told myself to focus on what was important.

Sick?

CHAPTER TWENTY-EIGHT

Just Plotting My Top Secret Escape, Don't Mind Me

After two weeks in Tres Hermanas, I had learned a lot, but not enough. I knew the layout and routines of the place but was still fuzzy on the overall geography. Where was the highway? I knew who was in charge and roughly how many women lived there. I knew about their livestock, their crops, their water and power supply. I had a pretty good idea who was sleeping with whom. And who wanted to be sleeping with whom. I had figured out who the major players were and who was in what clique. Jesus, so cliquey! Worse than school. All of that intel was well and good, but what still eluded me was the location of our gear. I hadn't had much of a chance to poke around in town yet. I was fairly certain our backpacks were locked up in one of the small unmarked buildings in the innermost loop, but all of our Utility crew jobs had taken us away from the center of things. So far, at least.

I wondered if East had heard or seen anything useful. Since she was usually working in the kitchen during meal times, I hadn't talked to her much. We would see each other in passing—or I would see her as Nancy, Marta and I strode by on the way to our next filthy and back-breaking task. I'd caught a glimpse of her that morning through the open flap of the cooking tent, singing a work song with the rest of the kitchen crew as they chopped and whisked. I didn't even know she liked to sing. Someone had done her long brown hair in a French braid. One more girly thing I could never have done for her. I scowled and walked a little faster. Those latrine pits weren't going to dig themselves.

That night was the weekly meeting. I showered before dinner, and my hair was still damp and spiky as I made my way down the stairs of the amphitheater, searching for East. In the crowd, the ladies were all agog with plans for their annual harvest festival. I spotted her in the thick of the kitchen crew and was debating trying to worm my way in amongst them versus catching her after the meeting.

"Kell—*venga aquí*," Marta summoned me to a spot next to her and Alma. I hesitated, but the meeting was about to start, plus Marta was giving me The Look, so I hurried to join them. Nancy was up on stage, seated on the benches with the other crew leaders behind Simone.

The meeting was much the same as the previous ones—status updates from the various crew leaders and then the floor opened for new business. New business being mostly complaints and hogwash, with nothing getting resolved as far as I could tell. The hot issue that night was: Is It Or Is It Not Okay For One Woman To Address Another Woman As Dude? The complainant was originally from the east coast. The native Californians shouted her down. They all seemed to enjoy the bickering thoroughly. I hated it.

The highlight of the meeting for me was Pinto's security update.

"Sisters," she told us in her methodical way, "there have been no further sightings of the intruder. However, food and other small objects have gone missing at some of the outermost tents, so we believe he may still be in the area. My security patrols continue to be on high alert. Please remain vigilant. Anything out of the ordinary should be immediately reported to Security, Sarge or your crew leader."

After the updates, Simone recaptured center stage.

"Just one more week 'til festival!" she proclaimed to much excitement from the crowd. She had to wait a moment for them to settle down before continuing. "Volunteers are still needed for the barbecue pit. See Buffalo for that. Oh, and our deejay has confirmed the stereo system is in good working order."

A burst of applause met that dual announcement, and I turned in my seat to see Beefy McGee (aka Buffalo) rise from her seat among the kitchen staff and wave to the crowd. She smirked, her bowl cut freshly trimmed. The deejay, a graceful older woman who went by the odd and less than melodious name of Euterpe, also rose to receive her due.

Music was something I missed from home. On special occasions at the Settlement, they'd fire up a generator and treat us all to some recording from the past. As with everything, the music that had survived from Before was a hodgepodge. I remembered at the last Aptitude ceremony, there was Bach, Cole Porter, bluegrass and flamenco on the program. We had musicians back home too, playing either instruments salvaged from the devastation of San Tomas or ones they'd made themselves. We sang in school. God Bless America…

There was lots of singing at Tres Hermanas. I'd heard other workers singing like the kitchen staff, but it wasn't part of the utility crew's routine. On Sunday nights, there was recorded music playing as dinner was served. Made me feel almost civilized.

The meeting was over soon after that. Nancy joined us as the audience slowly climbed the amphitheater steps with much stopping to talk and laugh with friends.

"East!" I finally succeeded in getting her attention at the top of the stairs. She waited for me, the crowd parting around her like a river flows past a rock. I caught her arm when I got to her, not wanting to lose her before we had a chance to talk. Nancy, Marta and Alma stopped when I did and stood there expectantly, waiting for me so we could make the walk back to our tent in the dark. Would they let me speak to East alone? I gave it a shot.

"Um, that's okay, I just want to talk to my friend for a minute. I'll catch up, all right?"

Marta looked at Nancy. Nancy looked at me. A long, cool, assessing look. I summoned up what innocence I had and met her gaze. Nonchalant. Just plotting my top-secret escape, don't mind me. I don't think I fooled her one bit, but she merely said mildly, "Okay. Do you have a flashlight, *chiquita*?"

I showed her the one she had issued me.

"Let's go," she said to Marta and Alma.

East and I found a semi-secluded tree just off the path. I noticed they'd given her a jacket that fit as well. A flannel-lined barn coat—nice. Maybe that was number three on the official Tres Hermanas Recruit Proselytization Checklist: feed 'em, checkup with the doctor, outerwear...

Women were straggling past us, singly and in small groups, calling good night to each other as they headed for their dwellings. I knew we only had a few minutes alone together for our first truly private chat since we'd stumbled upon Tres Hermanas. Anything more would be suspicious.

"Are you okay?" was my first question.

"Yeah. You?"

"Yeah. But we've got to get out of here."

She couldn't have been expecting me to say anything different, but it seemed like her face fell a little bit when I said it. I knew why—she'd found the safe place she'd been looking for. With plenty of food, shelter and people to admire her. Maybe it was wrong of me to judge her so harshly. She couldn't help being what she was. Me neither. Lot of that going around.

And truly, why should she want to go? She didn't have family waiting for her in Segundo. Although...I was never going to say this out loud to her, but if her brother Baird miraculously returned alive—to find the Settlement destroyed—and then even *more* miraculously found Segundo as the logical next step—that was her one chance, her one-in-a-zillion opportunity to ever see him again. I didn't know if East had thought of that highly unlikely scenario. I wasn't about to bring it up because I didn't want to be cruel—I knew in my heart that Baird was dead. That was the fate that awaited every Messenger. It was waiting for me right now, probably on the road to Segundo, but I had no choice. Segundo or bust.

And if East didn't care enough about me to make that her reason to leave Tres Hermanas, well, fuck her. Fuck all of them.

It was just a few seconds between my words and her reaction, and the uncomfortable pause that followed—but it seemed like a lot of information passed between us in those few seconds.

"I'm going with or without you, East," I finally told her gently as I could.

She looked away. "I know," she said, her voice low and distant.

I could see Buffalo and her kitchen crew approaching. Our time was almost up. I stepped forward and grabbed both of East's arms, up on my toes so I could whisper directly into her ear. "Do you know where our stuff is?"

The crew was almost upon us.

East stared down at me, her eyes wide in her pale face. She shook her head just a fraction, a movement so small I doubt the other women saw it. I wasn't sure if I believed her.

"Everything all right, Elinor?" Beefy/Buffalo called. "You coming?"

Without another word, East leaned in, planted a soft kiss on my temple, then hurried off to join her coworkers.

It was a long, lonely walk back to the tent.

The next day dawned clear and cold. I was glad for my leather jacket as Nancy, Marta and I rode out to a distant ridgeline to inspect and fix a fence. Horseback riding was a new skill for me, but the docile and sweet-natured gray mare Nancy chose was tolerant of my inexperience. Her horse was a muscular piebald gelding called Buster. When I asked, Marta told me her horse's name was *Caballo*. I think she was joking. It was a beautiful morning with brilliant blue skies and the earthy aroma of the freshly harvested fields filling my senses.

And then I caught myself. I hated those moments when I realized I was enjoying my time at Tres Hermanas. What the hell was I doing enjoying myself? Every minute I was there was time I wasn't using to find Segundo and my sister. No matter how much I liked Nancy and Marta and Alma—no matter how safe or warm or well-fed I was—I had to get out of there. With or without East.

Our destination that day was far from the central rings. After the first hour of riding, the only other women we saw were a couple of kitchen workers on horseback leading a solitary cow back toward town. I recognized the black and white markings—my old pal Bovine Nancy. Her bell sounded pure and sweet in the clear morning air.

Nancy and Marta were both capable of long, comfortable stretches of silence, so it was not unusual for us to not have much conversation on our way to work. That morning, however, I became aware there was some tension between them. I had never heard them argue before, so that was awkward. I didn't catch more than a word or two in their terse, but quiet, exchanges in Spanish—too quick for me—but it was clear they weren't in perfect agreement. Something about *la fuga*, which was not a word I knew. And Simone. I was straining to hear them while pretending not to pay attention. From their tones, Marta sounded worried with Nancy trying to placate her. Whatever it was, I figured they would work it out.

After a long ride which ended with a steep climb, the horses were content to graze while the humans worked. All morning long, we righted saggy fence posts and restrung barbed wire.

We were on the summit of one of the hills overlooking Tres Hermanas's pretty little valley. We could see for miles from up there, even to San Francisco Bay sparkling in the distance to the west and south of us. Of course, I couldn't see all the way to San Tomas, but I shaded my eyes with my hand and tried to discern any landmark or reminder of the only home I'd ever known—not knowing if there was anything or anyone left to see.

We broke for lunch midday, sitting in the shade of a venerable oak and admiring the remarkable view. The big tree reminded me of Gran's favorite spot in the dim coolness of the woods behind our cabin. I'd buried her there. I would likely never see that spot again, but Gran was with me in everything I did—my thoughts, my words, my attitudes. She was the blood that moved through my veins.

"See the bay, Kell?" Nancy said, pointing south to the shimmering water. I took a long swig from my Tres Hermanas-issued water bottle, then wiped my mouth with the back of my hand.

"I see it," I said.

As always, I was alert for any hints, verbal or visual, as to where the highway might be. That and my missing gear were the two things I needed before I took off. Without that information, Plan B was to simply head back the way we had come, backtracking many days and miles in the hope I could relocate the freeway. Plan B sucked. I scanned the scenic vista again, but saw no identifiable highways. The problem was, so much of it was so torn up and overgrown, a former road looked just like the rest of the landscape unless you were standing on it.

Nancy continued, "Okay, follow the coastline on the left down to where the greenery stops. And then see those few thin plumes of smoke at about ten o'clock?"

I followed her pointing hand. There. I nodded.

"That's Oakland," she told me.

"Right." I remembered me and East sitting by the side of the road there, right before I'd gotten sick.

"I grew up there. Marta and Alma came from further south, a place called Holmesville."

Oh, shit. Were we doing show and tell now? Well, I had nothing to show and less to tell. From the corner of my eye, I could see they were both looking at me, waiting for my response. Time to change the subject.

"Do you think there are any towns left out there, Nancy? Or other places like Tres Hermanas?"

To my surprise, she answered with certainty.

"Of course! There are a handful of small villages, I guess you'd call them, that we know of here in the Bay Area. We barter our wine and dried fruit with some of them. And swap information, more importantly. One of them has been willing to take in our mothers with boy children when they reach ten years old."

As so often seemed to happen, what started out as me asking her a question somehow turned into Nancy asking me questions.

"Isn't your sister at a place like that? She's with a group, right?"

I had never mentioned my sister to Nancy or Marta or anyone at Tres Hermanas. Damn you, Elinor Eastman. Heaven only knew what expression was on my face as I stared back at Nancy, but Marta did one of her small snorts.

"You think like a soldier, Kell," Nancy said approvingly. "But you are too young to be a soldier, so someone must have trained you well, eh?"

I nodded slowly, thinking of Gran and Gabriel. And how much I missed them. I blinked away the tears that sometimes sprang upon me without warning, pretending I had dust in my eyes.

Nancy was saying, "Your friend, however, is not as strategically minded as you are."

"Which is a nice way of saying she has a big mouth," I said sourly. I knew it was only a matter of time before East cracked like an egg and shared all our secrets with these strangers. Strangers who were beginning to feel like friends.

"She has a big heart as well," Nancy said. "A trusting heart. She is already very popular here."

Marta snorted again.

"So you kids are from San Tomas?"

The cat was out of the bag.

"Yeah," I said slowly.

"I used to go to the beach there in the summer with my girlfriend," Nancy said.

"*Que bonita playa*," Marta threw in. Holmesville was only about twenty miles south of San Tomas. Or had been. We were practically neighbors.

We were quiet for a while then, each staring off into the distance, into the past. The horses' bits clinked as they cropped at the grass. Nancy's voice brought me back to the present.

"Kell."

I looked at her. Marta chose that moment to get up, announce very uncharacteristically that she was going for a walk, and stomped off toward the horizon.

Nancy glanced after her with a look I couldn't read, then turned her attention back to me.

"Do you want to know where the freeway is?" she asked me without emotion.

We locked gazes. I did want to know. In fact, I had to know. If I admitted that to her, would I be giving up too much information? Would she use it against me? Would she lie? I came to three conclusions. First, that I did trust Nancy. Well, pretty much. As much as I trusted anybody. Second, that this was an exercise in trust for both of us. Third, that I had nothing to lose.

"Yes."

She pointed again to the plumes of smoke marking her hometown. I told her I knew the 80 ran north and south at that point—that was the way East and I had come.

"Right. Now if we move up the coastline, that's north. See how it curves and kind of bumps out there? That's Richmond. Or...where Richmond was. The freeway split there, with the 580 heading west and the 80 continuing more or less north."

I suddenly remembered East and I had been there too. I recalled a hill that stood out from the otherwise flat landscape. And standing on the freeway in my feverish daze, seeing a few hundred feet up the road where the freeway split to form a V— one route curving west around the shoreline of the bay, the other continuing north. It all snapped into perspective for me now. I could see the big hill too, now that I knew what I was looking for.

Nancy looked where I was so intently staring and seemed to understand.

"That hill was by a town called Albany," she told me. "Not that it matters anymore. That's where 80 starts bending northeast, more and more. In the old days, by the time it got to the California/Nevada border, it was headed practically straight east."

"And now?" I asked, perhaps too eagerly.

"I don't know. Last year, a few of us rode up the 80 to the bridge over the Carquinez Strait. That's about thirty miles from here. Needless to say, the bridge is out. We camped there overnight, then turned around and rode home."

Carquinez—that rang a faint bell. Maybe Gabriel had mentioned it to me.

"So..." I squinted, trying to see the map in my mind. "From Tres Hermanas, the best place to intersect the freeway is..."

"Just on the other side of that hill," she told me. "About a three-hour walk." She pointed this time at the northeastern side of the valley. The tent where we slept was at the foot of "that hill," which was the middle of three nearly identical peaks. The middle one was a little bit taller than its sisters.

"For real?" I said, dumbfounded to hear that the freeway I'd been so concerned about was just on the other side of the hill next to my tent. Duh.

"For real," she said solemnly, then gave me one of her first-class smiles. She held out her fist and I bumped it with my own, like I'd seen Marta do.

"But I want you to know something," she continued.

"What?" I said warily.

"Just that both you and your friend are welcome here, Kell. We see how valuable you two are in your different ways. You both bring skills and traits that we respect, and frankly, that we need here at Tres Hermanas. You may have noticed many of our sisters are older. Your youth and strength would make you much appreciated additions to our community."

She spoke persuasively but also from the heart. I believed her. If Simone had made me the same speech, I would have dismissed it without a second thought. There was something about Ole Fluffy Hair that I just didn't trust. I'd overheard a few mutterings here and there among the women that implied I wasn't the only one with misgivings.

But I liked Nancy, so I chose my words carefully.

"That's nice to hear, especially coming from you, Nancy. And both East and I are grateful for the welcome we've received at Tres Hermanas."

"Then stay with us, Kell," Nancy said passionately. "You two could have a life here, a really good life with friends and purpose. You fit in here, Kell—you're one of us. You have a chance for happiness with us you may never find anywhere else in this fouled-up world."

There was a lump in my throat. Tears stung my eyes again as I felt the truth of her words. I fought for control so I could answer her. Even if I knew where Segundo was and survived the journey, I'd still be a freak when I got there. An outsider once again, just like at the Settlement. And Gabriel wouldn't want to come to Tres Hermanas. She was looking for her own soul mate and he sure as hell wasn't at a lesbian feminist commune.

It was all such a mess. But it didn't matter. None of it mattered. I had to find my sister. There was no other choice for me. First, find Gabriel, my heart told me. Then…we'll see.

I shook my head slowly and then more firmly, finally regaining my composure. I looked Nancy in the eye. She looked so sad it almost made me want to cry again.

"I have to go, Nancy. I have to find my sister."

"I know," she said, after a moment. "I guess I'd do the same in your shoes."

I took a chance and asked the question that had been in my mind since our arrival. "Will Simone let us go?"

She shot me a troubled look and said, "Only Simone can answer that."

Not exactly the reassurance I was hoping for.

Nancy took a deep breath and let it out, then nodded as if she had reached a decision. "I hope you'll change your mind, kiddo," she said seriously. "But it's your choice and nobody else's."

"Thank you, Nancy. I mean…thanks. Really." Words failed me, but she understood. That was the great thing about her— she *got* me. A rare friend, indeed.

CHAPTER TWENTY-NINE

Secreto

On Saturdays, we worked half a day and then had the afternoon off to do as we pleased. Well, in theory we did. Somehow, there was always a reason for me to not see East or otherwise wander off on my own. Part of it was our conflicting work schedules—mine was regular Monday through Friday with the half day on Saturday, while the kitchen crew had three shifts working nearly 'round the clock, seven days a week. On the previous weekends, either Nancy or Marta had found some innocuous, yet effective, way to keep an eye on me.

Cleaning our tent from stem to stern was the Sunday ritual. One Saturday afternoon, there was a trip to the library with Nancy when I let it slip I was a reader. And I had to admit, all those books would have been a powerful incentive for me to stay, if the pull of family was not even stronger. Another afternoon was a picnic for the four of us by the creek that ran through the vineyards with Alma delightedly splashing her feet in the water.

This Saturday was different, though. For the first time ever, when I got up, Nancy was still in the lower bunk, face turned to the wall. I stood there uncertainly, wondering if I should awaken her. Marta stuck her head through the tent flap, however, and put a cautionary stubby brown finger to her lips. Further semaphoring made it clear I was to get dressed in a hurry and join her outside.

"Is Nancy okay?" I asked in a low tone as we started down the trail toward the dining area. I could see Alma ahead of us with her gaunt-faced friend, who I now knew to be part of the laundry crew.

"*Enferma*," Marta muttered. Sick.

"How bad—" I started, but she cut me off.

"*Enferma*," she repeated in a tone that brooked no further discussion.

The heart of Tres Hermanas was jumping with more than the usual hustle and bustle that particular Saturday. That night was the much-anticipated start of their harvest festival. After a quick breakfast, our job was to help anywhere and everywhere with festival preparations. The celebration would begin at sunset in the amphitheater. We assisted the willowy Euterpe with setting up her deejay platform in the meadow where much of the serious partying would take place. This bit of information I heard from others passing by—not from Marta, who labored in her usual stoic silence. I supposed it was restful. All my attempts to get a little more intel out of her regarding Nancy were unsuccessful beyond grunts and under-the-breath bilingual imprecations.

After rolling wine barrels, stacking hay bales, stringing garlands of flowers through the trees lining the main avenue and digging some new latrine trenches (a job at which I now excelled), it was time to knock off for lunch. Clambering out of our brand new and outstanding trench, I turned to extend a hand to Marta to haul her up. Before she could grab it, however, her foot slipped on a rock and she went down hard on one knee, crying out in pain.

"Marta!" I jumped down in the ditch beside her. She was clutching her knee and grimacing.

"Is it—? Are you—?" I searched my inner lexicon in vain for the Spanish word for sprain.

She reached for me and I helped her slowly to her feet. Gingerly, she tried taking a step but it was clearly painful. With her leaning heavily upon me, we limped back to town (as I now thought of it) at a snail's pace. I deposited her at the clinic, where she was greeted by the doctor with warm Gallic sympathy and cool medical efficiency. With nothing further to contribute, I started backing out the door, visions of a free afternoon dancing in my head.

"Kell," Marta said sharply, her eyes dark, her face lined with pain as the doctor gently examined her leg. "You find Alma, *sí*?"

"You want me to bring her here?"

"No, no...You are with Alma, okay?"

All day? All night? This was not what I had in mind for my Saturday.

"Please, Kell—you are with Alma."

"Okay, okay," I said. "I'm with Alma. I got it, Marta."

"*Gracias, Kellito.*"

As I trudged off in search of Alma, I mused on the fact that Marta trusted me to take care of her sister. On the other hand, on such a busy day, who else could babysit on such short notice?

Lunch hour was more than half over. I found Alma easily enough at one of the long wooden tables under a shady tree, seated with the laundry crew. She was delighted, as always, to see me, although her enthusiasm dimmed when she heard the words "Marta" and "doctor." I did my best to assure her the injury appeared minor, but tears were imminent. The laundry crew's chief, a kind-faced woman everyone called Maytag, said she would take her to the clinic for a quick visit while I got some lunch. Alma, cheerful again, was back at my side before I'd started dessert. Her smile and attention were equally divided between me and my pudding.

A peaceful silence had descended upon the dining area as I ate. The tables around us were all but empty. It looked like everybody was either busy getting ready for the festival or perhaps indulging in a pre-fiesta siesta. I'd kept an eye out for

East, but she was nowhere to be seen. I knew the kitchen crew was working on a special feast which was to be held under the stars in the meadow. She was probably deep into peeling and dicing somewhere.

I'd been waiting for this opportunity.

"Say, Alma—have you ever been on a treasure hunt?"

She smiled and nodded, which was her go-to conversational staple. I was never quite sure how much she understood in English or in Spanish, as she talked even less than her sister. But she was game, even more so after I shared my pudding with her.

Licking the spoon, which she insisted on bringing, she followed me to the first of the small unmarked structures on the inner loop.

"¡Hola, Alma! Hey, Kell!" We passed the carpentry crew who were headed toward the meadow. Alma waved her spoon at everyone, caught up in the festival-related excitement which had slowly been building all day.

There were a few people coming and going on the main thoroughfare, but when we surreptitiously ducked around the back of a building, all was quiet. It was little more than a shack, but it had windows. I peeked in, which Alma immediately copied. Stacks of boxes, shelves of jars and bottles—it was all food, neatly organized. Didn't seem like a likely place to store our dirty gear. The one and only door was in the front, right on the street. I paused there to shake out an imaginary pebble from my boot, Alma watching me avidly. When I looked around to make sure no one was watching us, she copied that too. Not the most covert of companions, but what could I do? With no one else in sight, I tried the front door. Locked.

Alma tried the knob too and rattled it mightily.

"Come on," I hissed, already moving toward the next unmarked building.

With an ear to ear grin, she galloped after me. Again, we casually cruised around the back. This was one of their military-style tents erected on a wooden platform. The plastic windows were cloudy with age and tough to see through, but it appeared this was more storage, this time of clothing, shoes and bedding.

"*Ropas*," I said to Alma, who nodded emphatically as if she already knew that.

Come to think of it, she probably knew what was inside every building. She'd practically grown up at Tres Hermanas. I tried asking her in two languages if she knew where my stuff was, but either I wasn't getting through or she genuinely didn't know.

On to the next building, which was a little larger, and, to my disappointment, mostly empty. When I casually tried the front door, it opened to my surprise. Alma peered over my shoulder with interest, then sneezed on the dusty air within. There was nothing much in there—a few small tables and chairs, one larger table and a cabinet which held a few papers and some pencils.

I looked a question at Alma, who was carefully and affectionately touching each chair, each table. She said proudly, "*Mi escuela*." My school.

I guess I'd put school right out of my mind after I (sort of) graduated. There were a few kids here, although I'd seen them in the fields with their mothers during the day. Probably all hands on deck during harvest season, with classes to resume afterward.

I grabbed Alma and ducked beneath the window at the sound of horses coming up the street.

"So let's be extra careful tonight, all right, ladies?" Pinto's voice carried. "This guy may still be out there and we don't want him crashing the party."

We waited a minute and then exited the school. There was no one on the street as we followed the loop back toward the dining area. I was running out of places to look. I tried to remember which way Marta had gone when she took our gear that first day, but it was a blur. All I could say for sure was that she hadn't been gone long. It made sense that our things were somewhere here in town. But where?

There were two places left between us and the back of the dining area. One was a locked and windowless shed, the other Simone's office trailer. If my backpack was in the trailer, I was sunk. People were in and out of there all day, I'd observed. At the moment, I could see Simone's fluffy white hair through the rear window. Looked like she was alone, but I couldn't think how to flush her out. And where were her constant companions, Violet and Rain Cloud? I'd never seen her without them before. Maybe they were off somewhere working on festival preparations like everybody else.

I turned my attention to the locked shed. There was one door and it was secured with a padlock. I put my eye to a knothole in the wooden door, but was rewarded only with the darkness inside. Alma tried out the knothole herself and seemed as disappointed as I was at the view. I checked out the lock, the hinges, the exterior of the shed, searching for any weakness that might allow me to get in, but to no avail. I'd read stories where locks were picked, but that was not one of my skills. Bashing it with a rock seemed likely to draw unwanted attention. Frustrated, I sighed and sat down, my back to the shed. I was out of ideas.

Alma touched my sleeve and gestured with her right fist, a twisting movement. She did it again, more insistently.

"I don't have the key, Alma. We can't get in."

A door slammed nearby, claiming our attention. Simone was out of her office, heading away from us and toward the latrines, moving with a purpose. Alma smiled down upon me beatifically and held up one index finger, perfectly copying her sister's peremptory gesture.

I watched, eyebrows raised, as she walked to the office, up the stairs and inside. Simone had disappeared from sight. There was no one else around. I held my breath as Alma emerged and started back toward me. I could not get her to accelerate, despite my urgent gestures and hissed "Alma! Hurry up!"

Still smiling, she deposited a ring of keys in my hand. A few high-speed minutes later, what seemed like the forty-second key finally worked and we were inside a nearly empty shed. East's backpack lay on top of mine in a corner. Moving quickly, I retrieved both bags, relocked the door, sent Alma to restore the keys to the office and huddled behind the shed with my treasure trying to figure out where to hide it. In front of me was a line of trees, separating the inner loop from the next ring. With no one else in sight, I ran to the trees, found the most easily climbed one and stashed the bags up and out of sight in its branches.

To my dismay, Alma was right there waiting for me when I returned to earth. I had hoped to hide them without her seeing. Owlishly, she peered upward into the leafy boughs, then back at me, puzzled by my actions.

I put my finger to my lips and said, "It's a secret, okay, Alma? *¿Secreto?*"

She grinned and put her finger to her lips, copying me again. Did she understand? But then she leaned close, her forehead against mine and whispered one word to confirm our arrangement.

"*Secreto.*"

CHAPTER THIRTY

Party Time

I spent the rest of that afternoon unsuccessfully searching for East, with Alma happily tagging along after me. Everywhere I went, East was nowhere to be found. She was "around here somewhere" or "I think she just left." Was it simply bad luck that I kept missing her? It was a busy day for the kitchen crew and they were all over the place, with frenzied preparations at the cooking tent and in the meadow. It looked like it was going to be one rager of a party.

I couldn't repress an uneasy whisper of paranoia. I tried to ignore it, but where was East? Surely, they couldn't be purposely keeping us apart.

Could they?

It was close to sundown when Alma and I finally returned to our tent. My stomach was rumbling, partly from hunger and partly from tension. I was curious to see what the big harvest feast was going to be like—every meal at Tres Hermanas had seemed like a feast to me. But I was also keenly aware that, if my plan worked, this would be my last meal there.

Marta, with her knee wrapped, was slow but ambulatory. She clucked at and scolded Alma in rapid-fire Spanish, hurrying to get them both ready for the party. Matching cotton dresses with embroidered flowers and birds were laid out on the lower bunk for the sisters—orange for Alma, yellow for Marta.

My wardrobe choice was easy. I decided to go with what I was already wearing. We'd seen other women on the path, some dressed up (either formally or outlandishly), some dressed down—and I mean way, way down, like body paint only. Good thing it was a warm night.

"Hey, Marta, where's Nancy? Is she feeling better?" I'd noticed her bed was neatly made.

The festive mood must have infected even Marta, who deigned to answer me while rebraiding Alma's pigtail.

"She's good. She's riding with Pinto tonight."

It made sense that not everyone could go to the party. Some crews would have to have women working, like Security and Kitchen. Marta and Alma, it transpired, were off to the childcare tent after the opening ceremony in the amphitheater to help out with the kiddy version of the festival.

Which meant I was on my own. Perfect.

In the distance, I heard the drum circle start up in the meadow, signaling the commencement of the celebration. The drummers had been practicing all week with more enthusiasm than talent, but it did look like fun.

"*Vámonos*," Marta said. She held out her hand to Alma, who took it and then grabbed mine too. I was grateful for the gathering darkness as we walked down the trail. I was going to miss these sisters and Nancy. What the hell was I thinking, making friends?

The tantalizing food smells wafting over from the meadow distracted me from the lump in my throat. There was music in the air too, some sort of intoxicating, primeval, thumping rhythm that already had a few of the ladies dancing in the aisles of the amphitheater. I hoped the speeches would be short. We found three seats in an upper row. The place was packed.

My plan was to leave Tres Hermanas that night. I wanted to leave. I had to leave. But an unexpected rush of sentiment had me seeing the assemblage as if for the first time. A joyous and excited crowd of hundreds of women, laughing, talking, calling to their friends. Black, white, Asian, Hispanic and more. Every kind of queer I could think of and others I hadn't had time to ponder yet. Maybe it was all the marijuana smoke drifting up from the rows below us, but in that moment, I felt only love for Tres Hermanas and its residents.

"Sisters!"

The music and the lights cut out abruptly. A single spot bore down dramatically on Simone at center stage, flanked by Violet and Rain Cloud. All three wore matching loose-fitting tunics and trousers with rainbow sashes. The minions' outfits were cream-colored, while Simone's was black, providing contrast to the fluffy white hair. Her speech was the usual bombast laden with platitudes. I could have written her script myself—blah blah bountiful harvest, blah blah sisterhood, teamwork, gratitude. There were gaps between her phrases in which the excited crowd was supposed to clap and stomp and hooray. They readily complied.

There was only one item of interest for me.

"One last thing before we sit down to our feast."

The crowd again screamed its approval, either at the proposed cessation of the oratory or in anticipation of the food, or maybe both.

"Pinto asked me to remind you all to be safe in your revelry, my sisters. Stay within the meadow and the first two rings and you'll be fine. Both Pinto and Sarge are leading patrol squads tonight to ensure our security and our right to...PARTY!"

That must have been the signal, because the music and lights came back up. The crowd rose as one and started streaming toward the meadow. I was swept along by the momentum, all the while scanning the women around me for a glimpse of East. I caught hold of a post at the top of the stairs and paused to get my bearings. Marta and Alma appeared, with Marta telling me they were off to their dinner at the childcare tent.

"But you go to the meadow, Kell," Marta told me. "Have some fun, but *cuidado*, okay? *Mira—la fiesta va a ser muy loca*."

Fun was the last thing on my mind, especially when I realized this was my final farewell to the two of them. I hadn't noticed before that moment that Alma still had the spoon from lunch and was waving goodbye with it. Somehow, that nearly undid me. I forced back tears, doing my best to appear nonchalant. Marta would normally have picked up on my emotion, but between her knee and her sister, and with the manic crowd surging around us, her antennae were down. We exchanged quick *hasta mañanas* and then they were gone into the darkness. I felt even shittier that I would soon be sneaking off without saying goodbye to Nancy. But if anyone would understand, Nancy would.

The amphitheater was empty. I could see a few stragglers headed in the direction of the meadow. I couldn't decide whether to go eat or continue my search for East. Before I could make up my mind, a voice hailed me from the dark road.

"Ah, there you are, *mon petit* Kell. Nancy asked me to escort you to the party as we are both on our own tonight."

It was the French doctor, Pinto's girlfriend, cheerfully accosting me. "You are going to dinner, *oui*?"

I didn't see how I could say no without raising suspicion. And I was hungry.

"*Oui*," I responded, which made her smile. She looped her arm through mine and marched me down to the meadow, all the while regaling me with tales of festivals past and painting a mouthwatering picture of the feast that awaited us. She also gave me a few tips.

"Tonight is all about having fun, Kell, and letting loose. This will be some party, I promise you. You might even find it a little scary. You have nothing to fear, however, from anyone at Tres Hermanas. If it gets to be too much, you can always go to your sleeping tent. No one will bother you there."

"Bother me?"

"Well," she said, considering me while somehow managing to look very French. "There will be a lot of drinking tonight, you know? Drinking and dancing and making love. Do you know what I mean?"

One of Gran's phrases came to mind.

"Sex and drugs and rock 'n' roll?" I asked her.

She grinned. "*Exactement.* And you are welcome to participate as much or as little as you want to. Since this is your first festival, I encourage you to take it easy. And…"

"Yes?"

"How can I put this? You may be offered things tonight."

"What kind of things?"

"All manner of things, *chérie*, but I am thinking of alcohol, marijuana, other drugs. Sex too."

I was a little shocked but did my best to hide it.

"I don't do those things," I told her, sounding primmer than I liked. Even if I did, that was not the night to indulge. I needed to stay sharp for the big escape.

"*Très bien*," she replied, slapping me on the back. "As your doctor, I commend you. Anyhow, if anyone offers you something or asks you something, just remember you can simply say no. This night always gets out of hand, but no one will force you to have more fun than you want. And you can always stay with me in the first aid tent—it's the one over there with the red cross on it."

Dinner was all that I had hoped for, gastronomically speaking. What I remember most from that meal, however, is not the food, which was as divine as it was varied, and in sumptuous portions. No, what I remember best was the kindness of the women around me. Maybe it was because I knew I was leaving, but it struck me afresh that night. There I was, without my crew, without East and yet I was hailed as a friend. Family. And I knew their names, their faces, their jobs, where they lived and with whom. I'd only been there a few weeks and they could have still viewed me as the stranger, the outsider.

But instead, it was "Kell, how are you doing? You're gonna love the festival!"

"Kell, have you tried the roast potatoes? They're fantastic! Here, try these."

And "I'm saving a dance for you, Kell, don't forget!"

Their affectionate, guileless welcome was in jarring juxtaposition to the thoughts racing through my brain.

Find East.

Get our stuff.

Escape!

But I smiled and nodded and ate my fill. As the evening progressed, the wine and what Gran called "shine" were flowing freely. The Tres Hermanans were celebrating with wild abandon. Voices got louder, laughter grew harsher. The doctor excused herself early to take command of the medical tent. I looked around at all the long tables set up under the stars in the meadow, the darkness held at bay by torches, and saw more than one accident just waiting to happen.

The food was served buffet-style that night, with some of the kitchen workers on hand to help. Others came and went with trays heaped high to restock the serving tables. But East was not among them.

Like everyone else, I made multiple trips to the buffet. I made a point of circulating through different sections of tables each time I returned to my seat, casually glancing at all the diners.

No East—where the hell was the woman?

If anyone noticed I was stashing extra food in my pockets, they were too polite to say so.

Dinner turned to dessert turned to the party itself. I strolled alone through the assorted entertainments, frustrated by my inability to find East and all too conscious that the clock was ticking. I was convinced that that night was our best chance to leave Tres Hermanas on our own terms.

I was a realist. I knew my chances of finding my sister were slim. I knew I could make a life at Tres Hermanas if I wanted to. I would have friends there, people to talk to. I'd be a valued citizen and worker, no longer the freak, the other. The shunned and reviled. Different is dead, Gran had warned me. But not at Tres Hermanas. My differences were welcome there.

But…Gabriel. My flesh and blood. My only true family. I had to find Segundo and Gabriel. And if I died trying, well, then all my problems would be over.

If I did reach Segundo, maybe I could establish a connection between the two communities. Nancy had said they traded with other groups. So perhaps, someday…

I shivered in the warm night air. I was dreaming about second chances and that was dumb. The world I lived in wasn't big on second chances.

I found I had wandered to the center of the meadow, where the deejay was blasting and the dancers writhed and leaped. I stood and watched from the shadows for a time. East was definitely not among them. Her hair, her height, her lithe gracefulness would have stood out.

Dancing was far from the only amusement that night. The drum circle was still pounding away. And there were booths in the meadow—a fortune teller, massage tables, games of skill and chance, exhibits of arts and crafts, and an incredible (to me), and aptly named, creation called a "slip and slide"—a pathway of slick black plastic doused with running water. Shrieking naked women ran full tilt and launched themselves down it for a wild ride of short duration, but high velocity. I would have liked to try that one, except for the naked part. Crowds lined each side of the slide, laughing and yelling at the participants, and passing judgments on distance and style. I heard one woman say it was better in the old days with "gel-oh." Whatever that was.

Flasks and bottles were passing from hand to hand, and the smell of weed was rich in the air. They had that back at the Settlement too, although I'd never wanted to partake. I could not afford to be off my guard—not then or now. I could tell from the pupils of some of the partygoers that other substances were in play that night as well. It was truly a *muy loca fiesta* as Marta had warned me, and nothing like the far tamer occasional festivities back at the Settlement. I'd read descriptions of such carousing in books, but they were nothing compared to the real thing. The real thing was torch-lit, surreal, sensual, loud and exciting. A little alarming, to be honest. No one was hassling me, but there was a lot of incidental contact in the crowd. A lot of bodies rubbing up against each other. A lot of couples making out. I wasn't used to any of it. I wasn't sure how it made me feel. How it was supposed to make me feel.

The meadow was ringed with tall trees, a mix of evergreens and deciduous. The leaves on the latter moved with the night air as seductively as the dancers. I'd been wandering the meadow for what felt like hours since dinner had ended and the festivities had not yet peaked. Whenever they did peak would be the best moment to slip away. But I couldn't—I wouldn't—leave without East, or at least without talking to her. I still didn't know if she would come with me. Were we even friends anymore? Had we ever been?

My feet brought me to the barbecue pit at the edge of the meadow. Aromatic smoke billowed from the coals. An entire cow had been roasted for the feast. Two of the burlier kitchen staff were still turning what was left of the carcass on the spit. Both looked drunk and were giggling as they struggled with their task. Buffalo ("Beefalo" was my churlish thought) slumped in a chair nearby, simultaneously supervising, drinking, and sharpening a very large knife on a whetstone. A dirty bell on a leather strap lay beneath her seat. I decided to never mention that to East.

The smoke parted to reveal several workers approaching with empty trays, East among them. I grabbed her arm and pulled her aside, out of earshot. "Jesus, where have you been? I've been looking all over for you!"

She seemed surprised by my intensity.

"What? I just woke up. I was working the spit all last night. I've been asleep in my tent."

The one place I hadn't thought to look for her. Shaking my head at my stupidity, I pulled her a step further into the shadows. None of the kitchen people were paying attention to us. They were all busy teasing Buffalo, who couldn't seem to get up out of her chair on her own. One of the burly women tried to help her and ended up on her butt to gales of laughter from her pals.

"This is it, East," I said, my voice low. "This is our chance to go—now, tonight."

She jerked her arm out of my grasp. "Now? You mean right now, this minute?"

I noticed she was clutching her serving tray tightly to her chest—a shield between us. Warding me off?

"Yeah, look at 'em, they're all drunk. We can escape tonight, East, but we gotta move fast."

"Escape…" she said uncertainly.

"Yes, escape," I said impatiently. "Look, you knew this day was coming. If you want to come with me to Segundo, well, now's your chance."

She looked at me. There was just enough moonlight for me to see her face. She looked beautiful, as always. Beautiful and remote.

"Don't you want to come, East?" I said softly. *Oh, God, don't make me go by myself.*

"I do," she said, "but—"

"But what?"

"But they have food here, Kell, and water and beds! It's safe here, for Christ's sake. These people are my friends."

We stared at each other.

"I thought I was your friend," I said.

"Of course you are! That hasn't changed. But you have to remember what it's like out there. Do you?"

I felt like I was turning to stone, to ice. My muscles were stiff, my fists clenched. But my blood was red hot in my veins. The anger felt good.

"What I remember is my sister's at Segundo, Elinor Eastman. And you're either with me or you're not. And it's time for you to decide, right now, because I'm going. Tonight."

She bit her lip and looked away, then looked back at me. Really looked at me. Took in a deep breath and then exhaled.

"Well, damn," she said, tossing her tray into a convenient nearby bush. "Can we at least wait until morning?" The sweetest words I'd ever heard.

And then I was hugging her, holding her tight, squeezing the breath out of her. I don't know which one of us was more surprised. When I let her go, she was laughing, but I was hoping the dark of night hid the tears in my eyes.

"Sorry, no," I said. "It's now or never. Let's go get our stuff, okay?"

"You found our stuff?"

I filled her in on the plan as we rapidly skirted the edge of the meadow, avoiding the torch light. Now that we were really doing this, my heart was in my throat that someone would see us and raise the alarm.

But everyone was at the party. The only women we came across were lovers in the shrubbery and they were far too busy to notice our passing. We made a quick stop at East's sleeping tent where she got her jacket and a few small things she'd acquired during her time at Tres Hermanas, then we found the tree with my cache. It was but the work of a moment to scale it and toss down our stash.

I had the flashlight Nancy had given me and used it to check the contents of our backpacks. Everything was as we'd left it with two notable omissions—our remaining MREs and the gun were gone! Silently cursing, I thought quickly. They'd probably locked up the gun in the office trailer, which was nearby. I did a fast risk versus reward calculation. I could try to break into the office—but I might not be successful, the gun might be elsewhere, we might get caught. Although I hated to leave without it (and was more pissed than ever at Simone for filching it), I had to conclude a midnight raid on the office wasn't worth it. Ditto for the food storage shed.

Heck, I hadn't even used the gun since I'd taken it off Lookout Dude back at the bomb-blasted observatory. But it sure had been comforting to feel it on my hip. At least they'd left me my hunting knife. I threw it and everything else back in my pack in my rush to get moving.

Shrugging off the loss, I handed East her backpack and donned my own. Best case scenario, we'd be in Segundo in a matter of days. The worst case wasn't worth thinking about.

"Which way?" she whispered as we filled our water bottles from the nearest spigot. So long, spigot. With the familiar weight of our packs on our backs, she seemed more like her old self to me already.

"Behind that hill is the freeway," I told her, pointing. "Let's get up and over it tonight, then we'll see what tomorrow brings."

I hoped it wouldn't bring a search party on horseback looking for us. My expectation was that we wouldn't be missed until later in the day, after the hangovers wore off. Maybe longer with a little luck. And surely they realized they couldn't hold us against our wills forever?

We hurried to my sleeping tent where I hurriedly tossed the rest of my things into my pack. We then continued on the path to the foot of the hill we needed to climb. That path was fairly smooth and well-maintained. The narrow trail up the hill I'd sussed out earlier was neither. Knowing that Security was on patrol, I couldn't risk using the flashlight. Moving as silently as possible, we saw no one. The moon was still bright in the sky, so that helped. Even so, we stumbled slowly up the hill.

Halfway up the incline, we crouched behind a boulder to catch our breath. Gazing back at the valley, we could see the torches of the party and hear the deep-throated BOOM BOOM BOOM from the deejay's speakers. I started to stand, then froze as I heard horses approaching. A woman spoke, just a few yards above us.

"Perfect night for it, eh?"

Someone grouchy answered her. "Be a lot more perfect if we were down there instead of up here."

"Well, you heard Pinto. The quicker we catch the bastard, the quicker we're at the party."

One of them chirruped to her horse, the sounds of creaking leather, jingling metal and hooves on a dirt road fading as they moved further away from us. As startled as I was, it was good to know we hadn't been missed already. They were looking for the intruder we'd been hearing about, not alert for fugitive teenagers. Plus, if the patrol had just passed us, with any luck the next one wouldn't be along for quite some time.

We waited a minute more, then climbed up to the horse path and beyond. In near silence, East and I finished our ascent. The undergrowth cleared near the top of the hill. A few lone pines provided cover. I made sure we were hidden behind one of them before I turned to look one last time at the valley behind us. East, close beside me, took my hand.

"We'll be fine, East."

How many times had I told her that? Well, it had been true so far.

We carefully picked our way across the clearing, straining in the darkness to see an opening to lead us down the other side of the hill. I still wasn't ready to risk the flashlight.

It was quiet on the hilltop. The Milky Way dazzled above. If we could safely descend and find a place to sleep for a few hours before dawn, I'd be satisfied. By the time all the party girls woke up and staggered out of their tents/bushes, we'd be long gone.

In the shadows under one of the big pine trees, a twig snapped. I froze, as did East. Animal? Wind? Security?

It was a man. Stepping out from behind the bole of the tree, not twenty feet away. He had a flashlight too, but kept his hand wrapped around the end of it so only a weak beam exuded. In his other hand was a gun.

To my horror, he said, "I've been waiting for you."

His voice was hoarse and shaky. But when he shone the light upward briefly to show us his face—filthy and overgrown with dirty matted whiskers—his lips were distorted in a triumphant snarl. He wanted us to look at him, to recognize him. It wasn't easy with all the dirt and hair, but I did.

As unlikely as it seemed, I was expecting Matteo.

It wasn't him.

We watched as the man kissed the barrel of his gun, then extended it to the sky, his raspy cry hardly more than a whisper.

"Long live the Ship of State! Death to all traitors and cowards!"

Lookout Dude.

"Mister, I thought you were dead—"

"They told me to take out the school bus, to send a message to all those weak-minded liberal fools at the university. They said I was the only man for the mission, that I had the vision, the courage to do what others feared to do…"

His tone was rapturous, jubilant at his conquest. The words poured out of him, tumbling over one another now that he finally had an audience. And all the more sickening to hear it in that raspy-voiced whisper.

"And I did it! I did it, except for you two and that other boy. Where's he at?"

He squinted suspiciously at us.

"He's dead," I said. My voice sounded calm, bored even, but every fiber of my being was focused on survival. I had no weapon other than my wits. The knife in my backpack might as well have been on the moon.

Lookout Dude went back to raving about the moral decay of an America infested with mongrel blood, government interference with his God-given rights, the end of days and a bunch of other shit. He seemed to have forgotten about the flashlight in his hand. With each wild gesture, the weak beam skittered about the clearing.

"Run when you can and yell for Security," I muttered to East through clenched teeth. I took a step toward Lookout Dude.

"No, Kell, no," East moaned.

She reached for me, but I shrugged her off, walking slowly toward him on legs which seemed to have lost all feeling. The whole moonlit scene was dreamlike. I felt hyperalert, flooded with adrenaline and out of my body at the same time.

Lookout Dude stopped waving his flashlight around and shakily pointed his pistol at me.

"Yeah, that's good," he said, wiping his mouth with his sleeve. "You come on over here, you little faggot, and I'll take care of you first."

He wasn't a huge guy, but he had more than six inches on me. It looked like the road had taken a toll on him, though. Whereas I was strong and fit from three square meals a day and my work on the Utility crew, he was emaciated. He looked like

one good puff of wind might blow him over. The hand holding
the gun was wavering all over the place. Unfortunately for me,
it was wavering from my head to my chest to my gut and back
again. My legs weren't working too well. I stumbled, went down
hard on all fours, then slowly picked myself up.

I now had a handful of dirt in my right fist. Maybe I could
throw it in his eyes and blind him for a second. I could scream
too, but that might startle him into shooting me or East sooner
rather than later.

"That's right, keep coming," he breathed.

It was hard to keep an eye on him and the gun while scanning
the ground in the moonlight for a stick, a rock, anything I could
use to bring him down. Unfortunately, Death By Pinecone was
not among the repertoire of dirty tricks Gabriel had taught me.
Strangling was, though. If I could somehow jump him from
behind and get an arm around his neck, I might have a chance.

One more step. And another.

"Stop right there," he commanded. "Turn around and put
your hands up."

I slowly did as he said. And took a deep breath.

"Now, in the name of the Ship of—"

My schoolmates had made the mistake of thinking such a
small person as I would never conceive of fighting back. They
were wrong. So was Lookout Dude. As he ceremoniously laid
a heavy hand on my shoulder, my fist flew back and opened
wide as I flung the dirt in his face. I ducked and threw myself
backward into his legs, knocking him down as he squawked and
scrabbled at his eyes. His flashlight flew off into the shadows.

"Run, East!" I yelled. He bucked and heaved beneath me,
throwing me to one side. Before I could get away, he was on top
of me, pinning me down with one hand on my throat, the other
still holding the gun, unfortunately. He grabbed my collar and
hauled me to my feet, his ugly face just inches from mine.

"Say your prayers, abomination," he whispered.

I closed my eyes. Sorry, Gabriel, I thought. Sorry, East.

The shot was so loud I jumped and then felt myself falling, falling onto a soft dense bed of pine needles. I hadn't expected to feel anything. Ever again.

"Kell! Kell!"

Voices. Two voices. I didn't feel any pain yet. I found I could open one eye.

So many stars. And two faces bending over me—East and Nancy. East looked appalled, Nancy stern but with a gleam in her eye.

"You do realize you're not actually shot, right?" she said.

"Uh…what?" I sat up, checking myself for bullet holes, but thankfully finding none.

I jumped up then, not seeing Lookout Dude anywhere.

"Holy shit—he missed!" I cried. "Where'd he go?"

"Shh," Nancy said, finger to her lips. "He didn't miss, Kell. And neither did I."

I belatedly noticed her large handgun. She shone her flashlight at a dark mass at the foot of a tree. Lookout Dude, dead. A bullet hole in the center of his forehead and a real mess coming out the back.

"Holy shit," I said again, though less loudly.

"We don't have much time," Nancy said. "Pinto and the others will have heard the shot. Some of them will be here soon. They won't hurt you, but they won't let you leave either."

"Are you going to stop us?" East asked her. My tongue was still stuck on "holy shit." I kept patting myself to make sure I really was alive.

"I'm not going to stop you. In fact, I'm going to help you."

She strode quickly to the edge of the clearing, then returned a moment later with her arms full. She tossed a small bag to me, which I promptly fumbled and dropped.

"It's not much, but there's a few days' worth of food in there. And here, Elinor—thought you could use a sleeping bag."

She helped East secure it to her backpack while I shoved the food bag in my own pack.

"One more thing," Nancy said. From the back of her waistband, she pulled out my gun, now ensconced in a worn leather holster, and handed it to me. "You're gonna need this on the road, kid."

"Thanks, Nance!" My brain was finally restarting. "But how did you know we were leaving tonight? How did you find us up here?"

"Because if I were you, this is the night I would have chosen. I signed up for Security tonight so I could patrol this hill. I was down at the bottom when I saw a light waving around."

Our eyes met for a long moment. *We are the same*, hers said. I owed this woman so much.

"Time to go, *chiquita*."

She shone her flashlight on a spot behind us.

"There's the path that will lead you down the hill. Be careful and use your flashlight—I'll distract them up here. They'll be focused on our dead intruder, I promise you. No one will know you're gone 'til tomorrow."

She pulled us both in for a hug.

"Thanks, Nancy," I said, holding her tight, my throat closing up on me. "I can't thank you enough for all you've done. You and Marta and Alma."

Her eyes sparkled with tears as she let us go.

"Until we meet again," she said.

CHAPTER THIRTY-ONE

The End Of The Road

It was weird being back on the road. Weird and yet familiar. East hardly spoke a word to me the first few days. That was fine—I had a lot on my mind too. Like what an idiot I probably was for walking away from food, water, shelter, fire. Pudding. While at the same time, I was excited to be heading toward Segundo, toward my sister. It was all right—I was used to the duality. Sadness/excitement. Fear/freedom. When you're a boy in a girl's body, you're more aware than other people, perhaps, that most things have at least two sides.

The small bag of food Nancy had given us, plus what I'd stashed in my pockets from the feast, only lasted a few days. That first morning, I took stock of the bag's contents while East made breakfast. (Perhaps all that time in the kitchen tent hadn't been a total waste.) Besides the food, there was a map, telling us how to find our way back to Tres Hermanas. The freeway ran along the foot of three almost identical hills, which the map called The Three Sisters. Tres Hermanas must have been named for them. The hill we'd descended was the middle one.

The map identified other landmarks and gave relative distances to places both remembered and still existing. I ran my thumb over Nancy's handwriting and thanked her again in my head. I missed her already, the first real friend I'd ever made. Not like East, exactly—I couldn't make up my mind what East was to me. Or I to her.

My plan was to hike up the 80 freeway about thirty miles to the Carquinez Bridge Nancy had mentioned. She had also said the bridge was out, but the Segundo crew would have gone that way, I thought. I was following in their footsteps, I hoped.

It took a little more than two days to reach the Carquinez Strait. We didn't see another living soul, which was a relief. We found it was easier to walk beside the freeway instead of on its once smooth surface. There must have been major earthquake activity in the area. It was as if the road had risen and writhed, shucking any vehicles to the sides. After a while, I quit my attempts to scavenge those vehicles. There was nothing left. It had been too long.

There was no sign of pursuit from the women we'd left behind. I saw East cast a few glances over her shoulder almost as if she wished there were, but we didn't discuss it. There was nothing to say.

We'd seen so little of each other at Tres Hermanas, it was almost like we had to get to know each other again on the road. On the morning of the third day, East finally broke her self-imposed silence to say, "You cut your hair." It was a moody, overcast day with a light rain falling. Just enough to be annoying. Not enough to easily fill our water bottles.

I touched my damp locks self-consciously. Nancy had trimmed it one evening after supper, joking that the Utility crew was known for a certain fashion sense. Marta gave one of her snorts, saying much without saying a word, and Alma giggled and clapped her hands. It was a small, warm, happy memory. I'd probably never see any of them again.

I don't know what look was on my face. But I was glad for the rain then, hiding my tears.

"It looks good," East said, not entirely believably.

I wiped my face and cleared my throat, wondering why I bothered to hide my emotion from her. I lengthened my stride to move a few paces in front as we neared the top of a hill.

"Hey, check it out—the bridge," I said, stopping in my tracks.

We had been climbing steadily since the previous afternoon up a series of hills, some gentle, some challenging. We now emerged onto a plateau overlooking the strait, seemingly gashed out between two halves of a mountain. Steep hillsides ran down to the water. To our left, the strait broadened to meet the Pacific in the distance. To our right, it continued up into the hills.

What had once been a town could be seen across the water. It must have been a port in its day. The remains of a gigantic cargo ship or maybe more than one were smashed and scattered upon a rocky shoreline. On both sides of the water, enormous cylindrical tanks once painted in pastel shades dotted the hillsides. Many were badly damaged or knocked askew, but several still stood tall. I had no idea what they were.

Just as Nancy had said, the bridge was no more. It had collapsed in what must have been spectacular fashion across the strait. I could see parts of it still rising from the whitecaps below, like some fantastic, half-submerged, aquatic beast. East and I walked as far as we dared to the edge of the road. Looked like several hundred feet down, maybe half a mile across. There was no question of crossing here, on foot or by swimming. Even from on high, the water looked black and foul. Maybe some of the huge tanks had leaked into it. The winds were strong off the water, the formerly light rain now pelting us unmercifully.

"What's the plan?" East asked.

"I guess we'll have to follow the water inland until we can find a place to cross, then cut back to the freeway on the other side."

"How long will that take?"

"I don't know."

She glared at me from under her brows. I waited, but no words followed. I didn't know what to say to her. After a moment,

I turned and started walking in our new direction. After another moment, she followed.

By nightfall, we had hiked several miles along the shoreline. We found shelter in the ruins of another, although much smaller, collapsed bridge. I hadn't even known there was another one in the area. Which was a reminder that I had no true map and was navigating by faith and instinct. I kept my worries to myself.

Wildlife was abundant in this watery region. We saw rabbits, foxes, deer and elk, and countless varieties of birds. Not to mention the bugs. No sign of fish, however. Even if the black water's appearance had not been so disheartening, the lack of fish warned me not to try swimming across it.

In addition, the strait showed no signs of narrowing. On the contrary, it had widened significantly as we wandered alongside. Its character had changed as well. What had clearly been a harbor deep enough for ships back to the west was turning to more of a swamp the further east we traveled. Presumably shallower, but no less treacherous. All I could do was hope an opportunity to cross it would somehow soon arise.

Although teeming with flora and fauna, this was a ghost land, this marshy country. Apart from the second bridge, I hadn't seen a single sign that another human being had ever set foot here. And all the little creeks and streams feeding into the swamp with its tiny islands—so different from the redwood forests of San Tomas. And so quiet after the noises of Tres Hermanas. Women calling to one another, little kids running and playing, the thunk of my shovel digging into the warm earth, the dinner bell, the singing of the cooks in the kitchen tent…

"Sing me a song, East," I said that night. We sat inside our tent, each of us cross-legged on our sleeping bags, as we did every night after dinner. Twilight was waning, but I could still see her in the shadows as she sat across from me. "Sing one of those songs you learned back there."

She cocked her head to one side, considering. I thought she would say no, but then she sat up straight and prepared to sing. I was hoping for one of their rollicking, bawdy work ditties, something to enliven the mood, but the song she chose was more a lament, a slow and melancholy ballad Gran would have labeled "country western." East's voice wasn't strong, but she could hold a tune. It sounded sad but sweet in the gathering darkness of our tent.

No angels
Watching over me
Lately
I've begun to see
If there's a heaven up there
It's only blue sky and air
And memory…
Won't you throw down a rope for me?

We were quiet for a moment. An owl hooted in the distance. Finally, I reached to switch on our little lantern, then clapped softly and said, "Hey, thanks for cheering me up."

She laughed and threw a balled-up sock at me. I batted it away, then got up on my knees to "douse" her with a cup she didn't know was empty. She squealed and tackled me, pinning me down. I admit I put up little resistance. We were both laughing by then. Flat on my back, I had a particularly excellent view of her breasts in a thin T-shirt as she labored to catch her breath.

She seemed to become aware of this. I can't say the temperature actually changed, but it felt like that. Like the chemical composition of the air itself had subtly altered. She was still on top of me, still pinning me down. But there was something different in her eyes, her breathing, the way she held her body above me.

I suddenly felt acutely uncomfortable, like some small creature of the night hearing the rush of wings, knowing it was about to be carried off into the dark sky by unseen, fiercely gripping talons.

I wriggled out from under her, mumbling "sorry." I wasn't quite sure why. She seemed to have lost interest as well, shrugging it off with a gusty sigh as she climbed back onto her sleeping bag and lay down. She was silent and avoided my gaze. I felt like a fool. Why didn't she speak?

I cast about for something else to occupy ourselves with—something, anything. "Hey, remember Mr. Giovanni's little red notebook?" I finally said when the silence seemed like it might go on forever.

"The one with the Aptitudes list? Sure."

"So would you have done it? Been a Pioneer, no questions asked?"

"Well, yeah, of course. It was our duty, right? We had to do it." She paused, frowning. "Why? Wouldn't you have done it?"

"Probably not."

"But you have to. I mean had to," she said seriously. "It was your job."

"It was my job if I was going to stick around the Settlement, but that wasn't my plan. As soon as we graduated, I was going to leave for Segundo."

East looked both surprised and troubled at my theoretical desertion.

"But you owed it to the Settlement. That's what they taught us. For keeping us safe and fed, fulfilling our Aptitudes was how we repaid the group."

An almost word-for-word quote from class.

"Well, I don't mean to be rude, but fuck your group. I don't remember them keeping me safe when I was getting beat up in school, or chased through the forest after class. They didn't feed me—my Gran did, and I fed myself after she died. And in case you haven't noticed, those fucking Aptitudes took your brother and my sister away from us!"

I was getting a little heated, but it felt good to be mad. I *was* mad. Shit, why was I always apologizing to her? I hadn't done anything wrong. And anything was better than feeling stupid. Anything was better than the fear that I was leading us to our deaths. That I would never see Gabriel again. The fear that seemed to have doubled inside of me since we hit the road again. The fear that I could never speak of to East.

I was hoping she would argue with me, fight back. I didn't know why. Instead, she was silent and looking a little sad.

"What?" I said, still fired up. If she started crying, I would feel like a prize jerk.

"Nothing. It's just that, if you did become a Messenger, maybe you would have run into Baird. Maybe you would have both ended up in the same place. Maybe you could have helped each other."

"Oh, East," I said, compassion welling in my chest.

"You're not the only one hoping to see family again, Kell."

"I know."

I could hear her breathing. Not crying, but not far from it. Maybe I should have left it alone, but my curiosity got the best of me.

"East, did your brother ever talk about the Messenger stuff? Like training or instructions?"

Maybe they had given the Golden Boy a few extra tips. If so, we could certainly use them now.

"He didn't really talk about it with me. I'm just a girl, you know." She gave me a lopsided smile.

We were quiet then, stretched out on our bags, listening to the night sounds of the marsh—water trickling, frogs and insects in full concert mode. A coyote howled, far away in the darkness.

"You would have been a kickass Pioneer, East," I eventually said by way of a good night.

"I always thought they'd make me an Educator," she replied languidly. Her almost falling asleep voice.

That surprised me, since she hadn't been much of a student. "Teaching what?"

"If you come over here, I could show you." Her languid tone had shifted to something I hadn't heard before.

"Ha, ha, very funny." I decided to answer as if I hadn't understood her. She was making me nervous and I didn't like it. The rush of wings...

I heard her sit up.

"Come on, let's talk about it, Kell. We can talk about it, right?"

Coaxing.

I sat up too and wrapped my arms around my knees.

"Talk about what?" I said warily.

"You know. Like, did you hook up with anyone back there?"

"What?" I wished the word hadn't come out so shocked-sounding. I hated how she made me feel sometimes—like a kid. Like an ass.

A freak. Always the freak.

Her sleeping bag rustled as she crept to my side. My heart was in my throat. I started as her arm brushed mine.

"Jeez, chill out," she chided me. "We're just talking, all right?"

I was trying to steady my breathing. Trying to be cool. Trying to not be me.

"Seemed like you were pretty tight with those women—Nancy and Marta? I just wondered, you know…"

"They were my friends, East," I said gruffly. "Just friends."

She lay back, propped up on her elbows, long legs sprawling across the tent floor. It was so easy for her, so comfortable in her own skin.

While I was jumping out of mine.

She said, "I made some friends too." And left it at that.

Was I supposed to ask her if she had hooked up? I didn't want to know. And I burned to know.

"Kell?" she said softly.

First, there were fingertips, gently touching, tracing unknown designs on my skin. Her hand finding mine and placing it on her back, under her shirt. She was warm, even hot to the touch. Lips on my neck. Hips pushing against me.

I panicked. I pushed her away, stumbling over my words. "Wait—I can't…I never—"

How could I tell her what I meant, how could I make sense out of the jumble of my thoughts? I'm a boy, East, I'm a boy. What you're touching, that's not really me, that's not how I'm supposed to be.

But it's all I have. And it feels so good.

What if this was my only chance—ever? How many days and nights had I dreamed of Elinor Eastman touching me, kissing me? Of anyone wanting to be with me? But I felt so agonizingly self-conscious. So mortified and confused. I couldn't say any of it to her. I never had, not to anyone. Not one word.

"It's okay," she whispered after a bit. And blew her gusty sigh again as she returned to her sleeping bag, switching off the lantern on the way. "Good night, Kell."

CHAPTER THIRTY-TWO

The Coyote

The next morning wasn't as bad as I had feared, mostly because we had our routine, our mundane housekeeping tasks to perform as we did every morning. Breakfast, packing up, breaking camp, resuming our hike.

We didn't talk much.

I couldn't tell if she was pissed or not. Hell, I couldn't tell if I was pissed or not.

The marsh seemed never-ending, but I could tell by the sun it was taking us due east. North was not yet an option—the swamp was too broad to traverse, and the nearly vertical hills on the other side looked unclimbable as well. We plodded eastward, cursing the sun that blinded us, the thorny vines that clutched at us, tearing our skin and clothes, and our soggy boots that never failed to find puddles much deeper than they looked. Not to mention the one million insects that called the marshlands home—clouds of gnats, swarms of mosquitoes, wasps and dragonflies, caterpillars and worms.

Ravens cawed at us from the tops of tall, dark green pine trees, then flapped away to some unknown avian destination.

There were more, wheeling high in the sky above. When I was little, Gran taught Gabriel and me a rhyme or a riddle about ravens, something rattling around the back of my brain that I couldn't quite recall. How did it go? The raven follows the... something. Or the something follows the raven? If all the bugs hadn't been driving me to distraction, I probably could have dredged it up. Instead, it played over and over in my head, another random singsong shred of memory. The raven follows the...what?

"Hey," said East behind me. "Can we take a break?"

We had been walking along the side of the black water for a couple of hours. The footing was difficult and the sun was hot. I agreed—time for a break.

One of the tall pines, complete with noisy ravens in its branches, was nearby. I wondered what had them so frisky today. Were they reacting to us, the interlopers in their territory? We sat down at the base of the tree. East mopped her brow with her sleeve as I murmured under my breath.

"Raven follows...tree? Wind? Water?"

"What are you babbling about?"

"Something my Gran taught me. Did you ever hear that one? Something about ravens and following? I can't remember if it's a poem or a saying or—"

"I don't know what the fuck you're talking about," East interrupted with asperity. She was always crankiest just before she ate. Plus, she was most definitely still pissed at me for the night before.

We were down to the last of our food—a couple of government issue protein bars. I wanted to conserve them and eat off the land as much as possible, but our last real meal had been the squirrel I'd snared two nights before. A scrawny squirrel at that. Even with the plentiful game in the area, there was no guarantee I would catch any of it. I felt like I was getting better at my hunting skills, but the critters didn't always agree. So I broke one of the protein bars in half and handed East her portion. They tasted awful, but it was something to chew.

We sat quietly for a few minutes, savoring the break and the slight breeze that cooled our faces. I kept an eye on our surroundings as always. The water there was not nearly as dark as before. It had changed from black to the deep brown of very strong tea. Still no fish, though, and still fetid and slow moving, with little hummocks of islands occasionally dotting its expanse. One such tiny island was directly across from us. Its sole inhabitant was a hardy-looking shrub. There was a lot of happy bumblebee activity going on. I took a closer look—blackberries! But fifteen feet of nasty brackish water separated us.

On the opposite bank, a coyote suddenly appeared. I probably never would have seen it if I hadn't been looking directly at the spot where it materialized from the bushes like a grayish brown wraith. It looked around cautiously, sniffing, then lapped at the water. High above our heads in the pine tree, a raven cawed. The coyote stiffened and cocked an ear, almost as if it were a signal, then slunk back into the undergrowth.

"I'm going in," I said to East.

"What? Where?"

I pointed out the blackberries, so enticingly close.

"You're gonna swim in that?" She sounded skeptical, but I could tell she wanted the berries too.

"It's a marsh, right? I mean, how deep can it be?"

About knee deep as it turned out, but the bottom was a layer of mud so thick and sticky it threatened to pull off my boots. When I fell down—of course—my pants and the front of my shirt were soaked with stinky swamp water. The mud on my hands smelled worse, like something that had been putrid when it was alive had died and gone bad. Way, way bad.

East thought it was hilarious. At least she was smiling again. I wiped my hands on the seat of my pants, persevered and finally climbed up on the islet only to realize I had nothing in which to carry the berries. Except the hat on my head, which I swept off with a flourish to East who was still mocking me from the shore.

Some animal had beaten me to one side of the bush and eaten all that fruit. There was more than enough left to fill my hat. I would've thought the swamp water would produce only stunted and bitter berries, but these were just about perfect—plump, juicy and luscious. I noticed other tiny islands in the marsh were also sporting blackberry bushes, but they were too far from shore for me.

"That's right," I said loudly to East. "Keep making fun of me. That's the way to get some blackberries."

She laughed. A raven circling overhead added his cawing to our racket. Something finally clicked in my brain:

The coyote hears the raven
The raven follows the bear
And when they get together
You better not be there

That was it! I turned to East to tell her this gem, one of several bits of doggerel Gran had made up to teach us about nature. In this case, to tell us how ravens are smart—they follow bears and feed on the pickings the bears leave behind. Coyotes are smart too—when they hear the ravens cawing, they invite themselves to the party.

But East was looking downstream, back the way we had come.

"Hey," she called uncertainly, still staring down the channel. "Is that a dog?"

I turned to look. Quite a ways downstream, but still too close for comfort, a big light brown head could be seen against the black of the deeper water in the middle. Bobbing up and down. Splashing. No—two light brown heads, one big and one not so big. Coming right at us. Mama bear and a cub.

You better not be there.

"Oh, shit," I said, shoving my full cap down the front of my shirt and wading as fast as I could back to shore. Which was nightmarishly slow.

"Those are bears, East!" I hissed. "Grab the packs!"

We scrambled up the hillside, putting as much distance as we could between us and them.

"Are they after us?" East gasped as we fled through the brush.

"More likely the blackberries," I told her. I knew bears were omnivores—I could only hope those two were strictly vegetarian.

After about half a mile, we found ourselves breaking free of the dense undergrowth. To my surprise, we were on the remains of a broad asphalt street. I'd pictured the swamp and forest stretching for miles. But no, here was a formerly residential neighborhood, where either earthquakes or bombs had torn the houses apart. Maybe both. A street sign still stood on one of the corners: Grizzly View Road.

Now you tell me.

Although the road was buckled and broken, we still made good time over it compared to the rough going in the swamp. There was no sign of the bears trailing us. I kept my ears peeled for the shrieks and caws of the ravens, but I heard none of that either. After an hour or so, the road began to both climb and curve, first northward and finally back to the west. We had rounded the swamp and were on our way back to where we'd started. We caught glimpses of the channel (but thankfully, no bears) through the dense trees. The sun sparkled on the dark water, making it look almost pretty from a safe distance.

"Look!" East cried out, late in the day. "I can see the bridge again."

The Carquinez Bridge, or rather the mess that was made when it collapsed, was now on our left. Before long we had regained the freeway. I was tempted to get down and kiss it, I was so glad to see it.

But my elation was short-lived. The freeway led us up a short, steep hill and at the top—it simply disappeared. We stood looking down at a vast chasm maybe a mile in diameter. Towering sandstone cliffs lined the bowl. So steep were the sides that little vegetation could cling. Far down at the bottom—five hundred feet? a thousand?—was more of the awful black water. The setting sun glinted on man-made debris as well, although it was too far to tell if it was cars or buildings or something else. I tried not to dwell on the something else. I'd seen a picture of such massive destruction like this once before in a book back at the Settlement. The caption described an asteroid exploding into the earth's surface in some faraway country. The impact had created an immense crater like this one. Was that what had happened here? An asteroid. Or maybe a bomb or an earthquake beyond all imagining.

It made no difference. Its only significance to me was as another obstacle between us and Segundo. East had silently slipped her hand into mine as we gazed, awestruck, at the devastation. A lot of people had died here once upon a time.

"C'mon," I finally said, but she didn't move. Her eyes were wide and unblinking.

"East?"

I put my arm around her waist and led her slowly away like a child, tears rolling down her face, but no sound to accompany them.

CHAPTER THIRTY-THREE

Food

It only got harder for us after that. Food was our biggest concern. We were fortunate to find water fairly regularly, or it found us in the form of rain. The conundrum was to stay put for a few days and set traps and maybe catch a squirrel or a rabbit, or keep moving to try to reach Segundo as quickly as we could. Sometimes we happened on a source of food and would set up camp there for a day or two, like we had so long ago on the beach with the shore birds and their eggs. I knew that the longer we were out on the road, though, the more our odds of survival decreased.

It would have helped if we knew where we were going.

After the road ended and the blast zones we found beyond that first crater forced us so many miles off our planned route, I tried to think what Gabriel must have done. After all, her group had to have encountered the same obstacles, assuming they had made it to the end of the freeway. I finally settled on a plan of hiking as near to due north as possible in the a.m. and due east in the p.m. It seemed like a logical approach to staying on track with the original course. And I couldn't think of anything better. Having a plan was preferable to blind wandering in any event.

But sometimes our need for food and water interfered with that orderly scheme. Streams were good, because they provided us with water and sometimes fish. Cattails as well, which were edible if not delicious. But streams don't run perfectly north and east, so my attempts at orienteering were all too often cast aside in favor of the search for sustenance.

I found I had better luck fishing than I did with trapping. One trick Gabriel had taught me was the fish dam. Even East grew skilled at this tactic. First, you needed a small stream. At a narrow spot, you piled rocks in the stream to block it with a more or less circular enclosure. One with a small, fish-sized opening. The next step was to put leafy branches over the top of that rock circle to create a dark and welcoming haven for the fish. Lastly—and this was East's area of expertise—one person went a little bit upstream to thrash and splash the water to drive the fish into the trap. Where I was waiting to spear them with a sharpened stick or simply scoop them out of the water onto the bank, where the challenge was to keep them from flopping right back into the drink.

We ate a lot of fish.

One chilly afternoon, we were huddled by our luncheon campfire trying to remember what bacon tasted like. East claimed she could still recall the flavor, but I was skeptical. We'd had only leftover cattails to eat that day and our water was running low again. I looked across the dwindling flames at her. The girl from high school was all but gone. Her face was drawn and dirty, her hair a mess, her cheeks hollow and her beautiful eyes had dark shadows underneath. I was sure I looked even worse, considering where I'd started from.

We were running out of time, plain and simple.

With a grunt, East rose to her feet and stretched. Without a word, she set about extinguishing the fire, kicking dirt on the embers and concealing the most obvious evidence of our passing. Our routine was well set by then. No conversation needed. I stood as well. It was overcast, but the distant landmark

I'd identified as due east the day before—a hill where fire had cut a swath through the forest, leaving a prominent bald patch— was still visible.

I shrugged into my pack and picked up East's bag to hand to her.

"Ready?" I said.

Before she could answer, we heard it. The unmistakable sound of a turkey. *Gobble gobble.* And not far off.

East's face lit up, but she nodded silently at my finger to the lips. She raised her eyebrows and held out her hands, palms up. *Where is it?* We listened, hearing the wind in the trees and nothing else for a long minute or two.

Gobble gobble. There! At about the same distance. Another turkey answered the first, helping me to pinpoint the direction. Between us and the bald hill. A flock, perhaps? My hopes soared. The more turkeys to aim at, the better chance I had of bringing one down. I'd filled my time at night around the fire recently by constructing a new weapon. Gran called it a *bola*. One day long ago, when I was maybe nine and Gabriel twelve, we were fussing and fighting over something, or more likely nothing. Gran pulled us apart, set us down on the porch, and told us to pipe down and learn something useful. She had Gabriel cut three lengths of cord as long as her arm and sent me off to gather three small spherical rocks "no bigger than a golf ball."

"A what, Gran?" I asked, confused.

"Round," she explained. "Half the size of my fist." She held out her bunched fist for me to compare. Small, but strong, like her.

When I didn't move fast enough, she told me to just go find a bunch of round rocks and not come back until my baseball hat was full of them. She was always adept at assigning small tasks to us that would ensure her at least ten minutes of peace and quiet.

When I returned, Gabriel had tied the three lengths of cord together at one end. Gran showed us how to attach a rock to each of the strands. You then grasped the knotted end, whirled the *bola* about your head and flung it at some unsuspecting critter, entangling its legs long enough for you to run up and brain it.

In theory, at least. At nine, I wasn't much of a marksman, but Gabriel managed to catch us a few dinners that way. Possum, as I recalled. I hadn't had much opportunity to practice with my newly made weapon, but long, skinny turkey legs were perfect for a well-aimed *bola*. I pulled it out of my pack and double-checked the knots.

"Let's go," I whispered to East.

It turned out to be a small group of turkeys, just four. A flockette. My attempts to stalk them were hampered by the wind, which insisted on unreliably shifting, and by East, who was constitutionally incapable of going more than five minutes without speaking. The turkeys were unhurriedly moving east, more or less, pausing to feed on whatever turkeys eat from time to time. They were in no hurry, just grazing, but every time I'd get set, they'd move again.

My plan was to sneak up on the dumbest and slowest turkey, throw the *bola* and then club it to death with a rock. No doubt all the other birds would scatter at this, but one turkey would provide plenty of meat for us. So far, though, the fowl had managed to keep a safe distance from me. I was almost desperate enough to use a bullet. But with the shifting wind and shaky aim on an empty stomach, my confidence level wasn't high. A couple of cattails and a few sips of water only takes you so far.

And I knew in my heart that it was more important to save our limited ammunition for truly dire circumstances. We were hungry, yes—but we weren't quite starving. Yet.

I probably would have given up after a couple of hours, but the birds continued to move east, so it made sense to keep following them. I kept an eye out for anything else edible as we crept along, which was a pace well-suited to our waning strength. The sun finally appeared late in the afternoon and was warm on our backs as we crested a small hill. The turkeys had paused again to feed in a small meadow just below us. The good news was there was plenty of cover on the downslope of the hill for us to get close. Closer, in fact, that we had all afternoon.

The bad news was what lay beyond the meadow. First, a fence. A serious fence—tall, imposing, eight feet high chain-link with razor wire on top. Gabriel and I had climbed numerous fences just like it in our scavenging trips in San Tomas. From right to left, the fence stretched as far as I could see, disappearing in both directions into the dense forest which bordered the meadow on both sides. It wasn't a new fence—time and weather had taken a toll on it. Portions sagged. I could see a rusty spot where someone had long ago cut through the links and made an opening. Weeds and shrubs flourished on the near side of the fence, but the far side was a barren, jumbled area of broken up concrete and asphalt. A few lonely dandelions poked their heads up through the cracks, but this was one of those rare places where the hand of man still dominated the landscape.

Thankfully, no actual man was present. From my vantage point on the hill, flat on the ground beside East and behind a concealing bush, I saw no evidence of the current or even recent presence of humans. That was comforting.

A hundred feet beyond the fence was the first of many enormous circular tanks, like the ones we'd seen on the hills around Carquinez. Metal or concrete, I wasn't sure. Each tank was easily fifty feet high. There were dozens of them, some collapsed, some still standing. All had once been painted white or pastel blues, greens, pinks and lavenders. White for water? Pink for petroleum?

All of this I took in at a glance. I wanted no part of it, whatever it was. Any water was likely to be contaminated. My focus was on the turkeys.

"What is it?" East breathed into my ear.

I shrugged. Did it matter? Something from Before—something for their power, their water, their communications. Just one more ridiculously giant eyesore those people had built before fleeing or dying.

"Stay here," I whispered to East, who was all too happy to comply.

I wormed my way down to the foot of the hill, as close to silent as all my years of training with Gabriel and Gran could make me. The wind was in my favor for the moment. One of the turkeys, a young male, was grazing closer and closer to my spot. My muscles tensed as I silently readied my *bola* for a throw. I held my breath. One more step…

I jumped to my feet and hurled the *bola*, all in one smooth movement.

And, of course, the not-so-dumb turkey was a split second faster. My weapon flew harmlessly by as he raced away, sounding the alarm. The other birds, infected by his panic, joined in the mad dash for the fence. I grabbed up my *bola* on the run, thinking I might get a second shot. To my chagrin, however, each of the birds zipped through the gash in the fence, leaving me on the wrong side. In a moment, they had disappeared behind the tanks. I heard a faint *gobble gobble* in the distance. Taunted by poultry. How rude.

I pondered our options as East came down the hill with a scowl on her face. I checked the sun, which was getting low in the sky directly behind us. That meant our eastward path ran right through the power plant or tank farm or whatever the hell you called it. I'd heard tales of strange men being drawn to such places, to the remnants of the technology and machinery that once ruled their lives. But I was reassured again by the stark absence of any sign of people. The turkeys certainly had no fear of it. I still had hopes of bagging one—I hadn't missed by that much.

On the other hand, it was late afternoon and I had no idea how many miles across this place was. I didn't like the idea of spending the night in there.

But if we meekly followed the fence line instead, who knew how far we'd have to go out of our way?

As usual, all our choices sucked. By the time East arrived at my side, I'd made up my mind.

"You giving up?" she asked.

"Hell, no," I told her. "We're going in."

CHAPTER THIRTY-FOUR

The Tank Farm

A rusty and mangled NO TRESPASSING sign dangled above the slit in the chain-link fence. Well, the birds hadn't heeded it, so why should we? I wrenched back the flap of fence for East to squeeze through, then followed.

Walking among the giant, decaying tanks was spookier than I had feared. It was dim in there, for one thing, with the huge metal structures casting shadows and blocking the setting sun. And with the tanks being curved, there was never a corner around which to see. The circle just kept going—and you were never sure what the next step might reveal.

So far, not much had been revealed. We continued to hear the turkeys every once in a while. But sound was distorted amongst the tanks. Vibrations bounced off one metal surface and on to another. It was hard to tell how far the birds were from us.

It felt colder in there too. The wind was picking up as dusk approached. Normally, that was a time of day when birds were most active—feeding, swooping through the sky, calling to each other. Apart from the intermittent gobbles, however, there was no birdsong in the tank farm. No squirrels darted across our path. It was not a place for growth and life. It was sterile. Eerie and abandoned. The not so ancient ruins of another failed civilization.

We had silently crept past several of the colossal tanks—blue, white, pink, green. All the colors were starting to look alike as the light faded. I was worried about finding our way out of there. The tanks had rusty metal staircases spiraling up and around their sides and I would have liked to see the view from the top, but they looked dangerously decrepit. I decided the climb wasn't worth the risk, not yet, at least. Just how big was the place? Well, if a bunch of bird-brained turkeys could get in and out, surely East and I could too.

Gobble gobble. They were close. Very close. I put up a hand to signal East. *Stay here.* She nodded and crouched down to wait, giving the icy wind less of a target. I slunk around the side of a lavender tank. The four turkeys had their backs to me, alternately scratching at the dirty concrete with a clawed foot, then pecking at whatever they'd found. Bugs? Weeds? Grit? Didn't look like much of a foraging spot to me. But then I was concerned with what I was going to eat, not them.

The wind was helping me now, keeping my scent from them and concealing the small sounds of my movements. Closer and closer I snuck, my *bola* at the ready. Now! I flung the weapon at the nearest turkey, entangling its legs and sending it flopping to the ground. It squawked its outrage, while the other birds ran off at a surprisingly high rate of speed. Good thing this hadn't been a footrace—I definitely would have lost.

I did my "thank you, Mr. Turkey" bit in my head, then dispatched him with a loose chunk of concrete. He flopped once more, then was still. I took in a long breath.

"East! Come over here! I got him!"

She came rushing around the tank and let out a war whoop when she saw me with the turkey. She gave me a big hug. I think she would have hugged the turkey too if the next problem hadn't occurred to us simultaneously.

As in how hard it is to cook an eight-pound turkey without firewood. We looked around in some dismay. We were deep in the heart of a tank-filled maze with maybe two hours of dwindling daylight left. Going forward seemed like the lesser of two evils. At least, per my compass, it was the desired direction.

"Let's look for wood and a place to camp," I told her. "Maybe there's a way out of here just past the next tank."

The only thing waiting for us after the next tank was another tank. And then another one. We couldn't even set up the tent on the hard concrete surface.

But I killed a turkey, my brain insisted. Like I was due points for that. Yeah, right, because life is so fair.

I was beginning to fear we were walking in circles, compass or not, when we emerged from the rows and rows of tanks to find something different. Another chain-link fence with a gate keeping the forest at bay was a few hundred yards away. Up close were three, beat-up old trailers arranged in a U-shape. Dozens of rusty barrels were stacked on pallets to one side. The scorched skeleton of an overturned tractor trailer reposed on the road leading out toward the gate.

East, fumbling, put her hand on my sleeve. She had turned around, staring behind us at the tanks with her mouth and eyes wide open. I whirled, expecting some new threat, but instead found my eyes drawn up to the tanks as well.

Messages. They covered the sides of the tanks, from top to bottom. Some small, some very large, from ground level up to the highest point, fifty feet above our heads.

Most were in paint, which led me to a pair of conclusions. Those people had come prepared, so this was a known spot to leave messages. I nervously glanced around, but again saw or heard nothing out of place. No people. Just the wind among the shadowy tanks. And realized none of the messages looked particularly new. Some had faded to illegibility.

It was an amazing display of diversity, if nothing else. Hastily scribbled pleas for help. Text so beautifully painted it was practically art. Messages in different languages, different colors, different sizes, different tones. Human nature being what it is, some of the messages were rude. THIS BITES was one of the milder ones.

Someone had scrawled ten-foot-tall Shipright slogans in red, white and blue paint. Someone else had painted "stupid fuckers" underneath in elegant black script.

Most of the messages were personal. R. I. P., DONTELLE.
I LOVE YOU, MOLLY NGUYEN.
JURGEN S. WAS HERE!

There was one in particular that stuck with me.
WE DESERVE THIS.

I wandered from one tank to another and read all of the messages that I could. Twice. But there was nothing from anyone I knew, no name I recognized, no mention of Segundo. If Gabriel and her group had come this way, there was no sign of it now.

East was still standing where I'd left her, fists clenched by her sides.

"I want to leave a message for my brother," she announced. Her tone dared me to disagree.

"Good idea," I said mildly. "What can we use for paint?"

"Oh," she said blankly, looking around and seeing a whole lot of nothing like I did. None of the previous artists had conveniently left us brushes and a can of paint. But East brightened and pointed—at me.

"The turkey! I can use its blood."

It was unnerving how she was starting to think like I did.

"It won't be that much," I cautioned her. "You'll have to keep it brief."

She nodded. I gave her the bird, my knife, a cooking pot and some quick instructions, then headed off to investigate the trailers. All three had been occupied in the past—two of them, disgustingly so. What is it in some people that they get off on destruction? Original sin, Gran would have said. Whatever that was.

The third trailer was okay and would give us shelter for the night. The pallets provided plenty of firewood. I had the camp set up and a fire going when I went back to East to retrieve the entree.

"I made it short," she said almost defiantly, tears running down her cheeks, while absentmindedly plucking feathers with her blood-stained fingers from the dangling corpse in the crook of her arm.

"I see."

BAIRD—AT SEGUNDO. ELLIE.

She wiped her face with the back of her hand, which only rearranged the dirt.

"He calls me Ellie," she said. "He's the only one who calls me that since our mom died."

I nodded, since I could think of nothing useful to say. One good rain and her message would be gone. It was almost dark. I reached out to take the turkey from her, but she surged into my arms and held on to me fiercely, her tears trickling down my neck.

We stood there like that long enough that the blood-red letters of her message faded into black as the first faint stars appeared overhead.

CHAPTER THIRTY-FIVE

Special Delivery

Days went by, then weeks, then I lost count. The sheer tedium of it was challenging. Sure, there were moments of adrenaline, but those were few and far between in the long hours of walking. Walk, camp, sleep, repeat. I found that East and I spoke less and less, and when we did speak, we argued more.

I would argue when I disagreed with her on something important or needed to make a point, but for her it almost seemed to be entertainment. Was this how her family had communicated? I couldn't imagine that household. Her jabs hurt my feelings more often than not, but I hid that from her.

Screw her for making me feel bad about not wanting to have sex with her. Screw her for not even trying to understand.

One more thing to never talk about.

Whatever I had thought of her back in school seemed completely childish. She was a totally different person to me now. As I knew I was to her.

I sometimes wondered if she would even still talk to me if we made it to Segundo. Still be my friend. Maybe take another shot at being more than friends if I could ever figure that out?

Or was it all just a matter of convenience for Elinor Eastman? Convenience and proximity. Back at the Settlement, she had her boyfriend, the not so dearly departed Hunter Cohen. On the road, she had me. At Tres Hermanas...

Just how many women had she slept with at Tres Hermanas?

Again and again, she made me ask myself if there was anything real between us, or if I was just a means to an end.

There was way too much time to think on those unending days of long marches. I tried to focus—I was on a mission and the only thing I needed to think about was getting us to Segundo. But then my brain would throw something random in like *that's right, you're on a mission and when you get to Segundo, you'll have proved you've got what it takes to be a Messenger.*

Where did that come from? I wasn't taking on their freaking Aptitude. One million-mile hike was more than enough for me.

Just concentrate, I told myself. North in the a.m. and east in the p.m.

One day, due north took us down a broad and well-worn grassy path which I suspected was once a dirt or gravel road. Animals clearly had found it be an easily-traveled trail. The countryside was rugged with many rocky outcroppings and no trace of any former human habitation. Our tree-lined track wound steeply down a hillside. I was glad it was comfortably wide—the drop-off to our right was severe. I could hear but not see a stream or maybe even a river far below, merrily rushing. The promise of replenishing our water bottles kept me following the path, although I was already worried about what exactly was down there. I hated not being able to see further than the next bend in the road.

East was quiet and lagging several steps behind. Tired, no doubt. Cranky, for sure.

A sizeable tree marked the next turn, a sharp ninety-degree angle. I paused in its shade and shrugged out of my pack for a moment, seizing the opportunity for a quick back scratch against the tree's gnarled trunk. Something had inflicted significant damage to it in the past. Lightning strike? Had someone tried, but failed, to cut it down? Or maybe something had crashed into it Before. And yet the tree continued to flourish, while whoever or whatever had struck it was long forgotten.

"Hear that stream, East?"

"Yeah. How much farther do you think?"

I stepped out of the shade and crossed to the side of the road to stare down toward the sound of moving water, trying to guess the distance. I still couldn't see it, not even a flash of sunlight reflecting off it. Although precipitous, the hillside was covered with scrub oak and pine, shrubbery and rocks, all of it obscuring my vision.

"Not too far," I told her.

Four things happened rather quickly.

East came over to take a look for herself.

A squirrel leapt from a bush right next to her and ran toward the tree.

Startled, she yelped and jumped and, in doing so, knocked into me as I peered over the edge.

I flew.

East's screams rang in my ears as I tumbled ass over teakettle down the steep incline. It felt like all the major body parts managed to bounce off the hillside at least once. Including my face. I was grabbing frantically at every passing shrub, root and branch, but it was all such a mad whirl that I only succeeded in ripping up my hands.

My furious plunge came to an end as sudden as its beginning. I caromed off the hillside one last time, was briefly airborne, struck a smallish tree whose branches broke my fall by beating the shit out of me and then landed hard on my back on a flat, leaf-covered surface with a dull "clonk."

The impact knocked the breath out of me. I could hardly believe I was still alive. I lay there without moving for at least a minute, trying to collect my thoughts and simultaneously convince my lungs to take in some air. Finally, with respiration returning, I managed to sit up and take inventory. Limbs, check.

Torso, check. Head, still attached. Although I was battered and torn, I was grateful to realize I was not badly hurt. No broken bones, thank goodness.

On a not so positive note, my compass, which I'd been wearing on a string around my neck, was shattered beyond repair. I categorized this as bad, but not a full-blown catastrophe. The sun would help us stay on our basic north-then-east path. It wasn't like I'd been navigating to a specific and known point on a map.

Throughout all of this, I'd heard East hollering my name and the sounds of her following me down the hill in a much slower, but obviously panicked, fashion.

"Kell!" she yelled again.

I tried to speak and found that I couldn't. I took a deep breath, winced at the pain that resulted and tried again.

"I'm here, East! I'm okay," I called to her, somewhat truthfully.

"Jesus Christ," I heard her say to herself. I could see her a ways up the hill, cautiously testing each hand-and foothold as she descended. And glory be, she had my pack with her. She'd come a long way since the Worst Field Trip Ever started.

Wait a minute—*clonk*? Just what had I landed on? I seemed to be about ten feet off the ground. I could see the stream not far away, sparkling in the sunlight. The flat surface I found myself on was approximately eight feet wide by fifteen feet long, thickly covered with leaves. In retrospect, there had been two clonks. The first one when I landed flat on my back, then the second one after I bounced up and back down. I was fortunate the leaves—rotting underneath, more or less dry on top—had acted as a safety net to cocoon and catch me on the second bounce.

East was still grumbling her way down the hill and had reached the ledge that must have served as my launching point. She stared at me in disbelief.

"Are you sure you're all right?"

"Yeah. Shook up, but unstirred."

"What does that mean?"

"I don't know, my Gran used to say something like that." Although it didn't sound right when I said it. Maybe I'd hit my head harder than I realized. I cautiously rose to my feet, testing the surface beneath. It seemed solid enough.

"Do you know what you're standing on?" East said from her vantage point.

"What is it?"

"It's a truck," she said. "It's a big, brown, boxy truck. You're on its roof. It must have crashed down the hill a long time ago."

She found a way down from the ledge while I did a few careful stretches and deep knee bends on the roof. My ribs were sore on one side and there was a goose egg developing on the back of my head. I knew I was lucky to have escaped with such minor injuries. I'd probably feel like hell tomorrow, but for now, the next order of business was to hang off the side of the vehicle and drop to the ground below. I washed my cuts in the icy clear water of the stream while East refilled our water bottles.

We then went back to the truck at my insistence. The front and the sides were thrashed, evidence of a headlong dash down the densely wooded hill that must have ended when the truck rammed into a very large tree. The pancaked engine compartment bore silent testament to the violence of the impact. A gaping, driver-sized hole in the windshield suggested a sudden and fatal exit for that individual. He or she was nowhere to be seen for which I was grateful. The last thing we needed was another grisly sight to add to our memories.

I had quite a bit of experience salvaging cars and trucks, thanks to Gabriel's tutelage and plenty of practice back in San Tomas. Better safe than sorry was the first rule. Don't expect much, if anything, was the other one. Water usually found a way into a vehicle long before my sister and I arrived, leaving the interiors a rotting, mildew-y mess with nothing worth taking. Once in a while, though, we'd come across something worthwhile—something that had withstood the passage of time and the elements. Maybe a sentimental relic of the past that we could trade to some gormless Settlement adult for an actually useful item.

The passenger side door was partially open, but just a few inches. East and I pushed and pulled, and finally managed to pry it further open enough for me to climb inside the mangled cab. It was a tight squeeze, but occasionally being small and skinny is a good thing. I told East to stand watch while I took a look.

"Anything?" she asked after all of five seconds.

"Oh, yeah, sure—fried chicken, clean underwear and a feather bed."

"Ha, ha. Very funny."

Five more seconds.

"But, seriously," she said. "Anything?"

I set aside an empty plastic bottle with its cap screwed on. We could use that. The seats were moldy and decayed. I was careful not to catch myself on the exposed springs.

East stepped up on the running board and rubbed her sleeve on the passenger mirror. Her sleeve was no match for years of muck and exposure.

What else? I had no tools to remove any mechanical parts, even if I could think of a purpose for them. A screwdriver under the seat was a find—rusty, but still serviceable. I used it to pry open what Gabriel called the glove compartment. No gloves, just a decomposing glob of papers.

"Kell?"

"Okay, I'm coming. Just a sec."

With the help of my trusty new screwdriver, I got the keys out of the ignition, then climbed out to an expectant East.

"That's it? A fucking plastic bottle and rusty screwdriver?"

"And keys," I said, jingling them in her face. "Which might just open the back."

The rear end was the least damaged part of the vehicle. It took several tries and a fair amount of cursing, but in the end, we got the door open. A hodgepodge of boxes of different sizes and colors filled the interior. Envelopes too. The air inside was stale, but dry. By some miracle, no water had seeped in over the years. I had no hope of finding anything edible in the packages, but thought it was worth opening a few just to get an idea of what the truck was carrying.

"What is all this?" East asked.

"I don't know. I guess the driver was taking all these boxes somewhere. Here, let's try the big ones first. Help me get 'em out on the ground."

The last thing I wanted was to be caught inside a small dark space if two-or four-legged predators were nearby.

Some of the boxes were too heavy to easily move. I let those be, as the chances were slim we could make use of anything so unwieldy. As I slashed at a box with my knife, East ripped open a few of the smaller pouches that lay scattered about. As far as I could tell, all she was finding was paper. I wasn't having any better luck, but I was starting to see a pattern.

"East, see the names on the label? Check out the one at the top left."

She started reading them out loud.

"*Visions of Beauty*—I call dibs on that one. Boring, boring. Toss. Ooh, *Rockridge & Piedmont, Purveyors of Fine Soaps*! Here, I'll set aside the good ones and we can open them up like it's Christmas."

I tuned her out while I took another look around the interior. A red metal dolly was secured to the wall close to the door. It was of no use to me, but the bungee cords dangling from it were still in decent condition. I stuck them in my backpack. Above the dolly was a metal box, also secured to the wall. A first aid kit! Excellent timing, considering my banged-up state. We'd used up the contents of the Tucker box first aid kit some time back. I sat on the tailgate and doctored myself with some stinging antibacterial pads while East continued her sorting. My ribs were increasingly sore and my head was starting to throb. I popped some of the powdery aspirins from the kit.

In the end, East had set aside only three packages. I took a quick look at what she had tossed and kept a couple, but the rest was all the same: paperwork, electronics, ruined stuff, useless stuff.

"Why do you think nobody's found this truck before?" she asked me.

I'd been wondering along the same lines.

"I think it came off the road up there about where I fell. And this spot's nowhere near the road. Remember how it curved?"

It seemed to me that the road must meet up with the creek several hundred yards downstream. Which meant we were in an off-the-beaten-path kind of spot. A rather idyllic one too. The creek rushed and gurgled. Just upstream, a waterfall cascaded down the bare rock face of a cliff, filling a pool below which narrowed at one end to become the creek. The big tree that must have stopped the truck so long ago provided shade for us and housing for multiple squirrels. (Whose demise I was already plotting.) The ground was level. It would have been a great place to make camp if it wasn't early afternoon. Although between my ribs and my head, I wasn't looking forward to several more hours of hiking.

"How long do you think it's been here?" East said, shivering a little in the dappled sunlight. It was a little creepy—going through packages sent by and to a bunch of dead Before people.

"Well, if they were still out on the roads delivering mail, it must have been before the Bad Times really kicked in, right? Maybe just before, since they apparently never found it. I wish they'd been smart enough to be shipping each other survival gear and weapons, instead of all this paper and crap."

"So why did he crash then?"

"I don't know. I didn't see any bullet holes. Maybe it was just a simple accident—a deer in the road or an earthquake."

"Hmmph," she said, a little downcast.

"What?"

"Well, dang, I never would have figured all that out. You know you make me feel pretty stupid sometimes, Kell."

I stared at her. I wanted to tell her no, she had that backwards. But I chickened out and asked her instead if she wanted to start opening packages.

"No, you go first. What have you got?" she asked, excited again.

I sat down next to her on the tailgate. I held up the first of my two packages, a small, square, plastic envelope.

"*Presidio Custom Guitarworks.*"

"Uh, pretty sure it's not a guitar," she said sarcastically.

Much better, actually. Guitar strings. Thin metal cables which I immediately set about twisting into squirrel snares while East opened one of her selections.

"*Visions of Beauty*," she intoned with great solemnity. To her disgust, the little box contained only a pair of eyeglasses. Ugly ones, at that. She tried them on, blinking and squinting at the result.

"Do I look smarter?"

"Oh, absolutely, Professor," I told her. "Wait, don't throw those away—we can use them to start a fire."

She made a silent "oh" with her mouth and stuck them in her backpack. She held the next box up to her nose and inhaled deeply.

"Here, smell this." The fine soaps had weathered their stay in the back of the truck well. East kept one bar for herself (French lavender) and tossed me the other, which smelled divinely of grapefruit and watermelon.

Her third box was a knee-high rectangular tower, but she insisted on opening that one last. I handed her my other package—a lumpy cardboard envelope addressed to Mrs. Lois Pomeroy which had caught my eye solely due to the colorful kid's drawings adorning it. East drew out a fat wad of photographs, a letter and a shiny compact disc labeled "photos for Grandma Lo." East promptly began to use the CD as a mirror, tilting it this way and that to get the best look at her reflection.

"Oh my God, I'm a mess!" She started fussing with her hair.

I unfolded the letter and began to read it aloud. *Dear Mom*, it began, *I printed all the pictures from Logan's birthday party, but made a CD for you too in case you want to put them on the computer.* I stopped there. I couldn't go on. The words were so ordinary, so innocent, so completely unaware of what was coming. Normal people, normal lives, a birthday party with the neighborhood kids, one of the twins skinned her knee and the dog got into the cupcakes. My throat just closed up on me and the words on the page swam.

East was thumbing through the photographs.

"Nice party," she murmured. "Nice family."

Out of the corner of my eye, I saw her tuck one of the pictures in her back pocket when she thought I wasn't looking. But then she caught me trying to clandestinely wipe my nose on my sleeve.

"Oh, Jesus, don't you start crying," she told me irritably. "You'll make me cry. Plus, check it out—I got one more box here. And I saved the best for last!"

"Where's it from?"

She gave me her best devilish grin. "*Bay Area Whiskey Lovers Club.*" She held up the package and gave it a jiggle. "And it sloshes!"

She had it open in no time and took a sniff at the contents.

"Smells good," she declared. "Probably even better after a few extra years in the dark."

"I don't know, East, I don't think this is such a good idea."

"Oh, come on," she said dismissively, then downed a healthy slug. She grimaced appreciatively, patted her chest, then took another drink.

"East!"

"Oh, sorry, here you go." She passed me the bottle despite my continuing protestations and watched me expectantly.

I cautiously sniffed it. Well, maybe one swallow wouldn't hurt. Might help the pain in my ribs and the dull thudding in my head. Whoa—liquid fire passed from lips to sternum, searing a path to my stomach where a pleasing warmth then developed.

East screwed the cap back on the bottle, then rose to her feet. "So are we done here?"

I must have stood up a little too fast. I felt dizzy all of a sudden and little black dots swarmed my vision. I swayed a bit and sat down rather heavily on the tailgate.

"You lightweight, Dupont," East scoffed. Then, with some concern, "Wait, are you all right?"

I put a hand to my head. The dull thudding had upped its tempo to more of a sharp pounding.

"Is it the whiskey?" she asked. "You don't look so good."

"I think I'll just lie down for a little while, okay?"

"Sure. I'll set up the tent. No, don't argue, it'll only take a couple of minutes and the bugs won't bother you in there."

I couldn't remember East ever putting up the tent before, although she'd watched me do it a hundred times. To my surprise, she chose a good spot without prompting from me and had it set up quickly. I was feeling too punk to compliment her, however. It was all I could do to crawl inside and lie down on my sleeping bag. I could not keep my eyes open, but I never did quite drift off to sleep.

An odd afternoon ensued in which I lay there in a dreamy twilight state, keenly aware of various aches and pains announcing themselves, while I listened to East move about the campsite. Talking to herself, singing, laughing. I was pretty sure the whiskey bottle was keeping her company, but I simply felt too unwell to protest. I finally drifted off to sleep when darkness fell.

When I awoke, the particularly beautiful light of early morning was illuminating the tent with its rosy pinks and cheerful yellows. The harmonious sounds of the forest—stream gurgling, birds singing, leaves rustling in the breeze—were unfortunately overwhelmed by the sounds of East retching down by the creek. Ah, Nature.

I stretched and put a tentative hand to the bump on my head. Didn't seem to be any bigger. No swarm of black dots appeared when I sat up, so I crawled outside to greet the day. The landscape briefly whirled about me when I stood, but settled back down when I closed my eyes. As much as I hated to admit it, I knew hiking was out of the question for at least the next twenty-four hours. I knew the smart decision was to listen to my body. And it was saying ow.

The remains of a fire were down to a few winking embers. I built it back up and put some water on to boil. East joined me, looking even worse than I felt. I silently handed her a cup of water when it was ready.

She eyeballed me, then finally spoke. "Just say it," she said. The knife edge of her temper gleamed in those three short words. It was like the fun we'd had the day before with the packages had never happened. Mean East was back.

I shrugged, hoping to avoid confrontation but she seemed dead set on it.

"So big deal," she said angrily. Her rage seemed to grow, feeding on itself with each succeeding word. "So I took a little vacation day. So did you. I wasn't the one sleeping all day in the tent. Don't you think we deserve a holiday once in a while from this freaking wild goose chase?"

I thought it a bit unfair to call the day I'd had a vacation, especially since she was the one who had knocked me down the hillside in the first place. But there was no point in arguing.

"One more day," I told her. "One more day here, then we hit the road again tomorrow. Okay?"

As far as I could tell, she spent the rest of the day feeling absolutely shitty while I fished, set up my squirrel snares and otherwise enjoyed relative leisure. The highlight was washing up in the pool beneath the waterfall with my new bar of soap. It smelled so good I was inspired to do laundry as well. Mine and hers.

Saint Kell.

Dinner that night was trout with a side of trout. East picked at her food. Finally, she thrust her plate aside.

"I'm sick of fish."

I was tired and hardly in the mood to take her crap. My head was pounding again.

"Yeah, well, why don't you catch us something better tomorrow?" I said.

"Very funny," she said savagely.

I didn't get where all her hostility was coming from except we were both exhausted and scared. I dealt with it by working hard and pushing myself to ever greater limits, anything to avoid dwelling on thoughts of failure. But she always had to vent, always had to take it out on me.

"I'm serious, East," I told her. "You need to learn how to do these things for yourself. Just in case."

She went off on me then, a tirade of cursing and blame and insults and imagined slights. I sat there silently, staring into the fire and thinking what a bunch of immature nonsense it was. I was trying for no expression whatsoever on my face, but I'm not sure I succeeded.

"Fuck you, Kell," was her closing statement as she stalked off into the darkness. I heard her throwing rocks in the stream and angrily muttering to herself.

I let her go. If she wanted to be an idiot, I couldn't stop her. I did the dishes and went to bed. Another long, lonely night. I wished I could at least dream of Segundo or even of the Settlement—escape in my subconscious to a better place than this. But those dreams had stopped some weeks back. And Gabriel's image was fading as well.

I rolled over and shoved my face in my sleeping bag when I heard East come in the tent. I was damned if I would let her hear me cry. The truth was, I was losing hope. What I would do when it was finally gone was one more thing I couldn't let myself think about.

CHAPTER THIRTY-SIX

Rabies Stew

My squirrel snares came up aces overnight, but that turned out to be the last meat we'd see for quite a while. Our north and east path had taken us into stony foothill country where both game and vegetation were scarce. The lack of sustenance was a constant and worrisome reminder of the food chain of which we were clearly not the top. We found things to eat here and there—occasional fruit, a stream now and again in which to fish, the much-despised cattails. But we were always hungry now. Always.

In my head was a near-constant fight—should we stick to the north-and-east plan that, in theory, might lead us to Segundo? Turn back to a more fertile area where at least we were assured of finding food? Give up altogether and head back to Tres Hermanas?

You're a mule-headed Dupont, all right, Gran said in my head.

I doggedly kept us moving forward—north in the a.m., east in the p.m.

One morning, we awoke to a fine white mist enshrouding everything. It was hard to tell what time it was, but it felt early. The fire had died in the night, quenched by the wet enveloping vapor. I couldn't get it restarted. Everything was covered with dew. We'd found some nuts the day before and the few remaining were our less than hearty breakfast. My stomach was growling as we set off into the sluggishly receding fog. I knew from yesterday's bearings that north was uphill. There was no point sitting around a non-existent campfire with nothing to eat. So up and at 'em.

But it was a cold, hungry, clammy way to start the day. Visibility was limited and East was not a morning person, so we were moving both slowly and quietly up an uneven slope when I heard something. I stopped and motioned to East to halt as well. I could tell she had heard it too. We strained to see through the ragged remains of the mist. We could see a stone's throw in each direction before it swallowed up the world.

A drumming, thrumming sound. Louder. Faster.

Hoofbeats.

Maybe fifty feet away, a stag burst through the mist and ran like hell straight up the hill. It all happened so fast I hardly had time to blink before he'd disappeared again. Half a moment later, something else big, but making a lot less racket, raced past us, just out of sight. Seconds passed. I held my breath. A faint cry in the distance held no clue as to the outcome. The terrified final shriek of the prey? The predator's disappointed snarl?

I had my fingers crossed for the former. Better it than us.

"Did you see it?" East whispered. "What was that?"

"Cougar, I'm guessing," I said loudly, startling her. You want to be big and loud and intimidating if there's a mountain lion around. And don't run. At least that's what I'd been taught. I threw a few rocks in various directions while continuing to loudly declaim, rattling my pack and stomping about. East looked at me like I was daft. Not the first time that had happened.

We knew there were predators around us, though we rarely caught a glimpse of them. We heard howls in the night, found their scat on the trails we followed, sometimes came across the very little that was left of some creature they had savaged.

We were lucky, I guess.

Hard to feel lucky on an empty stomach.

We walked. After seeing the one deer, I had hopes of finding more, but the game seemed to be thinning out the further we went. I couldn't understand it. An overabundance of predators? That was a scary thought. I wasn't as worried about pumas and other larger-than-Kell critters as I was about the wild dogs. At least a puma or a bear would be quick. Being torn to shreds by a pack of dogs, though—that was the stuff of nightmares.

We were traversing a ridgeline late one afternoon when I heard them yipping and baying in the meadow below. We were high above them and the wind was in our favor, for which I uttered silent thanks. Nevertheless, I motioned East to take cover with me behind some rocks. I made sure the gun's safety was off—if the dogs were coming our way, I would be ready.

From our hiding place, we had a good view. A good view of a horrible sight. The pack—half a dozen slinking, snarling curs—had chased down a doe and her fawn.

"Oh, God," East whispered, distressed. "Kell, can you—can we do something?"

I just looked at her. Do what? It was an impossible shot from that distance with a handgun, even if I were willing to give up the six bullets.

"Don't watch," I whispered to her. But it was as if she couldn't—or wouldn't—look away.

When the slaughter and the feeding were over and the dogs had moved on down the valley—farther away from us, thank God—East had one more question. Her voice was high and a little shaky.

"Can we eat that? Now that they're gone? I'm so hungry…"

"No," I said. "It's not safe." And there was none of "that" left, I was pretty sure. The pack had ripped the poor creatures apart and devoured them.

"But you've got the gun. And there might be something left, maybe bones for a soup or a stew or something…We've got to eat, Kell."

I explained to her about the possibility of rabies, and that a rabid dog would have infected the meat and the blood. We couldn't take the chance, not even as hungry as we were.

She stared at me angrily. Desperately. I could tell she wanted to argue. I could see in her eyes that she would have eaten the sickening remains of the deer if I weren't there to stop her. I put my hands on her shoulders. So thin now.

"Come on, East. We'll find some food. Soon, I promise. You help me look, all right?"

She was in no mood to be coaxed. I knew it was the wrong approach as soon as I said the words, but the damage was done. The whirlwind of her anger was unleashed upon me again. Such a waste of energy.

To summarize, it was all my fault. I treated her like a child. I'd failed to train her properly. I thought I was such a know-it-all, but she could do shit too if I'd only give her a chance.

She was really starting to piss me off.

"Well, step up then," I said rather heatedly.

"What the fuck does that mean—step up?"

I took a deep breath. I knew how bad it was to be out of control like this. We had no margin for error left.

"Look, we both want food, water, fire and shelter. Right? So just tell me what you want to learn and I'll show you."

But she was still too angry to be reasonable. And her anger always made her cruel.

"Oh, I'm supposed to learn from you, but you have nothing to learn from me?"

That again. I felt the heat rise in my cheeks. I stared at her for a moment, then looked away, stung by her words.

At school, sometimes I thought I was the only one who ever read the books which had survived the bombing of the university campus. I was surprised then to find a group of the older girls surreptitiously passing around a tattered paperback held together with string. They didn't notice me noticing, but they hid it from the boys and the teachers. An empty-headed junior left it in her bag one day and left the bag behind at lunchtime. The shabby little novel went home with me that weekend, where I showed it to Gran.

"Of all the damn things to survive the end of the world and we got Fabio," she said, laughing her head off.

The book made about as much sense as Gran did. It was supposed to be about love, but it was all messed up, I thought. When I made up my own stories in my head about true love, the people were a lot less irritating.

A heck of a lot less irritating than Elinor Eastman.

Dinner that night was dandelions and a little lizard I roasted on a sharpened stick. Outside the dancing flames, the darkness was absolute, the chill and starry sky immense above us.

"And this is better than rabies stew," I heard her mutter to herself as I offered her one half of a petite and well-done reptile.

Of all the damn things to survive the end of the world and we got sarcasm.

CHAPTER THIRTY-SEVEN

One For Her

Before I opened my eyes the next morning, I experienced those wonderful few fleeting seconds of simply being. No thoughts, no worries, no nagging emotions or sensations—just free-floating existence inside my head. I was alive. I was awake. I was me.

Then, those pesky thoughts and sensations crept back in. Gnawing hunger. The frosty nip in the air. I opened my eyes to see a new hole in the tent wall. I'd have to find a way to patch that. Although just about everything I owned, including my boots, had holes, so why should the tent be different?

I put on a few more layers of dirty clothes and my holey boots, trying to find something positive to think about. Maybe one of my snares had captured some breakfast. East was already out of the tent—not having to face her first thing in the morning was a plus. At least it was quiet.

BAM! BAM! BAM! BAM!

I nearly leaped out of my skin at the unexpected and violently loud sounds of nearby gunshots. I tore out of the tent like my hair was on fire—probably not the smartest move, but sometimes instinct takes over. East was a hundred feet away, calmly aiming a gun—*my* gun—at a small and inoffensive tree downslope.

"East!" I screamed.

She swung around, which meant she was pointing the gun at me. I dropped to the ground.

"Put the gun down!" was my next scream. In my head, I added the words *you stupid fool!*

She put the gun on the ground. I got up and ran over to her at top speed, thinking there was so much wrong with this scenario I hardly knew where to begin. One, she was using up precious ammo. Two, she was calling unnecessary attention to ourselves—any predator, human or beast, within half a mile or so must have heard those shots. Not to mention frightening any nearby game. Three, she had scared the shit out of me. And all of this before breakfast!

"What the fuck are you doing?" I demanded, angry and aghast. The fact that she was smiling and apparently self-satisfied only stoked my ire.

"You're the one who told me to be more self-sufficient. Fine. I'm learning how to shoot the gun. Look—I think I hit that tree down there!"

She was proud of herself.

"Check it out," she continued, bending down to pick up the weapon. I put my boot on it before she could reach it.

"Hey," she said, irritated.

It was all I could do not to punch her in the face. My hands curled into fists at my sides. East noticed and backed up a step.

"Whoa," she said. "Hey, I'm just trying to learn stuff like you said."

"We have very little ammunition," I said with my teeth gritted. I spoke slowly and with each word evenly spaced in an attempt to control the rage I was feeling. Rage that threatened to spill out of me if I wasn't careful. "We can't afford to waste it on target practice. Not to mention you just advertised our presence to everyone and everything within earshot."

She glanced around, but seemed unconcerned. "No, no, it's cool," she insisted, smiling again—almost smirking. "I got it covered."

Her bag was on the ground nearby. She knelt down to rummage through it, then turned to me, holding up a small box.

"See? We've got plenty of ammo."

I grabbed the box out of her hands. "Where did you get this? When, I mean?"

"The night we left Tres Hermanas. Remember, we went by my tent to get my jacket? Buffalo had an emergency stash under her bed. You were so hyped up to leave, I couldn't think what to take. So I just grabbed the bullets and some jerky and then we split."

"You've got jerky?"

A pause.

"Well, no. I ate it. A while back." She looked away.

She had hidden the jerky from me. And she was sharing a tent with Buffalo...

I shook my head like there was a flea in my ear. Shook away the unwelcome thoughts.

"Get up," I told her. I all but threw the box of bullets at her feet.

"But, Kell..."

I could tell she didn't get why I wasn't excited about the ammunition. But she got I was pissed. "Take another look at the box, East. Wrong caliber—wrong size."

"There's different sizes?" She stared confusedly at the box while I checked the number of rounds left in the gun.

Two bullets left.

One for her. One for me.

CHAPTER THIRTY-EIGHT

An Old Friend

The gently sloping foothills became steeper foothills divided by wide and windswept valleys. A great fire had swept through the region in the not-too-distant past, leaving it barren and dismal. There was no smoke, no heat. Indeed, it was bitter cold and gusty with the land stripped bare of vegetation. The animals, even the insects, had fled the area. The occasional cawing of a crow was the only indicator of life besides us.

I grimly kept to my north-in-the-morning, east-in-the-afternoon schedule, but it was only because I had no other idea what to do. There was no question of trying to walk around the area that had burned—from the tops of hills, we'd seen it went on and on as far as the eye could see. So I stuck to my north/east plan. Slower and slower we paced the imaginary grid each day. The only destination we seemed to be nearing was starvation. Population zero.

Ever desolate, ever upward, the hills were leading us to a high ridge. Another half hour—make that an hour—and we would top it. I decided we would take our morning break there and see what the vista revealed. If the blaze had gone up and over the ridge for more than another day's worth of walking... Well, there was no point in thinking about that. We were a good three days into the burn zone. Too late to turn back.

Our last meal had been the night before last—cattails from a small stream that replenished our water bottles.

Bottles that were close to empty now.

East had taken to wearing Mr. Giovanni's stretched-out wool sock on her head as a hat. The chill wind tore the warmth from our bodies like a bird ripping meat from a carcass. The beautiful girl I remembered from school was barely recognizable. She must have lost twenty pounds on a frame that started out slender. I'm sure I looked no better. Gaunt, dirty, shivering. Cracked lips and matted hair.

The wind was brutally raw at the top of the hill. There was little cover to protect us from its bite. East and I huddled amid the ruins of a stand of pine trees, somber charred fingers stretching toward a morose gray sky. The temperature had steadily dropped in the last forty-eight hours to below freezing at night and not much above it during the day. At least we hadn't seen much snow. Yet.

There was no food left, but we each took a sip of water, neither of us speaking. There was nothing to say. What with the hunger pangs, the cold, the sheer mental fatigue of the neverending parade of cheerless days—it was hard enough to think, let alone speak.

The panorama before us was bleak. The same stark desolation as was behind us. The fire that had raced through here days—weeks?—before had killed everything, erased it with smoke and flame and cinders.

The hill descended steeply to another meadow with its heather gray blanket of ash. Occasional rocky outcroppings dotted the slope. Another burnt-out hill lay beyond. The icy wind stirred the ashes at our feet into tiny dust devils. Dancing little dervishes, mocking us with their frivolity.

I had hoped, time and again, that the next ridge would show us the end of the fire's destruction. The next ridge. And then the next one. That we'd be back to greenery and game. Food and water. Life.

This was it. It was too far to go back to where we'd entered the fire zone. We'd never make it. Our food was gone with no way of replenishing it. We had less than a day's worth of water between us.

I had gambled and lost. I had killed us.

My legs suddenly gave way and I found myself on my knees in the ashes. Mumbling. Sobbing.

"I never should've brought you with me. Should've left you at Tres Hermanas with Nancy and Marta. You wanted to stay and I made you change your mind."

East was staring at me with a mixture of shock and confusion. Like *what are you doing down there, dumbass? Get up.*

"Jesus Christ, East," I cried. "Can't you see we're going to die out here?"

She clutched the collar of my jacket and yanked me to my feet so fast I thought I had levitated. And then promptly pushed me so hard I fell right back down.

"Don't you dare," she yelled at me. "Don't you dare say that to me, Kell Dupont. It was my choice to come with you. MY CHOICE. Don't you even think of giving up now, you little shit!"

She was towering over me, angrily shaking her first in my face. I scooted backward on my butt through the ashes, trying to find enough purchase to regain my feet. My hand brushed against a rock. I grabbed it and jumped up, holding it like a weapon.

I stared at East, her face distorted with rage, so haggard and thin. She looked like a stranger to me. But then an image of her flashed through my mind as I'd seen her on the school bus that day so long ago. Swaying down the aisle, trailing her fingertips over the backs of everyone's seats, giving me just the glimmer of a nod…I looked at her, then down at the rock in my hand. I opened my fist and it fell to the ground.

East sank to her knees, much as I had a moment before. I could feel the Arctic wind in my eyes, in my lungs. It seemed particularly awful to know we would die in such a barren and frozen place, never to be warm again or see the ones we loved. I stumbled over and threw myself down beside her, my arms around her as tight as I could make them. A tear ran down my cheek and onto my neck. I didn't know if it was hers or mine.

She said quietly, "I'm not stupid, you know. I know you think I'm stupid, but I'm not. I knew this was the only chance I had to ever see my brother again."

"Oh, East," I said, my heart aching. "I don't think you're stupid. In fact, I think you're kind of wonderful."

She leaned back to look at me.

"Kind of?" she said pointedly. Which brought a smile to my lips. And then hers.

"Kind of," I said, shrugging. "In a way."

"You ass, Dupont."

She took a handful of ashes and released it over my head like confetti, then slowly climbed to her feet.

"I'm going to pee behind those rocks and then we're going to go on, all right?"

"Okay," I said, bent over trying to shake the ash out of my hair.

What else could we do?

Even in the few minutes we'd lingered there, the weather had worsened. An ominous mass of gray-white clouds now dominated the western horizon. Where had that come from? Overhead, smaller, darker clouds had formed. A few flakes spiraled down from the sullen sky. I put my tongue out. Hydration.

"Kell," East said from behind the rocks. Her voice sounded odd.

"What?"

"C'mere." Still that odd, flat tone.

As quietly as possible, I pulled out the gun. I warily approached the head-high rocks, dropping down to peer around the corner from ground level.

But there was no death awaiting me on the other side—at least not my own. East stood there, motionless, her arms hanging down by her sides as if she'd forgotten they were there. Staring down at something on the ground, her face looked drawn and white beneath the layers of grime. The pallor of shock.

A small plateau had been carved into the side of the hill with the rocks as its backdrop. It might have once been a pretty little spot, overlooking a green meadow. Maybe there were wildflowers. I tried to imagine it. Soft grass underneath our feet, lush trees, a view of the rolling hills surrounding us.

Now all was ashes. Wind and stone.

East stood staring at a grave. A stone marker that even the fire could not destroy. Someone with some skill had hammered an inscription into it: *Sola Sanchez*. Years of birth and death. *Our teacher, our friend*, it said. A horseshoe was affixed to the stone.

Miss Sanchez, the math and Spanish teacher who had joined Gabriel's group as their Educator, chosen even more for her skill with horses than her undeniable knack for imparting knowledge. A woman of many talents. A young woman, now gone.

But they had been here! The first feeling of shock was passing quickly. They had been here! How long ago? A month? A year? I looked around desperately for any other hint of the group, but there was nothing. Not even a clue as to what direction they'd taken.

East knelt to brush the ashes away from the stone.

"It's Miss Sanchez," she said in a small voice.

"I know, East," I told her gently. I reached down and put a hand under her elbow, easing her back to her feet.

"She was nice..."

"Yeah, she was. Come on, we gotta go."

"But look, Kell—look!"

She pointed to where she'd cleared around the base of the marker. A tiny and tentative little sprout. Green life pushing upward from the ashes.

"Maybe it's a sign," she said hopefully.

"Yeah, maybe," I said, taking her hand and pulling her with me away from the grave, down the hill.

I didn't believe in signs. My grandmother had taught me to believe in things that were real, things that meant something—a hot meal, a good book, a hug from someone you loved.

I believed we were going to die. Soon.

We camped that night halfway up the next ridge. Our energy had flagged mid-afternoon. We were out of water. The few snowflakes that had fallen were just that—few. Not enough to quench our thirst. We'd been unable to find any firewood, not even the half-blackened stumps that had sufficed so far. The numbing cold, the fierce wind and the steep terrain all conspired against us in our sorry state. We pitched the tent and huddled together inside for warmth. The wind was noisy, ripping and roaring through the night. East wanted to talk, but my exhausted silence finally shut her up.

I found a grim amusement in imagining Gran's exasperation.

"You mean you survived all those bloodthirsty critters and crazy bastards just to poop out now?" she said in my head. *"Just to die from...from* nothing?"

I was miserable and ashamed and too tired to sleep.

CHAPTER THIRTY-NINE

The Compromise

We got a late start the next morning, but what did it matter? For a fleeting moment, I thought about leaving the tent and all our gear behind. There almost didn't seem to be any point in continuing to haul the extra weight. But then I caught East's questioning eye. She was obviously curious as to why I wasn't doing my usual pack-it-all-up-and-go routine. I couldn't stand the thought of having to explain it to her, so I packed it up. Slowly. Every movement seemed to have its own aches and pains now, every breath a conscious effort.

There was less to pack than before. After the ammunition fiasco, we'd sat down one night to go through both packs together and take a careful inventory of our meager supplies. A few rotting or busted items well beyond repair got tossed. East wanted to start carrying the gun. We argued, then compromised. One of us would carry the tent and sleeping bags, the other would carry the gun, cooking gear and other implements, and the few clothes we weren't wearing. The next day, we would switch.

It was my day for the tent and bags—I automatically made certain they were securely attached to my pack. It was good not to have them bouncing and banging against me as we picked our way up the dangerously steep incline, careful amongst ash and loose rocks. One wrong move and it would be a quick slide to disaster. It was no less cold than the day before, but the skies had cleared again to a delicate pale blue.

At the top, I was panting and faint with exertion, my mouth parched, my stomach twisting and empty. I leaned against a boulder, struggling to catch my breath. East lagged wearily behind, clearly hurting with each step. I reached out a shaking hand to pull her up the last stride. She looked wretched.

There was nothing but the sound of the wind and our heavy breathing for several minutes. Finally, she said, "It's another burnt valley."

"Yep," I said, my head still hanging. It was an effort just to speak.

"We've gotta keep going," she said. I didn't bother to answer.

"I'm heading down," she told me, tightening the straps of her pack. "Maybe there's a creek in this valley."

The fire hadn't had much to feed on on this hill. It was mostly bare rock with a scruffy weed here and there clinging hard to its windswept face. The wind must have carried sparks and embers from the valley behind to the one in front of us, setting it alight as well.

Myriad stones, pebbles and loose dirt made the footing treacherous. The bare rock was cracked and weathered by eons of exposure and who knew how many earthquakes. A fissure as big as my hand was easily crossed, but gave me the shivers as I peered into its dark depths.

If the climb up the other side had been dangerous, the way down was doubly so. We resorted to cautiously sliding on our butts. East was maybe ten feet ahead of me, which meant she'd be in the path of any rocks I dislodged. I eased up even further to avoid that.

"Be careful," I called to her. This time, she was the one who didn't bother to answer, merely flapping a dismissive hand at me without looking back.

"Slow down, East! You're going to start a slide."

"Do you want to get down there or not?" she yelled back.

She'd apparently elected herself team leader for the day in the wake of my meltdown. Which would have been great if she knew what the hell she was doing.

"East, stop! You're going to bring the whole damn hillside down! Wait for me on that ledge, all right?"

She had almost reached an outcropping on the slope, a brief flattening of the otherwise sharply descending terrain. What lay beyond and below it was not visible to me from my higher position, but we were still well above the valley floor. I moved down a few inches and then a few inches more. *Easy does it*, Gran said in my brain. Or maybe it was Gabriel.

Irritatingly, East didn't pause on the ledge as I'd asked, but turned her head to glance back for my reaction. Laughing at my expression, she scooted herself over the edge without looking.

She vanished.

She screamed.

CHAPTER FORTY

The End Of The Beginning

"East!" I shouted, abandoning all caution and scrambling down to the ledge as fast as I could. Pebbles and larger stones came rolling down with me, but I got to the ledge without setting off the avalanche I'd been so worried about just a moment ago.

Once there, I saw, to my horror, what she had not. The slope beneath was fractured by a large fissure, a crevasse four to five feet wide. There was no sign of East. She must have slid right into the chasm, unable to stop her forward momentum after she pushed off the ledge. Even more alarming than her sudden disappearance was the total lack of sound. Her one heart-stopping scream had cut off abruptly. *Had* she fallen in? Could someone—or something—have attacked her? I listened fiercely as I cut my eyes around in all directions, but heard only the wind. Saw only rocks and dirt.

I climbed carefully off the ledge, then wormed forward on my belly, my body at nearly a forty-five-degree angle. I was praying to every deity my various ancestors had imagined that the hole wasn't deep. Maybe she was just winded. Maybe she wasn't dead at the bottom of a bottomless pit.

I peeked over the side, still wary that some enemy other than gravity awaited me.

"East!" I yelled, relieved to at least see her. And only her. The crevasse narrowed as it deepened. She appeared to be wedged in pretty good about twenty feet down. Better than a bottomless pit, but not much. This was bad. Really bad. I fought back the panic churning in my stomach and tried to breathe, tried to remember everything I'd been taught.

"East!" I tried again. She wasn't moving or responding. I didn't see any blood. She might have been knocked out by the fall. I looked around me despairingly. The barren hillside was markedly devoid of handy resources. No tree limbs, no vines. The sides of the crevasse were fairly smooth—no handholds there. I had no way to climb down. I could jump down there, but I didn't see how that would help either one of us get back up, even if I somehow managed to land without injuring myself or East. Resources—I had my gear and the clothes on my back.

East stirred below. I saw an arm move slightly, then her head. That was good.

She screamed. Not good. It was a scream of pain, not fright. Somehow, I could tell the difference. I was in agony as well. I had to help her—had to. But how?

She was moaning now, sobbing.

"East," I said, just loud enough for her to hear.

She jerked her head up to look at me which clearly hurt. A lot. She gasped and tried to clutch her right leg. I presumed it was broken.

This is bad, my brain said unhelpfully. Shut up, I told it. Think about resources. My gear…and hers. As luck would have it—dreadful, devastating luck—she had the pack with the cord in it that day. I thought there was about thirty feet left—but how to get it from her to me? And did I really think I could pull her out? One step at a time, I told myself sternly.

"East, the cord's in your pack. Can you reach it?"

The look she gave me was stark and full of fear. Pain was etched in every line of her tear-streaked face.

"I think my leg is broken," she said. "Christ, it hurts so bad." Her breath was coming short and fast.

"I know," I said. "Don't worry, I'm going to get you of there." Or die trying.

"Try to slow down your breathing, East. I know it hurts. Come on, I'll breathe with you."

We tried some shallow, measured breaths. It took a while, and I hated how much it was hurting her, but she managed to get the cord out of the side pocket of the pack.

"I don't think I can throw it to you," she said weakly, shading her eyes with her hand as she stared up at me.

I'd been busy up top as well, cutting my flannel shirt into long, thin strips with my knife. I finished tying them all together to make a rope of my own. I attached a small rock to one end to keep it steady and lowered it down to East.

"Tie the end through your coiled cord and then I can lift it up to me."

"And then what, Kell?" Her voice was flat. Bleak. The full measure of her calamity seemed to be sinking in.

"I'll figure out a way to secure it up here, lower one end back down to you, you tie it around you and I'll pull you up."

Great plan, but what the hell was I going to secure it to? There was no handy tree or boulder. One look at East's face told me she knew that too.

Not to mention I seriously doubted I could pull her up. I'd heard of people exhibiting superhuman strength in emergency situations, but I felt weak. Feeble. I was on a steep downward slope, with nothing to brace against, and slippery footing. East weighed at least twenty pounds more than I did. Jesus, I wouldn't pull her out, she'd pull me right in. The panic surged into my chest, like acid, but ice cold.

Stop it. One step at a time. I scanned the hillside again, desperately searching for something, anything that could help.

But there was nothing.

"Kell."

"Hang on, East, I'm gonna get you out of there. Just give me a minute to figure this out."

"You can't."

I looked down at her.

"We both know you can't," she said simply.

"You shut up!" I yelled at her angrily. "I'm getting you out of there and that's that."

"Kell," she said almost gently. "You should go. Go on to Segundo. It's okay."

"It is *not* fucking okay! I'm not going anywhere, all right, East? Just let me figure this out. We've been through worse, right?"

That wasn't technically true, but I needed to keep her talking. Keep her positive. You lose heart in a survival situation and the odds against you go way, way up. *You never quit,* Gran said in my head. *Never.*

"We're never giving up," I said out loud to myself, to Gran, to East. "Now tie my line through the cord. We're doing this, East. We're a team."

She laughed or sobbed or maybe both, I couldn't tell. But she sent the cord up to me.

"Okay, that's good. You're doing great. Just give me a minute to think, okay?"

I shut my eyes and concentrated. I could dig a hole and… what? Rappel down there somehow and…Run down to the valley, find something useful and run back up—but she didn't have that kind of time. She must have already been going into shock, her body trying to protect her from the trauma of her injuries. I could hear her moans and sobs and the scrape of fabric on the rock walls as she struggled with the pack, probably trying to find a more comfortable position.

She needed a doctor. If I got her out—*when* I got her out, I corrected myself—we were fucked. If she couldn't travel and I couldn't leave her…I blanked my mind to all of that and ignored everything that wasn't helpful—like the horror and distress threatening my self-control.

"Kell," she said in a small voice. I opened my eyes and looked down at her. She smiled up at me. So beautiful, even then.

The gun was in her hand. At her temple.

"I love you," she said. And pulled the trigger.

CHAPTER FORTY-ONE

The Seagull

I sat by the crevasse for the rest of the day and into the night. I couldn't move. I couldn't think. My bones, my muscles, my brain had all forgotten how.

I didn't look down.

A cold, drenching rain passed through shortly before sunrise, bringing me out of my bewildered, stuporous grief and rousing me to fresh waves of misery. I was freezing, for starters, shaking from head to toe. Starving, but at least the rain let me quench my thirst. Tired, so goddamn tired. Heartbroken and shattered as the pinkish gray light of dawn slowly revealed the world to me again. I felt old—I was seventeen when I got on the bus, but I was much, much older now.

I had the same choices as the day before—give up or go on. It really didn't matter. Either way, the clock was just about all ticked out. I hadn't eaten since…I couldn't remember. I had maybe one more day's worth of walking in me, if that. It was hard to think, hard to focus. Hard to care anymore. Without

East, my journey was done. We'd reached the end of our road together. How could I leave her now?

The rainstorm moved on just as quickly as it had come. The gray clouds sailed on serenely to their next destination. The sky above me was clearing to a pure pale blue.

A lone white bird soared overhead—a seagull, cruising with the air currents first this way, then that.

Get up, said a voice in my head. I couldn't tell if it was Gran or Gabriel or East this time. Maybe it was my own. It was just a voice, but it wouldn't stop. *Get up. Go.*

A hot tear trickled down my face as I struggled to stand. My joints were stiff, my voice broken and hoarse from all the screaming I'd done since she left me.

"I gotta go, East," I said quietly as I painfully donned my pack. *Go*, the voice agreed.

I took a big breath and leaped over the abyss that had taken my girl. I paused on the other side for one more moment. I looked up, not down, watching the white bird glide.

"I love you too," I said finally.

And then I walked down the hill into the burnt-out valley. There was no creek. Just ash. What did it matter? I staggered onward. One more hill to climb and maybe then I could lie down and sleep forever. The rasp of my breathing was the only sound besides my footsteps. My feet kept moving, shuffling mechanically forward. One more step. One more. I didn't know if it was hours or minutes that had passed when I reached the foot of the hill on the far side of the valley.

Looking up hurt my eyes with the sky so bright and blue. Why I was even bothering to climb this hill when every step was painful, every inhale a knife in my chest? But something deep inside simply would not let me stop. Not yet. Walking was easier than thinking. There wasn't as much ash on this hillside as it was all rock. No dirt, no vegetation, just bare, gray stone.

But it was steep. Panting, I dropped to my hands and knees as dizziness overcame me, little black dots once again swarming my vision. I was close, so close to the top. The black dots withdrew. I tried crawling a few feet. The dots returned. Stop, breathe, crawl.

It was no good. I had to rest, at least for a few minutes. I wrestled out of the pack and sat with my back against a boulder. There wasn't much of a view, just the fire-ravaged valley. I averted my eyes from East's hill. The top of my hill was only a few feet above my head. I glanced up and saw what had not been visible before. Green. The waving tops of a few green tendrils of the most beautiful grass I'd ever seen. The steep and rocky incline must have stopped the fire. Green on the other side meant life. Green meant maybe one more day, if not more.

I hadn't even had time to stand up when the second miracle occurred. Faintly, but distinctly, came the small but unmistakable sound of someone clearing his or her throat.

Wait—do mountain lions clear their throats? Do bears?

I wondered abruptly if I was hallucinating all this—if there was no grass, no throat-clearing, just me face-down in the bitter cold ash at the bottom of this hill, ready to rejoin the earth from which I'd sprung. I looked at my hands. They were shaking and scratched and dirty—but they looked real. I took a deep breath and slowly, silently crept up the final few feet to the summit. I peeked over the edge.

The ocean. Whitecaps and dark blue swells, a quarter mile away. It looked cold and turbulent. A winter sea.

Beneath me the green hillside gently sloped to an off-white beach where people were moving about at the water's edge. Looked like a work crew, gathering food. I saw no buildings or encampment, no sign that they lived here. A young guy slumped under a tree halfway down, fidgeting. Every thirty seconds or so, he would glance around in a half-hearted attempt to be vigilant. He looked familiar.

Suddenly I knew him—Burroughs! The butterfly-chasing kid from the Settlement, my erstwhile baseball pal. I could have told them not to put him on sentry duty. That kid had the attention span of a three-year-old.

And then I was running, running down the hillside. The people on the beach—one stood out. A young woman with long dark hair.

"Hey!" shouted a startled Burroughs as I shot past him like a deer.

The young woman on the beach stopped, turned, put a hand to her forehead to better see.

My mind was a jumble of random words and images, each like a separate jolt to the brain with each jarring footstep.

Gran.

Nancy.

Me, the freak, the outcast.

East. My whatever-she-was.

Mr. Giovanni and the Aptitudes list with "Messenger" written next to my name.

Burroughs was still yelling behind me, but I didn't care. My brain was clearing as I ran faster and faster. I wasn't a kid anymore. I wasn't the same person who got on the bus in October. I didn't know everything, but I knew my life had to be my choice.

The young woman on the beach was running now too. Running up a path to meet me.

Gabriel.

Then she was holding me tight, kissing my hair, saying my name over and over again, both of us crying like maniacs, I so filled with joy and relief and sorrow and fatigue I thought I might break in two.

And over her shoulder, in the distance, beyond the surging deep blue of the Pacific, were the forbidding sheer cliffs of the west coast of Nevada. Where the earth had torn asunder from this island of California.

Bella Books, Inc.

Women. Books. Even Better Together.

P.O. Box 10543
Tallahassee, FL 32302

Phone: 800-729-4992
www.bellabooks.com